LEIGH RUSSELL

KILLER PLAN

A DI GERALDINE STEEL MYSTERY

NO EXIT PRESS

First published in 2015 by No Exit Press,
an imprint of Oldcastle Books Ltd,
Harpenden, UK

noexit.co.uk
@noexitpress

ISBN
978-1-84344-539-5 (Print)
978-1-84344-540-1 (Epub)

4 6 8 10 9 7 5

Typeset in 10.5pt Times New Roman
by Avocet Typeset, Somerton, Somerset TA11 6RT
Printed in Great Britain by CPI Group (UK) Ltd, Croydon, CRO 4YY

CRITICAL ACCLAIM FOR *DEADLY ALIBI*

'Curves I never saw coming' – *For the Love of Books*

'You are not going to want to put it down' – **Jo Robertson,**
My Chestnut Reading Tree

'Of all the Steel books so far, this will be one that stays with me
for a long time' – *So Many Books, So Little Time*

CRITICAL ACCLAIM FOR *MURDER RING*

'A great murder mystery in its own right and highly recommended'
– *Fiction Is Stranger Than Fact*

'Smoothly professional fare from the always-consistent Russell'
– *Crime Time*

CRITICAL ACCLAIM FOR *KILLER PLAN*

'Her previous six novels featuring DI Geraldine Steel marked her out
as a rare talent, and this seventh underlines it' – *Daily Mail*

'I will be looking out for more from this author' – *Nudge*

'A fast-paced police procedural and a compelling read'
– *Mystery People*

CRITICAL ACCLAIM FOR *FATAL ACT*

'A most intriguing and well executed mystery and…
an engrossing read' – *Shotsmag*

'The best yet from Leigh Russell – she keeps you guessing all the way
through and leaves you wanting more' – *Crime Book Club*

'Another fast-paced and complex mystery – a fabulous read'
– *Fiction Is Stranger Than Fact*

'Another corker of a book from Leigh Russell… Russell's talent for
writing top-quality crime fiction just keeps on growing…'
– *Euro Crime*

'The plot is strong and the writing just flows with style and panache'
– *Goodreads*

CRITICAL ACCLAIM FOR *STOP DEAD*

'All the things a mystery should be, intriguing, enthralling, tense and utterly absorbing' – **Best Crime Books**

'*Stop Dead* is taut and compelling, stylishly written with a deeply human voice' – **Peter James**

'A definite must read for crime thriller fans everywhere – 5*' – **Newbooks Magazine**

'A well-written, a well-researched, and a well-constructed whodunnit. Highly recommended' – **Mystery People**

'A whodunnit of the highest order. The tightly written plot kept me guessing all the way' – **Crimesquad**

CRITICAL ACCLAIM FOR *DEATH BED*

'*Death Bed* is a marvellous entry in this highly acclaimed series' – **Promoting Crime Fiction**

'An innovative and refreshing take on the psychological thriller' – **Books Plus Food**

'A well-written, well-plotted crime novel with fantastic pace and lots of intrigue' – **Bookersatz**

'*Death Bed* is her most exciting and well-written to date. And, as the others are superb, that is really saying something! 5*' – **Euro Crime**

CRITICAL ACCLAIM FOR *DEAD END*

'All the ingredients combine to make a tense, clever police whodunnit' – **Marcel Berlins, *Times***

'I could not put this book down' – **Newbooks Magazine**

'A brilliant talent in the thriller field' – **Jeffery Deaver**

'An encounter that will take readers into the darkest recesses of the human psyche' – **Crime Time**

'Well written and chock full of surprises, this hard-hitting, edge-of-the seat instalment is yet another treat... Geraldine Steel looks set to become a household name. Highly recommended' – **Euro Crime**

'Good, old-fashioned, heart-hammering police thriller... a no-frills delivery of pure excitement' – **SAGA Magazine**

'A macabre read, full of enthralling characters and gruesome details which kept me glued from first page to last' – *Crimesquad*

'*Dead End* was selected as a Best Fiction Book of 2012' – *Miami Examiner*

CRITICAL ACCLAIM FOR *ROAD CLOSED*

'A well-written, soundly plotted, psychologically acute story' – **Marcel Berlins, *Times***

'Well-written and absorbing right from the get-go... with an exhilarating climax that you don't see coming' – *Euro Crime*

'Leigh Russell does a good job of keeping her readers guessing. She also uses a deft hand developing her characters, especially the low-lifes... a good read' – **San Francisco Book Review**

'*Road Closed* is a gripping, fast-paced read, pulling you in from the very first tense page and keeping you captivated right to the end with its refreshingly compelling and original narrative' – *New York Journal of Books*

CRITICAL ACCLAIM FOR *CUT SHORT*

'*Cut Short* is a stylish, top-of-the-line crime tale, a seamless blending of psychological sophistication and gritty police procedure. And you're just plain going to love DI Geraldine Steel' – **Jeffery Deaver**

'Russell paints a careful and intriguing portrait of a small British community while developing a compassionate and complex heroine who's sure to win fans' – *Publishers Weekly*

'An excellent debut' – *Crime Time*

'Simply awesome! This debut novel by Leigh Russell will take your breath away' – *Euro Crime*

'An excellent book...Truly a great start for new mystery author Leigh Russell' – *New York Journal of Books*

'A sure-fire hit – a taut, slick, easy-to-read thriller' – *Watford Observer*

'*Cut Short* is not a comfortable read, but it is a compelling and important one. Highly recommended' – *Mystery Women*

Titles by Leigh Russell

Geraldine Steel Mysteries
Cut Short
Road Closed
Dead End
Death Bed
Stop Dead
Fatal Act
Killer Plan
Murder Ring
Deadly Alibi
Class Murder
Death Rope
Rogue Killer
Deathly Affair
Deadly Revenge
Evil Impulse

Ian Peterson Murder Investigations
Cold Sacrifice
Race to Death
Blood Axe

Lucy Hall Mysteries
Journey to Death
Girl in Danger
The Wrong Suspect

To Michael, Joanna, Phillipa and Phil

Acknowledgements

I would like to thank Dr Leonard Russell for his expert medical advice, and all my contacts on the Metropolitan Police for their invaluable assistance.

I would also like to thank the inimitable Annette Crossland for her loyal support.

Producing a book is a team effort. I am fortunate to have the guidance of a brilliant editor, Keshini Naidoo, and I am very grateful to Ion Mills and Claire Watts, along with all the dedicated team at No Exit Press, who transform my words into books.

My final thanks go to Michael, who is always with me.

Glossary of acronyms

DCI   – Detective Chief Inspector (senior officer on case)
DI   – Detective Inspector
DS   – Detective Sergeant
SOCO – scene of crime officer (collects forensic evidence at scene)
PM   – Post Mortem or Autopsy (examination of dead body to establish cause of death)
CCTV – Closed Circuit Television (security cameras)
VIIDO – Visual Images Identifications and Detections Office

1

THE BENCH JOLTED AS someone sat down. From the wheezing, she judged it to be an old man. Annoyed that someone was sharing her seat, she stared stonily ahead.

'Caroline?'

Beneath her puffa jacket she felt her body tense.

'It *is* Caroline, isn't it? Caroline Henderson?'

She hadn't been called that for years. It was Caroline Robinson now, worse luck. She turned to the stranger and glared at him. She had noticed him in the park before. Once or twice she had suspected he might be watching her, but they had never spoken. Until now. At close quarters he wasn't as old as she had imagined, probably not much older than her, with a scraggy face and thinning ginger hair. She nearly stood up but she sat on this bench every day. It had the best view of the grassy area where the boys liked to kick a football around. They called it their pitch. Besides, she was curious.

'How do you know my name?'

'You remember me, Brian from Cartpool Juniors.'

She trawled through her memories. There had been a Brian in her class in junior school, but she could barely remember him. She certainly didn't recognise the innocuous-looking man sitting beside her on the park bench.

Pale eyes peered at her from a pock-marked face. Despite his stooping shoulders, he gave an impression of latent physical power. He wasn't bad-looking, in a way, although there was something off-putting about the coarse yellowy hair sprouting from the backs of his large hands. It even grew on his stubby fingers. He was wearing a grey raincoat and grey trainers. There was nothing remarkable about him. No wonder she couldn't remember him.

'Brian, of course!' Beneath her falsely effusive greeting, she was wary. They might have been at junior school together, but that was twenty-five years ago. 'How are you?'

He shrugged. 'You know.' His eyes slid away from hers.

The breeze picked up and she thrust her fists into her jacket pockets with a shiver. It was chilly for May, more like late autumn than spring.

An awkward pause followed the brief disturbance of mutual recognition.

'Are you married?' He was looking at her again.

'Yes,' she replied firmly, not meeting his eye.

'You don't sound very happy about it.'

He was fishing. All the same, she hesitated before replying. 'We're fine.'

'I was married,' he said, although she hadn't asked.

'How long have you been divorced?'

'We weren't divorced. She's dead.'

'I'm sorry.'

He looked away. 'Suicide.'

Caroline felt a tremor of guilt at having jumped to conclusions, and pity for the softly spoken man seated beside her. He had been through a terrible experience. Besides, he knew she was married. There was no harm in expressing sympathy. 'Oh my God, I'm so sorry. Do you want to talk about it?'

'There's not a lot to tell, really. She killed herself after I found out she'd been cheating on me. She was having an affair.' He shuddered. 'It was horrible at the time...'

It wasn't clear if he was referring to his wife's infidelity or her death.

'I can imagine.' It was a stupid remark. Of course she couldn't imagine what he must have gone through. 'I'm so sorry,' she repeated. She didn't know what else to say.

'We were fine until she met someone else.'

Studying his profile, she saw his lips press together, contorting his face. Afraid he might break down, she was relieved when he spoke calmly.

'It had to end. It couldn't go on.'

Wanting to comfort him, she couldn't think of the right words.

Only his disgusting hairiness restrained her from reaching out and putting her hand on his.

'I know how you feel,' she said quietly.

'Really?'

She turned away, unnerved by the intensity of his gaze. The bench beside her creaked as he shifted position.

'How could you possibly understand?'

A few yards away on the grass the boys were playing football. With nothing else to distract her, she had a sudden urge to confess her unhappiness. Brian had told her about his wife's suicide. That must have been a painful confidence to share, inviting her to divulge secrets of her own. It would be heartless to hold back. What did it matter anyway? Barely a vague recollection from the past he was, effectively, a stranger.

'My husband's unfaithful,' she blurted out. All at once she thought she was going to cry. She had never spoken the words out loud to anyone but her husband who doggedly denied her accusations, claiming she didn't understand his relationships with other women. She had believed him at first when he used to say he was working late, but it had been impossible to ignore the evidence. He was permanently besotted with one young girl or another. No amount of pleading on her part made any difference.

'Bastard!' Brian said.

She warmed to his anger. There was no reason for him to care about her distress. He didn't know her, not any more. The fact that they had once sat in the same class room was irrelevant. The past had been overshadowed by a more immediate bond: betrayal.

Ed ran towards them, waving and calling out something she couldn't hear. As soon as she waved back he ran off again.

'Yours?' he asked.

'Yes. They're football mad.' She chuckled. 'Have you got kids?'

'No. I'd have liked a family but somehow it never happened. We never did get to the bottom of it, and then...' He paused.

They watched the twins in silence for a few moments.

'Your boys look as if they're enjoying themselves.'

She followed his puzzled gaze.

'They're identical.'

'Of course. Thought I was seeing double there for a minute.' He smiled. 'Must be hard work. How old are they?'

'Ten.'

'How could your husband even think of cheating, when you've got kids their age?' He turned to her. 'Tell you what, why don't you let me help you? If I can, that is.'

Instantly on her guard, she asked what kind of help he had in mind.

'I was just thinking,' he paused, 'it might be a good thing if we could wake your husband up with a dose of jealousy. What I mean is, he's busy playing away from home, right?'

She nodded cautiously.

'And all the time he knows you're sitting at home. You're always there whenever he wants to come back to you. I expect you even cook him dinner.'

She was tempted to tell him it was none of his business what went on between her and her husband, but she kept quiet, intrigued.

'What he needs is a bit of a scare, something to make him think he might lose you if he's not careful.'

'Lose me?' Her gaze wandered back to the boys, kicking their football around. 'I could never leave him. Not before they're grown up anyway.'

'Good lord, no! I'm not suggesting you leave him. But there are other ways.'

'I don't know what you're talking about.'

He must have realised that she was irritated, because he spoke quickly.

'What I'm suggesting is that I could maybe go to your house and make him think I'm interested in you. I can turn up on the doorstep and pretend I'm looking for you, didn't expect him to be there, that kind of thing. Put the wind up him a bit. Let him wonder who the hell I am and what I want with you. People who are playing away from home always suspect everyone else is doing the same. It's the way their minds work. That's all I'm suggesting. Make him sit up and notice you.'

She smiled at him. 'That's sweet of you, but he'd never believe it. If you told him you fancied me he'd just laugh. He knows I'd

16

never leave him. Not while the boys are around.'

She didn't add that she was afraid Dave simply wouldn't care if she found someone else. He might jump at a chance to get rid of her so he could pursue every little tart that took his fancy, without fear of recrimination.

'Tell you what,' Brian went on, warming to his idea. 'Let's take a selfie together, and I'll make sure he sees it. "This is the woman I'm looking for – do you know where she lives? I seem to have come to the wrong house." That kind of thing.' He grinned. 'What's he going to think when he sees a picture of me with my arm round you? He won't carry on taking you for granted, that's for sure. You can brush it off by explaining I'm just an old friend, we met in the park – all true. But he'll always have that doubt in his mind to keep him on his toes.'

She couldn't help laughing at his childish enthusiasm. He had lost his hangdog air and looked quite attractive. He was a man, anyway. It could work.

'Oh, go on then.'

He put one arm round her shoulders, extended his other arm and took a few pictures.

'You choose.'

Wriggling out of his embrace, she scrolled through the images. They weren't bad. She picked out one where they were both smiling, and wrote down her address on the back of an old receipt he had in his pocket.

'Add a message,' he urged her.

'What sort of message?'

'Nothing too incriminating. How about: "See you soon", something along those lines, and sign it with a kiss.'

He watched her writing, then tucked the slip of paper away in his pocket.

'When will he be at home by himself? I'd better do it when you're not there.'

'You could come round tomorrow afternoon. I take the boys to football practice at two, and we're gone all afternoon. They're football crazy. We don't get home until five at the earliest.'

He nodded briskly and stood up with the air of a man who had concluded a satisfactory business transaction. She felt as though she had hired a hit man. In reality all she had done was arrange for an old school friend to go and have a talk to her husband. The innocent subterfuge gave her a guilty thrill. For so long she had been the victim with Dave. That was about to change. She started to thank Brian, but he was on his way to the exit and she would have had to shout. Watching his figure striding through the gate, she smiled, imagining Dave's surprise when another man came to the house looking for her.

2

GERALDINE GLANCED AT HER watch. It was only seven o'clock. There was no need for her to get up yet. As a detective inspector working in Serious Crime Command in London, she was prepared to work round the clock if necessary, but right now she wasn't on a case. The paperwork for her previous investigation was finished, and she was on call waiting for the next job. Plumping up her pillow, she lay back in bed and gazed at the blind on her window. The slats were slightly open, allowing narrow shafts of bright sunlight to penetrate. That was what had woken her up. It was only May, but blue skies already held a promise of warm weather to come, heralding summer. She smiled and stretched out her legs, luxuriating in the knowledge that she could stay in bed all day if she wanted. For the first time in years, she felt at peace with her world.

After dozing for another hour she got up and opened the blind. Dazzling light hit her. It was a beautiful day. She couldn't decide whether to have breakfast in her flat or walk down the road and treat herself to a pastry and cappuccino in one of the smart cafes along Upper Street. Early promotion to the rank of inspector, together with a generous inheritance from her mother, had enabled her to buy a flat in Islington when she had relocated to London from the Home Counties. It was expensive living in Central London, but she loved the area. Added to the lively atmosphere, it suited her working hours that shops stayed open through the night. She didn't miss the slower pace of life on the Kent constabulary at all.

Half an hour later she was sauntering along Upper Street in bright sunshine, alone in a seething metropolis. Even at that hour the streets were busy with people hurrying by. Cafes had already put tables and chairs out on the pavements, in expectation of fine weather, although it was too chilly to sit outside that early. Only a few smokers were perched on the pavement, huddled in jackets, warming gloved hands on steaming mugs of coffee. Geraldine walked past them, enjoying the atmosphere. She had lived there for nearly two years, but walking along Upper Street still gave her a holiday feeling. In England's capital city, all it took was a little sunshine to make her feel she could be in a Mediterranean town, with its cafe culture spilling out onto the street.

After a leisurely breakfast in one of the cafes, she walked briskly back to her flat. When she had finished a few household chores, she planned to catch up on a DVD box set she had been given for Christmas that she had not yet got round to watching. That, and a takeaway, would complete her lazy day.

The breeze had picked up and she wished she had worn a warmer jacket. She rounded the corner into Waterloo Gardens and her building came into view. The ground floor was occupied by offices, closed at the weekend. The first and second floors of the block were private flats, accessible only through electronically controlled metal gates. For a detective working on murder investigations it was perfect, discreetly tucked away in a side street, yet central, and, above all, secure.

Reaching her building she hesitated, and her good intentions vanished. She couldn't bear the thought of a case being opened while she was at home messing around. It would be different if she had something useful to do with her time off. It was shameful to hanker after the challenge of a murder investigation, but she sometimes felt that her work was all that stood between her and despair about the futility of her life. In another era she might have become a missionary, or a suffragette. As it was, she dedicated herself to the pursuit of justice in an attempt to find purpose in her existence. It was ironic that she felt most alive when investigating the circumstances of someone else's death.

Twenty minutes later, instead of loafing around at home, she was sitting in traffic on her way to work. By mid-morning she was gazing despondently at a pile of claim forms piled neatly on her tidy desk, regretting her decision to go into her office. No new case had turned up demanding her attention. She had merely exchanged her chores at home for mundane tasks at work. As she turned to stare out of the window, she heard the door to her office open and a voice broke into her reverie.

'You're looking thoughtful today.'

Geraldine recognised the drawling voice of Nick Williams, the detective inspector who shared an office with her. She looked round to see him smiling at her, his eyes fixed on hers.

'Penny for your thoughts,' he said softly.

'I'm busy,' she fibbed, resenting the intimacy his tone seemed to imply.

'I can see that.' Nick heaved an exaggerated sigh. 'I just thought you might be ready for a little distraction.'

'I don't like being distracted when I'm working.'

He laughed. 'Your powers of concentration are enviable. You know, I'm just the opposite. I find it almost impossible *not* to be distracted when you're in the same room as me.'

She laughed, trying to quell her irritation at his flirting. She knew his reputation for womanising. Out of the corner of her eye she watched him meticulously arrange papers on his desk into neat piles. It looked as though he had forgotten all about her. So much for him finding her impossibly distracting. They worked in silence, side by side for a while.

'Geraldine.' He spoke so quietly she could barely hear him. 'You haven't heard anything about a white van on an undercover op?'

'No.'

'Or seen a white van hanging around outside?'

'I haven't seen a white van, or heard anything about a white van. Why?'

'It's nothing. Oh shit, I nearly forgot. Reg asked if you were in today. I said I'd let you know he was asking for you when I saw you.'

'Thanks.'

It couldn't be important or Reg would have sent a formal summons rather than passing a casual message via Nick. All the same, she was apprehensive about going to see the detective chief inspector. She hoped she wasn't in trouble.

'Ah, Geraldine, I thought you'd be in at some point today,' Reg greeted her.

He knew it was her day off but had assumed she would turn up anyway. She wasn't sure if he considered that was to her credit. Being unable to switch off from work wasn't healthy. They all knew of cases where officers had suffered burnout from overwork. She hoped he wasn't about to suggest she take some time off.

'I want you to meet Max Grey,' Reg continued affably, 'drafted in from West London to cover for Samantha Haley while she's out of action. He's in his early twenties, a graduate on the fast track, a bright young lad, should go far. Take care of him, won't you?'

Geraldine nodded. The sergeant she had been working with, Sam Haley, was recovering from an injury she had suffered on their last case.

'You'll find him,' Reg added with a nod at the door.

Geraldine understood she was being dismissed. Relieved, she left the room and went to search for Max Grey. She eventually found him in the canteen, where he was chatting to another young officer over coffee.

'That's Geraldine,' she heard his companion say as she approached their table.

Max leaped to his feet. Small and wiry, he had closely cropped dark hair and sharp pointed features.

'Hello, I'm Max Grey,' he announced. 'Fast track graduate, DS, and posted here to work with you. Reg told me to look out for you, and here you are.'

Geraldine was impressed, but at the same time wary. Max carried himself with an air of confidence that bordered on arrogance. Knowing that Reg would have told her about him, there was no need for him to boast about his rapid promotion to sergeant. She had met youngsters like him before, clever young men who thought they knew it all. Resisting the temptation to introduce herself as, 'Geraldine Steel, experienced DI, and your superior officer,' she sat down as Max's companion left.

'Hello. Would you like to get me a coffee, and then you can tell me all about yourself.'

Without a word he turned and went to join the queue at the

canteen. She didn't particularly want a coffee, but it was important to assert her authority right from the start. Watching Max move slowly along the counter, she hoped he would live up to Reg's description.

3

'ARE YOU GOING TO come and give me a hand with the shopping?' Caroline called out again, with growing exasperation.

No one answered. She could hear thumping through the ceiling. Putting down the bags she was holding, she crossed the hall.

'It's not a trampoline up there!' she yelled from the foot of the stairs.

The dull thuds continued, beating out a regular rhythm. The boys were jumping on their beds again, oblivious to her return.

'Dave! Come out here and give us a hand, will you?'

Her husband didn't answer. He was probably asleep, if he was still at home. It would be typical of him to go out, leaving their two ten-year-old boys alone in the house while she was spending her Saturday morning at Tesco.

'Mum'll be home soon,' he would have warned them as he left, 'so don't go making a mess.'

Fuming, she carted the shopping bags into the kitchen and went back for the next load. Just as she had finished putting the last of the shopping away, Dave sauntered into the kitchen.

'Hello, love.'

'Bloody hell, Dave, where have you been?'

'In the shed.'

'You could have helped me bring the shopping in. Why the hell didn't you answer when I called you?'

She knew the reason. He was a lazy sod.

'I told you, I was out in the shed. I didn't know you were back. You should've come to get me.'

'You could have listened out. You knew I'd be back with the shopping.'

Heaving a noisy sigh, she put the kettle on and followed him into the living room. Sprawling in his armchair, frowning at his phone, he didn't even look at her when she spoke to him. She wondered which young floozy he was thinking about this time. If he noticed her disapproving scowl he paid no attention. There might as well have been a wall between them. If it hadn't been for the twins, she would have sent him packing a long time ago, if she had married him in the first place. She suspected he felt the same. She watched him scrolling down his screen, muttering under his breath.

'Are we going to see anything of you this weekend?'

He didn't reply.

'Dave, I'm out of cash.'

He shrugged.

'If we got back all the money you've wasted, we'd be out of debt by now.'

He grunted without looking up. It was a familiar gripe. Above their heads voices rose in shrill anger as the boys began squabbling. Yelling up at them to behave, Caroline went to fetch the ironing board. Dave glanced up as she dragged it into the living room.

'Do you have to do that here?'

'Where do want me to do it?'

Annoyed, he jumped up out of his chair. It was typical of him to vent his irritation on their ten-year-old sons.

'Shut up! You're doing my head in,' he bawled up the stairs.

She glanced at her watch. It was nearly time for the boys to change into their football kit. She had only ironed a couple of Dave's shirts, not that she would get any thanks for it. Grumbling, she shouted up to the boys to get ready. They began clattering about overhead. A few moments later they charged downstairs. She could hear them in the hall, swiping at each other and shouting cheerfully.

'You're dead!'

'Well, I'm a zombie, so you're dead!'

'I'll get you!'

'You can't kill a zombie.'

She had to raise her voice to be heard above their clamour.

'Stop making all that racket and get your boots. It's nearly time to go.'

Dave leaned back in his chair and stretched his legs. His eyes were closed. Seemingly oblivious to her attempts to calm the boys down, and the din that signalled her lack of influence, he could have been lying on a lounger on the beach.

'Don't go to sleep, Dave. Aren't you taking the boys to football practice?'

'Can't you take them?'

'I went last week.' And the week before. And the week before that.

'I would, only I need to stay here and cut the grass. It's going to rain later.'

'Oh, all right. I'll take them again.'

Dave knew her grumbling was put on. She liked taking the twins to football.

'See you later then.'

He sprang to his feet and ruffled the boys' hair so it stood up in spikes.

'I'll get the grass cut so we can have a kick around out there later,' he said, and the boys cheered.

Caroline couldn't help smiling. For all his faults, Dave was a good father. The boys adored him.

'See you later then, love. And don't fall asleep before you've cut the grass.'

He leaned forward and pecked her on the cheek. 'You're not a bad old girl.'

4

IN THE SHED, a man was struggling to untangle the cable of a lawnmower from the legs of a garden chair. Absorbed in his task, he was unaware of Brian's arrival. Stepping over a bright green hose coiled loosely by the entrance, Brian stole towards him. The other man had cheated on his wife. He deserved what was coming to him.

With trembling hands, Brian reached for a large garden spade. Using a weapon that was already there meant it couldn't be traced back to him. Gripping the handle, he imagined the racket that would ensue if he disturbed the shelf it was leaning against; dirty tins of creosote and flower pots crashing to the ground in a cascade of broken opportunity. Breathing silently, eyes stretched wide with the fear of discovery, he raised the spade. Even slamming it down with all his strength, he wasn't confident the blow would be enough to knock the other man out cold. His arms shook. Intending to hit his target with the flat of the spade, he watched in horror as the handle twisted in his gloved hands. The spade slid from his grasp, its edge slicing into the side of the other man's head as it fell.

His victim let out a grunt. His legs gave way and he sank to the floor, hitting his head on the lawnmower with a loud thud. The impact disturbed some blades of dry grass. A few came to rest on a dark pool of blood that was oozing across the floor. The felled man began to moan and his arm twitched in a convulsive movement. Brian swallowed a mouthful of sour vomit. If he threw up in the shed, he would never get away with it. The spade felt heavy when he picked it up a second time. Blood on the handle made it slippery. The man rolled over and he finished the job.

Arms aching, he dropped the spade. It hit the floor with a startling clatter. As he backed away, his elbow knocked a tin off the shelf. The lid must have been loose. Thick black creosote oozed out, mingling with the pool of blood. With a whimper he turned and darted out of the shed, pushing the door shut with his elbow. The stench of creosote followed him as he sprinted away, wiping his shoes on the grass as he ran. His chest was burning but he kept running until he reached his car. He peeled off his gloves, taking care not to touch the outer surfaces, and kicked off his shoes.

Tearing off his jacket, he laid it on the passenger seat beside him, inside out, and rolled it up with his blood-spattered shoes inside it. He wasn't so worried about being seen now. In the darkness blood stains didn't show up against the black fabric of his trousers. As far as he could tell, his jumper was clean. He hoped there were no bloody smears on his face. A trace of his own blood near the scene of the crime could be enough to land him in the nick. But he had been careful. No one had seen him. All he had to do now was get home, shower, and dispose of the incriminating clothes, and it would be over.

Caroline was free, and her husband had been justly punished. He smiled to himself as he turned the key in the ignition. It had been so easy.

5

IT WAS GROWING LATE by the time they returned home. The boys were grouchy, and Caroline was tired. It had been cold standing on the touch line. The Labrador was whining in the hall. Dave had forgotten to put him out. Irritably she sent the boys upstairs to shower while she went to the freezer.

'I'm putting on some chicken nuggets for the boys!' she shouted. 'Do you want some?'

Dave didn't answer.

'Do you want some chicken nuggets?'

Dave still didn't answer. She threw the whole packet on the baking tray and shoved it in the oven. It was too late to take the dog for a walk, so she let him out in the back garden. The soppy animal shot through the door, yelping. She cleared the work surfaces before trotting upstairs to check on the boys. On the way she glanced in her bedroom, half expecting to see Dave lying on the bed, fast asleep. He wasn't there.

After telling her he wanted to stay at home to cut the grass, he had slipped off while she was taking the boys to football. As if that wasn't bad enough, he had forgotten to let the poor dog out. Angrily she stabbed at his name on her phone. He didn't answer.

'Lying toad,' she muttered.

'Mum, where's dad?' Matthew asked as he joined her in the kitchen.

A moment later his brother followed him in. Caroline forced a smile at them as she dished up their supper. Apart from inheriting his blonde hair, they were already developing into miniature versions of their father, slightly built with classic good looks.

'You both played really well today,' she fibbed, feigning enthusiasm.

'Where's dad?' Matthew repeated. 'I want to tell him about my goal.'

'It was just a lucky shot,' his brother said. 'You were rubbish.'

'It was brilliant. I was brilliant,' Matthew replied.

'You were rubbish. He was rubbish, wasn't he, mum?'

The boys settled down to eat.

'Slow down, Matthew,' Caroline said.

The boy looked up from his supper. 'Where's Dobby?'

'He's out in the back garden.' She glanced at her watch. It would be dark outside. 'I'll go and get him.'

When she opened the back door cold air struck her like a slap, making her eyes water. Somewhere in the garden the dog was whimpering. She called him and stood in the doorway, waiting for him to bound over to her. There was no sign of him.

'Dobby!' she yelled. 'Get in here now!'

Only his whimpering alerted her to his presence in the darkness, but he refused to answer her summons.

'Oh, stay out there and get cold then!' she snapped, slamming the door, aware that she was venting her anger with Dave on the dog.

It wasn't unusual for Caroline to feed the boys and put them to bed by herself during the week, but Dave was generally around on a Saturday. Doggedly she kept up a pretence of being cheerful until, finally, the boys were settled in bed. Dave still wasn't home. Furiously she tried his mobile again. There was no answer. Her anger turned to a familiar aching bitterness. It was all right for Dave. He did whatever he wanted, leaving her alone with the chores. They might as well not be married at all. She put the television on. At least she could choose what to watch, while he was out throwing hard earned money at some little tart.

With a guilty start she remembered Dobby, outside in the cold. The dog almost knocked her off her feet in his haste to come in. He dashed past her so fast she couldn't make out what he was holding in his jaws. Afraid he was bringing a dead rat into the house, she hurried after him.

'Dobby, drop it! Drop it!'

Head lowered, tail down, the dog obeyed. She gazed at the

misshapen lump on the kitchen floor. It took her a few seconds to recognise Dave's shoe, glistening with Dobby's saliva, the dirty white fabric stained with blood.

The next few minutes passed in a blur. To begin with Dobby dashed ahead of her, barking and yelping, as she made her way across the garden. It was beautiful in the moonlight. As they approached the shed he hung back, cowering, his tail between his legs. Apprehensively she peeked inside. The shed door creaked and groaned as it swung on its hinges in the cold night air, while the dog's howling echoed eerily across the garden.

At first she didn't see the body lying at her feet. As her eyes grew accustomed to the darkness she made out a shape on the shadowy floor.

'Dave? Dave? What's happened? Is that you?'

It was impossible to believe that her husband was lying there on the filthy floor. Crouching down, feeling the hard mound of his shoulder cupped in her hand, touching the skin on his stiff cold neck, she was momentarily baffled. Only when she felt slippery wetness on the side of his head, slightly sticky on her fingers, did she have a glimmering of understanding.

Apart from the sound of Dobby, whimpering softly, the night was still. Trembling, she scrambled to her feet and stumbled back to the house to call for help. As she stepped indoors, she saw her fingers were bloody. Her legs were shaking. She was afraid she would collapse before she reached the phone. As she heard it ringing, she realised she had left the back door unlocked.

6

GERALDINE WAS POURING a glass of wine when her phone rang. She felt a familiar thrill at the summons. As a detective inspector working in Serious Crime Command, a call at home could mean only one thing. Within seconds of answering the phone, she was pulling on her shoes, still listening to the call.

'I'm on my way.'

She arrived half an hour before the briefing was due to begin and went straight to her office, expecting to find it empty at that hour. To her surprise, her colleague Nick Williams was still at his desk.

'I thought you'd gone home,' he greeted her.

'You're working late.'

He grinned at her. 'I couldn't think of a nicer way to spend the evening than looking at you.'

Preoccupied by the pending case, Geraldine wasn't sure she appreciated Nick's flattery at that hour. It sounded insincere, and was quite frustrating because she couldn't tell if he fancied her, or was just being friendly. Taking everything into account, she hoped it was the latter. Sharing an office, it could become uncomfortable if they grew intimate, or fell out.

Normally clean shaven and smartly dressed, Nick appeared uncharacteristically unkempt. His hair was a mess, the lower part of his face grey with stubble. Aware of her scrutiny, he turned away and began to fidget with files, straightening them so they lay parallel to the edge of his desk.

'Are you OK? You look a bit rough.'

He countered with a flippant comment about some women liking 'a bit of rough'.

'I'm serious, Nick.'

'Well, I'm fine. You don't need to worry about me.'

He forced a laugh, and mumbled something about going drinking with some mates. He refused to meet her eye as he spoke.

'Is something going on here, or is it problems at home?' she probed gently.

He shrugged. 'A bit of both, to be honest. But how about you? What are you doing here at this ungodly hour?'

Geraldine told him she had been summoned to a short briefing at the station before the investigation began.

'Reg cracking the whip?'

Geraldine had a grudging respect for Detective Chief Inspector Reg Milton, the senior investigating officer on the case.

'He probably just wants to keep us all out of bed,' she said, lightly dismissing Nick's comment.

He turned away from her with a shrug. 'If that's what you think.'

She was drawn in, despite her reluctance to engage Nick in conversation. 'What do you mean?'

Undecided what to make of Reg, she was curious to discover what Nick thought of him.

'I've got a lot of time for Reg,' Nick said. 'We go back a long way.'

'But?'

Prompted, he came over and perched on the edge of her desk, very close to her. She restrained herself from shifting her chair further away from him.

'But nothing. Reg is – well, he sometimes comes across as more interested in himself and the progress of his own career than in the case, if you get what I mean. Not that there's anything wrong with that,' he added quickly. 'There are plenty of very good career officers on the force. But not all of them have the same passion for the job that we have.'

Geraldine nodded. If she was honest, she had entertained a few reservations about Reg's motives herself. He was clearly ambitious, and she suspected he would probably prioritise his own career over any other considerations. It could be dangerous to make a mistake on a case where he was senior investigating officer.

'Fortunately his promotion depends on carrying out successful investigations,' she said, 'whatever his personal motivation.'

'I didn't mean to say he isn't dedicated to the job,' Nick seemed to backtrack. 'He's a bloody fine officer.'

There wasn't time for Geraldine to reply. The briefing was due to begin.

'The body of a man has been discovered in his own back garden, just off Ballards Lane,' Reg announced to the assembled officers.

He turned to a picture of the dead man as he spoke. It looked like a passport photograph. In his thirties, with short curly fair hair and wire-framed glasses, the victim stared levelly back at them. 'David Robinson, living with his wife and ten-year-old twins.' He read out an address in Finchley, North London.

Someone asked who had found the body. The victim's wife had discovered him in his garden shed. A faint sigh rustled round the room.

'Imagine if he'd been discovered by one of his kids,' someone muttered, voicing what everyone was thinking.

'It was his wife who found him,' Reg repeated firmly.

Geraldine drove to the victim's house, accompanied by her new sergeant, Max Grey. He seemed enthusiastic and conscientious, but they hadn't worked together before. She was pleased to find that he was impatient to view the crime scene before too much had been moved. As far as they knew, the body had not yet been taken to the mortuary.

It was Saturday evening, and everyone had had a busy day. The usual crowd of spectators had not yet gathered, hungry for information and gossip. In the light from the street lamps uniformed officers were visible, guarding the entrance to the house, but the street was otherwise deserted. Passing through the cordon, they followed a constable down an unlit side passage that ran alongside the house and into the back garden.

'He was found by his wife,' the constable told them as they pulled on their protective suits. 'It's lucky she happened to spot him, really. There are two kids living here who could've found him. His kids. They're only about ten. His own kids. Can you imagine? He's not a pretty sight.'

Geraldine thanked the constable and turned to enter the protective tent that had been erected over the entrance to a garden shed.

'I wish he hadn't said that,' Max muttered as he followed Geraldine.

She didn't answer. Beneath his dark hair, the young sergeant's sharp face looked pale in the brilliant lighting that had been rigged up inside the tent. She hoped he wasn't going to turn out to be squeamish. It was a surprisingly common handicap for a detective working on a murder investigation team. Geraldine herself had never been fazed by the horrors they witnessed in the course of their work. She liked to attribute that to her single-minded focus on the job. The dead gave invaluable clues to the identity of their killers. But apart from her professional interest, she found them intrinsically fascinating.

'His wife and kids are in the house with a constable,' they were told as they went in.

'Widow,' Max said.

Geraldine noted his pedantic remark with silent approval. Attention to detail could be crucial to the success of a case.

A scene of crime officer and a doctor were inside the tent, the former gathering data, the latter kneeling by the corpse conducting a preliminary examination. Any question over whether the death might have been accidental vanished as soon as they set eyes on the body. The victim lay on his back. With thin arms and legs sticking out from his slight frame, he resembled a monstrous four-legged insect. One side of his face had been smashed in. A large metal gardening spade lay on the floor nearby, the blade stained with blood. Blobs of soft tissue clung to it, like rock barnacles.

'Jesus,' Max mumbled.

The doctor turned to greet them and Geraldine was pleased to see Miles Fellowes. She had worked with the young pathologist on previous cases. He had been summoned straight away, since there was no doubt this was murder.

'Can you tell us the time of death?' she asked.

'Between four and five this afternoon,' Miles said. 'It looks as though he was taken by surprise, felled from behind and then repeatedly hit when he turned to face his attacker.'

Geraldine stared at the dead man's pulverised head.

'It was a violent attack,' she said.

'You can say that again,' Max agreed. His voice shook slightly.

The pathologist nodded. 'There were multiple blows to the head, possibly none severe enough on their own to kill him, although I'll be able to tell you more about it once I've had a chance to carry out a full examination. The killer hit him repeatedly with the flat of the spade, but the edge of it caught him a couple of times too, slashing the side of his head. The murder weapon was a heavy garden spade...'

'Suggesting it wasn't premeditated?' Max interrupted him. 'The killer didn't bring the murder weapon with him.'

'Yes, it looks as though the killer used whatever came to hand.'

'But we can't be sure of that,' Geraldine said.

They looked down at the body.

'Is it possible to say how many times he was hit?' she asked.

Miles shrugged. 'At least six times, possibly as many as a dozen. I'll know more once I've examined him properly.'

'It's possible the killer wasn't very strong, if he had to hit him repeatedly before he managed to kill him,' Max said.

'It's possible,' Geraldine concurred, 'but it might have been a frenzied attack. We can't be sure of anything yet.'

'We can be sure he's dead,' Miles pointed out with a slight grin.

Geraldine suppressed a smile. She suspected the killer had hit the victim repeatedly in a rage. Someone who wasn't very strong would be unlikely to seize a heavy spade and use it to beat a man to death. Not only that, but the longer the attack lasted, the more chance there was of discovery. The nature of the attack suggested the killer had been out of control.

'He fought back,' Miles went on, 'but he was already on the ground. The first blow must have caught him off guard because it felled him. He didn't stand a chance really.'

While Max went to speak to scene of crime officers again, Geraldine went in the house where the dead man's widow and two sons were sitting huddled together on a sofa in the living room. The woman looked older than her thirty-five years, her dark hair streaked with grey. Two identical blond-haired boys were sitting on either side of her, leaning against her. Both children were crying. Their mother stared straight ahead, the desolation in her eyes more desperate than tears.

Geraldine approached. 'Mrs Robinson?'

The woman nodded without looking up. Geraldine introduced herself and asked if she would answer a few questions.

'We can do this later, if you prefer. But we're keen to find out what happened as quickly as we can.'

The woman gave another nod to indicate she had understood and was prepared to talk. After a female constable had taken the two boys to the kitchen, Geraldine sat down.

'Can you tell me what happened? Take your time.'

7

It was only natural for Caroline to be distressed. As the recently widowed mother of ten-year-old twins, she would be expected to be shocked by her husband's sudden death. That was lucky, because it gave her time to think. But she couldn't delay answering the sharp-eyed inspector indefinitely. The detective was watching her, waiting for her to regain control of herself. With her head down, Caroline wondered what would happen to her sons if the truth ever came out. Shaken by a bout of crying, she glanced up at the inspector who was sitting perfectly still, waiting.

'I'm sorry,' she stuttered, 'I can't think straight. What did you want to know?'

'There's nothing to apologise about.' The detective smiled. Her huge black eyes stared at Caroline without blinking. 'This can wait. I can come back tomorrow.'

Tomorrow.

Caroline struggled to understand the implications of her husband's death. Dave hadn't been mugged in the street. He had been killed in their own back garden. Worse than that, it was her fault he was dead. She shivered. She had never meant it to end like this. Whatever else happened, the police must never discover that she had not only met her husband's killer, but she had given him their address and told him when the coast would be clear so he could find Dave alone. The police would never believe the truth. They would assume she had arranged for Brian to kill Dave.

'I want to know who did it,' she muttered fiercely. 'I want to help. Ask me anything you like. Anything at all.'

She wasn't sure what she was talking about, or what she would be saying if she was innocent. She tried to imagine how she would be feeling if she hadn't been involved in the murder. Of course

Dave's death had come as a total shock, but there was no escaping the dreadful truth. She may not have been wielding the murder weapon, but she was responsible for the death of her husband, her children's father, the man she had once loved more than life itself. All that mattered now was her sons. She felt herself trembling with fear in case she slipped up and betrayed her guilt. If the police suspected her, they would take the boys away from her. Wherever this nightmare carried her, she mustn't lose the boys.

If the questions were too difficult for her to handle she would have to break down in tears, or complain of a headache, and postpone the interview. She almost did. It was crazy, allowing herself to be interrogated in her present state. But leaving the detective unsatisfied meant the prospect of yet more questions. Far better to get it over with as quickly as possible. At least she had a cast iron excuse for sounding confused right now.

All she wanted was to be left alone to rebuild her life quietly, in her own way. Things were going to be very different now. She dropped her gaze, afraid the detective would see through her lies. It was hard to take in the reality of the situation. Never again would she sit downstairs by herself, wondering if her husband was going to return home before morning. Worse than his infidelity had been his deception. Lies had fallen easily from his lips, as though he hadn't cared whether she believed him or not. Losing her trust had meant nothing to him. Her own lies had to be convincing.

The inspector's words cut through Caroline's chaotic thoughts.

'Can you think of anyone who might have wanted to harm your husband? Take your time. Think carefully.'

'No.' She answered, too quickly.

'Was there anyone who might have held a grudge against him for some reason?'

Caroline tried to speak slowly and make her words sound considered, but she could hear herself gabbling, close to hysterics.

'No. No one. He wasn't that sort of man.'

'What sort of man?'

Caroline hesitated. She wasn't fooled by the inspector's sympathetic expression. Behind a show of compassion, the woman was waiting for her to slip up so she could pounce. Caroline could see it in her eyes. She was desperate to pin this murder on someone, and the victim's wife was bound to be a likely suspect, especially if they ever found out about his other women.

'He wasn't the sort of man to get killed,' she announced firmly.

The inspector's eyes widened slightly. That was bad. Caroline's reply had surprised her. In all her years as a detective, the inspector had obviously never heard an innocent person say that. It was as good as a confession of guilt. Any second now, Caroline expected to be arrested. She closed her eyes in an effort to stop shaking, and waited for the inspector to speak. What would happen to her sons if she went to prison? But when Caroline opened her eyes, the inspector was rising to her feet.

'If you can think of anything else, call me.'

Stunned, Caroline took her card and stared at the name: 'Detective Inspector Geraldine Steel'.

'If you think of anything else that might help us,' the inspector repeated, 'you can call me at any time.'

Caroline nodded.

'I'll see myself out. Would you like PC Perry to wait with you until your neighbour gets here?'

Caroline shook her head. 'No,' she whispered. 'I'll be fine.'

She just wanted the police to go away and leave her alone. On top of having to deal with the shock of Dave's death, she had to cope with the stress of telling lies to an inspector trained to detect the truth. She could barely control herself from confessing her guilt just to put an end to the terror. But she had to stay strong for the sake of her boys.

As soon as the inspector had gone, Caroline dropped her head into her hands and began sobbing uncontrollably. At last she pulled herself together and went upstairs to wash her face. The boys had been taken to a neighbour's house. They hadn't wanted to go, but the police had suggested it would be best.

'We need to get on with our work here,' they said quietly.

Caroline understood that they wanted to move the body. It would be better if the boys weren't around when that happened.

'But what about you, mum?' Ed insisted. 'We can't leave you here by yourself.'

She had to promise them she would be fine on her own before the boys agreed to leave. She didn't add that she needed time to rearrange her face, and her thoughts. She was a widow. Her husband had been violently murdered in their own back garden. She told herself fiercely that she hadn't the faintest idea who had killed him, or why. He must have been the victim of a random attack by a maniac, or a drug addict. His death made no sense. It had nothing to do with her chance encounter in the park the previous afternoon. The best thing she could do right now was forget all about that. There was certainly no point in mentioning Brian to the police. Even in her confused state of mind she understood that they were bound to suspect her of being implicated in Dave's murder. For the sake of her sons she had to ensure no hint of suspicion fell on her.

When her neighbour finally brought the boys back, Caroline had her crying under control. No one could have suspected she was feeling overwhelmed not by grief, but by fear.

8

BY THE FOLLOWING MORNING A team of constables had been assembled to speak to residents in The Ridgeway where Caroline lived. Leaving Max to co-ordinate the door-to-door questioning, Geraldine turned her attention to the neighbours on either side of the Robinsons' house. She would have liked to speak to all the residents in the street herself, but she had to be practical. First she walked along the pavement to the first corner in one direction, then back the other way as far as the next side turning, observing.

The door to the adjoining property was opened by Arthur Mortimer, a stout ruddy-faced man who enquired her business in a brisk tone. As soon as she introduced herself his demeanour altered.

'It's all been a terrible shock,' he admitted solemnly. 'My wife's very upset about the whole thing.'

'Were you close to them?'

'Close? No. I wouldn't say we were close, exactly. But we knew them to speak to. We were neighbours, you know. We were... neighbourly.'

Arthur took Geraldine through to a tidy little kitchen where he introduced his wife, Mavis. Wide-eyed with dismay, she ducked her head deferentially to Geraldine.

'We heard all the sirens going, but it never occurred to us there'd been a murder, just the other side of the fence. We watched all the comings and goings, but when we saw the ambulance we thought there must have been a terrible accident, didn't we? It wasn't until we saw the tent in the garden that Arthur told me what had happened. "There's been a murder," he said, didn't you, Arthur? He knew straight away.'

Arthur's face turned a deeper shade of red.

'Of course we knew something was wrong,' she went on, 'but we weren't sure whether to go round there or not. There are children in the house.'

'It wasn't our place to go interfering,' her husband interrupted her firmly. 'We're not family.'

Geraldine had the impression this wasn't the first time they had discussed it.

'After all they've been through, as well,' Mavis continued, 'to have it all end like this.' She shook her head. 'It could have been them that found their father out in the garden like that. After all they've been through, poor things.'

'What do you mean by that?' Geraldine wanted to know. 'What have they been through?'

'What?'

'You said, "after all they've been through." What did you mean?'

Mavis threw a worried glance at her husband before mumbling about hearing shouting next door.

'We heard them a few times,' Arthur agreed, 'shouting obscenities at each other. I don't think they got on well.'

'They had no business using language like that in front of their children,' his wife added.

Having established they had nothing more to tell her, Geraldine left. It had begun to rain so she pulled up the hood of her raincoat and walked quickly along the road to question the neighbours on the other side.

A woman with straggly blonde hair came to the door.

'What?' she demanded.

Geraldine introduced herself and explained the purpose of her call.

'First I knew about it was when your lot arrived. Why they needed to turn up with sirens blaring, beats me. I mean, what was the rush? The poor bloke was dead, so where was the hurry?'

Fortunately there was a narrow porch overhanging the front door, because the woman didn't invite Geraldine in.

'I don't want to be unhelpful, Inspector, but I really don't know what you want me to say. It's not like we were mates or anything. They just live next door. I know them to say hello to, I know they've got twins. Always making a racket, those kids, but they seem all right, I suppose. He's – he was...' She broke off in confusion. 'I'm sorry but I don't know what I'm supposed to say. I hardly knew the bloke. But they used to do a hell of a lot of swearing and yelling, especially in the summer, with the windows open. I hope you catch the maniac that killed him before it gets dark.'

Geraldine didn't say they had no idea yet who had committed the murder.

'Did you have the impression they were a happy household?'

The woman snorted. 'What's happy when it's at home?'

Geraldine tried again. 'What impression did you have of them?'

The neighbour shrugged. 'Like I said, I don't really know them. They're – they were – just the people next door.'

'Did you ever see them going out together as a family?'

The other woman shook her head. 'We keep ourselves to ourselves. I'm not one to go snooping.'

The neighbour in the house opposite was more forthcoming. She invited Geraldine in straight away, without even pausing to glance at her warrant card. But although she was keen to help, she could offer no useful information either. She seemed to want to talk about the victim.

'He was a lovely man,' she repeated, dabbing cautiously at heavily made-up eyes. 'And those poor boys, orphaned at such a young age, without any warning.'

Geraldine didn't point out that David Robinson's sons were not orphans while their mother was still alive.

'And to go like that,' she continued, 'savagely butchered in his own back garden. It's horrible.'

Outwardly impassive, Geraldine wondered how much the woman knew about the nature of her neighbour's death, and who had told her. The man had been dead for less than twenty-four hours and already gossip was spreading. With neighbours talking in terms of butchery, she hardly dared speculate how the local media would sensationalise the fatality. None of it made any difference to the victim, but publicity didn't make life easier for his family, or for the police who were already under pressure to find the killer quickly. Until he was caught, there was always a chance he might strike again.

9

THE DETECTIVE CHIEF INSPECTOR summoned the team to a briefing early next morning. Geraldine was already at her desk, having left home at six thirty to avoid the Monday morning traffic.

'The violent nature of the assault suggests a crime of passion, which makes the wife a suspect. What do you think, Geraldine? You questioned her. Do you think she could have killed him?'

Choosing her words with care, Geraldine said she thought Caroline had been afraid rather than upset.

'I mean, I can understand why she might feel frightened. It looks like this was a frenzied attack,' she added, repeating the pathologist's words.

'It certainly looks as though it could have been done in the heat of the moment. So do you think she's responsible?'

She shook her head. 'It's hard to say. The neighbours reported hearing heated arguments, but I can't believe she would have left him in the shed like that, with her children in the house.'

Reg scowled. A tall man, he stood with his shoulders slightly hunched, in an aggressive posture.

'You don't think she did it then?'

'No, I don't.'

'What about evidence? Does she have an alibi?'

Geraldine turned to Max who had been checking out Caroline's movements at the time of the murder. Caroline claimed to have taken her sons to football training on Saturday afternoon. Her husband had wanted to stay at home to cut the grass. She had left the house at around two o'clock and hadn't left the football club until around six, arriving home at about a quarter past.

'She was a bit vague as to the exact times. As soon as they reached home, she got their dinner on while the children went

45

upstairs to shower.' Max looked up from his notes with a frown. 'We've already spoken to half a dozen of the other parents who were there, and to the football coach. They've all confirmed that she was at the training ground with her kids on Saturday, watching them play football, and that she didn't leave early. So she wouldn't have reached home till past six.'

'He was killed between four and five,' Geraldine said.

'She would've had to slip away from the football without anyone noticing, race home, kill him and then be back again without anyone realising she had gone,' Max pointed out.

'So we all agree it's unlikely, but is it possible?' Reg persisted. 'She might not have returned home intending to kill him. She might have forgotten something, gone home to fetch it, and come across her husband by accident, as it were. Is the timing feasible?'

Geraldine understood his eagerness. If they thought Caroline had murdered her husband, they would at least have a line of enquiry to pursue, and Reg would have something to tell his superiors.

'Are you confident she couldn't have gone home in the time available?' Reg repeated.

'Just the travelling home and back again would have taken half an hour, at least, whatever route she took. I've checked all the possibilities. Plus her alibi checks out,' Max said firmly. 'We checked CCTV at the sports ground as well as asking other parents who were there, and Caroline's vehicle never left the car park. The evidence shows she was there the whole time.'

'Excellent work, Max, very thorough,' Reg said. 'Carry on like that and we'll make an inspector of you before you know it, eh, Geraldine?'

She nodded. Reg had never praised her so generously, but she had to agree Max was an impressive young man. For all his air of breezing through tasks, there was no denying he worked hard, and he seemed to grasp that any detail could be significant until it was ruled out. What was even more impressive was his easy manner when standing up to the detective chief inspector's questioning. But Geraldine would happily have forfeited Max's confidence for her usual sergeant's presence at her side. It was true that Sam could act rashly, but only because she was driven by a passion for her work. Despite her impetuous nature, she had an instinct for the job which Geraldine suspected Max lacked.

With a snort of impatience, Reg turned to Geraldine. 'She was his wife. Maybe she isn't directly responsible for his death, but she must know something. Didn't you manage to find out anything at all?'

Geraldine did her best to ignore the implication that she hadn't been conscientious in her questioning. She repeated her earlier statement.

'What was she afraid of?'

'I don't know.'

A sergeant made a quip about anyone in their right mind being afraid of being questioned by Geraldine, but she didn't smile. Caroline had made her feel uneasy, although she couldn't say why.

That afternoon Geraldine went along to the mortuary to find out what Miles could tell them. His reports were invariably submitted promptly. All the same, she wanted to go and speak to him herself. Not only would she hear the results of his examination straight away, but he was often willing to share information with her in person that he would be reluctant to commit to a written report. 'Off the record,' he liked to say, and she was grateful to him for sharing his impressions. Not all pathologists were so relaxed in their approach.

Miles looked up and smiled at her when she arrived. In his white apron he looked like a plump butcher as he raised a bloody gloved hand in cheerful greeting.

'This is all pretty clear cut, for once,' he announced cheerfully. 'He was struck on the side of his head with some force, probably with the edge of the spade which was then swung at the back of his head, again with some force. He must have been knocked down – probably knocked out – by the initial blow. The edge of the spade caught him and sliced right through the skin, fracturing the parietal bone.'

'Was that what killed him?'

Miles nodded. 'Brain damage, intracranial bleeding and shock all contributed to his death.'

'What can you tell us about his killer?'

'Anything I say would be guesswork.'

'Guess away.'

Many pathologists would refuse to speculate about crime scenes, at least in the presence of a detective on duty.

'This is most unscientific,' Miles protested feebly, his eyes alight with excitement.

'Yes, yes, off the record, I know. So…?'

Grinning, Miles rubbed his bloody gloves together. 'The first blow was to the side of the head. Presumably he didn't see it coming because there's no evidence he tried to defend himself, no bruising on his arms from an attempt to ward off the blow. He was standing in the shed, and it's possible – there's no evidence for this, mind – but it's a reasonable supposition that someone came up behind him. There's no other way of making sense of his being hit so soundly on his head.'

'Soundly?'

'Fiercely, strongly – it was a blow strong enough to knock him out. It would have knocked him off balance anyway. He must have flung his arms out as he fell, cutting his forearm on a rake. Scene of crime officers have confirmed blood on the rake, and these lacerations match the prongs of the tool.'

Geraldine leaned forward to peer at a line of parallel scratches on the victim's arm.

'He also hit his face on a lawnmower when he fell.' Miles nodded to a colleague who turned the body over, exposing a large bruise on the side of the dead man's forehead. 'Once he was down, he tried to stand up.'

'How far did he get?'

'I'm only telling you what might have happened,' Miles reminded her. 'I think before he could get to his feet, the killer struck again, this time making a nasty dent on the back of his head. His attacker then hit him about six times, but by then he was already dead.'

Geraldine frowned. Miles hadn't really told her anything useful.

'What about the killer? How tall was he? Would this have taken a strong person? Do you think a woman could have done it?'

'Now that really would be moving into the realms of pure guesswork. I'd like to be able to give you a full description, but all

I can tell you is that you're looking for a very dangerous killer. A maniac.'

'Aren't they all?'

'Yes, but this was a particularly ferocious assault.' He glanced up at Geraldine. 'Someone as violent as this could be a danger to the public. He needs to be locked up.'

10

BY MONDAY AFTERNOON, CAROLINE was struggling to cope with the twins.

'Why did it happen, mum?'

She tried to explain that a bad man had attacked Dave for no reason. Violence like that hardly ever happened where they lived. The bad man would never come back to their street. The police would soon lock him up and never let him go.

'But why did it have to be our dad?' Ed kept asking.

She had no answer. All she could do was try to comfort the devastated boys. There were moments when their distress distracted her from the memory of Dave's body, lying on the floor of the shed. But such respite never lasted long.

The head teacher suggested the boys keep to their normal routine, as far as possible, assuring Caroline that their teachers would keep a close eye on them. Caroline could see the sense in what the head said, but she didn't argue with her sons' demands to stay at home. At first inconsolable, the boys cheered up when they realised they didn't have to go to school. Always keen to know exactly what was going on, Ed asked when they would have to go to back.

'When you're ready,' she replied stupidly, and was rewarded with a grin from Matthew.

'We'll never be ready,' he crowed, flapping his arms.

Ever serious, Ed disagreed. 'What about our education?' he asked. 'We'll have to earn lots of money so we can look after mum when we're grown up.'

Caroline was relieved when they started squabbling again.

Although they weren't keen to return to school, they were bored at home. Apprehensively, Caroline allowed them to cycle round the block. As long as they didn't try to cross the road and kept each other in sight, it was safe enough.

'Dad would have let us,' Matthew pointed out.

It was probably true.

'What if the killer's out there?' Ed asked.

'Good,' Matthew replied promptly. 'We can zap him.' He mimed holding a gun. 'Peeow! Peeow!'

Caroline smiled anxiously. 'You'll be fine. Just stick together, boys, and don't go on the road.'

Promising they would be careful, the boys raced off. Caroline watched them through the window until they disappeared from view. They seemed to be gone for hours, although it was only actually about twenty minutes before they ran back in, squabbling.

'Don't,' she heard Matthew say. 'She won't like it.'

'We have to. We promised.'

'We didn't want to.'

'But we did.'

'You did, I didn't. We're not allowed to talk to strangers.'

'We never talked to him. He talked to us.'

'You told him we'd tell her.'

'I only said yes. One word doesn't count.'

Caroline went out into the hall and asked what they were talking about. The boys hesitated. Matthew glared at his brother.

'We got a message to tell you,' Ed muttered.

'Shut up,' Matthew hissed. 'She won't like it.'

'From a man,' Ed went on, his face rigid with determination. 'It was a message for you.'

Caroline smiled weakly, waiting to hear another expression of condolence from a neighbour she barely knew.

Ed cleared his throat. 'He said to tell you it's your turn now. He said he's done what you wanted.'

'And now it's your turn to do what he wants,' Matthew echoed.

'He said it's your turn to do the same for him,' Ed corrected his brother earnestly.

'Who was he?' she asked, trying to quell the feeling of dread that had gripped her.

Ed shrugged. 'Don't know.'

'What did he look like?'

'He had a spotty face!' Matthew shouted, eager to join in as much as possible, now that Ed had spoken out. 'He was ugly. He had ginger hair and pokey eyes.'

Caroline suddenly felt as though she couldn't breathe.

'What's pokey eyes?' Ed interrupted. 'No one has pokey eyes. You're an idiot.'

'We didn't like him. He had hairy hands.'

'He likes us. He told us to be sure to tell you he said it was nice to meet us.'

'Who was he, mum?'

Caroline shook her head. 'I've no idea,' she lied.

'Well, I didn't like him, not one bit,' Ed agreed with his brother. 'He was weird.'

Afraid the boys would sense her panic, Caroline sent them to watch television before she double locked the front door. Then she bolted the back door and went round the house checking all the windows were shut. In the morning she would think about going to the police to insist they move her and the boys to a safe house until Brian was locked up. She had to convince the police that Brian's threat was serious, without explaining how she knew he had killed Dave.

11

THE DEAD MAN HAD been quite short and slight, with curly fair hair. Despite his good looks, there was something effete in his cleanly delineated features. Max had been working with the borough intelligence unit, looking into the victim's circumstances. Geraldine wanted to quiz him about what he had found out. She found him in the canteen. Over coffee, Max told her that Caroline and Dave had been married for ten years.

'Do you think they got married because she was pregnant?'

'I guess. But listen.' Max leaned forward. 'They were in a bit of financial difficulty, thanks to him.'

'I thought he was an electrician? They had quite a nice house. Finchley's not that cheap.'

'It was his parents' house. He was living with them when they were both killed in a car crash, about ten years ago. He never moved out. His wife – widow, I should say – works part-time at a local café. Between them they managed to earn enough, but the point is, he was spending a hell of a lot. According to his workmates he was a bit of a player, always chasing after women.'

Geraldine wondered whether they had been rash to dismiss Caroline as a suspect.

'I looked into their finances,' Max went on. 'He'd remortgaged the house, he was maxed out on credit cards, they had the bailiffs round more than once repossessing their stuff – they lost a TV and a car – and last month they were being threatened with repossession which would leave them with massive negative equity. As far as his wife was concerned, someone bumped him off just in the nick of time.'

Geraldine nodded. The sergeant's youthful conceit was irritating, but she was continually impressed by his industry. If she could train him to control his tendency to jump to conclusions he would be an excellent officer, as Reg had intimated.

'And I suppose you're going to tell me next that he had a life insurance policy...'

'Taken out when the twins were born. No doubt that would have been cashed in next...'

'If he hadn't gone first.'

Looking up, Geraldine saw Nick in the doorway. He saw her and raised his hand. Before she could acknowledge the greeting, Max stood up.

'Come on, we'll be late for the briefing,' he said.

Geraldine was surprised to realise how quickly she had come to depend on Max to remind her of their schedule. She was used to being in control. As she passed Nick in the doorway, he touched her arm. Meanwhile, Max was striding on ahead.

'Fancy a drink later?' Nick muttered.

It seemed as though he wanted to catch her attention without anyone else noticing. Flustered, she hurried after her sergeant without stopping to answer.

At a nod from Reg, Max stepped forward. He looked around the room. Once again, Geraldine was struck by his self-assurance. She was beginning to feel he had earned the right to feel confident. Not yet in his mid-twenties and already a sergeant, he had entered the service on a fast track graduate scheme which promised rapid promotion. Not all entrants made the grade, but Geraldine thought Max would be fine. He brought the team up to speed about the victim spending virtually all his money on other women. A mutter rippled around the room. Everyone understood how powerful a motive Caroline had for getting rid of her husband.

'It's only hearsay,' Max concluded.

Reg's broad square face creased in a smile.

'Who was it interviewed the wife?'

'That was me,' Geraldine replied sharply. He couldn't have forgotten that she was the officer who had spoken to Caroline. 'I spoke to her. There was something uneasy about the way she answered my questions, as though she was on her guard, but she has an alibi. She might not have been heartbroken, but I can't believe she would have killed her children's father, not at home where they could have found him.'

'Yes, yes, you made that point before, and if we're dealing with a normal mother that would be significant. But if she's a killer who brutally assaulted her husband, well, the rules of normal behaviour are hardly going to apply to her.'

'She has an alibi,' Geraldine insisted.

'She might have paid a hit man,' someone suggested.

'It's possible,' Reg agreed.

'With what?' Geraldine asked. 'They were about to lose their house. They were skint.'

Reg turned to Max and instructed him to investigate Caroline's financial circumstances further. If the widow had somehow managed to get her hands on a reasonable sum of money, then she might indeed have arranged for her husband to be removed while she was out, watching her sons play football, in the presence of several witnesses. Geraldine hoped they wouldn't discover Caroline was responsible for her husband's death. The woman had two young sons who had already lost their father.

It wasn't the first time Geraldine had found herself at odds with Reg. He wasn't an easy man to challenge. As her senior officer, she found him quite intimidating. Bombastic and self-opinionated, he seemed to solicit her views only to overrule her response when her ideas didn't coincide with his own. As if that wasn't sufficiently irritating, Reg favoured the opinions of a useless profiler. Apart from Jayne, all the profilers Geraldine had worked with had offered invaluable insights. Geraldine couldn't understand why an intelligent man like Reg would have time for this woman's inane views.

Jayne shook her long curly hair and looked around the room with a warm smile.

'Wives killing their husbands isn't as extraordinary as you might think. Think of Agamemnon, the king of Greece who led an army to recover Helen of Troy.'

'Is he a suspect?' someone called out.

Jayne gave a tolerant smile. A few people sniggered. Geraldine heaved a sigh of quiet protest. She wanted to focus on the investigation, not waste time listening to a lecture on ancient Greek mythology. Even Reg looked disgruntled.

'While Agamemnon was away for ten years fighting, his wife took a lover,' Jayne continued, apparently indifferent to the ribbing. 'When Agamemnon returned, his wife and her lover killed him. It's a pattern that has been repeated time and again. A wife takes a lover and they kill the husband and take his estate and make themselves rich.'

'Rich in debts,' Geraldine muttered. 'And who's the accomplice in this case?' she demanded out loud. 'It's all well and good establishing her motive – a lot of wives probably want to see their husbands killed.'

There was a ripple of laughter. Jayne raised her eyebrows. Someone called out that it was no wonder Geraldine was single. Ignoring the reaction, she carried on.

'Don't forget Caroline has an alibi for the time of her husband's murder.'

'I heard about your little outburst earlier on,' Nick said when he joined her in their office later that afternoon.

Geraldine hesitated, her eyes on her desk. She wasn't sure what to say. His comment was tolerant, yet once again he was implying an intimacy that made her feel uncomfortable. There was no sensible reason for her to feel awkward in his company, but she did. If she knew for certain that he was seriously attracted to her, the situation would be easier to deal with. They hadn't exactly been on a date, but several times he had asked her out for a drink, and they had stayed on for something to eat. She enjoyed spending time with him, and would have liked him to confide in her. At the same time, she was wary of making a fool of herself with a man she would have to see every day. He worked with her colleagues, and knew them far better than she did. His flattery was gratifying. She just wished she knew for certain what it signified.

'Do you want to talk about it?' he went on, moving closer until he was standing beside her chair, leaning on the back of it. She could smell his aftershave.

'I'd like to stop and chat,' she replied brusquely, panicking, 'but I've got to go.'

She stood up and hurried from the room. She couldn't allow anything to distract her from her investigation.

12

CAROLINE HADN'T SLEPT SINCE she had discovered Dave's body. It wasn't that losing him had broken her heart exactly. She had given up hoping to reclaim his affection a long time ago. What worried her was her meeting with Brian. She had dismissed the encounter as irrelevant, until the boys had delivered a message that could only have come from him. They had both been clear about the wording. 'He said he's done what you wanted, and now it's your turn to do what he wants.' They had described Brian, right down to his hairy hands and his bad complexion.

Brian wanted Caroline to do something for him. Only the memory of Dave's body prevented her from dismissing his message as a sick prank. Whatever Brian expected of her, it wasn't going to be good. She wanted to tell the police, but that would mean admitting she had known in advance that Brian was going to see Dave. Worse, she was the one who had set up the meeting, telling Brian where to find him, and taking the boys out of the way. The police were bound to suspect her of being complicit in the attack.

She tried to reassure herself there was nothing Brian could do if she ignored his demands. He could hardly report her to the police. But he knew where she lived. She had volunteered that information herself. He had spoken to her sons. He was capable of murder. There was no knowing what he might do if she refused to carry out his request. She wanted to discover what he was after, and she was terrified of finding out. Meanwhile, all she could do was wait and worry. Brian knew where she lived, but she had no idea where to find him.

She tried to imagine his reaction when she refused to do as he asked.

'I killed your husband, just like we agreed. Now it's your turn.'

It was a surreal scenario, with an unspoken threat hanging between them. Fragments of memory slipped into her mind. She recalled Brian as a nasty boy in school uniform. But now 'I'll tell the teacher' had turned into 'I know where you live,' and 'You know I'm not afraid to kill,' and, worst of all, 'I know your children.' She slept badly again the following night, disturbed by snatches of nightmares in which strange monsters pursued her children along dark streets. The boys were laughing as though it was all a game. Only she knew that the boys were going to be torn to pieces. She struggled to call out a warning, but she had no voice.

By Wednesday she was worn out with anxiety and lack of sleep. She hadn't slept properly for three nights, not since Dave's murder. She was sitting at the small breakfast bar in the kitchen, watching the boys eating spaghetti hoops on toast, when the doorbell rang. Shocked into immobility, she watched Ed jump up and run to open the door. Trembling, she forced herself to her feet. It was an effort to cross the kitchen and go out into the hall. Her mother was standing there, smiling at Ed.

'I came as soon as I could.'

Caroline shrugged. It didn't take three days to travel to London from Brighton. Nevertheless, she was pleased to see her mother. Her fussing would be a welcome distraction.

'You look terrible,' her mother said. 'How are you coping?'

Caroline turned away. She couldn't be bothered to try and explain. Only she and a pock-marked stranger knew that they were accomplices in a terrible crime. An encounter of just a few seconds had plunged her life from normality into the depths of a nightmare world of unbelievable horror. After explaining that she couldn't stay long, her mother chattered to Ed and Matthew with forced cheerfulness until Caroline wanted to scream at her to shut up. She felt like locking herself in the bathroom, crouching on the floor and clutching her knees to her chest, crying. But she couldn't allow herself to fall apart, for the children's sake.

Her mother put the kettle on to make tea. They were out of milk. All at once, Caroline was desperate to escape the claustrophobic stuffiness of the house.

'I'll pop along to Morrisons.' There was a small local store just across the main road. She hadn't been out to the shops since her encounter with Brian. 'I won't be long.'

'Off you go then. We'll be fine here, won't we, boys?'

'Yes, granny.'

'Get some Jaffa Cakes, mum.'

'Get some chocolate fingers!'

With a promise to return with treats, Caroline left the house. She was preoccupied, thinking that someone would have to sleep on the sofa. Now Dave had gone, there was no reason why she shouldn't give up her own room to her mother. On the other hand, if she made her too comfortable, her mother might never leave. She was startled out of her planning by a voice calling her name in an urgent whisper. It took her a second to realise someone was lurking among the trees at the end of her road, just out of sight.

'Caroline! Caroline! Over here!'

She spun round. Brian was standing almost close enough to touch, his pale eyes seeming to glow in the shadow of the branches under the streetlight. Instinctively Caroline backed away, resisting an urge to turn and run. There was no point. Brian knew where she lived. On trembling legs, she stepped closer. Without warning he reached out and seized her arm in a pincer-like grip, propelling her further away from the road. In the silence, Caroline thought she could hear the pounding of her own heart. After a few steps, she recovered her senses and stopped. With a rough movement she shook herself free of his grasp.

'What do you want?'

'It's your turn,' he whispered. 'I did what you wanted. Now it's your turn.'

'I don't know what you're talking about,' Caroline whispered, furious with fear. 'Leave me and my boys alone, or...'

Brian stepped closer. 'Or what?'

13

ON HER FIRST VISIT Geraldine had to park halfway along a street packed with police vehicles. This time she parked right outside Caroline's house, ignoring the parking restrictions. It was dry but breezy when she left the car, unexpectedly chilly after a bright start to the day. She had left her jacket in the car and almost went back for it, but it hardly seemed worth the bother, the house was so close.

A grey-haired woman came to the door. 'My daughter's not here.' There was a hint of aggression in her voice.

She took a step back from the door, as though to close it, but her expression softened when she learned who was asking for Caroline.

'She told me not to answer the door to anyone,' she apologised. 'I think she's worried about all this getting into the papers, you know.'

Geraldine guessed they were worried about the effect any publicity might have on her sons.

'It's not right,' Caroline's mother went on. 'She's lost her poor husband – not that he was much use to her – isn't that enough for anyone to cope with? She shouldn't be hounded like this. It's not fair. Can't you do something to protect her? I'm doing what I can, but I can't stay long. I have to get off first thing in the morning.'

Geraldine put on a sympathetic expression. 'Has your daughter had many callers since you arrived?'

'I got here today,' came the reply, a trifle too quickly. 'I couldn't get away earlier.'

Geraldine was interested to hear that Caroline's mother was dismissive of her son-in-law, even at such a time.

'He wasn't what you'd call a bad man, not really.'

'Just not good enough for your daughter?'

'It's not that. You make it sound like I thought no one could be good enough for her. I'd be the first to admit she's no saint, but...'

'But?'

'He wasn't good enough for any woman, that one.'

Geraldine listened patiently as Caroline's mother talked around the subject, finally admitting that Dave had 'gone' with other women. 'I'm not talking about just one affair either. This was all the time. He had no shame. She tried to cover it up, but we all knew. The worst of it was the way he flung money at them. Caroline had to go back to work...' She broke off, worried she might have been indiscreet. 'They were happy together,' she added lamely, conscious of the damage she had done.

Unintentionally she had confirmed that her daughter had a strong motive for wanting her husband dead.

'Caroline loved him. She would never have done anything... '

They both knew it was too late.

She had no idea how long her daughter would be out. 'She went shopping.'

'Shopping?'

The other woman bristled. 'She might have lost her husband, but she still has to feed her children.'

'Please tell her I'll come back tomorrow.'

Geraldine made her way back to the car. There was nothing to be gained from hanging around, waiting. There was no way of knowing how long Caroline would be out. Her next task was to visit the dead man's workplace to find out what she could about him. As she drove towards Hayes, she wondered if she was going in the wrong direction. She couldn't help feeling that Caroline knew more about her husband's death than she had yet confessed.

The building company Dave had worked for was a small outfit employing only a handful of men. Geraldine hadn't expected to find anyone at the builders' yard but three of them were there, a middle-aged foreman and two younger men. The foreman returned her greeting sombrely.

'We heard he was dead.' He put down the mug of tea he was drinking and stood up. 'What can we help you with? He was a good electrician,' he added, and the other two grunted in agreement. 'Bloody nice bloke too.'

The others nodded glumly.

Dave had been working with them for about five years. They didn't seem to know much about his life outside his work.

'He had a wife,' the foreman told her.

'And twin boys,' another man added helpfully.

Geraldine didn't stay long. She couldn't afford to waste time.

14

CAROLINE WANTED TO TURN and run, but she had to stay and protect her children. They had just lost their father. They couldn't lose her as well, not so soon. There was no point in blaming Brian. He knew what had happened as well as she did. If it weren't for the situation they were in, she might have felt sorry for the wretched creature standing in front of her. But all she could think about right now was her two boys.

'Brian, look, you mustn't think what happened…' she broke off, unable to find the right words. She tried again. 'Brian, I won't tell anyone what happened.' Her voice quavered. Gulping for breath, she went on. 'I'll keep quiet about it if you leave me alone. What happened can stay between us, as our secret. But you must see that you need help. You have to go to a doctor…'

She was crazy, hiding in a copse of trees, attempting to reason with a psychopath. She edged away, struggling not to cry.

Brian took a step forward. 'I did it for you.'

She stared at him, outraged.

'What are you talking about? I loved my husband.' That had been true once. 'Like I'm sure you loved your wife.'

'That's why they had to die. Both of them. You know that. I couldn't let her walk away from me. Not after everything we'd been through together. You understand that. You know better than anyone why he had to die. It's what he deserved, after all he put you through. You're free now.'

'You're insane.'

A cloud drifted across the setting sun. It cast dappled light through the trees. She wondered if she would ever be rid of the lunatic laughing softly at her, teeth and eyes gleaming in the shadows. She fought to keep her terror under control and speak calmly. 'If you don't leave me alone, I'll go to the police and tell them what happened. I'll tell them it was you who did it.'

Brian stepped away and she heard him laughing. 'You can't tell anyone, can you? Because I didn't do it alone. We did it together.'

'What the hell are you talking about? I wasn't there.'

'You told me where and when to do it.'

'You know it wasn't like that. I had no idea – it wasn't meant to be serious. You were only supposed to make him jealous, make him think someone else was interested in me...'

As if a scrawny weasel like Brian could ever be a threat to Dave.

'You told me when to do it, and where to find him,' Brian insisted softly. 'You set the whole thing up. It was all your idea.'

'No, no, stop it. That's not true. You know it wasn't like that. I'm going home now. I never want to see you again. I never want to speak to you again. If you ever try to contact me again I'll go to the police.'

Brian's quiet tones cut through Caroline's hysterical whispering.

'If you go to the police, I'll tell them you talked me into killing your husband. They'll take your children away from you.'

'This has nothing to do with my children. What makes you think the police will believe your lies, anyway? I'll deny knowing anything about it. You can't prove we even met.'

As she was speaking she remembered the photo on his phone, and how she had written down her address for him, signed with a kiss. He had set it all up to implicate her.

'Don't be silly,' he said. 'If you refuse to do what I want I'll tell the police we're having an affair, and we planned your husband's murder together. If you go to the police, you'll be signing away your future as well as mine, and you'll lose your children. You'll go to prison and they'll be taken into care. That's not always a very nice experience for young boys.'

He reached out and grabbed her by the arm again. The hand now clutching her sleeve had battered Dave to death. Shocked, she jerked free of his grasping fingers.

'Get off me!'

She drew back, trembling.

Brian stepped closer. 'It's your turn. Whatever you say, you can't wriggle out of it. I did what you wanted. You can't back out now. Don't worry. We've been too clever for them. But if you don't carry out your side of the bargain, you'll be sorry. Remember, I know where you live. And don't even think of going to the police. I'll tell them what you made me do. They'll think you're not fit to be a mother. They'll take your children away from you... if I don't kill them first. You know I can do it. I might just decide to kill one of them – or it could be both – if you don't do exactly what I want.'

His eyes were shining. She hoped he couldn't see her legs were shaking so much she could barely stand.

'If you really think you can push me around, you're even crazier than I thought. You're completely nuts. There's no way I'd agree...'

'You already have agreed. We had a deal.'

In the shadows of the trees, she thought he was smiling. 'Don't tell me you've forgotten that you wrote your address down for me,' he went on quietly. 'You can't deny it, not when it's got your finger prints all over it. And there's the photo. That's more than enough proof for any judge and jury. But no else ever needs to find out, not unless one of us tells them. And why would either of us want to do that? We're in this together. We get through this together, or we go down together. We had an agreement. I've done my bit. Now it's your turn. But we shouldn't stand around talking like this. Someone might come, and we can't be seen together. I'll make it quick. It's quite simple. No one will ever find out it was you, as long as you're careful. Don't underestimate him and don't take any chances. Whatever happens, don't let him see you. If he sees you then we're both screwed.'

'I don't know what you're talking about. What the hell do you want me to do?'

'You're going to kill the man who was fucking my wife.'

Caroline had never been so frightened, not even when she had seen Dave's body in the shed. Meanwhile Brian continued talking in a quiet monotone, like someone reading out a shopping list.

'It'll be best if you kill him in the street, in case you leave any traces, DNA and such. Listen carefully. Here's what you have to do.'

'You'll never get away with it,' she whispered when he had finished.

'Oh, do stop fussing. No one's going to know it was us. Not if you do it right. Now stop worrying. Listen, it'll be fine. We got away with the last one without any bother, didn't we?'

Caroline gasped. Brian was completely demented. It seemed Dave's death was just the beginning of his madness.

15

NICK COULDN'T HELP BEING aware of Geraldine when she was in their office. Her predecessor had been a rugged older male officer, a decent bloke, and far less distracting. Being attracted to a good-looking woman was nothing new, but he had never before pursued a woman who sat beside him every day, tantalisingly off limits. Despite the temptation to flirt, he couldn't afford to make a fool of himself. They had been out together a couple of times, but it was impossible to work out what she thought of him. Once or twice she glanced in his direction and he dropped his gaze like an awkward teenager. He didn't want her to see him watching her. He found it difficult to keep his eyes from lingering on her. Unconscious of his gaze, she sat like a beautiful statue, gazing at her screen. Several times he caught her staring fixedly at the window where a small patch of sky was visible, boxed into a corner. Usually he would have challenged her, 'Penny for your thoughts.' But he remained silent. Finally, against his better judgement, he turned to her and suggested they go for a drink later. She hesitated before agreeing. Her unexpected grin raised his spirits, and he returned to his mundane tasks with renewed enthusiasm.

After work they walked round the corner to the nearest pub. It was a large saloon bar with a flickering mock log fire, red patterned carpet and rows of gleaming copper ornaments. A pleasant change from the fashionable bars closer to Central London, it prioritised comfort over style. Most of their colleagues dropped by from time to time, and a group of young constables were already there, chattering and joking. With a sigh, Nick thought back to his early years on the force, before he had risen up through the ranks to become an inspector. Back then life had seemed so full of promise. But that was before he had married Eve.

'Cheer up.' Geraldine's voice reached him across the table.

He smiled. She always seemed to understand how he was feeling. He wished he had taken her somewhere less public, but it was too late now to suggest they go to a quieter bar. They couldn't leave without having at least finished their pints, and by then she would probably want to go home. There was a time when he would have been happy to have a drink or two with an attractive colleague, flirting and chancing his luck. Right now he just felt depressed.

'Sorry,' he muttered into his pint. 'I'm a bit tired.'

She saw through his words straight away.

'Would you like to talk about it?'

Her sympathy thrilled him. Their physical closeness no longer seemed important. He wanted to confide in her, tell her all about his miserable marriage, as though he was a child again and she could make him feel better. But he couldn't share his wretched story in a place where they might be overheard or interrupted by colleagues. What he wanted to share was private.

'Maybe we go somewhere…' he stammered.

She shifted in her seat and he cursed his crassness as his invitation dissipated in a clumsy misunderstanding.

'No…' he blundered on, 'that's not what I meant. I just want to talk.'

It was too late. Avoiding his gaze, she pulled on her jacket and picked up her bag. Her words were brisk, but there was a sadness in her eyes as though she too regretted the way the evening was ending.

'I really need to get going. Early start in the morning.'

He wanted to reach out to her and beg her to stay. They could go out for dinner, or go for a walk, anything as long as she would listen to him, really listen. He hadn't been able to talk to anyone – really talk – for such a long time.

'See you tomorrow then. Thanks for the drink.'

He leaned back, defeated, as they retreated into polite formality.

'We must do this again.'

'That would be nice.'

Nick was furious with himself. It had taken him so long to find a woman who would actually listen to him talking about things that mattered, and he had driven her away. No doubt Sam Haley would have taken great glee in warning Geraldine about his reputation with women. It had been slow going, but finally he had begun to gain her trust. A couple of times she had even gone out for a meal with him. And now he had blown it. With a sigh he walked slowly out to his car. His wife would be waiting for him at home. He had never felt so alone.

Only a sixth sense, drummed into him during training, compounded by years of vigilance, alerted him to a white van pulling out from the kerb as he drove away. Recently he had noticed a van just like it several times when he had been leaving work. He sped up. Glancing in the mirror he saw what could have been the same van, still right behind him. Dismissing a vague unease he slowed down. He was in no hurry to get home. Studying his rear mirror when he stopped at a red light, he was relieved to see the van had gone. The traffic was heavy along the main road. In the mirror, he saw what could have been the same van again, one vehicle away. He considered calling for backup, but all he could report was that he thought a van might be following the same route as him. Only his instincts warned him to be on his guard, but he could hardly report a feeling.

Over the years he had put away so many vicious characters, there could be any number of ex-cons wandering around, bearing a grudge against him. Next day he would check if any villains had recently been released from the nick. If one of them owned a white van, Nick would arrange a visit. The threat of going back inside would be enough to put a stop to any nonsense. It wouldn't be the first time this had happened to a police officer. For now, he would shake off the van – if it really was pursuing him. He didn't want anyone following him home. As he put his foot down, there was a sudden downpour.

There were a couple of cars between him and the van he suspected might be following him. He pulled into the kerb and took a few deep breaths as he watched several cars pass in the pouring rain. There was no sign of the van. Puzzled, he pulled out and headed towards home. And saw the van immediately behind him again. With a curse, he veered suddenly off to the left into a side street. Tyres squealing, he almost crashed into a car parked near the corner. He swerved across the road, clipping the kerb as he slammed on the brakes, and was lucky not to burst a tyre. The van had no chance of following. Shaking, he drew into a space between two parked cars and waited until he felt calm. Then he pulled out and drove home by a circuitous route.

Eve didn't respond although she must have heard him call her from the hall. Hungry, he went into the kitchen. She wasn't there, although the oven was on. It was empty.

'Hello,' he called.

When she didn't answer, he turned off the oven, and checked the rest of the house. She wasn't in. Relieved, he returned to the kitchen, put a couple of slices of bread in the toaster and took some cheese from the fridge. He wasn't aware his wife had come in until she spoke.

'You eat like an animal. Can't you use a knife and fork?'

He laughed bitterly. 'You want me to eat toast with a fork? *Is* there a clean fork in the place?' He looked at her in unbearable irritation. 'Jesus, just look at the state of you. You must be freezing. Go and get yourself dry, for Christ's sake. Why didn't you wear a coat? You're worse than a child.'

Smoothing down her drenched hair she stalked out of the room, muttering to herself under her breath.

'What's that?' he demanded sourly. 'Can't you at least try to behave normally? I've just come in from a long day at work, for Christ's sake. Most wives would be at home to put the kettle on, never mind have a conversation with me for a change, instead of talking to yourself all the time.' But she was already out of earshot. 'I ought to have divorced you a long time ago,' he called out.

16

GERALDINE REGRETTED HAVING AGREED to go out for a drink with Nick. At first morose, he surprised her by suggesting they go somewhere more private. When she rejected his suggestion, the evening ended abruptly. They walked back round the corner to the car park without exchanging a word. It was growing dark by the time they parted, and beginning to rain. With a terse goodbye she hurried away. If he had registered her disappointment it would have been humiliating, but he seemed too preoccupied to pay any attention to her feelings.

Pleased to get home, she fixed herself a simple supper of cheese and pasta, with a glass of red wine. She had finished clearing up and was flicking through channels, television remote control in one hand, glass of wine in the other, when her phone rang. Not having heard from her sister for over a week, it was no surprise to hear her slightly nasal voice at the other end. Expecting Celia to start grumbling about how she never called, and didn't want to spend time with her family, and hardly ever saw her niece, Geraldine prepared to make her excuses.

'Guess what?'

Celia sounded surprisingly cheerful. She usually phoned to complain. Feeling guilty that Celia always called her, Geraldine threw out a few suggestions: her niece Chloe had passed a piano exam; she had come top in a class test; she had been chosen to play the lead in the school play. Only news about Chloe could prompt such excitement in her mother.

Celia gave an impatient laugh. 'No, no. It's nothing to do with Chloe. Why are you so fixated on Chloe all of a sudden?'

'I give up.'

'That is, it is *something* to do with her, but it's more to do with me. I mean, it's going to change things for her. For all of us.'

Geraldine tried not to sound as tired as she felt.

'You've got a job?'

'No.'

'Oh, I don't know. You've booked a holiday?'

'No. Guess again.'

'I can't. You'll have to tell me.'

'I'm pregnant!'

'What?'

Taken by surprise, Geraldine didn't respond straight away. Not for the first time, she envied her sister. It wasn't that she wanted children herself. Far from it. Even if she had been in a relationship, she couldn't imagine allowing anything to distract her from her work. But she couldn't help feeling that her life would have been more fulfilling, if only she had been a different kind of woman.

'Aren't you going to say anything?'

'That's wonderful news!'

After a convoluted account of how she had been afraid she might never conceive again Celia paused, and Geraldine butted in with a promise to invite her niece to stay for a weekend as soon as she could.

'What does soon mean?' Celia demanded. 'When are you going to have her?'

'Oh God, please don't go all hormonal on me. I'm really up to my ears right now, but I'll see her as soon as I can,' Geraldine repeated, already regretting having committed herself that far, 'but you know my time's not my own when I'm on a case.'

'You're always on a case,' Celia complained. 'Since you moved, we hardly see anything of you, and it's almost impossible to get hold of you.'

Geraldine did her best to placate her sister. She knew exactly what Celia was after. Such exchanges usually ended with Geraldine agreeing on a date to take her niece out.

'You've got no idea how fast she's growing up,' Celia repeated a familiar refrain. 'Soon she'll be a teenager and then she won't want to go out with you. It's really important for you to establish a good relationship with her now, while she's still young enough to be excited about seeing you and being taken out.'

Since their mother had died, nearly two years earlier, Celia had been increasingly desperate for Geraldine to form a relationship with her niece. Geraldine had done her best to point out that she couldn't take their mother's place, but it was hard.

'It's different for you,' Celia had insisted tearfully. 'You weren't as close to mum as I was.'

There had been a good reason for that, although Geraldine had only discovered it after their mother's death. Not until she and Celia had been going through their mother's papers had Geraldine learned that their mother had been unable to have any more children after Celia was born. Not wanting Celia to be an only child, her parents had adopted Geraldine. What made the revelation more painful was that Celia had known the truth all along. She had been genuinely amazed by Geraldine's shock, insisting that she had always believed Geraldine knew her own history.

At last Geraldine succeeded in ending the call.

'You know I'd love to have her. I'll make a date with you as soon as I can. And congratulations again. I'm so excited!'

She was genuinely thrilled for her sister. But when she rang off, she unexpectedly burst into tears. She had hardly settled down to watch an old film on TCM when the phone rang again. Assuming Celia was calling back, she was pleasantly surprised to hear the voice of her former sergeant. Working together in Kent, they had developed an intimacy that frequently developed between officers who were together for a long time. They had only met occasionally since her move to London, since when Ian Peterson had also relocated. Recently promoted to detective inspector, he had gone to the North of England. She was really pleased to hear from him. In contrast to her sister, Ian was genuinely interested to hear how she was progressing on the Met. She told him about her current case.

'In his own garden shed?' he repeated, 'Blimey. And there I was, thinking my shed was a safe haven from the rest of the world, no phone, no internet, and the wife never sets foot in there. It's just me and the spiders.'

Geraldine laughed, but she felt an irrational pang of jealousy at the reminder that he was married.

'How is your wife?' she asked, and then wished she hadn't.

Sitting alone in her flat, she didn't want to be reminded that, like Nick, Ian had someone waiting for him at home. Sometimes it felt as though she was the only person she knew who was still alone. Some of her friends had met their partners through online dating. She had gone as far as registering with a couple of agencies, but somehow work commitments had always prevented her from following it up.

'What have you got to lose?' Sam had teased her. 'If a guy pushes his luck, you can always arrest him! A lot of men might like to be clapped in handcuffs.'

Ian was talking about his new post. A few minutes passed in discussing the difference between the workload and responsibilities of an inspector compared to the role of a sergeant. Having finished indulging in understated mutual congratulations on their success so far in their careers, they moved on to commiserating with one another about the loss of overtime pay they experienced as inspectors. From there they chatted in a desultory fashion about their former colleagues in Kent. Ian had only left recently but the memories had lost their immediacy for Geraldine, and the conversation moved on to the cases they had recently worked on. There was plenty to talk about. Chatting with Ian, she felt like a young girl talking to her boyfriend outside school. But she wasn't a schoolgirl talking to her boyfriend. She was a woman on her own, and he was a married man. She resolved to make more of an effort with Nick. A relationship with a colleague might stand a better chance of success than seeing someone outside the force who would never appreciate the constraints her work placed on her time. Even her own sister didn't understand.

17

THE NEXT MORNING NICK was in the office before Geraldine. He barely glanced up when she entered the office. She hoped their evening hadn't put him off her. Apart from the possibility they might actually hit it off if she gave him a chance, it would be tricky to fall out with each other when they shared an office. By late afternoon the atmosphere between them was tense and Geraldine decided it was time to do something about it. Turning her chair so she could look at him directly, she cleared her throat. She couldn't decide if she was nervous because he was a colleague with whom she shared an office, or because he was an attractive man who had taken her out for a drink several times and assured her he was estranged from his wife. His motive in inviting her out had been fairly obvious, whatever he now said.

'Nick?'

He grunted without glancing up from his screen.

'I was wondering if you were thinking of going for a drink after work tonight?'

That made him look up. He gazed around the room as though to find out whom she was addressing. Geraldine laughed at his charade but he didn't smile.

'Do you fancy going for a drink after work tonight?'

He hesitated. 'I don't think I'd be very good company right now. I've got a lot on my mind.'

'We've all got a lot on our minds,' she muttered, 'but if you'd rather not join me for a drink that's fine...'

'No, no, that's not what I meant. I'm just very tired, that's all.'

They returned to their screens, but Geraldine couldn't concentrate on reading witness statements, hunting for inconsistencies. Abandoning the search, she began to sort through a list of expenses claims, a mindless task that allowed her thoughts to wander. She had given up all hope of getting anywhere with Nick when he broke the silence, suggesting they go for another drink in the local pub frequented by colleagues after work.

To begin with when they had gone out together, Nick had taken her to a comfortable pub off the beaten track where they wouldn't be recognised. Although relieved he still wanted to spend time with her, Geraldine was faintly disappointed he didn't want to go somewhere more discreet. His suggestion seemed to signal he was no longer interested in her as a woman, if he ever had been. Shrewd in her reading of suspects and witnesses, somehow she never managed to understand her personal relations with men. Although she missed her friend and colleague who was off work injured, she felt a frisson of guilty relief that Sam wasn't there to see her going out with Nick. She could imagine her sergeant's scathing indignation.

'He's a snake, Geraldine.'

She left work early and walked to the pub where she found him waiting for her in a quiet bar. Taking their pints to a corner table, they sat down. Neither of them spoke for a few minutes.

'You're not your usual self,' she hazarded, in an attempt to break the silence. 'If I've said something to offend you, I'm sorry, but...'

He looked up at her in surprise. 'Not at all. Like I said, I'm just a bit preoccupied at the moment. You would be too if...'

He broke off and glanced around, as though afraid they were being watched. Geraldine remembered that he was in fact married, although he claimed to be estranged from his wife. She wondered whether Sam had been right all along, and she had completely misjudged his intentions. He was still living with his wife, after all.

When she announced she was leaving he sprang to his feet and followed close behind her. In the darkness, she thought she had misheard him when he asked if he could follow her to her flat. Despite the solemn warnings ringing in her head, she couldn't suppress a smile. She hoped he didn't notice. She turned away, muttering something inane about his wife.

'I've told you, it's over. We're separated.'

He was standing so close to her, she could feel the soft touch of his breath on her cheek. She didn't move away.

'Nick, you know as well as I do that just because people separate, it doesn't necessarily mean that's the end of it.'

'Look, I'm not suggesting any impropriety...' She wished she could see his face. 'But it's early, and I'll be on my own at home, so I just thought a coffee, a chat.' There was an urgency in his voice that startled her. 'Geraldine, please. I have to speak to someone.'

She knew it was a mistake to agree.

In the kitchen her fingers fumbled with the cafetière as she brewed coffee. She was aware of Nick standing behind her, so close she could detect a faint whiff of his aftershave. When she turned, holding the coffee pot between them, he leaned forward slowly until his lips brushed hers. She pulled away, clutching the pot, careful not to spill it.

'Careful, it's hot.'

'Forget the coffee. You're hot.'

His voice was low and his eyes stared intensely into hers. Geraldine's resolve crumbled. Wordlessly she put the coffee down and led him into her bedroom. It was a long time since she had last slept with a man. It crossed her mind that she ought to ask if he was going to stay the night, or if he intended going home to his wife. But they were both adults. If he was cheating on his wife, it was without Geraldine's knowledge. There was nothing wrong with her seeking physical comfort in the arms of a man who had assured her he had no ties.

Nick was a sensitive lover. Afterwards, when she snuggled up against his firm warm body, he began to talk in a low voice. Only half listening, she understood he was worried.

'I'm sure it will be fine,' she assured him sleepily.

Her head rose and fell as he sighed.

'That's what I need,' he admitted, stroking her hair gently, 'someone sensible telling me everything's going to be all right.' He paused. 'But what if it isn't?'

He half sat up, pushing her aside, and began to speak rapidly, as though talking against the clock. She raised herself up on one elbow so she could see his face, and was shocked to see he was close to tears. In silence she listened with increasing concern to what sounded like paranoid ranting.

At last she interrupted him. 'If what you're saying is true, you need to do something about it.'

'If?' he repeated indignantly. 'What? You think I'm making it up?'

'No, no, of course not. But you could be mistaken.'

Nick flung himself back on the pillow and stared gloomily at the ceiling for a moment. Then he turned a miserable face to look at her.

'At first I thought I was imagining it,' he said helplessly. 'I couldn't think why anyone would want to follow me. But you know how it is; we're trained to observe accurately...'

'And to report coherently,' Geraldine thought.

'It was the same van, the whole time. I drove all the way round the block, and it was there, right on my tail.'

'Did you get the number?'

He shook his head.

'Why not?'

'It was too close, and it was impossible to see. It was chucking it down with rain. But I could see it was the same van,' he added quickly.

'What about when you got home? When you got out of the car?'

'It disappeared.'

'Disappeared?'

Nick sat up, growing animated as he tried to explain. 'I live on a corner and before I knew it, he'd disappeared. I should have followed but, well, I know it sounds unlikely, me losing my head, but I panicked, all right? I wasn't thinking, and I let him get away. He just sped off and was gone before I had a chance to gather my thoughts. Do you think I should report it?'

'Report what?'

'What I just told you. That I think I'm being stalked.'

'If you're sure the van was following you.'

'That's just it, I can't be sure. I mean, I could be wrong. It could have been chance that it was going the same way as me, all the way.'

Geraldine refrained from pointing out that he was contradicting himself. He was clearly too flustered to think clearly.

'What did Reg say?'

'I haven't told him. I haven't told anyone else.'

'Why don't you wait and keep an eye out for it? If you see the van again, report it. And make sure you get the registration number this time.'

She felt smug, knowing he had confided in her alone. All the same, it had been a confusing visit. Her emotions were a mess. She was relieved when he climbed out of bed and told her he had to go. She didn't ask why. Uppermost in her mind was the thought that it might be wise to guard against falling for Nick. There were too many complications.

'Just take it easy,' she told him as he was getting dressed. 'No one's out to get you.'

'I find that very disappointing coming from you,' he replied, with a return to his usual good humour, 'after my performance just now, I can hardly believe my ears!' He bent down to kiss her. 'I'll have to try harder next time. Don't get up. I'll let myself out. See you tomorrow.'

And with that he was gone, leaving her confused and elated, and decidedly uneasy.

18

GERALDINE WAS DISAPPOINTED TO discover that Nick had the day off on Saturday. In theory his absence meant she was able to get on with some work without any distraction. In practice she couldn't help speculating about whether he might want to sleep with her again. She couldn't recall which of them had made the first move, but once he had set foot in her flat it had been inevitable they would end up in bed together. It would be embarrassing if he lost interest in her after they had spent just one night together.

Despite her impatience to see him again, she was glad to have time alone to consider the ramifications of their night together. In different circumstances she would definitely have wanted to see him again, but a relationship with a colleague was risky. For a start, it was bound to give rise to gossip, and anyway it might not last. That could be difficult. On balance, she decided to tell him she thought it had been fun the one time, but it was best left there. Only her pride made her hope he would be disappointed. Other than that, the whole thing really was best forgotten about. Yet it wasn't easy to forget his touch, or the movement of his body with hers.

Resolutely she turned her attention to her work, determined not to waste any more time thinking about him. Her sergeant, Sam, had dismissed him as a condescending liar. Geraldine had seen how tender he could be. The last thing she wanted to do was romanticise him, but she had been on her own for a long time. She was pretty much decided to give him a chance, if he was genuinely interested in her. She wasn't put off by his silence. She had hardly expected a bouquet of red roses on her desk. A text would have been nice. But she expected he was feeling as confused as she was, the morning after.

She was still going round in circles in her mind when there was a knock at the door. Max entered to tell her one of Dave's workmates had turned up at the station claiming to have information about the murder. Welcoming the distraction, she invited Max to tell her more.

'It's all in my report.'

'Yes, but I'd like to hear it from you.'

Max shrugged. 'He's a black guy, called Will Henry. He's about thirty and nervous as hell. He kept twisting his hands in his lap and he was sweating the whole time I was with him. Said he'd never been in a police station before. I'm not sure I believed him.'

'What did he want?'

'It took a while to get that out of him,' Max replied.

Geraldine hoped the sergeant wasn't going to spin it out like the witness had. She nodded and leaned forward, urging him to continue. All at once the words tumbled out in a monotone and she had to ask him to slow down as he read out what he had transcribed of the witness's account. Will had reported seeing Dave and one of his workmates, Greg, arguing. Apparently Dave had taken a swipe at the other man, swearing at him.

'He refused to repeat the words Dave used. He just said it was foul language.'

Greg swore back and soon they were both hurling insults. Finally, Greg threatened Dave.

'What did he say exactly?' Geraldine asked. 'Did the witness remember?'

'I'm coming to that. It's all in my report. Greg said, "I'll get you," and then he said, "You ain't seen the last of this." And then the foreman came along and Greg and Dave scarpered. Will was the other side of a pallet the whole time, watching through the slats. They had no idea he was there. He said he'd been afraid to show himself in case the other two turned on him. They were both pumped up. They thought no one had seen them fighting, but he was there the whole time, watching and waiting for a chance to escape. It's possible Greg decided to finish it.'

Geraldine frowned. 'When did this encounter take place?'

'That's just the point. It was on Friday, the day before Dave was killed, at about eleven in the morning. Looks like we've found our killer.'

His smugness implied that he felt responsible for solving the case. Geraldine was more cautious. She had been distracted by false leads before, especially ones she herself had stumbled upon. She wanted to know what the two men had been fighting about.

Max shook his head. 'I asked him that but he said he didn't know, it could have been anything. But that's hardly the point. And he wanted his identity kept quiet. I had to promise him anonymity before he'd say anything.'

'Is he still here?'

Max shook his head. 'He was nervous as hell and itching to leave.'

Greg Hawkins wasn't working that weekend. He was easy to trace and Geraldine was soon driving to Hackney where he lived with his girlfriend, Stacey, and her three children in a square grey building in a grey street unrelieved by any trace of vegetation. His block of flats was a replica of the blocks either side of it, exactly the same as those across the road. She crossed the narrow front yard and took the lift up to the fifth floor. No one answered the bell, which didn't appear to be working. When she knocked loudly a woman opened the door on the chain. Scrawny and pale-faced, she glared at Geraldine. Over her shoulder, Geraldine could see a small hallway cluttered with children's toys and shoes.

It was no surprise when Stacey refused to say anything, other than that Greg wasn't in and she didn't know where he was. Once Geraldine had reassured her that the police were questioning all of Dave's workmates, her sullenness turned to open hostility.

'Oh yeah? What's a bleeding inspector doing, asking questions of everyone that knew the poor bugger? It's the constables do that. What kind of fucking idiot do you think I am?'

'You don't want to believe everything they show you on the television. That's not how we do things in a murder investigation,' Geraldine lied. 'You might as well tell me where I can find him or we'll have to keep coming back. Wasting police time is an offence, you know.'

'Everything's a bloody offence to you lot,' the woman grumbled. 'I told you I don't know where he is. And if I did know, you're the last person I'd tell.'

She went to close the door but Geraldine stepped forward and put her foot against the door.

'Oy, piss off out of it!'

Before she left Geraldine wanted to take the opportunity to question Stacey about the previous Saturday.

'Greg was here all afternoon. He went out about eight.'

'Are you sure?'

'Yes. I'm fucking sure. I was working till seven. He's here with the kids every Saturday.'

Geraldine tried to wheedle more information out of her without asking outright if Greg was violent but Stacey refused to answer any questions about her boyfriend. Kicking Geraldine's foot viciously out of the doorway, she shut her out.

An old woman was peering out of the flat next door. 'You after Greg? Is he in trouble then? You from the council?'

'Do you know where he is?'

The neighbour told her to try the pub across the street. 'Only don't tell him I told you,' she added quickly. 'I don't get involved with them.' With a frightened expression, she slammed her door.

19

A MUSTY SMELL HIT her as she entered the pub. From the stained red patterned carpet to the grimy walls and chipped paintwork, the place was badly in need of renovation. Only convenience could attract customers. A dour-faced barman was staring at a newspaper on the counter. In the background a crackly sound track of seventies hits was barely audible. A few old men were sitting at tables gloomily nursing pint glasses. No one looked at her as she crossed the room. When she reached the bar the landlord looked up from his paper with a curt nod.

'I'm looking for Greg Hawkins.'

When he didn't respond, she repeated her statement more loudly. This time he raised his whiskery eyebrows and jerked his bald head towards a corner of the room where a man was sitting by himself.

'Thank you.'

Without buying a drink she joined Greg. He squinted up at her, scowling. Close up he looked younger than she had thought at first, no more than thirty. His bottom lip was split and his left eye was almost closed, bruised and inflamed.

'Greg?'

'From the social are you?'

'I'm a detective.'

She held up her warrant card and an air of muted hostility seemed to permeate the room. The chair rocked slightly on the uneven floor as she sat down opposite Greg.

'Tell me about Dave.'

'He was all right,' he mumbled into his pint.

'Did you get on well?'

'He was a mate.'

Geraldine leaned forward and spoke softly.

'We have a witness who tells us you and Dave had a disagreement the day before he was murdered.'

'What? I never...' He broke off, catching sight of her expression. 'Yeah, well, it was his fault.'

'What were you fighting about?'

'It was nothing.'

He dropped his eyes, but not before she had seen the flare of anger in them.

'Tell me about Dave,' she repeated. 'You know he's dead, Greg. This isn't going to go away. We're investigating his murder and that means we're speaking to everyone who knew him. You'll have to give us some answers sooner or later, so you might as well start co-operating or you can see how it's going to look. Now, let's try again. What were you fighting about?'

Greg sat with hunched shoulders. With his head hung forward, she could see the pale surface of his balding pate beneath his greasy comb over. At last he appeared to reach a decision. He sat upright, and faced her squarely.

'All right, I'll tell you what. We did have a bit of a scrap, I won't deny it. But he had it coming. It was all his fault.'

He took another swig of his beer, set his glass carefully on the table, wiped his mouth on the back of his hand, and began a rambling account of how Dave had lied about some money.

'He owed me. He knew it and I knew it. And he lied, trying to wriggle his way out of it. He kept fobbing me off. It was obvious he never intended to pay me back, and I ran out of patience. I'm telling you, he had it coming.'

'What did he have coming?'

Greg's overhanging brow lowered into a scowl. 'Look, he had my dosh, right. I told him I needed it back, but he just kept giving me excuse after bloody excuse. I told him if he didn't get me my money I'd make him sorry. I meant it too. So I had a bit of a go at him. So what? I wanted my money. He owed me. Now he's dead I'm well and truly screwed. No one's going to pay me back now, are they? I called on his wife and the bloody cow said he never borrowed anything from me, and that's a bloody lie.' He leaned forward suddenly. 'He owes me a hundred quid, all told, and you've got to get it back for me. You're the law, aren't you? I lent him that money, fair and square, out of the goodness of my heart, because I thought he was a mate. It's mine, that money. That's the law, isn't it? I should be paid interest and all.'

Max was convinced Greg had killed Dave.

'Sounds like we have our suspect. He must have gone after his money and lost his temper when Dave didn't pay him back. Where was he last Saturday afternoon?'

'He told me he was at home with the children while his girlfriend was at work. She confirmed his alibi.'

'No independent witnesses then.'

'Now hold on.' Geraldine appreciated the young sergeant's enthusiasm, but he was jumping to conclusions. 'I don't think he did it. He was genuinely upset about it. Actually, he was angry because Dave owed him a hundred quid that he doesn't think he'll ever get back now.'

Somehow Geraldine wasn't surprised that Reg agreed with Max. When she raised a note of caution, her senior officer raised his eyebrows sceptically.

'He could have been deliberately throwing you off the scent when he complained about never getting his money back. It looks pretty clear cut. Dave refused to pay back the money he owed him. Greg lost his temper. It was a vicious attack. We can't take his posturing seriously. We know he attacked Dave the day before the murder. We have a witness to that.'

On the face of it what Reg was saying made sense, but Geraldine wasn't convinced that Greg was guilty of murder. It was a stretch from being annoyed about his money to violently attacking Dave with a garden spade. When she remonstrated, Reg shook his head.

'The chances are Greg's our killer. We know he was violent.'

'If the witness is credible.'

'At any rate he was angry enough to start a fight with Dave, and then the next day, Dave was assaulted and killed. It's too much of a coincidence to ignore. Let's bring him in, Geraldine. Let's not pussyfoot around any longer. We need to get him behind bars, and the sooner the better, before someone else gets hurt. Or worse.'

On the point of protesting, Geraldine stayed silent. She despised herself for lacking the gumption to stick to her guns for fear of antagonising her senior officer. But she could offer no proof of Greg's innocence. Her opinion wasn't enough. Reg might quite reasonably deride it as mere 'feminine intuition', or worse. She needed evidence, and so far she had none. For all their efforts she was convinced they had the wrong man. Even if it meant working alone, she was determined to put that right.

20

EVERY TIME CAROLINE LEFT the house she was scared of bumping into Brian, but she couldn't stay indoors indefinitely. Apart from anything else, it wasn't good for Ed and Matthew to be cooped up all the time. Life had to go on for them. Bored after a whole week at home when all their friends were at school, they had both agreed to go back to school on Monday. Caroline had been dithering about whether to take them to football practice as usual on Saturday. At the last minute, she decided it would be good for them. Matthew was reluctant, but he didn't want to be left out.

It was a crisp day, overcast with an invigorating breeze. She felt uncomfortable stepping out of the house and enjoying the fresh air, as though she was somehow being disloyal to her husband's memory. She glanced up and down the street but there was no sign of Brian. No cars were driving past and the pavements were deserted. She hurried the twins into the back seat and drove off round the block to the park. Hearing the excitement in the boys' voices as they neared the ground, she felt reassured that she had made the right decision. The twins fell quiet as they arrived, and were subdued leaving the car, but before long they were busy kicking balls around. There was no need for any of the boys to speak beyond calling out for the ball to be passed, cheering raucously, and bandying muttered insults. It was an appropriate reintroduction into the society of their peers.

A few parents were scattered around the periphery of the makeshift pitch, where the grass wasn't so muddy. Most of them drifted over to express their condolences before moving away again along the sideline. The air was fresh with the scent of new mown grass, and a few birds flittered overhead, black against the bright lightness of the sky. A group of mothers sat huddled on the bench, gossiping, while others stood as close to the play as they could, shouting encouragement or criticism to their sons. One father, notorious for his zeal, clapped his gloved hands in an accompanying rhythm as he shouted out.

'Come on, Zak!'

A few women sniggered.

'Listen to him.'

'Thinks he's at bloody Arsenal.'

He carried on yelling, impervious to their catty remarks. The boys finished their training exercises and were divided into teams. A few stood at the side observing, waiting their turn to play. The loudmouthed father watched, alert, to make sure his son was selected. Normally, Caroline would have joined the chattering mothers. Today she walked away from the pitch, alienated from the eager supporters and the gossiping spectators alike. She felt a little awkward, and hoped the other parents would appreciate she was only there because it had seemed best for the twins to return to some sort of normality. She wasn't ready to socialise.

The fresh air seemed to crystallise her thoughts. As soon as she had dropped the boys at school on Monday morning, she would go to the police and tell them everything she knew. What she had said to Brian was true. She would never have told him where to find Dave if she had suspected his intentions. It was insane. Armed with nothing more than an address, no one in their right mind would kill a complete stranger. He was a psychopath. Moral considerations aside, someone might have seen her and Brian together. She had to go to the police and exonerate herself, before they caught up with her.

The more she mulled over the situation, the less responsible she felt for what had transpired. 'You can't foresee insanity,' she muttered to a non-existent audience, rehearsing her interview with the police. But whichever way she imagined the conversation, it didn't go well.

'Why did you come up with this plan to have your husband killed in your shed?'

'That's not what happened. He was only going there to make Dave jealous.'

'Jealous?'

'Yes. He was going to make out he fancied me. It was just a bit of fun. How was I to know he was a psychopath?'

Even to her own ears the truth sounded ludicrous. No one would believe her. She wouldn't, if she hadn't encountered Brian herself. She would have given anything to be able to walk away and forget all about her involvement in her husband's death. It should never have happened. She needed someone to advise her, and wondered whether she ought to hire a lawyer. The loudmouthed father watching the game was a solicitor. He had stopped shouting encouragement to his son and was now yelling out instructions.

'Don't pass, keep the ball! It's your shot. Your goal. Go on, you can do it!'

Caroline turned and watched. The boy missed. She walked away. Hearing a quiet disturbance in the shrubbery that ran alongside the pitch, she peered through the heavy foliage and glimpsed a hooded figure moving away from her. Pushing between the densely packed bushes she discovered a narrow track. She stared around in panic, but the figure had vanished.

21

As they set off for the grimy block of flats where Greg lived, Max reminded Geraldine she had found him in the pub sporting a split lip, an injury sustained in a fight he had instigated.

'He might resist,' he warned her as they climbed into the car. 'He obviously likes to use his fists. But don't worry. I can handle it.' He grinned as he put his foot down.

'You did remember to log this visit with the CAD, didn't you?' Geraldine asked, with sudden misgiving.

Max's youthful enthusiasm was making her nervous. If he was right about Greg, they might need to use a link via Computer Aided Despatch to enable the local station to locate them immediately from a radio signal and send the nearest car straight there.

'I mentioned it to Billy,' Max replied airily, naming the newest recruit who was in his first week and still learning his way around.

Geraldine's unease increased. When they had first met, she had assumed her colleague's self-assurance was a front. Now she was afraid his youthful arrogance might cause him to act impetuously, but this was not the time to challenge him. When they were back at the station she would take him to task over his slapdash approach. He must learn that it was never a mistake to be careful.

Greg's girlfriend came to the door again. She looked as though she had been drinking. Her slack jaw tensed when she recognised Geraldine.

'You again! Well he's not here, so you can bugger off.'

Swaying slightly, she started to close the door. As she did so, a man's voice called out and Greg appeared behind her. Catching sight of Geraldine, he swore and ran into one of the rooms off the hall. Stacey tried to shut the door but her reactions were too slow. It wouldn't have achieved anything anyway. They were on the fifth floor. As long as Geraldine could stop him leaving the flat, he was trapped. It wasn't worth the risk of going after him without backup. Concerned that he might have gone to fetch a weapon, she flicked on her phone to summon help.

'Where are you?'

Geraldine hesitated, realising the visit had not yet been logged. Either the new recruit had registered it incorrectly, or it was on his To Do list. Before she could say anything, Max darted past her into the flat. Shoving Stacey aside, he dashed across the hall after Greg. Geraldine was so startled she almost called out. There was no time for her to start reeling off the address. Max might already have put himself in danger. Stacey let out a yell and blocked Geraldine's way, shouting over her shoulder to Greg to watch out.

'We only want to ask him about his workmate who was murdered,' Geraldine snapped. 'What's your problem? Is there a reason you don't want us to speak to him?'

Muttering under her breath, Stacey let her pass. Following her colleague through a door at the far end of the narrow hall, she found the sergeant had pinned Greg up against the wall. One of Max's forearms was pressed against his throat, the other held one of his wrists against the wall. Greg's other arm was trapped behind his back, pressed against the wall. He looked terrified.

'Max, let him go. We only want to ask you a few more questions,' Geraldine explained, keeping her voice low and steady. 'There's nothing to be alarmed about. Let him go, Max. There's no need to restrain him. You can see he's not going to run off.'

'He was reaching for a weapon,' Max growled between clenched teeth.

'I was getting my keys,' Greg protested. 'I was just getting my keys, you crazy fucker. There was no need to attack me.' He looked helplessly at Geraldine. 'He's a maniac. He fucking attacked me. You should be sacked for that. He could lose his fucking job over what he done to me, couldn't he? I'm going to complain to your boss. Get you sacked for what you just done to an innocent man.'

'You can talk,' Max retorted. 'A man who attacks his own girlfriend.' He glared contemptuously at Greg.

Greg hung his head, rubbing his wrist and muttering about police brutality. Max put a hand on his shoulder and guided him towards the front door. They escorted him out of the flat. Stacey glowered at them hustling him past her in the hall. She appeared to be having difficulty focusing her eyes. As they stepped into the hall Greg darted off, racing towards the lift. With a cry of frustration, Max sprinted after him. Greg must have known the lift was waiting because the door opened as soon as he hit the button. Tall and long-legged, he moved fast, with an ungainly stride, but Max was fit. Geraldine's voice echoed down the grey corridor as she yelled at Greg not to be an idiot, while Max sprang forward and stuck his leg out. The lift door slid across. Desperately Greg hit the button again and again. Meeting an obstruction, the door slid inexorably back open and Max flung himself inside, slamming Greg against the side of the lift. It shuddered at the impact. Geraldine joined them and nodded when Max snapped handcuffs on him.

'What did I tell you?' Max said.

Geraldine didn't answer.

Greg was cowed but sober enough to answer questions. Max was pumped up and ready to make a formal arrest, but Geraldine hung back. She wanted to hear what Greg had to say, under the pressure of a police interview. He was miserable and sulked like a teenager for most of the session. Nevertheless he stuck to his story which tied in with what Stacey had told Geraldine, that he had been looking after her children at the time of Dave's death.

'Our problem is that we can't expect the children to be reliable about dates and times,' Geraldine told him. 'And Stacey might be lying to protect you.'

The colour deepened on Greg's cheeks.

'She wouldn't lie,' he mumbled, shifting uncomfortably on his chair.

'Well, we'll leave you to sleep on it until tomorrow,' Geraldine said brightly at last.

'What do you mean? You can't keep me here!'

Geraldine stood up and left the room. Max followed her. Neither of them said another word to Greg. They knew he was right. They could keep him locked up for the rest of the weekend but then they would have to let him go. They couldn't hold him without any evidence of his guilt, and right now all they had was supposition. If they failed to find any evidence soon, they would be right back to square one. A week had passed since Dave had been brutally battered to death, and they still weren't sure who had killed him. While they were hoping Greg would confess, the real murderer might be walking the streets, free to kill again.

22

DRIVING ALONG BALLARDS LANE, Brian passed Caroline's street. Leaving his car at the end of her road, he walked rapidly along the pavement, slowing down as he approached her house. At intervals, the roots of an occasional ageing tree had pushed against the paving stones around it, making the ground uneven. Beside the dusty kerbside packed with cars, the front yards were generally well tended. It was a pleasant enough road for London, with a suburban feel to it. There was nothing to gain from lingering there, but somehow staying within reach of Caroline seemed to bring the fruition of his plan closer. At first it had seemed no more than coincidence, his seeing her again after so long. But as soon as she had told him about her husband's adultery, he had known what to do. Her confidence had shown him the way to fulfil his dream of killing his own intended victim without fear of discovery. The idea had come to him in a flash. He couldn't have planned it better.

From that moment their lives had been inextricably linked. However much she tried to distance herself from Brian, they would never be free of one another until she paid her debt. He had played his part straight away. It was time for her to do the same. That was only fair. It was worrying that, after he had given her all the information she needed, she had made no effort to fulfil her side of the agreement. Perhaps he had been naive to trust her. But if she wasn't prepared to honour her obligation voluntarily, he would find a way to force her. When all was said and done, it wasn't that much to ask. It wasn't as though she even knew the man she was going to kill, so she could have no emotional bar to carrying out her side of the bargain. Having put his own liberty at risk, there was no way he was going to walk away now. If he had come too far to back out, so had she.

Walking back along the main road, he passed the entrance to the park near Caroline's house and wandered in for a stroll to try and clear his head. He needed to think clearly. The park was mainly grass, bordered by a wide tarmac path in turn surrounded by a screen of tall trees and shrubs. The earth beneath the trees was mostly concealed beneath a mess of brambles and bracken. Two young boys were playing football, running around, laughing and calling out to each other. One of them tripped. His companion collapsed on the grass in peals of laughter. The first boy scrambled to his feet and launched himself at the other boy, pummelling him. Both of them rolled on the ground, shouting with glee.

As they scuffled, a woman stepped forward, calling out to the boys to stop fighting. Brian nearly cried out in surprise. He had been thinking about Caroline, and suddenly there she was, standing just a few feet away from him. It was like a sign. Preoccupied with shouting at the two boys, Caroline didn't notice him as he slipped out of sight behind a massive tree trunk.

Noiselessly he shuffled sideways into the shrubbery, feeling the rough corrugated surface of the bark through his glove. Concealed behind overhanging branches thick with glossy leaves, he squatted in the shrubbery, an idea forming in his mind. Even if she had to be coerced, Caroline was going to do what he wanted. Smiling to himself, he turned his attention back to the two boys. Upright again, they were kicking their football backwards and forwards. All he had to do was wait. The grassy plot wasn't large and the boys were energetic. Every few minutes one or other of them kicked the ball into the bushes and went haring after it. Seeing them together, Brian realised they were identical. That made the task much easier, because they were both Caroline's sons. Either one of them would serve his purpose.

He waited. His legs grew stiff but he didn't dare move in case they noticed him hiding in the bushes. In spite of the discomfort, he began to enjoy a sense of power as he watched them, unobserved. They had no idea what was going to happen. Time passed slowly until impatience threatened to overwhelm him. Crouching in the shrubbery, watching and waiting, was a waste of time, not to mention painful. He might as well give up and go home. But a knot of hatred in his stomach kept him skulking there.

His attention wandered from the playing children. He watched a small fat shiny beetle crawl steadily along an overhanging branch, oblivious to its precarious position. He waited for it to fall but it carried on its steady progress. At last the tiny creature disappeared behind a leaf. Without thinking, he shifted position and felt a shooting pain in his leg, stiff from staying in one position for so long. Cautiously he stood up and stretched his back, and moved his legs, taking care not to disturb the branches around him.

There was a rustling in the bushes ahead of him. He froze as a football bounced out of the bushes and rolled past him. He could hear someone crashing about, chasing after it. This was his chance. He tensed, alert to every sound, every shiver in the leaves. He hardly dared move for fear of betraying his presence. The boy had no inkling he was lurking in the shrubbery nearby. Through the leaves he saw the boy bending forward, kicking at the undergrowth, scanning the ground for his ball, unaware to his watcher.

Brian held his breath. As he took a cautious step forward, he heard more crashing in the foliage. Boys' voices erupted in a noisy squabble as one of them seized the ball. They dashed off together while he remained, motionless, scarcely daring to breathe. His plan depended on finding one solitary boy. It would be impossible to overpower two of them at once. Cursing softly, he turned and crept away. There would be other opportunities. Next time he wouldn't fail.

23

GREG WAS ARRESTED AND charged with murder. To begin with he made a dreadful racket, cursing and complaining, and threatening to sue the police for wrongful arrest.

'You can't keep me here,' he ranted. 'I'm a law abiding citizen. I got kids at home. I got rights.'

After an initial tantrum he sat quietly on his bunk, staring miserably at the floor. Stacey didn't show up, and he only became animated when his solicitor arrived to speak to him.

'You get me out of here now! I got to see to my kids!' Geraldine heard him shouting as she walked away.

Greg's vociferous anxiety over what was going on at home was surprising. They weren't even his children. Recalling how unsteady Stacey had been on her feet, Geraldine guessed that Greg thought she was an unfit mother. Considering the two adults involved, the odds were stacked against her children enjoying a happy childhood. With a sigh, Geraldine turned back to her expenses claims. Sometimes she wondered if she had made a mistake, joining the force. She had wanted to make a difference to other people's lives. She might have served her fellow man better if she had become a social worker. In the meantime, all her training and experience lay in another area. It was too late for a career change. But she shared Greg's anxiety about the children he had been forced to abandon. Stacey didn't seem capable of taking care of them by herself.

A team was hard at work gathering information on Greg. They suspected him of subjecting his girlfriend to physical abuse, and there was an eye witness account of his altercation with Dave the day before he was murdered. In preparation for interviewing him again, Geraldine wanted to know as much as possible about him, every conviction, every charge, every caution. No detail was too insignificant to interest her. She wasn't convinced he was guilty, but if he was, it would be up to her to convince a violent killer to confess to his crime. So far all the evidence remained circumstantial. They needed more. She had to be able to say with complete conviction, 'There's no point in lying, Greg. I know all about you.' Only then might she manage to persuade him to confess. She wished she was feeling more confident.

Dave's body had not yielded anything that might secure a conviction. Scene of crime officers were still searching the shed for traces of Greg's DNA. A confession would make life easier all round. First thing Monday morning, Geraldine and Reg would begin the process of convincing Greg it would be in his interests to co-operate with them. If he realised they didn't have sufficient evidence to put him away without a confession, he would be a fool not to take his chances with a jury. He wasn't bright, but a lawyer would be there to advise him. While Reg was bullish about the outcome, Geraldine was worried. She had read everything they had on Greg. He had no previous convictions or charges of violence of any kind, nothing more damaging than the odd speeding fine, and one caution for being drunk and disorderly. On the latter occasion he hadn't even been involved in a brawl, but had been caught urinating in the street.

There was nothing more she could do. She could have taken advantage of her day off to have a lie-in, but luxuriating in the soft warmth of her empty bed reminded her of Nick. He had been pursuing her since they had first met but, after spending the night with her on Friday, he had made no effort to see her on Saturday. The entire evening she had kept her phone on the table in case he called. She hadn't felt so needy since her teens. He didn't ring, his silence calling into question his claim to be estranged from his wife. At last she had watched a film on television in an attempt to distract herself. It hadn't worked.

Brewing a Sunday morning cafetière, it was impossible not to think of Nick, standing with her in her tiny kitchen on Friday evening. Sipping her coffee, she considered calling him. There was no reason why she should wait for him to contact her. They were both adults. If she wanted to see him again, she was entitled to say so. He might make her feel like a hesitant teenager, but she was in her prime, a professional woman accustomed to making weighty decisions that affected the lives of other people. She was entitled to make important decisions for herself. At the same time, she acknowledged there was very little point in calling him just then. Leaving late morning, she was going to spend the afternoon with her sister's family. No doubt she would allow Celia to talk her into staying for supper. She sighed, conscious that she ought to be pleased her sister wanted to see her.

'You can't go yet,' Celia would say. 'We hardly ever see you. Now you're here we want to make the most of it, don't we, Chloe?'

Excited, Geraldine's niece would cry out happily as she seized the gift Geraldine always brought her.

'Geraldine, you shouldn't have,' Celia would scold, watching Chloe tear the wrapping paper off Geraldine's latest peace offering. 'You don't need to bring anything. We're just happy to see you. I just wish you'd come more often.'

Geraldine would launch into her habitual apology. She would love to see them more often but her work kept her busy. It had been impossible to get away. They replayed the conversation at every visit. Thinking about it, Geraldine sighed. At the last minute, she picked up the phone. If Nick wanted to see her that evening, she would have to leave Celia early, so she told herself it was for the best when Nick didn't answer her call before she set off. That way she didn't have to hurry away early from Celia's. She would see Nick in the morning anyway. There was no rush. If Nick wanted to take things slowly, that was sensible.

There were no hold ups on the road. Her sister was pleased to see her. Geraldine felt a stab of guilt that she had been prepared to leave early to see Nick.

As she closed the door, Celia whispered to her. 'We haven't told her about the baby yet.' Her eyes were shining with suppressed excitement.

Before either of them could say anything else, Chloe came charging into the hall. 'Aunty Geraldine! Aunty Geraldine!' She flung her arms around Geraldine who hugged her back, laughing.

They spent a relaxed afternoon, chatting and playing with her young niece. Geraldine had bought her a bright pink leather satchel. Chloe loved it and danced around the room, with the bag swinging from her shoulder. Celia scolded Geraldine for spoiling her niece, but it was obvious she was pleased. Celia's husband was out for most of the afternoon but came home in time to sit down for supper with them. Once Chloe had gone to bed, and her brother-in-law was in the sitting room dozing in front of the television, Geraldine sat in the kitchen with her sister over a coffee before setting off home. Quietly Celia talked about her excitement at finding herself pregnant again.

'I thought it was never going to happen,' she said. 'We've been trying for so long. I don't want to tell Chloe until she really needs to know. To be honest, I was afraid I was going to turn out to be like mum, only we wouldn't have adopted...' She broke off abruptly. 'Sorry. I didn't mean...'

Geraldine shook her head with a smile. 'Don't be silly.' She reached out and touched her sister on the arm in an uncharacteristically tender gesture.

Putting her cup down, Geraldine cleared her throat. 'I've decided to try to find my mother.' She faltered at Celia's startled expression. 'My birth mother, that is,' she added quickly, 'not our mother.' She fell silent, aware that she had spoken clumsily. 'I'm sorry. I didn't mean – I'm sorry...'

Celia shook her head, as though brushing away an annoying fly buzzing around her face.

'That's OK, you don't need to apologise. You're entitled to look for your mother. I would, if I were you. You ought to try and find her. One day it's going to be too late so you should try to find her now, while you still can.'

'It might already be too late,' Geraldine said, with a return of her earlier misgivings. 'I did manage to trace an address for her but, by the time I summoned up the courage to visit her, she'd already moved away.'

'Surely it can't be difficult for you to find out where she's gone? You must have access to people's addresses and stuff.'

Geraldine sighed. It wasn't that easy. For a start, she wasn't sure she wanted to face the mother who had steadfastly refused to meet her. Still, she was relieved that Celia had raised no objections to her plan. It felt as though she had overcome an unforeseen hurdle. Maybe Celia was right, and it wouldn't be so very difficult after all.

24

FIGHTING TO QUELL HER panic, Caroline was relieved her voice sounded normal.

'I don't know what you're getting yourself all worked up about. He'll be back soon.'

'He wouldn't just go off like that without saying anything. Something's happened to him, I know it has.'

Caroline was worried. Matthew was right. *He* might wander off thoughtlessly, but Ed was the responsible twin. He would never disappear like that without telling her where he was going. With a pang of grief she recalled their father complaining that Ed was too sensible.

'Of the two of them, he's the one that'll go off the rails,' Dave had predicted. 'He's repressed. I know Matt's a pain in the arse, but there's no turmoil under the surface with him.'

Caroline shook her mind free. She couldn't be sidetracked by memories just now, not when one of her sons had vanished. Ed had gone out to Morrisons to buy sweets. Matthew had a stomach ache so he had stayed at home. The shop was only five minutes away. Ed knew he had to cross at the lights. He had been there by himself before. But this time he hadn't come home. After an hour she had walked to the shops and back, looking for him. Another hour had passed, and he hadn't returned. Matthew was on the verge of tears.

'Did you two have a row?' she asked.

'No.'

'Well then, he must be hiding.'

She did her best to inject a note of fun into her voice. 'Come on, let's go and find him. Where would he have gone, do you think?'

'He might have gone to the park.'

'Come on, then. Let's look there first.'

'Maybe he's fallen over in the bushes and banged his head,' Matthew suggested, brightening up as he began to appreciate the drama of the situation. 'Or he's lost his memory and wandered off and he doesn't know who he is or where he lives. Or he might have been recruited.'

'Recruited?'

Distracted by worry, she had forgotten Matthew's obsession with children's spy thrillers.

Reaching the park, she pushed her way between stout leafy rhododendron bushes, holding onto branches to prevent them snapping back and hitting Matthew in the face as he followed her.

'Stay close to me,' she called out to him over her shoulder. 'I don't want to lose you as well!'

Of the two boys, Matthew was the one who was always getting into trouble. Ed had never given her a moment's worry – until now. As she struggled through the bushes to the perimeter fence, she studied the ground to left and right. There was no sign of her missing son. She wished she had brought Dobby along. He would have found Ed. She considered going home to fetch him.

It was hard going. Underfoot the earth was hidden beneath weeds and brambles, hard to traverse. Several times she stumbled over concealed roots and only managed to save herself from falling by grabbing onto protruding branches. Matthew had a point. It was perfectly possible that Ed had tripped and knocked himself out. They just had to find him. He couldn't be badly hurt. Thick foliage would have broken his fall. Besides that, she refused to believe that anything terrible could have happened to her son, not so soon after his father was murdered. Life couldn't be so cruel.

Painstakingly they traversed the overgrown terrain, calling Ed's name and searching the ground, until the daylight began to fade.

'Mum, I can't see where I'm going. Ow!'

Desperately she pressed on until they were both stumbling around blindly. When an overhanging tree branch whacked her on the head, almost hitting her in the eye, she had to accept it was time to turn back.

'What about Ed?' Matthew wailed, reversing his opinion once he knew they were leaving.

As they made their way back home, Matthew began chattering excitedly about search parties. He wanted Caroline to call the police.

'They'll send a helicopter. They always do. And it'll have a ginormous light on it so it looks like it's day.'

Caroline hesitated. She tried to ignore the words floating in her head: 'I'll tell them what you made me do. They'll think you're not fit to be a mother. They'll take your children away from you... if I don't kill them. You know I can do it. I'll kill them if you don't do exactly what I want.'

She couldn't risk it. 'No police,' she said firmly.

'But mum, they'll bring dogs, and we'll be wrapped in silver. We'll be on the TV. Please, mum.'

'We'll come back with Dobby,' Caroline said firmly, 'if Ed's not found his way home by now. Come on, I expect we'll find him there waiting for us.'

Trotting at first, they both broke into a run as they neared the house. But Ed wasn't sitting on the doorstep and he didn't open the door when Matthew rang the bell frantically, while Caroline rummaged in her bag for her keys.

There was an envelope on the door mat addressed to her by her maiden name. Her heart seemed to pulse in her throat as she reached down. Matthew ran into the kitchen calling Dobby. Caroline slit the envelope open and withdrew a single sheet of white paper. On it were two letters, written in small neat capitals. 'ED'. That was all. It was enough. Caroline let out an involuntary sob. Brian must have been watching them. He had followed Ed to the shops. He had known Caroline wasn't home yet when he posted the letter through the door. 'I know all about you,' had been no idle threat. Before she could gather her thoughts, Matthew emerged from the kitchen, dragging Dobby by the collar.

'You're a lazy lazy beast,' he admonished the dog. 'We're going walkies.'

Dobby wagged his tail and gave a short bark.

Caroline clapped her hand to her head. 'I totally forgot,' she blurted out in a panic. 'A friend of mine called, and I arranged for Ed to go home with her. And then I forgot all about it. Silly me.' She forced a stupid laugh.

Matthew accepted the ridiculous story without question. Guilt at his absolute trust in her was swept aside by her terror about what was happening to Ed.

'Why?' Matthew demanded after a brief hiatus. He was kneeling down, scratching Dobby's head. 'Why?' he repeated.

'Why what?'

'Why did you let him go without me?'

'You had a tummy upset. I thought you were better off staying at home.'

It was a stupid lie, as well as a desperate one, inviting an obvious response.

'I'm better.'

She almost snapped and screamed at him to shut up and go to bed. She had to be left alone to think.

'Go and put the telly on,' she said. 'I'll make us some supper. Ed'll be home soon.'

She hoped that was true. The flimsy piece of paper trembled in her hand.

25

'HERE WE ARE,' BRIAN announced cheerily. 'This is my house.'

His young passenger frowned. 'I want to call my mum.'

'That's the last thing we want to do right now, start troubling her all over again at a time like this. I told you, she wants to be left alone for a while. She's got a lot to sort out. Now come on, let's go inside and have some tea.'

'Then can I call my mum? '

'Look, if you really want to bother your mother, you can call her, but I really think it would be kinder to leave it until tomorrow. Unless you're too young to manage this?' The boy shook his head uncertainly. 'Come on, then. I've got chocolate biscuits.'

The boy followed him dutifully into the house. Brian settled him in the front room with the curtains drawn and a cartoon channel on the television that neither of them was really watching. It was just as well the boy was behaving sensibly. Brian was feeling so wired, he struggled to maintain an outward appearance of calm. He wasn't sure he would be able to control his temper if the kid turned difficult. Besides, it would be easier to keep the boy out of sight if he was behaving himself. Having gone to all the trouble of capturing him, there was no way Brian was going to let him go. Not until Caroline had completed the job.

'Where's the chocolate biscuits? You said you had chocolate biscuits.'

Brian went to the kitchen and returned with a plate of Jaffa Cakes. After complaining his favourites were chocolate Swiss rolls, the boy tucked into the biscuits. 'They're my second favourite,' he admitted solemnly, as though it mattered.

'Have another one.'

He hesitated. 'Mum never lets us have more than two.'

'Your mother's not here.'

With a grin, the boy reached across the table for another biscuit. It was the first time Brian had seen him smile. He watched him as he munched happily, wondering whether the boy trusted him. He seemed to like the Jaffa Cakes anyway.

'When am I going home?'

It was an effort to keep his voice level. 'That all depends on your mother. I told you, she needs to rest. But you don't need to worry about her, she's going to be fine and you can go home very soon. You'll only be staying here for a few days, and your brother's gone to another friend of your mother's, just while she sorts herself out.' He put on a sad face. 'I wanted to put you both up here, but there's not enough room. It won't be for long anyway. Your mother just needs a little time to herself. I'm sure a clever boy like you understands that, don't you? Go on, have another one. We won't tell her.'

Looking thoughtful, the boy reached for another biscuit. 'Is she cracking up?'

Brian forced a laugh. 'No, of course not. She just needs to rest. It would really help her if you stayed here without making any fuss, just for a few days. I'll take good care of you. Plenty of Jaffa Cakes and I'll get you some chocolate Swiss rolls.' He laughed again, far too heartily.

'I'm thirsty.'

'You haven't drunk your juice.'

'I don't like it. The orange juice we have at home is nice but this is yucky.'

'That's because this is a healthy sort of orange juice. It'll make you strong. I can put some sugar in if it's not sweet enough?'

'OK.'

Brian hurried to the kitchen. It was vital he settled the boy down soon. He wasn't sure how easy it was going to be to keep him hidden in the house. In some ways it would be easier just to get rid of him, but then there would be the problem of disposing of the body. Even though he was only ten, he was quite tall. It could be more trouble than it was worth to get rid of him. Still, there was that option if the boy started causing trouble.

A single bed was made up in the spare bedroom although no one ever slept there. He would take the boy up there as soon as he finished his juice. Scooping up a teaspoonful of sugar, he paused. The boy had already eaten nearly a whole packet of biscuits. If he was sick it might be impossible to remove obvious traces of his DNA. Besides, too much sugar could make a child go wild. He tipped most of the granules back in the packet and dropped a tiny amount into the glass of juice. It wouldn't make much difference to the taste, but that was too bad. The boy would drink it if he was thirsty. He didn't have to like it.

When he returned to the front room, the biscuit plate was empty. Brian hoped his young visitor wouldn't be sick. He didn't look ill, just worried.

'Can I call mum now?'

'I thought we'd already agreed you would call her tomorrow.'

First Brian needed to think what he was going to say to Caroline, if he was going to allow the boy to communicate with her at all. It would certainly convince her Ed was with him. That was, after all, the whole point of the kidnap. Then again, the boy might have seen a road name that would help his mother find him. If that was the case, Brian wasn't confident the boy would keep his trap shut.

'Why didn't mum tell me I was coming here?'

He had been expecting that question, and trotted out a pat answer about it being a last minute decision.

'This wasn't her idea at all. When my friend and I suggested it, at first she didn't want you and your brother to go away, but we persuaded her it was for the best, just for a day or two. It gives her a chance to have a good rest, and she agreed it might be a bit of an adventure for you and your brother to go somewhere new completely by yourselves!'

It wasn't hard to inject some enthusiasm into his voice. In a funny way it was exciting to have a child in the house. He wondered whether he ought to offer the boy supper. He had eggs and bread in the fridge, but no sausages or burger or pizza or chips or anything like that. Boys were supposed to have huge appetites, but he had already eaten the best part of a packet of biscuits. Surely that was enough for anyone. Besides, Brian wanted to pack him off to bed before he could ask any more tiresome questions.

'Come on, it must be past your bedtime. I'll show you where you're sleeping.'

'I'm not tired.'

'Well I am, so come on, and I'll show you to your room.'

The boy stood up. 'What about my teeth?'

'What?'

'What about my teeth? I haven't got my toothbrush.'

'Teeth cleaning is overrated.'

'I don't know what that means. Mum says I have to clean my teeth.'

The boy's bottom lip trembled. Brian was afraid he was going to cry.

'I checked with her and she said it was OK. It won't matter for a few days.'

'How long am I staying here?'

'You'll be going home soon enough. Now come on, I'm getting really sleepy.'

To his relief, the boy obediently followed him upstairs to the spare bedroom. The wallpaper had pale blue flowers and the bed cover and tiny hand basin were light blue too. The brown carpet didn't quite go with the rest of the decor, but that didn't matter.

'This is your room.'

Brian was surprised when the boy grinned.

'I've never ever had my own room before!'

His glee was infectious. For the first time in years, Brian felt happy.

26

MATTHEW SAT GLUED TO the television while Caroline fiddled around in the kitchen making his supper. She didn't want to have to field any more of his questions about his brother. 'Where is he? Why couldn't I go? When's he coming home? It's not fair!'

She told herself she had put him in front of cartoons on the television to give herself time to think. In reality, she wasn't thinking at all. Her brain didn't seem to be functioning. Through a haze she watched her hands empty a tin of baked beans into a saucepan, then put two slices of bread in the toaster. She seemed to stir the beans forever to prevent them sticking to the bottom of the pan. When the toast popped up, she cried out, startled.

Brian had taken Ed. That much was certain. Equally certain was that Brian was a psychopath. Without going to the police, Caroline had no way of finding him. But if she went to the police, Brian would kill her son. He might already be dead.

'Mum, mum, the toast's burning. I don't like toast when it's all black and horrid.'

Caroline came to with a jolt. Matthew was shaking her arm. Delicate wisps of white smoke were rising from the toaster. She was still stirring the beans, but the sauce had thickened and was sticking to the bottom of the pan. She darted over to the toaster. The charred slices burned her fingers. She dropped them onto the work surface. Catching sight of Matthew's stricken face, she hurried to reassure him.

'Don't worry, we'll throw those away and put more on. You go back and watch telly.'

'I'm hungry now.'

'It'll be ready soon.'

'When's Ed coming home?'

'He'll be back tomorrow.'

It was a desperate lie. She didn't know what else to say. The next day she might have to think of something else to tell Matthew, but for now she couldn't think how else to deal with the situation. It was tempting to hand the whole nightmare situation over to the police and let them deal with it. They had the resources to find Ed. Stifling a sob, she put some more toast on and tried to salvage the beans. The gooey sludge resisted the stirring motion of her spoon and a nasty charred smell rose from the pan. The beans would taste bitter. She chucked the whole lot away and started again. She would have to be careful not to incinerate the toast again. She was dimly aware how absurd she was, struggling to make beans on toast. She had chosen that supper precisely because it was so simple to prepare.

Stirring a second tin of beans, she tried to calm down. It was too risky, going to the police. Brian might be watching, and she knew he had no compunction about committing murder. He had already killed her husband. She wasn't going to let him kill her son. Brian had terrorised her into a state of virtual paralysis. She didn't have to take that. If she could track him down, she might be able to find a way to scare him off. It was better than sitting at home, doing nothing. First, she would have to try and get hold of a list of pupils who had been at school with her. As far as she could remember, there had only been one Brian in her class, but even if she managed to obtain a list of names of boys who were with her at school, she had no way of finding out where he lived. Only the police would have access to that kind of information. A couple of times she reached for the phone, then stopped. Brian had told her he would know if she went to the police. He might be watching the house. Even an unmarked police car might warn a suspicious observer that she had contacted the police. Knowing what he was capable of, she couldn't risk provoking him.

The toast popped up. The beans began to bubble. Matthew was hungry. Miserably she poured beans over his toast. There should have been two plates.

'Time for bed!'

Matthew glared up at her sullenly. 'What about Ed?'

'Yes, well, Ed will be back with us tomorrow. Now, off you go. You've got to be up early for school tomorrow.'

'But...'

'No more talking. You've got school tomorrow.'

'Will Ed be there? How will your friend know where he needs to go?'

She nearly broke down in tears, but she had to remain in control of her emotions, at least until Matthew was asleep.

'Don't worry,' she said. 'You're always worrying.'

As she spoke she remembered that Ed was the worrier, not Matthew.

Once Matthew was in bed she set to work cleaning the kitchen. She had to keep busy. If she allowed herself to stop and think, she would go mad. No one could help her. Dave would have known what to do. Now she was facing the most terrifying ordeal of her life on her own. Perched on a stool in her kitchen, gazing into a pan of mushy beans, she shivered. She had never been so frightened before, or felt so helpless. Somewhere out in the darkness, Ed was waiting for her to rescue him. He might already be dead. And there was nothing she could do.

27

THERE WAS NO SOUND from the spare room when Brian got up the next morning. He pulled the door open slowly, wincing when it creaked on its hinges. Peering round, he saw the low mound of a body and the back of a small blond head on the pillow. He stood for a few moments, watching and wondering what to do. Lulled by the sound of rhythmic snoring, he was startled when the boy turned over without warning, so that he was facing his unseen watcher. Only the boy's head was visible above the covers, his eyes still shut. Sleep had smoothed away his worried scowl. He looked angelic, spreadeagled in the bed, a faint smile lifting the corners of his lips.

Brian hesitated in the doorway. It was a shame to wake him. Softly he stepped into the room and approached the bed. The boy's long fringe had flopped forward over his eyes. With the tips of the fingers of one hand Brian reached down and brushed it back off his face. He stirred then and opened his eyes. Watching him wake up, Brian felt a curious pang of loneliness. It was a long time since he had shared such an intimate moment with another human being.

'It's time to get up,' he said, stepping away from the bed.

He was afraid the boy was going to demand to be taken straight home, but instead he grinned up at Brian.

'Your clothes are all clean,' Brian went on.

He had washed and dried the boy's clothes before he had gone to bed the previous evening. They now lay folded in a neat pile on a chair beside the bed.

'Do you want a shower?'

The boy screwed up his nose. 'Do I pong?'

'No,' Brian laughed. 'You don't pong. And you don't have to shower here unless you want to.'

'That's never!' the boy crowed joyfully, sitting up, and they both laughed.

'My mum makes us wash all the time,' he added as he reached for his clothes. 'She's obsessed with it.'

'Well in this house you do exactly as you like,' Brian said, and was rewarded with another smile.

'I never get to do whatever I like at home.'

At the door Brian turned and announced he was going downstairs to make breakfast.

'Is there sausages?' the boy asked, his face alight with expectation.

Brian hesitated. 'There can be if you don't mind waiting. Tell you what, why don't you let me know what you'd like and then you can stay in bed for a bit while I nip out to the corner shop? There's no need for you to get up yet if you don't want to.'

The boy flopped back on his pillow, grinning broadly and Brian relaxed slightly. As long as the boy stayed in bed, he couldn't get up to any mischief.

'Sausages, waffles, and chocolate milk!' he announced with an air of cautious triumph, as though he was afraid Brian might balk at his temerity.

'Sausages, waffles and chocolate milk it is,' Brian replied promptly. 'I'll give you a shout as soon as I get back and then you can be getting dressed while I make the breakfast.'

A light drizzle was falling as he hurried along the deserted street to the little grocery store. The goods in there weren't always fresh, but he couldn't waste time going to the supermarket. Predictably, the shop was empty. A small Asian man sat hunched behind the counter, gazing at a newspaper with a bored expression on his face. It wasn't a very stimulating way to pass the day, sitting and waiting for someone to enter the shop and buy a paper, or a sliced loaf. Quickly Brian walked along the first cramped aisle, scanning the shelves. The shopkeeper rang up his purchases without a word, barely glancing at him when he paid.

There was no reason why anyone would look at him. He was just an unremarkable bloke out buying some ordinary items of food. He knew people would look askance at him if they thought he had brought the boy home with him without his mother's permission, but she knew all about it. He had made sure of that. There wouldn't have been much point in bringing the boy home with him if she hadn't. It was up to her now, how long the boy stayed with him. It was hardly his fault if she didn't do what was necessary to get her son back. He was sure she would see sense before too long. Any mother would do what he had asked. He smiled. It was a shame only he and Caroline would ever know just how clever he was.

It was raining more heavily when he left the shop. Clutching his carrier bags, he dashed back home, eyes down, avoiding puddles on the uneven pavement. Dumping the wet shopping bags in the kitchen, he shuffled into his slippers and called up from the bottom of the stairs.

'I'm home. You can get dressed now.'

There was no answer.

He half turned back to the kitchen to start getting the breakfast ready. Thinking better of it, he clumped up the stairs, calling out as he went. 'Are you awake? It's time to get up!'

The door to the spare room was open. As he reached the landing he had a clear view of the bed. It was empty. He started forward and ran into the room. There was no sign of the boy. Brian spun round in a panic and saw that the neatly folded clothes had gone from the chair.

He wasn't sure what to do. He had to find the boy, but he had no idea where to look. He must have gone out to try and find his way home. Brian had only been out of the house for about fifteen minutes, getting the breakfast the boy had asked for. He couldn't have gone far on foot. Panicking, Brian ran downstairs and out to the car. Driving around the streets seemed to be his best chance of finding him but, if the boy returned while he was out searching, he wouldn't be able to get in. Brian cursed himself for leaving the boy unattended. When he found him, he was going to be far more careful.

28

REG MARCHED ALONG THE corridor ahead of Geraldine, his arms hanging stiffly at his sides. His large square shoulders didn't seem to shift beneath his jacket as he moved, rigid from the waist up. He wasn't overweight, but even from behind he looked solid. Reaching the interview room, he flung the door open and strode in without pausing to hold the door for her. With his air of self-importance, he dominated the room. Geraldine found him intimidating. She could only imagine the effect he would have on a suspect.

Greg's face was grey and drawn from lack of sleep. Scruffy ginger hair skimmed hunched shoulders which were dusted with dandruff. He looked unwashed, and his eyes seemed to exude misery. Geraldine almost felt sorry for him as he seemed to shrink into his chair on the far side of the table, his head lowered so that his large forehead hid his eyes. He flinched as Reg launched into the formalities.

'It wasn't me,' Greg growled hoarsely, without looking up. 'I never laid a finger on him. Never touched him.'

Ignoring the interruption, Reg continued his impassive recital. 'Also present, Detective Inspector Geraldine Steel.'

Greg raised tormented eyes to Geraldine as though pleading with her to intercede on his behalf. His left eye was still slightly swollen, the bruising stark against his pale face.

'It wasn't me,' he insisted.

Reg reached the end of the obligatory preamble. 'Just answer the questions,' he said heavily.

The duty solicitor leaned forward and muttered to Greg who slumped back in his chair again, mumbling under his breath about being wrongly accused.

'Let the process take its course,' the lawyer said quietly.

'Not much else I can do, is there?' Greg complained.

'Just answer the questions,' Geraldine echoed the chief inspector.

She found Greg's response to the situation worrying; cowed but not angry. The more aggressive Reg grew in his questioning, the more Greg seemed to retreat into himself. He didn't strike her as sharp enough to be putting on an act. Withdrawal seemed to be his natural reaction to hostility. When they took a break Geraldine tried to discuss her impression with Reg, but he dismissed her reservations with a wave of his hand.

'It's only a matter of time now until he slips up. We'll nail him sooner or later. Let's hope he doesn't string it out too long.'

Reg was in a hurry to wind up the case, but Greg remained quietly intransigent.

'You're not helping your case, you know,' Reg said at last, heaving an exaggerated sigh. 'Let's go through it all over again. I suggest you give your answers some careful thought, and listen to your lawyer when he tells you it will be better for you if you stop wasting our time and tell us the truth.'

'Please don't put words into my mouth,' the solicitor said.

He sounded thoroughly bored with the situation. His blasé attitude infuriated Geraldine. Both he and the detective chief inspector seemed to have made up their minds that Greg was guilty of murder. Maybe they were right, but their cavalier attitude flouted the principle that a man was innocent until proven guilty.

Reg grilled Greg about his whereabouts on the day Dave was killed. Greg stuck to his story that he had been at home all day with Stacey's small children while she had been out at work. Stacey had returned home late, he said, but he couldn't give them a precise time. Heaving another of his exaggerated sighs, Reg changed tack and asked about the suspect's relationship with the deceased.

'Dave? He was all right.'

'All right?'

'Yeah, he was all right. I mean, we weren't mates or anything. I hardly knew the guy.'

Reg pounced, with the clear intention of catching the other man off guard. 'What were the two of you fighting about?'

Greg glanced at the solicitor who didn't appear to be following the interview.

'What do you mean?'

'It's a perfectly simple question. What were you and David Robinson fighting about before he was killed?'

'We were never fighting.'

'We have an eye witness. You were seen fighting.'

'I don't know what you're talking about.'

Reg spoke slowly. 'Someone saw you fighting with David Robinson the day before he was killed.'

Greg's eyes widened in terror as he registered the implication. 'That's a lie. I never touched the guy. We had a few words, that's all. You couldn't call it a fight.' He became animated. 'This is a set up. Who said we were fighting? What's been said about me? Who was it? Someone's telling you lies about me. Why do you believe them and not me?'

Reg leaned forward. He spoke very softly.

'Would you mind telling us where you got that black eye?'

Involuntarily, Greg's hand fluttered to his eye.

'That's a nasty shiner. It must be about a week old. And you've got a split lip where someone must have punched you in the face.'

Greg mumbled incoherently.

'What was that? I didn't catch what you said. You'll have to speak up for the tape.'

'I said I walked into a wall.'

Reg gave a bark of genuine laughter. 'No, you had a fight with Dave Robinson. He got the better of you, didn't he? You threatened to come back and kill him, and that's exactly what you did, creeping up on him from behind when he wasn't looking. We know what happened, so you might as well come clean. You're going down anyway, so you might as well co-operate. You'll only make things worse for yourself if you insist on denying it.'

When Geraldine repeated her reservations to Reg after the interview, he refused to take her concerns seriously.

'With respect, sir, a man's freedom is at stake.'

'He'll have the full force of the law on his side if he's innocent.'

In the hands of a skilled prosecuting barrister, juries could be swayed by the balance of probabilities. 'Reasonable doubt' was a tricky judgement call. History showed that miscarriages of justice weren't impossible. As things stood, Greg appeared to be in the frame and guilty as charged. But that wasn't the same as a certainty. The longer he remained in custody, an accused man, the more likely it was he would be condemned. Already he looked more desperate than he had when she had first seen him in the pub, as though a stain of villainy had rubbed off on him from previous inmates of his cell. She couldn't have pinpointed the difference in his demeanour, but he had developed a furtive air which made him look guilty. Meanwhile, he had stopped protesting his innocence and sat in his cell in sullen silence.

According to Reg, Greg had stopped complaining because he recognised the game was up.

'Probably true,' Geraldine conceded, 'but we need to be sure.'

'That's for a jury to decide.'

Reg spoke firmly, in a tone of voice that ended the discussion. Seeing Geraldine's vexed expression, he added, 'Why don't you go and talk to the witness who reported seeing Greg and Dave fighting? We've got his statement, but we have to make sure he's prepared to give evidence in person, and you can set your mind at rest at the same time.'

She nodded and set off at once, relieved to escape the police station for a couple of hours. Wherever she went in the building she bumped into either Reg or Nick, both demanding her attention in different ways. She was beginning to feel hemmed in. She missed her usual sergeant. Max was pleasant enough, but she couldn't have a laugh with him like she could with Sam.

29

BEFORE GOING TO SEE Will Henry, Geraldine telephoned the mortuary to check a few details. She was hoping to speak to Miles. Fortunately he was at work that morning and the technician was able to put her through to him straight away.

'Hello, Inspector. How can I help you?' his familiar voice asked breezily.

'I have a question about the body.'

'And I thought you were calling to invite me out for dinner as a reward for working on a Sunday. Oh well, life's full of disappointments.'

'I need to speak to you about Dave Robinson.'

'Fire away, I'm all ears.'

His lighthearted tone didn't faze her. She knew he took his work seriously.

'What I want to know is whether there were any injuries that could have been inflicted a little over twenty-four hours before he was killed? Specifically around eleven on the Friday morning.'

'What sort of injuries are you talking about?'

'Injuries consistent with being in a fight.'

Miles spoke slowly. 'Nothing I can recall offhand, nothing that I noticed, but I was focussing on evidence of the attack that killed him. I wasn't looking for anything else.' He hesitated. 'Let me check and get back to you on this. Give me an hour.'

Miles was as good as his word. Before the hour was up, he called her back. He was quite clear that he had seen nothing to indicate the victim had been involved in a fight the day before he was killed.

'Of course it could have been a scrap with no physical injuries inflicted, leaving no trace of the attacker. What I'm telling you isn't conclusive.'

'Absence of evidence rarely is. But how likely is it that someone could come away from a fight without any physical signs at all? Not so much as a bruise or a scratch?'

Never normally slow to express an opinion, on this occasion Miles refused to commit himself. 'I'd like to give you an answer but I've really no idea. It's quite possible that many of the victims I see were involved in fights shortly before they died, without being injured. I couldn't tell that from examining them, not unless they sustained injuries while they were fighting. Sorry I can't be more helpful.'

Nick hadn't arrived at work by the time Geraldine set off. She was tempted to wait until she had seen him before she left the office, but there was no sensible reason to postpone speaking to a potential witness just in order to see Nick. She saw him every day. He would be at his desk by the time she returned. In the meantime, she had to focus on her investigation.

Will Henry stared morosely at Geraldine. He was younger than she had expected. If anything, he appeared even more anxious than Max's description had suggested. He shifted awkwardly from one foot to the other, while his eyes slid past her without once looking at her directly.

'What do you want? I went to the police station and spoke to someone there. I gave my statement. I got nothing more to say to you.'

Geraldine considered. She was going have to proceed carefully. He would be easily scared off.

'We're investigating a murder,' she said firmly. 'Everything has to be thoroughly looked into.'

'I get that, but I already told the policeman everything I know.'

'Let's go over it one more time. I'd like to hear it from you.'

'Don't you trust your colleague to get it right?'

Geraldine ignored the provocative remark. Will was riled at being questioned again.

'What happened the day before the murder? What did you see? Describe it to me.'

'Nothing happened. There was a row. I told the policeman about it. There's nothing else to say.'

Geraldine tried to sound reassuring, hiding her sudden alarm.

'What do you mean, a row?' she asked quietly.

Will looked at her for the first time, reacting to a change in her voice. 'They were having a row,' he repeated, frowning. 'Like I said, they were having a row. You know, a barney. Jesus! I thought you people were supposed to be clever. I don't know what more you want me to say.'

'Who started the row?'

He shook his head, growing defensive in response to her intensity. 'I don't know. I didn't see. They just started having a go at each other. They were so busy at it, neither of them noticed me behind the pallets, but I could see them all right through the slats. I was scared to come out in case they thought I'd been watching. They were pumped.'

Geraldine chose her words carefully. 'Who threw the first punch?'

'I didn't see any punches.'

'But you said they were fighting.'

'I wouldn't call it a fight, exactly.'

He fidgeted, seeming to appreciate that her tone had altered without understanding what had worried her.

'Tell me everything you saw.'

'I heard voices first off. They weren't shouting or anything, but I could tell they were angry.'

'How did you know they were angry?'

A faint smile flitted across his dour face at the question.

'Because I could hear them. And then Dave give him a shove.'

'A shove?'

'Yes. Pushed him, you know.'

'Where?'

'What?'

'Where did he push him? Show me on your own face or body exactly where he pushed him.'

Will shrugged. 'Here.' He touched his right shoulder.

'Not on his face?'

'Does it look like my face?' he retorted, pointing at his shoulder.

'And then what happened?'

She forced herself to be patient, remembering Max's complaint that getting information out of Will had been hard work. She held her breath, waiting to hear that Greg had retaliated violently. She was disappointed. According to Will, far from launching a counter attack, Greg had stepped back, dodging Dave's second lunge completely. Dave had sworn, Greg had sworn back, and they had hurled insults at one another. Just as Greg warned Dave it wasn't over, and he hadn't heard the last of it, the foreman walked in and the two men had hurried off.

Geraldine frowned. 'I need you to be absolutely clear about this. You're saying Greg didn't fight back?'

'Him? Stand up to anyone in a fight? Are you joking? He's a right chicken…' He broke off abruptly, afraid of saying too much.

'Why did you tell my colleague you witnessed a fight between them?'

'I never said I saw them fighting. I said they had a row.'

'You said they were fighting.'

'Well maybe that's what I said. What's the difference?'

'So there was no physical fight?'

'No. They were still fighting though.'

Geraldine reminded him that he had told Max he was convinced Greg had killed Dave. Will nodded energetically.

'What makes you so sure?'

'Stands to reason, doesn't it? They had a fight – all right, a row – and Greg was threatening Dave. Said it wasn't over. The next day, Dave's killed. It's obvious what happened, isn't it?'

Will meant well, but his statement was a waste of time. He had no proof Greg had killed Dave. On the contrary, if anything, his ambiguous testimony seemed to imply that Greg had avoided a physical conflict with Dave. Max had been too ready to take what Will had said at face value. Now Geraldine had another problem to address. She would have to find time to make it clear to her sergeant that he must constantly guard against jumping to conclusions. She wished she could point that out to her detective chief inspector as well, but it wasn't her place to do so.

She returned to the police station, excited about seeing Nick again, yet apprehensive. To her disappointment, the office was empty. He was often away from his desk all day. It was absurd to worry that he might be avoiding her. More than once she stopped herself phoning him to check if he was thinking about her. He would not appreciate her calling him, for no reason, while he was working. But the more she tried to put him out of her mind, the more she was plagued by the memory of their night together.

30

As Caroline approached the end of her road, her legs felt weak. She tensed with the expectation of hearing a voice summoning her from the shadows in the trees. Shaking with fear, she struggled to keep going.

'Come on, mum,' Matthew called to her. 'It'll be dark soon.'

She hurried after him. Once she had passed the trees, her mind cleared. It felt strange to be taking Matt to the park by himself. His lone figure looked horribly solitary on the pavement up ahead of her. It was hard to imagine, but this must be what it was like for people who had only one child. Dreadful to her, for many parents it was normal. She trotted to catch up with him and then regretted it because as soon as she reached him he started whining about Ed again.

'When's he coming home?' he asked. 'It's boring without him.'

She didn't answer.

The park was empty when they arrived. Matt kicked the ball around on the grass in a desultory fashion. She could tell it was no fun for him without Ed. He perked up after a while when a few other kids appeared and asked to play. Matt was the one with the ball, so he took charge. For a brief time he seemed to forget about his missing brother as he shouted out directions. Watching him engrossed in his game, she wondered what their lives would be like if Ed never returned. It wasn't a prospect she had allowed herself to consider before. She blinked as her eyes began to water. Whatever happened, she had to stay strong for Matt.

The bench jolted almost imperceptibly. Someone had come to sit beside her. Without turning her head she knew who it was. She stared doggedly at the boys kicking the ball around. It wasn't clear where the goal posts were. For no apparent reason the group of boys all started shouting at once. Matt was jumping up and down, yelling something. There must have been a goal, but it wasn't clear who had scored.

'It's a lovely evening,' he said quietly.

An outside observer would have agreed. A slight breeze ruffled the leaves overhead. A single bird sailed across the clear sky, high above them, ragged wings and curved beak marking it out as a bird of prey. The boys were playing happily on the grass. The scene was idyllic. Only she knew the sinister truth behind this conversation in the park.

'Don't you think it's a lovely evening, Caroline?'

Her name crackled on his lips like a threat.

'Where is he?' she muttered without looking at him.

At her side she thought she heard muffled laughter, but when she glanced sideways Brian was staring ahead with a tranquil expression. She followed his gaze. He was watching the boys playing football. Matt was preparing to kick the ball, his face set in ferocious concentration. Several of the other kids were yelling at him, but she couldn't hear what any of them were saying.

Brian hissed so softly she barely caught the words. 'He must miss his brother.'

'You have to bring him home right now.'

'All in good time. It won't be long now.'

Her heart seemed to miss a beat. Brian had agreed to bring Ed home, if not now then soon. Her son was alive. She struggled not to cry. Her throat seemed to close up with the effort to speak.

'When?'

'As soon as you've done what I asked.'

Disappointment threatened to choke her. Then came an anger so sharp, she wanted to lash out. Dave was dead and Ed's life was in danger. Now Brian wanted her to commit a murder. She would do anything in her power to save her son, but she couldn't deliberately kill a stranger. The one man she hated enough to kill was the only person who knew where Ed was being held. The situation was complicated. She would have to be cunning to outwit Brian. Instead of rejecting his demand outright, she would play along with his crazy plan and see where it led. Perhaps she could warn the man Brian wanted her to kill. That way, her intended victim could go to the police on her behalf, and put an end to this insanity. It was an unlikely plan, but she had to do something.

'What if I agree to do what you want? What then? How can I trust you to bring Ed back home?'

'You can trust me.'

'Tell me again where to find the man your wife ran off with.'

'She didn't run off with him. She wanted to, but he was already married. She wanted him to leave his wife, but then she died.'

A horrible thought struck Caroline.

'She didn't kill herself, did she? You did it. You killed her.'

He was silent for a moment.

'Ed's waiting for you,' he said at last.

She understood he didn't want to talk about his wife. Best not to provoke him. To change the subject she asked again about the man she was supposed to kill. With a sense of unreality she listened as he gave her the details again. He spoke as calmly as though they were arranging a trip to the cinema.

'Now give me your word that you will carry out your part of the bargain,' he concluded.

Despite the fact that she had never entered into any such agreement with him, she had no choice but to humour him for now. It was too late for regrets. If only she hadn't met him in the park that first time. If only she had never spoken to him that day. If only she hadn't rushed to give him her address or let him take a photo of the two of them together. If only she had warned Dave, and gone straight to the police – but no one would have believed her. In any case, he had given her no indication of his true intentions at their first encounter. She had believed him when he had said he was going to make Dave jealous by showing him a photo of her with another man on his phone. It had never occurred to her that he was going to kill her husband.

'Remember, if you go to the police, or if you fail to finish the job, you will never see your son again. If you try to double cross me, I'll know. As soon as the police knock at my door...'

He drew one hand across his throat making a horrible choking noise in his throat to indicate someone dying. She looked away. His reference to committing murder as a 'job' was chilling.

'If I'm arrested, I won't be able to take care of him. No one will ever find him. He'll be left locked in a room to starve, all alone. You wouldn't let that happen, would you?'

His face relaxed into a smile. She wanted to punch him.

'What if I can't do it? What if someone stops me?'

'You know the terms. A life for a life. Either you end a guilty man's life, or your son dies.'

Brian smiled at her. He sounded so reasonable, she struggled to believe what she was hearing. She had no choice but to play along with his madness. Completely insane, he alone knew where her son was. If she contacted the police, she believed Brian could actually be crazy enough to keep Ed's whereabouts to himself. He had been crazy enough to kidnap him in the first place. Unless he had told someone else, it was possible no one would ever find Ed. She couldn't risk alienating Brian.

'I'll do it,' she agreed wretchedly. 'I'll try.'

'I knew you would,' he said. From his voice she could tell he was smiling. 'But remember, if you go to the police, you'll never see the boy again.'

They sat in silence for a moment. When she looked round, the bench beside her was empty.

31

CAROLINE HAD DRUMMED INTO Matthew that his brother had gone to stay with a friend of hers, and wouldn't be home for a few days.

'You said he'd be home today,' Matthew whined at breakfast.

'I know, that's what I thought too, but then my friend called this morning before you woke up and invited him to stay on for a few days. I spoke to him and he said he wanted to stay there and I said he could.'

Matthew was only ten and he trusted her. Nevertheless, she was relieved when he accepted what she had said, although he continued to complain that it wasn't fair.

'How come *he* gets to miss school?' he grumbled into his Coco Pops. 'If *he's* not going to school how come *I* have to go? It's not fair. I'm having to do stupid work and he's not.'

'My friend's a teacher,' she lied desperately. 'She'll be giving him lots of work to do so he doesn't fall behind.'

Matthew sniggered and she relaxed slightly. The problem of keeping Matthew quiet about his brother's disappearance had been resolved for the time being. Now she had to face the real problem of rescuing Ed.

Matthew dragged his feet as he crossed the playground. Standing at the school gate, Caroline watched him make his way up the steps to vanish in the throng of children entering the building. Without his brother he looked isolated, in spite of the other children milling around him on the steps. As soon as he was out of sight, she telephoned the school office and explained that Ed was struggling to come to terms with his father's sudden death. He was too upset to return to school just yet. She was keeping him at home for a day or two. Matthew had a lively imagination. No one would take any notice if he gave a different explanation for his brother's absence. She had a couple of days' grace. Soon Matthew would start asking questions again. It wouldn't be long until the school grew suspicious. Neighbours might become curious, noticing she was now accompanied by only one child. But apart from the fear of discovery, she had to find Ed and bring him home. She refused to consider it might already be too late to save him.

First she had to discover Brian's full name. Without that she had no chance of tracking him down. As soon as she reached home, she googled her primary school and phoned up. Understandably, the secretary was reluctant to divulge the names of boys who had been in her class.

'You don't understand.' Caroline tried to stay calm. 'I went to Cartpool Juniors. I was there. It's my own class I'm asking about. I want to organise a reunion.'

'If you give me your contact details I can certainly pass those on, but we can't give out any personal information from our records.'

'I'm not asking for any personal information. I just want the names.'

However hard Caroline tried to persuade the school secretary to help, the other woman refused point blank to give her the names she wanted. Unless she could discover where Brian was living, there was no way she could find Ed. She had to think fast. Even if she broke into the school, she might not be able to find class lists from over twenty years ago. They might not even exist any longer. Brian had warned her not to speak to the police, but they were the only ones who could possibly have access to the information necessary to trace Brian's address. Afraid of what he might do if he discovered she had defied him, she was apprehensive about going to the police, but she had no alternative. By herself, she was helpless. Somehow she had to speak to a detective without his knowledge.

'If you go to the police, I'll tell them you talked me into killing your husband. They'll take your children away from you... if I don't kill them. You know I can do it. I'll kill them if you don't do exactly what I want.'

The words seemed to ring inside her head as she reached for the phone. She wasn't sure whether to dial 999 or try to contact her local police station. Probably it would be best to speak to someone local, but she didn't know the number. The police station wasn't far away. It would be easier to just go there. It would certainly be difficult to explain herself over the phone without prompting a visit from the police. As soon as she mentioned a missing child, they were bound to send a police car to her house, with flashing lights, and sirens blaring. She had seen it happen so many times on TV shows. It had always looked so exciting on the telly. However careful she was to insist they didn't come to the house, the policeman on the other end of the line might misunderstand her concern. Brian had warned that he would be watching. It was too risky.

After dithering for a while, she raced upstairs and rummaged in her wardrobe. Five minutes later she left the house, a large handbag over her shoulder. She crossed the main road and headed straight for the Tesco a few blocks away. She walked up and down the aisles for a while, looking at the shelves, surreptitiously studying the other shoppers. There was no sign of Brian. Finally she slipped into the toilet. Once she was safely inside a cubicle, there was no time to waste. Quickly she unzipped her bag and pulled out a rolled-up beige mac, a paisley scarf and leather gloves that were too big for her. Hurriedly she pulled them on, tucking her hair out of sight beneath the headscarf. Tears welled up in her eyes as her fingers groped their way inside Dave's gloves. Now only her ankles, shoes and face remained the same as they had been when she had entered the toilets. Blinking furiously, she felt in her bag for a pair of sunglasses she had brought with her. She was undecided whether to wear them or not. On such an overcast day they might attract attention. With sudden inspiration, she pushed out the lenses. The empty frames made her look as though she was wearing ordinary glasses. She was ready. Before leaving the cubicle she took a quick gulp from the small bottle of whisky she had brought with her, to give her courage. Stepping out into the shopping centre, she glanced around. There was no sign of Brian. It didn't matter anyway. He thought he had outwitted her, but she could be clever too. If he saw her leaving the toilets, or going into the police station, he wouldn't recognise her.

32

As a rule Detective Constable Timothy Clarke was conscientious, but after spending most of the weekend at a stag do he was too tired to think about anything but getting through the day without any cock ups. With luck, he would have slept off his hangover by the next morning. All he wanted to do was sit quietly waiting for the day to finish so he could go home. Staring at his computer screen was giving him a headache, so when a woman turned up at the desk to report a problem, he was happy to go and listen to what she had to say.

He sat down and studied the woman carefully. Head down, collar turned up, her hair concealed beneath a patterned scarf, he could see little of her face other than her black-framed glasses. There was something odd about her appearance, although he wasn't immediately sure what it was. When she raised her head, he realised her glasses had no lenses. Seeing him looking at her curiously, she removed the frames and placed them on the table.

'I had to come here in disguise,' she explained earnestly. 'He knows everything I do. He's watching me. He knows where I go.' Her hoarse voice trembled.

Timothy sighed. This was going to be a waste of time. Noticing a faint aroma of whisky, he supposed that alcohol had rotted her brain. Either that or she was mentally ill. Whatever the cause, she was paranoid.

'What seems to be the problem, Miss – er – Farmer?'

The woman blinked nervously, twisting her gloved hands in her lap. As if reading his thoughts, she said quietly, 'Freda Farmer isn't my real name. I just made it up when they asked me at the front desk. The policeman out there said I had to give my name if I wanted to talk to someone. My real name's Caroline Robinson. But

I gave him my real address. You're going to have to know that.' Her lips twisted and she began to cry.

Timothy decided to give it five minutes. If she hadn't come up with anything coherent by then, he would send her packing. He waited but she didn't stop crying. When he pushed his chair back to stand up, she finally pulled herself together. Carefully removing her gloves, she fished a tissue out of her bag, and blew her dripping nose.

'My boy's missing.'

Timothy sat down again, frowning.

'Are you reporting a missing child?'

'Yes.'

'How old is he?'

'He's ten.'

She began to cry again.

Timothy noted down the boy's name and address, and the name of his school, and when and where his mother had last seen him. If she was telling the truth, the boy had been missing overnight. When they had gone all through the details, and established a few facts, he questioned her about her disguise. Instead of offering a predictable account of an abusive ex-husband or boyfriend, and a vicious custody dispute, she launched into a convoluted story about a man she had been at school with. Timothy did his best to make sense of her narrative.

'Let's go back to the beginning. You said you met this man in the park?'

'Yes, in the park, although we weren't exactly strangers. Like I said, we'd known each other years ago, at primary school. He recognised me straight away. He came and sat next to me in the park, where no one else could see us. And there aren't any security cameras there. That's how clever he is.'

Timothy looked up from his notebook.

'And a few days after meeting you in the park he kidnapped your son?'

'Yes.'

'Can you think of any reason why he might have done that?'

She hesitated too long before blurting out, 'You have to find him.

Oh, please hurry. He could be hurt, or frightened, or...'

That didn't answer his question, but she was crying again.

'And you've had no contact with this man since you were at primary school, other than that one time you met him in the park?'

'Yes, that's right.'

'Can you think of any reason why he might want to kidnap your son? What does he hope to gain by it?' He paused, wondering if the woman facing him in tears was more wealthy than she appeared. 'Have you received any demands for money?'

'No, nothing like that. I haven't got any money anyway. But...'

'Yes?' he prompted her, glancing at his watch.

'He wants me to kill someone, a man I've never met.' She stared at him, wide-eyed. 'His name's Brian. I've tried and tried, but I can't remember his other name. You have to find him before he kills my son.'

Timothy sighed. 'You say he's going to kill your son? I thought you said he wants you to kill someone?'

'Yes. He wants me to kill a man I've never met. That's the point. If I don't do what he wants, he's going to kill my son. And he'll do it. I know what he's capable of. He's killed before.'

Timothy was no psychiatrist, but he could tell she was disturbed. She clearly had no idea how absurd her story sounded. He assured her the police would do everything in their power to restore her son to her. It was probably a waste of time, following up her ravings, but he went through the motions. He couldn't ignore a report of a missing child, even such a far-fetched report. After assuring her that the police would do everything in their power to help, he sent her home to wait there in case the boy returned.

Once she had gone, he phoned her son's school.

'Ed Robinson?' the school secretary said. 'Yes, he's off school today.'

Timothy's heart skipped a beat. Perhaps the distraught mother had been telling the truth after all, and the child really was missing. The secretary's next words reassured him.

'His mother called in to say he's staying at home today. I'm afraid there's been a tragedy in the family. His father died a few days ago and of course they're all very upset.'

Timothy answered hurriedly before she could hang up.

'His mother phoned to tell you he's at home, you say?'

'Yes, that's right.'

'Is she disturbed, would you say?'

'I can't comment on that. I'm sorry. I don't know her. But it would be understandable. She must be terribly upset. It wasn't a natural death, you see. I'm afraid the father was murdered.'

The penny dropped. Timothy couldn't believe he had failed to make the connection sooner. Robinson was the name of a recent murder victim. He checked his screen quickly. The addresses matched. No wonder the poor woman was raving. He thanked the school secretary, and explained about the call the school would be receiving from the social services. There was nothing more he could do. The school confirmed that Ed Robinson was at home with his mother. She had called the school to tell them where he was. Unhinged by grief, or confused by medication, she imagined that her son had been abducted by a stranger who was going to kill him. In reality, it was her husband who had been taken from her and killed. Timothy hoped her distress would pass, and she would recover her wits. If not, the boy would have lost both his parents. With a sigh, he returned to his daily duties. Having passed the situation on to the social services, there was nothing more he could do to help the poor woman.

33

MOST DAYS DENNY DIDN'T mind his job. He grumbled about it, along with the other lads at the depot. They all liked to moan about their hours, their exposure to the weather, the heavy sacks they had to carry, and the threat of vicious dogs. Urban legends had grown up about horrific injuries suffered by postmen. There was certainly no shortage of issues to complain about. All the same, if he collected his deliveries early, on a good day he could be finished by the end of the morning. On Tuesday morning he set off as usual, whistling cheerily. The clouds that had threatened rain earlier on had drifted away and the sun was shining. Tulips and wallflowers dotted the gardens with splashes of yellow and red, dazzling when he looked straight at them. The sky was a bright turquoise, reminding him of summer holidays, lazing on the beach.

He was checking the letters, not looking where he was going, when his foot kicked against something on one of the paths, and he stumbled. A couple of letters dropped from his hand. Regaining his balance, he bent down to retrieve them and saw what had tripped him up. Sticking out from a ragged hedge that ran along the side of the garden a trousered leg with a brown shoe lay across the path. Denny frowned. There was something peculiar about the leg. He had inadvertently kicked it quite hard, nearly falling over, but there had been no response. Its owner must be unconscious – or worse.

Intrigued, and curiously excited, he knelt down and placed his free hand on the calf of the motionless leg. It felt cold. He placed his hand on the ankle and shook it, calling out softly. The leaves on the bush rustled with the movement. Slipping the letters he was holding back into his bag, he carefully parted the branches of the shrub and gasped. A face was lying on the earth, staring straight

up at him. It looked ghastly, the complexion pale and streaked with
dried blood.

'Bloody hell!'

Startled, he released the twigs he was holding and sprang
backwards. Although his hands were shaking, he felt surprisingly
calm. The situation was clear. He had come across a corpse.
Cautiously, Denny leaned forward and parted the leaves again.
There was no doubt about the thin red line around the neck, or
the dried blood on the bruised face. This was what they called
'suspicious circumstances' all right.

His initial excitement rapidly faded with the realisation that this
was likely to be time consuming. He might be expected to hang
around for ages, answering questions. It was tempting to ignore
the few letters addressed to the people living in that house, and
continue on his round as though nothing had happened. But there
was no doubt about it. Denny had uncovered a crime scene. If he
had contaminated it, he had done so unwittingly. He couldn't walk
away. Apart from anything else, the police might somehow be able
to trace his presence from his brief contact with the leg and the
bush. He had seen too much television not to know the police could
do all sorts of clever tricks with DNA. He couldn't take that risk.
Plus he would have a great story to tell the lads at the depot. He
gave a guilty start because the prospect of telling his mates made
him smile.

'A dog barked at you?'

'It was a bloody big dog. Could've taken my hand off.'

'Yeah, that's tough. All I did was stumble on a dead body.'

That would make them all sit up and listen.

He stepped carefully over the leg and rang the doorbell. As he
waited, he rehearsed what he was going to say. It was going to
be tricky. He didn't know if the victim had lived at that address.
Perhaps he had been attacked on the street and staggered up the
path, seeking help, as he was dying. He might have been killed
elsewhere and dumped there, hidden from view. Whatever the
reason for his finishing up in that particular garden, it was going
to be a nasty shock for the householders. He waited with growing
unease, but no one answered the door. He looked around. Apart

from the leg lying across the path, there was nothing untoward about the garden. He rang the bell again. He heard it ringing inside the house. Still there was no answer.

Only a few minutes had passed since he had first tripped, but it felt as though he had been standing there for hours. People along the street might be wondering when their post was going to arrive. He would finish his round late. He looked around again. No one was going to answer the door. He couldn't wait there indefinitely. This was down to him. He had no choice but to make the call. Taking a deep breath he stepped back over the protruding leg as he dialled 999. It sounded funny to say he had found a body. He had to explain what he was doing there, in a stranger's front garden, and give his name and his own details. He had only just rung off when a patrol car drew up outside and a uniformed policeman jumped out and called his name. Denny's legs began to shake as he went down the path to talk to them.

34

INTENDING TO DRIVE TO work after the rush hour on Tuesday, Geraldine was gutted to be woken by a phone call just before eight in the morning. Still half asleep and cursing, she reached out to answer it. Recognising the number on the screen, she stretched, yawning, and propped herself up on one elbow.

'What is it?' she asked sleepily.

'You need to come in right now.'

There was no point in remonstrating. She wouldn't be able to get back to sleep now. All the same she protested feebly, on principle.

'The DCI wants you here right now.'

'Yes, so you said, but you haven't told me why.'

'Just get here without making a fuss, for Christ's sake, will you?'

'Why? What's happened?'

She knew the answer. The detective chief inspector must have found out that she and Max had gone to question a man known to be violent without logging their visit. Failure to follow protocol where the safety of officers was concerned was a serious infringement. She wouldn't have been summoned so peremptorily for any other reason, unless it was a second murder. But if that had happened, the sergeant would have told her.

'What is it? Tell me,' she demanded.

The sergeant on the line spoke gruffly. He said he had more calls to make, and rang off. Geraldine swore. However hard she tried, there was always something waiting to trip her up. This had been Max's error, but the buck stopped with her as the senior officer. Fully alert now, she dressed hurriedly, checked her equipment, and set off to the station. Irked that the duty sergeant had refused to pass on any details over the phone, she put her foot down and the car leapt forward. The summons had been urgent. She wracked

her brains to think of a witness who might have complained about
her, but she couldn't imagine what problem could be severe enough
to warrant her being called like that first thing in the morning. It
could only be the issue with Max.

The atmosphere at the station was tense. Everyone seemed aware
that something dreadful had occurred, although no one knew what
it was. A meeting had been convened for everyone working on the
murder case. Geraldine was puzzled. Clearly this wasn't about her
and Max after all. For once, Reg didn't keep them waiting long. A
faint murmur rippled through the assembled officers as he entered.
Ashen, he shuffled with stooped shoulders, seeming to have aged
overnight. Only a ferocious glare in his eyes when he turned to
face them gave any sign of vitality.

'This is hard,' he announced and paused.

No one challenged him. No one spoke.

Reg heaved an audible sigh, almost a groan. 'This is hard,' he
repeated.

He gazed around the room as though looking for help, seeming to
register the presence of his colleagues for the first time. Geraldine
wondered if he was going to announce that he was sick. With an
abrupt return to his customary brusqueness, he straightened his
shoulders. Speaking very quickly, he posted a photo on the screen.

'There's been another murder. This case concerns someone we
all know – all knew...'

Several of her colleagues blurted out an expletive of some sort.
Geraldine felt as though everyone was looking at her as the breath
caught in her throat and she felt a hot surge of blood to her face.
The room fell silent as they all gazed in horror at the screen. A
picture of Nick Williams stared down at them, his expression blank
as a passport photograph. Beside it another image was displayed
showing his face bloodless, with wildly staring eyes, his mouth
gaping blackly.

No one knew that Geraldine had dismissed Nick's desperate plea
for help. She might have been the only person in whom he had
confided, and she had dismissed his fears as nonsense. And now
he was dead.

Reg broke the stunned silence. 'As you can see, it was a vicious assault...' He paused and wiped his lips with the back of his hand. 'A vicious assault,' he repeated, looking around the room. His shoulders sagged again. 'He was attacked in the street outside his house. It looks like a random mugging that went wrong, but we have to keep an open mind. You know what to do,' he went on firmly. 'We're on this twenty-four seven. No one takes any leave, not a minute, until we've got the bastard who did this behind bars.'

'What about the Robinson case?' a female constable asked.

'This takes priority over everything else,' Reg snapped. 'Greg can wait. I don't want anyone being distracted from this, not by anything. Not till we've found out who did this. Let's focus on getting the ball rolling. We'll have no slackers on this one.'

The atmosphere was sombre. This had probably been a random attack, or it could have been personal. It was possible Nick had been violently murdered just because he was a cop. If that was true, they could all be at risk. But that was unlikely, and besides, they were already investigating a murder.

Geraldine took up the question about the Robinson case. 'I mean,' she faltered, realising everyone was looking at her in surprise, 'it's just that, well, we've already started...'

'If you don't feel comfortable working on this new case, you can opt to stay with the Robinson case,' Reg growled. 'I don't want anything half-hearted about this new investigation.'

'No, no, that's not what I meant,' Geraldine felt her face going red. 'I want to be part of it, of course I do. I just meant...'

She broke off in confusion.

'Right, let's get started,' Reg snapped.

For a moment no one responded. No one moved. Then everyone began talking at once. The room seemed full of officers rushing purposefully around. Checking the list, Geraldine saw she had been allocated the task of questioning Nick's wife. The widow had been informed, but no one had yet questioned her to establish whether she could tell them anything about the circumstances of her husband's death. Geraldine told Max to wait for her in the car. Then she turned and hurried after Reg. She caught up with him just as he reached the door to his office.

'Reg?'

He turned and raised his eyebrows in a weary expression of forced interest. 'What is it?'

'Can I speak to you about Nick?'

Without a word he opened his door and motioned to her to go in. He sat behind his desk and looked up at her, waiting. It was difficult to begin.

'It's about Nick...'

'Yes? What about him?'

Tentatively, Geraldine told him that Nick had been concerned that he was being followed shortly before he was murdered.

'Followed?' Reg repeated. 'As in someone was stalking him?' He sounded incredulous.

Geraldine nodded dumbly. Reg put his head in his hands for a second. She waited awkwardly, knowing this was too important to walk away from. At last he looked up.

'Listen, Geraldine, I know you're upset about what's happened. We're all upset.' He leaned forward as though to give his words emphasis. 'I worked with Nick for over ten years. He was a fine colleague. But it doesn't help to be hysterical. We need to be level-headed in our assessment of the situation, and work on facts alone. Speculation can lead us into all sorts of blind alleys.'

'Reg, I'm not being hysterical...'

'The fact is, when Nick was worried about anything, he spoke to me. As I said, we worked together for a long time. He used to tell me about his troubles. Can you give me one reason why he would have come to you with anything like this, and not breathed a word of it to me, or to his wife? No,' he shook his head, 'I'm afraid you've got hold of the wrong end of the stick. Misunderstood something he said, and made a drama out of it. You didn't know him for very long, but I...' He broke off with a sigh. 'He was a friend as well as a colleague. If he was worried about anything, he would have come to me, as I hope you would too, Geraldine. We're on the same team here, and we have to pull together, now more than ever. Come on,' he added, heaving himself to his feet. 'I'll come with you to see Eve.'

35

NICK WILLIAMS HAD LIVED in West Hampstead. The door was opened almost at once by a uniformed female constable.

'I'm just making her some tea, sir.'

'How is she?' Reg enquired in a subdued voice.

The constable shook her head. 'Not good, sir. This way.'

With a quick nod, he strode after her. Geraldine followed. A faint smell of mould hung in the air as they crossed the hall and entered the kitchen where a woman was sitting motionless on a stool. Her arms hung limply at her sides. She didn't look up when they walked in. Geraldine studied her furtively. With her head lowered, her fair hair fell forward hiding the top half of her face so that only the tip of a thin nose and a pointed chin were visible.

'Eve, you know what's happened?'

The thin woman nodded and her hair swung further forward.

'They told me about it,' she whispered. 'They were very kind.'

Looking around, Geraldine was surprised to see how untidy the kitchen was. It couldn't have degenerated into such a tip in the one day since Nick had been killed. The large kitchen could have been a nice room, but the sink was full of dirty dishes and the worktops were strewn with used saucepans, stained cups and foil takeaway containers. There was a stench of stale food. Geraldine couldn't help thinking about Nick's obsessively tidy desk at work, pens in a straight row, files neatly stacked, not a paper out of place. She wondered how he had coped with the chaos at home. Eve perched on a stool staring at the floor, seemingly oblivious to their presence as they sat down.

'Eve,' Geraldine said gently, 'we're going to find out what happened to Nick.'

The widow looked up on hearing her dead husband's name, but her expression was dull and she didn't seem to register that she was being addressed. Geraldine pressed on, determined to proceed as though this was a routine investigation and the deceased hadn't recently spent a night with her.

'Can you think of anyone who might have wanted to harm your husband?'

'No.'

'Was he worried about anything?'

'What do you mean, worried?'

'Did he say anything to you about being worried about anything, or anyone?'

The blonde woman frowned. 'Worried about what?'

Abandoning caution, Geraldine leaned forward and stared directly at Eve's face, half hidden behind a fair veil of hair.

'Did Nick say anything about being followed recently?'

'Followed?' Eve echoed.

Reg cut in officiously. 'We're just wondering if he might have been targeted by an ex-con with a grievance. We have to consider every possibility.'

He glowered at Geraldine, his heavy brows lowered. Ignoring his disapproving glare, Geraldine pressed on. Whatever the personal cost, she had to discover the truth. If she could do so without revealing that Nick had confided in her, so much the better. She wanted to avoid raising questions that could damage her reputation. She didn't want to risk appearing promiscuous as well as incompetent. She bitterly regretted having failed to insist Nick go to Reg with his suspicions.

Geraldine tried again. 'We knew Nick. He was our colleague...' her voice cracked. 'We all want to find out what happened to him, and see justice done. You can help us.'

Eve gave no sign that she had heard. Geraldine pressed on before Reg could cut in again.

'Did he seem uneasy about anything before he died? We wondered if someone was following him.'

Eve looked at Reg. 'Nick was careful. He would have told you if he was worried about anything. He was always careful.'

'Of course, we're just trying to find out what happened,' Reg interrupted forcefully.

Unable to prise any information out of the stunned widow, Reg asked her to contact them if she needed anything at all, and left.

'A constable will stay with you, and if you need anything you just ask, anything at all,' he added kindly.

Eve didn't even look up.

On the way back to the station, Reg reprimanded Geraldine for her crass questions.

'I would have expected better from someone of your rank.'

She was relieved to get back to her own office. Predictably, Max agreed with Reg when Geraldine gave him a sanitised version of the interview.

'She was in shock, poor woman. We all are. We can only hope she'll get over it in time,' he added pompously.

'They were estranged,' Geraldine reminded him.

Max grunted.

'He told me so himself.'

Geraldine didn't add that Nick had told her a lot more than that.

'Well?' Max asked. 'What did you make of her?'

Geraldine shrugged. Other than wondering what Nick had seen in the little blonde woman in her dirty house, she was preoccupied with what Nick had told her about being followed. She wished he had reported his suspicions to Reg, rather than confiding in her, or that she had taken him seriously. If she had acted on his fears, he might still be alive. But she couldn't bring herself to tell anyone what had happened between her and Nick. She suspected Reg would refuse to believe her. Whatever his reaction, confessing now could only damage her reputation. Worse, she would lose Sam's trust. And it wouldn't help Nick.

36

THE WHEELS HAD BEEN set in motion on Nick's investigation, with teams of officers drafted in to question the dead officer's neighbours and friends, even his colleagues. Yet more constables were checking criminals who had recently been released from prison, looking into any who might have held a grudge against the dead detective. Geraldine wondered whether they ought to be questioning husbands and partners of women Nick had seduced but she hesitated to make the suggestion to the detective chief inspector. He had already lambasted her for interfering with the investigation he was heading. He clearly didn't want to hear about Nick's infidelities.

With nothing more she could do to support the investigation into Nick's murder, she resolved to stay out of trouble and turn her attention back to Dave Robinson. Checking the most recent statements, she came across an odd report. His widow had come to the police station claiming that one of her sons was missing. Her statement hadn't been taken seriously, partly because she had been drunk at the time. Geraldine went to question the constable who had spoken to Caroline. She found DC Timothy Clark at his desk. A snub-nosed young man, he looked about sixteen.

'Oh that,' he replied airily to her question. 'No, that's all sorted.'

'What do you mean by all sorted?'

'The boy's not missing at all. The woman's just nuts. Crazed with grief and all that.'

'All what? How do you know he's not missing? Has she reported he's back home?'

'Not to us, but she'd already called the school to tell them he was at home, too upset to go to school after what happened to his dad, so the boy's not been kidnapped, even if he is at home with a crazy mother.'

'Why did she report him missing then? Has anyone seen him?'

Timothy shrugged. 'How am I supposed to know what's going on in her head? She's crazy, I told you. Maybe she's feeling guilty because the boy's fallen apart over losing his dad, and she hasn't. But I can follow it up.'

Geraldine agreed that would be a good idea, although she wasn't satisfied. What Timothy was telling her sounded strange, but she held back from openly challenging him for being so laid back about Caroline's report. She had been criticised in the past for being unwilling to delegate. Reg had already accused her of being interfering. She didn't want to be dogged by a reputation for being controlling. Without telling anyone, she decided to go and speak to Caroline again. If it turned out that Timothy had been correct in his conclusions, all well and good. No one need know she had been checking up on him. At the same time, she couldn't ignore her unease. Timothy was a constable, young and inexperienced. It would be a dereliction of her duty to refuse to follow her instincts out of a misplaced concern for her own reputation.

Caroline looked dreadful. There were grey bags under her eyes, and a lifelessness about her smacked of depression. She clearly hadn't been sleeping, which was understandable, and looked as though she hadn't washed for days, which was probably true. She started back when she saw Geraldine, and motioned to her to go inside the house.

'Quick, quick,' she muttered, 'before anyone sees you.'

That suited Geraldine, although it was odd that Caroline wanted to usher her inside so promptly, and she wondered why Caroline seemed so anxious that no one saw her. Before Geraldine could mention the purpose of her visit, Caroline turned to her in frantic desperation.

'Have you got any news?'

'News?'

'Yes.' Caroline's eyes met Geraldine's for a brief moment before sliding away. 'Have you found out who killed Dave?'

'You came to the station yesterday to report one of your sons

149

missing. You said he'd been kidnapped. Is that correct?'

Caroline gave an impatient shake of her head. 'No, no. That was all a mistake. I was just in a right old state.'

Her laughter sounded so fake, Geraldine was convinced she was lying.

'You reported he'd been kidnapped by someone called Brian.'

'Yes, that's what I thought, but I was wrong, see? Ed came home. He's back here now. He's not missing at all.' She gave another nervous laugh.

Geraldine didn't tell Caroline she had looked into her school records and traced someone called Brian who had been in her class at school.

'What made you think Brian took your son? Has he been in contact with you?'

Caroline hesitated. 'Yes, I mean no, I mean I'd seen him recently, bumped into him in the park. Then he met Ed and – brought him home. I got in a panic when Ed didn't come straight home, that's all. I thought he wasn't coming back. You don't know what it's like, without Dave here. But it's got nothing to do with the twins. They're fine. They're both fine.'

'I just want to understand what's going on, Caroline. Why would you think Brian had kidnapped your son?'

'I told you, he met Ed and he – took him out for tea, and then he brought him home. Why does that matter? I miss Dave.'

Caroline was clearly making up her story as she went along, but Geraldine was no closer to understanding why she would falsely accuse someone of abducting her son. She supposed Caroline was just falling apart after losing her husband, but the story of the kidnap didn't sound right. If anything, Geraldine felt even more confused than she had done when speaking to Timothy.

For all her desperation, Caroline clammed up when Geraldine attempted to quiz her more about the alleged kidnap. Unless she was prepared to talk, there was nothing much Geraldine could do. She couldn't pursue a report of a kidnap when the person who had made the claim had retracted it. All the same, she had a feeling Caroline was hiding something. Other than suspecting it must be connected to Dave's murder, Geraldine had no idea what it was, and she had no evidence that Caroline knew more about the murder than she was willing to say.

She gave it one last go. 'Unless you tell me what this is all about, I can't help you.'

Caroline raised stricken eyes, but shook her head. 'I don't know,' she wailed. 'There's nothing more to say.'

'So you're telling me both your sons are at home now?'

'Yes, that's exactly what I'm saying. Now for God's sake, find out who killed my husband.'

There was a desperation in her demand that was more complicated than grief. Caroline was frightened.

37

BRIAN WAS SO UPSET by the whole episode, he could barely stand up. Afraid he might collapse, he sat in his front room, physically shaking with shock. A police constable had been to his house asking questions. If the boy had been there, the whole carefully constructed plot Brian had set in motion would have unravelled in front of his eyes. It had turned out to be a stroke of luck, the boy disappearing like that before the police came calling.

His thoughts darted around wildly. Obviously Caroline had betrayed him. The constable had given some flimsy pretext for calling, pretending he was carrying out a house to house enquiry about the missing boy. He didn't fool Brian. He knew they suspected him of hiding the boy. They must be watching him. If they found Ed before he did, Brian might never see him again. The thought brought tears of anger to his eyes. Clearly it was risky for the boy to carry on staying in his house. When Brian found Ed, they would have to move away. The police might be back at any time. It was a pity, because they were comfortable together in the house, where Ed even had a room all to himself. He liked that. It was a shame they couldn't carry on living there.

It was Caroline's fault the police had called. He should have known she would be trouble. Women always were. Brian felt a brief flicker of pity for the woman who hadn't seen her son for three days, but Caroline had another son. Brian had no one else. It wouldn't be fair for Caroline to keep two boys for herself, when Brian didn't even have one. In any case, she had forfeited her claim to the boy. She had failed to do what was necessary to earn him back. It had been left for Brian to finish the job himself. He had been happy to do that because it meant he could keep Ed for himself. So it had all turned out well in the end. He just had to wait for Ed to come home. If he didn't, Brian knew where to find him. Next time, he wouldn't let him go.

Caroline was playing a dangerous game. It was because of her that Ed had run off by himself. He might be facing all sorts of hazards out on the streets alone. He was only a child. Caroline was crazy to let that happen. And Brian's wife had accused *him* of being mentally disturbed. Caroline was the one who should be locked up, not Brian. He was the victim. Him and that poor boy who was all on his own. When Brian found him, he would never let him out of his sight again.

He nearly didn't answer the door when the bell rang that evening. He was afraid it was the police returning. Worse, it might be doctors come to take him away again. Last time that happened, his wife had driven him to the hospital herself. Like a fool, he had gone with her in the car. In all fairness, he hadn't really understood what was happening. By the time he realised where he was, he had been too confused to protest. He still hadn't forgiven his wife for standing by and watching while a softly spoken stranger had stuck a bloody great needle in his arm and explained calmly that he wouldn't be going home for a while. He had no idea how long he had been sectioned in the hospital but gradually his thoughts had begun making sense, without the white hot anger that had sparked his incarceration. They called it treatment. Whatever else happened, he was never going back into a ward for mentally disturbed patients. He would rather die than return to that grey half-life. It had all been his wife's fault. The bitch had deserved everything that had happened to her.

The doorbell rang again. Peering out from the side of the curtains in the living room, he couldn't see anyone standing on the doorstep. Whoever it was, they were hiding. It must be the police, come back to lock him up. His legs felt wobbly but he forced himself to clamber upstairs. By standing on a chair by his bedroom window, he was able to look down onto the front step. Cautiously he leaned forward, holding on to the window sill. Craning his neck he saw the top of the boy's head. He leaped from the chair, knocking it over with a clatter. Leaving the chair, he raced downstairs, thrilled that the boy had come back to him, terrified he might reach the front door too late. If he let him disappear again, he would never forgive himself.

He flung the door open, panting. The boy looked up at him with an anxious smile. His eyes were bloodshot and puffy, his cheeks flushed. He was soaking wet and had been crying. His lips quivered. Brian reached out and seized his arm, pulling him inside the house. Quickly he glanced over the boy's shoulder, scanning the street outside. There was no one in sight, only empty cars. He closed the door and turned to the boy. First things first, he had to make sure the boy didn't fall ill. It would be difficult explaining what he was doing there if he had to see a doctor.

'You're sopping wet. Go upstairs right now and have a hot shower. You can come down for supper in your new pyjamas. Bring your wet things down with you, and I'll put them in the dryer.'

The boy smiled anxiously. 'I thought you weren't here. You took ages to open the door.'

Brian returned his smile. 'Hurry up and get changed, I've got a lot of sausages waiting to be eaten.'

Thank goodness he'd had the foresight to buy more than one packet.

'Sausages?'

'Yes, and waffles.'

'I'm starving. But aren't you going to have a go at me, ask where I've been and all that?'

Brian considered. 'You'll tell me where you've been if you want to.'

'My mum would never let me get away with it.'

'I'm not your mother.'

'No.' He gazed at Brian with his swollen eyes. 'You're nice.'

For a moment Brian was too happy to speak. Before long he was watching Ed tucking into a plate piled high with sausages and chips.

'You *are* hungry,' he said.

Brian guessed he hadn't eaten for the two days he had been missing, but he had undertaken not to quiz him about where he had been and he kept his word. It didn't take long for Ed to open up.

'I wanted to go home,' he explained as he gobbled his dinner.

'When I came downstairs and you weren't here, I tried to find my own way back home but I couldn't, and then I got lost and couldn't find my way back here so I just walked around. I didn't know what to do. I thought I was going to starve to death. And then I saw your house and so I'm here again.'

Brian hesitated, but he had to know. 'Do you still want to go back to your mother?'

Ed looked surprised. 'Well, yes, of course I do. As soon as you can take me there,' he added politely. 'I don't want to be any trouble.'

Brian chose his words carefully. 'You'd have to go back to school, and you'd be sharing your mother with your brother. He's with her now. She wanted to keep him, when she asked me to bring you home with me.'

'You said Matt was staying with another friend of hers.'

'I didn't want to upset you,' Brian answered quickly. 'You can stay here a little longer if you like. That way you won't have to go back to school straight away.'

Ed nodded uncertainly. Brian turned away to hide his triumph. He was going to stay after all. This time he would never leave. They would go to another town, start again with new names. It was no more than Brian deserved. He had given Caroline every chance to carry out her part of their bargain. After everything Brian had done for her, giving her freedom from a life of misery, she had been too weak and selfish to do the same for him. Brian had been forced to step in. Not that he had minded. It would have been less risky for Caroline, but Brian had been clever enough to do the job himself without being caught. He hadn't needed her help after all. Only now he had Ed, he had no intention of giving him up. Why should he, when he had earned the right to keep the boy? It was only fair.

'Everything's going to be OK,' he promised Ed softly. 'Don't worry. I'll take care of you from now on. You don't need to worry about a thing.'

The child nodded, yawning. He was exhausted. 'Thank you,' he said politely.

38

JANICE LOOKED AROUND THE class. For once they were all quiet, reading or looking at their books with glazed eyes. Her gaze lingered on a sandy-haired boy staring miserably out of the window. If any other child had been so blatantly inattentive, she would have snapped at him to focus. The teachers had been warned to keep an eye on Matthew. They had discussed whether it had been wise to keep him and his brother at home for a week after their father was murdered. Janice had thought it sensible. But they had all agreed something wasn't quite right when the mother sent only one of the twins back to school. Almost all of Janice's colleagues held strong views on that point, making for lively discussion in the staff room. Finally the head teacher had put an end to the discussion.'Matthew's ready to come back to school, and Edward isn't. The boys must be treated as individuals. We can't insist Ed returns to us before he's ready. But by the same token, his mother can't keep Matthew at home if it's better for him to be here and distracted.'

Sitting in the staff room at break time, Janice had been convinced the head was right. Now, watching Matthew slumped over a table, she wasn't so sure. It must be difficult enough for him, losing his father suddenly like that. It could only make him feel worse knowing that his twin brother was at home with his mother while he was packed off to school by himself. He was bound to feel excluded, as well as bereaved. She called his name three times before he heard her. At last he raised his head and looked at her with lacklustre eyes.

'Come here, Matthew.'

He was normally such a live wire it was heartbreaking to see him looking so downcast. His arms hung limply at his sides as he shuffled obediently over to her desk.

'Matthew, I know this must be very tough for you. If you want to talk about anything, you know you can talk to me, or there are other people who can help you.'

He looked up eagerly. 'Will they make Ed come back?'

'Ed just needs a bit more time at home. People cope in different ways…'

The boy shook his head vigorously. 'Ed's not at home. He's gone to stay with my mum's friend. She keeps saying he's coming home, but he never does. It's not fair. How come he gets out of school and I don't?'

Worried, Janice mentioned Matthew's complaint to the head teacher at lunch.

'Do you think we should tell Matthew's mother how upset he is? I don't think he's eating.'

The head thought it was probably better for Matthew that his brother had gone away, rather than staying at home with their mother. At least Matthew couldn't feel his mother was choosing his twin over him. All the same, she shared Janice's concern. Matthew was clearly missing his brother. It must be even worse for Ed who had been packed off with a stranger, leaving his brother at home with their grieving mother. It wasn't healthy for a ten-year-old boy. The boys should be together at such a difficult time in their lives. The fact that they were twins made it even worse to separate them. To leave just one of them at home with their mother was wrong.

'But whatever we think about it, perhaps it's best if we leave them to sort themselves out,' the head said firmly. 'It's bound to take time.'

'Shall I phone the mother?' Janice asked. 'Let her know Matthew's missing his brother? I'll be careful,' she added, aware that the person Matthew really missed was his father.

'If you want to.'

Janice wished the head had given a clear indication as to whether she thought it was a good idea to contact Matthew's mother. After lunch, she popped along to the school office to use the phone. There was no answer. Thoughtfully, she replaced the receiver. By the time she left work, the children had all dispersed.

Sometimes their parents hung around chatting, but it was raining and they had all gone. There was no sign of Matthew or his mother. It was only a short detour to drive past their house on her way home. Without giving it much thought, she turned into their road and drew up outside the house. She wasn't sure she was doing the right thing. The head had advised leaving them to sort themselves out. It was no doubt sound advice. But Janice was worried about Matthew. It wasn't just that he looked pale and depressed. She had worked with children for long enough to know when a boy was frightened.

Mrs Robinson opened the door. Given her present circumstances, it was hardly surprising she looked terrible. Even so, Janice was shocked at the change in her. At their previous encounters, Mrs Robinson had struck her as didactic. She must have needed to be bossy, raising twin boys. Now she stood in the doorway looking cowed and pale. She didn't seem to recognise Janice.

'Mrs Robinson, I'm Janice Threadgold, Matthew and Edward's teacher.'

'Oh yes,' the other woman responded dully.

'I've come to ask when Ed's coming back to school.'

Mrs Robinson started as though she had been slapped. 'Ed?' she repeated.

Janice hesitated to invite herself in. There was a sharp wind, and the rain wasn't letting up. She shivered.

'Can we discuss this indoors?' The other woman didn't respond. Janice forced a smile. 'No problem. We can talk here.'

'What do you want to talk about?'

'Mrs Robinson, we are wondering when Ed might be coming back to school?'

It was a question, but the other woman didn't respond. She wasn't making it easy for Janice.

Janice tried again. 'Where is Ed?'

'Gone to a friend.' Mrs Robinson sounded defensive. 'He's fine. It's just that – he's with my friend.'

'Where is he?'

The other woman grew unexpectedly sharp. 'I don't see that's any of your business.'

Janice gave up. 'We were just concerned about Matthew...' she muttered as the door closed.

The head teacher was right. The family would have to come to terms with their terrible loss in their own way. With a sigh, she turned away and walked briskly back to the road, wrapping her arms around her chest in an effort to conserve her body heat. There was nothing she could do to help.

39

'POOR COW,' REG MUTTERED as they picked up their protective clothing at the mortuary. 'That's Eve I'm talking about, his widow. I know we'll do everything we can to support her, but it's not the same, is it? I mean, it can't be, can it?'

Geraldine nodded without answering. She understood he was talking inconsequentially to distract himself from what they were about to witness. His mask dangled from one hand. She watched it swing gently as he continued.

'I mean, she didn't strike me as the sort of woman to cope on her own. She didn't seem to know what was going on. What did you make of her?'

The intensity of his gaze made it impossible for her to ignore the question.

'It's difficult to say, really. It's not like we saw her under normal circumstances.'

Reg nodded. 'I've met her a couple of times. She always struck me as lacking in confidence. A mousy little thing, wouldn't you say?'

His words sounded calm enough, but she could hear the tension in his voice and observed it in his set features. Reluctantly they finished fiddling around covering themselves. It was time to go in. Geraldine took a deep breath. Above his mask, Reg's anxious eyes stared straight ahead as he stepped forward to open the door. He hesitated with his hand outstretched, then shoved the door quickly and strode in. Geraldine followed.

Miles Fellowes looked up at them solemnly. Usually cheery and ready to crack jokes, he stared glumly across the body at Reg. 'One of yours, wasn't he?'

Reg responded so promptly, it sounded as though he had been

rehearsing his reply. 'Nick Williams was a fine officer and a remarkable detective.' Preparing to deliver a eulogy could well have been in his mind, as he went on to enquire when the body might be released for burial.

Miles gave a miserable grimace and turned away with a shrug. 'That rather depends on how you get on with your investigation, doesn't it?'

With a conscious effort, Geraldine turned to observe the body. Disturbingly, Nick's eyes were open. Gazing upwards, he seemed to be looking straight at her. Shocked, she saw that one of his eyes was slightly closed. Even in death he appeared to be winking at her, in a macabre parody of their brief physical intimacy. Below his staring eyes his flesh had been sliced through several times, his cheeks mere strips of white flesh slashed by dark streaks. Never normally fazed by cadavers, she was afraid she was going to pass out, yet she couldn't take her eyes off him. The lump of flesh, hacked about on the table in front of her, was almost unrecognisable as the man she had known. Almost, but not quite.

Dazed, she listened to Miles' account. She was barely able to control her trembling. Her conscious mind knew this was happening, but inside her head she was paralysed in a nightmare. Once before she had been to view the post mortem of a man she had interviewed only days before as a witness. It had been a shock seeing him on the slab, all the mannerisms and quirks that had made him an individual wiped out with one blow. But nothing could have prepared her for the sight of her lover, lying dead just inches away from her, his chest sliced open.

She struggled to follow what was going on. 'Obviously he was taken by surprise,' Reg was saying. 'There's no question about that. All my officers are trained in self-defence. Highly trained.'

'Yes,' Miles agreed. 'He could well have been caught off guard, because he was hit from behind.'

He nodded to his colleagues who turned the body over. When it was settled on its front, face down, he indicated a deep gash across the back of Nick's head, just at the nape of his neck.

'This was the first blow, and it knocked him clean off his feet, fatally damaging his spinal cord. He must have been stunned but he wasn't knocked out cold because he tried to fight back after he was on the ground. He was still moving around for a short time at any rate…'

'You mean…' Reg interrupted, excited. He broke off, staring eagerly at Miles.

Over the inert corpse, the pathologist looked miserably from Reg to Geraldine and back again. He shook his head.

'I know what you're both thinking,' he said, 'but I'm afraid it's unlikely we'll get anything from his defence wounds other than traces of mud and maybe a few bits of grit. We've sent off whatever we could scrape out from under his nails for analysis, of course, but I don't hold out much hope.'

Nick's body had been lying beside his front doorstep overnight.

'His wife never reported him missing,' Reg said.

'Perhaps she was used to him sometimes working nights,' Geraldine suggested, her voice curiously hollow.

Miles estimated the time of death to be between eight and nine o'clock on Monday evening. When he had been discovered on Tuesday morning he had been dead for nearly twelve hours, lying outdoors, abandoned to the wind and rain. The thought made Geraldine want to cry.

Miles turned back to the body, which was still lying on its front. Geraldine was fleetingly relieved at no longer having to see Nick's face, until she remembered running her fingers through his hair. Now caked with dried blood where his head hadn't been shaved, it was almost unrecognisable.

Miles turned to her. 'Did you want to ask me anything while you're here?'

He was probably thinking that it wasn't like her to be so quiet. She shook her head, too choked to speak.

'Are you all right?' He looked at her more closely. 'You look awfully pale.'

She mumbled something vague, determined her voice wouldn't tremble in front of Reg. Miles raised his eyebrows almost imperceptibly. Meanwhile Reg continued staring at the body.

'He was a valuable addition to our team,' he announced, 'and a good friend. A fine man. We will all miss him.' He was back to rehearsing his funeral eulogy.

Geraldine couldn't trust herself to speak.

40

GERALDINE DROVE CAUTIOUSLY ALONG Upper Street, her wipers making a faint scratching noise as they swept across the windscreen like a slow pendulum. She wished it would either stop drizzling or else rain properly. As it was, the wipers were smearing water across her field of vision. Passing people hurrying to the station beneath their umbrellas, their collars up against the wind, she turned off into her own street, and was soon driving through the gated entrance to the small car park at the back of her block. She had never been more pleased to arrive home. Throwing off her coat and shoes, she went in the kitchen to fix herself something for supper. For the first time in her life, viewing a dead body had made her feel faint. Now she was home, she was ravenous. It seemed somehow disrespectful, but she had hardly eaten anything all day. Nothing would be gained if she fell ill. She had to stay on top of her game and make sure she tracked down whoever had killed Nick.

Invariably, her sister contrived to pick the worst time to call, as though she had a sixth sense about what was happening in Geraldine's life. Cursing herself for answering, Geraldine muttered that she was about to make herself supper.

'Oh, well, if you haven't started on it yet, it can wait a few more minutes,' Celia said promptly, 'unless you've got someone coming round,' she added archly.

Geraldine sighed. Celia's calls were never over in a few minutes.

'How's it all going?' her sister asked finally, after talking about herself for nearly ten minutes. 'What happened with that guy you were being so secretive about?'

Celia had called one evening just after Geraldine had been out for a drink with Nick. Excited by his attention, she had vaguely mentioned him to her sister, saying only that she might be seeing someone. That had been enough. Celia had latched onto the throwaway comment and had been curious about him ever since.

'I've already told you, there's no secret,' Geraldine insisted wearily. 'Nothing happened between us, and nothing's going to happen.'

'Don't say that. You never know what's round the corner. He might phone tonight. You never know.'

'I do know, and he won't phone.'

'There's no need to be so hostile. And anyway you can't be sure. He might be thinking about you right now, plucking up the courage to call you.'

'Yes, I can be sure, and no, he's not.'

'You never know...'

'Celia, drop it, will you? I know he's not going to call me.' Geraldine held back from telling Celia that Nick was dead. She couldn't cope with sympathy. 'Look, Celia, I don't want to talk about it any more.'

'But...'

'I said I don't want to talk about it, so if you keep on about it, I'm going to hang up.'

Celia gave up, and the conversation moved on. At last Geraldine rang off and went in the kitchen. As she prepared her supper she could hear the phone ringing. She tried to ignore the shrill summons, just as she tried to ignore the tears that were streaming from her eyes. It took her a few minutes to recover her composure. The caller left a message. It wasn't Celia. She recognised the voice of her sergeant, Sam Haley, who was off work recuperating from an injury sustained during the course of an investigation.

With a pang, Geraldine remembered how Nick had saved her life, and Sam's too. Much to Sam's chagrin, Nick had come to their rescue like a knight in shining armour. What made it worse was that the situation had been entirely Geraldine's fault. Unwittingly, she had sent Sam to the house of a killer on her own. By the time Geraldine had realised her mistake, Sam had already arrived and was questioning a demented psychopath. Geraldine had raced after her sergeant too late to prevent them both being attacked. Only Nick's quick thinking had saved their lives. Geraldine had escaped relatively unscathed, but Sam was still recovering from her injuries. They were both lucky to have survived the encounter. To his credit, Nick had never mentioned it afterwards, but Sam was still smarting from the debt she owed him. She had never liked Nick, her dislike exacerbated by his friendship with Geraldine.

By the time Geraldine heated up something to eat she had lost her appetite so instead of opening a bottle of wine she made herself a cup of tea. She sat down in front of the television, trying to take her mind off Nick, but she couldn't stop thinking about him, wondering if he might still be alive if she had taken his concerns seriously. The thought made her cry again. Weak and lightheaded, she forced herself to eat something, still sobbing as she ate. She had never felt so alone, not even when she had first moved to the capital.

She wondered whether she ought to talk to a counsellor about what had happened. If she still felt upset in the morning, that might be sensible. Emotional distress could affect an officer's judgement, and in her job errors of judgement could cost lives. As she had just demonstrated. On the other hand, the only other person who had known about her secret was dead. She didn't have to confess her ineptitude to anyone else. What she did have to do was work out a way to deal with her secret. Finding Nick's killer would help alleviate her guilt. She would start with that.

After clearing away her supper things she called Sam back.

'I heard,' were the first words Sam said. 'How terrible. Are you all right? What happened? Or would you rather not talk about it?'

'No, that's OK. I mean, I'm OK talking about it. But there's nothing much to say except that we're on it, but we haven't got anywhere yet.'

'It's early days.'

'I know.'

'If there's anything I can do...'

'You can get better and come back to work!'

Sam gave an appreciative grunt before asking, 'Who's working the case with you?'

'You won't know him. He's called Max Grey. He's been brought over from West London. Thinks he knows it all. You know the type. Arrogant youngster, barely out of college...'

'Hey!'

Sam wasn't much older than Max.

'He's a graduate on the fast track to promotion, thinks he's going to be Commissioner by Christmas. And of course Reg falls for it. He thinks Max is a bright young lad. Well, he's clever all right, but as for being a good officer, you're worth ten of him. He's been decent enough so far, but he's ambitious as hell and I daresay he'll turn out to be a bit of a shit.'

'So you like him, then?'

Geraldine laughed for the first time since she had heard about Nick's death. They chatted for a while, avoiding talking about their dead colleague.

After Sam rang off, Geraldine remained sitting on her sofa, dozing fitfully. Finally she dragged herself off to bed. Nick flitted in and out of her dreams, sometimes alive and flirting, at other times a grinning death's head, drenched in blood. Once she woke from a dream in which her own hands were dripping with blood. In the dream she knew it was Nick's blood, but she didn't know why it was on her hands. She woke, trembling with terror and confusion, glad when morning came.

Before climbing out of bed, she leaned over to slide open her bedside drawer. Taking out an envelope, she pulled out an old photograph, the only souvenir she had of the mother she had never known. Having given her up for adoption at birth, her mother had refused to have any contact with her. Geraldine had spent some time searching for her mother. When she had finally traced her address she had summoned all her courage and gone to meet her, only to discover that the records were out of date and her mother had moved away. After a period of nearly unbearable expectation and apprehension, the disappointment had been acute. Fear of yet more disappointment had put her off making another attempt.

Nick's death had reminded her that life was short. If she had agreed to go out with him when he had first asked her, they might have had more time together. It was a mistake to hold back. Under her breath, she made a promise to the sad-faced woman in the photograph who stared back at her with her own eyes. Once Nick's killer was safely behind bars, Geraldine would look for her mother again. This time she would find her.

41

THE FOLLOWING MORNING, ED wanted to go in the garden to play football. Taking him out of the house was risky. Someone might spot them. Not only that, Ed might see his own face in a newspaper, or on a television news channel. Since the police had been round, snooping, he must have been reported missing. It had always only been a matter of time. He hadn't watched the news but the story of Ed's abduction must have hit the headlines by now. All the same, Brian realised he would struggle to keep the boy cooped up in the house forever. Although he had kept him occupied tolerably well so far, watching cartoons and playing games on the computer, he was becoming twitchy, asking to go to the park to play football, nagging to go home.

It was only four days since Ed had moved in with him, and Brian was already running out of ways to entertain him. They would have to move away soon, leave London altogether. If he could think of a way to get him out of the country, he would take him to France, or America. He would have to figure out how to get hold of a false passport for him if they were to go abroad. It was possible. People did it all the time, only Brian didn't know how. Wherever they went, it would be best to act quickly, but first he had to gain the boy's trust. Without that, the plan would come to nothing. Keeping him well fed was part of Brian's campaign to win his affection. He had given him sausages and waffles for supper. He served the same for breakfast.

Luckily the wet weather had offered an excuse to stay indoors for a couple of days. That wouldn't last. When the sun came out he would have to find another reason for him to stay inside. He couldn't keep that up forever. It might be as well to meet the problem head on and take him out, drive away from London to some remote destination where he could run around and let off steam.

'I thought we might go to the seaside. You'd like that, wouldn't you?'

Ed's eyes lit up. He bounced on his chair with excitement.

'When can we go? Can we go today? Can we take a football?'

Brian was gratified by his enthusiasm. 'Yes. We'll get a football, if that's what you want. We'll take a picnic and eat it on the beach.'

'And paddle in the sea!'

'And run on the sand.'

Their eyes met in mutual understanding, and Brian felt a rush of joy at this unexpected connection with his new friend. As he cleared away the breakfast plates, he considered the options. He could suggest they go out in disguise, but that might alert the boy to the need for secrecy. He didn't want him to start asking awkward questions. They couldn't travel by train for fear of being recognised. If they got in the car quickly, right outside the house, the chances of anyone seeing them were negligible. It had to be worth that slight risk. A deserted beach would be an ideal place to take him. It was impossible to be absolutely certain they wouldn't be caught on CCTV but that was unlikely. They were going to have a glorious day out, one they would both remember for the rest of their lives. What was more important was that the outing would cement their relationship. They would settle down together, and Ed would stop harping on about his mother and his brother.

'We're going to the seaside. And we can have lots more fun outings together after that. You like it here, don't you? If there's anything you want, you only have to say.'

'I want my mum.'

'But if you go home, you'll have to go straight back to school, and we want to have some fun first, don't we?' he insisted. 'You like it here, don't you?'

'I don't like it here. It's boring. And I haven't got a toothbrush.'

'You're bored because we've been stuck indoors for so long. But look, it's a lovely sunny day out there, perfect for going to the seaside. Let's go today! And on the way we can stop off and get you a new toothbrush and some new clothes if you like. Anything you want.'

Ed screwed up his eyes and squinted up at Brian. 'Why are you being so nice to me?'

'I promised your mother I'd take good care of you, and that's what I'm going to do. And besides that, I like you. You're a very special boy. You know that, don't you?'

'What do you mean?' He was still wary, but he was curious now as well. 'What's so special about me?'

Brian hesitated, wondering how much praise he could dish out without making Ed even more suspicious of him. With a flash of inspiration, he remembered that Ed was a twin. He was probably fed up of being lumped together with his brother all the time.

'You have an independent spirit,' he hazarded, taking care not to mention Matthew. 'You're an individual.' From the way Ed's shoulders relaxed, it was clear he liked that idea. 'And you're clever and funny. I don't have much time for most people I meet, but I like you. I thought we were friends. Of course, we don't have to go to the seaside today, if you'd rather go back to school.'

Ed shook his head, mumbling that he wanted to go to the seaside.

'Good. Let's get ready then. I've got some old shorts you can wear on the beach.'

'I can't wear your old shorts!'

Brian laughed at his outrage. 'Then we'll stop off and get you some new ones on the way. And you can help me choose the picnic.'

'We need a football.'

'Yes, we'll get one on the way.'

Beach ball, football, Brian didn't care. They were going to have a fantastic time at the seaside, just the two of them. They didn't need anyone else. It was frustrating that Ed was taking so long to grasp that. They couldn't afford to wait much longer. Soon they would need to start making plans to leave England for good.

42

Seconds after Brian slammed the front door they were inside the car and accelerating away from the house. He glanced at Ed, sitting beside him on the front passenger seat. His face partly concealed behind the sunglasses Brian had given him, he was grinning and chattering excitedly about what he wanted to buy for their trip. No one who saw him would recognise him behind the large lenses, and no one could possibly suspect he wasn't with his father. They drove out of London, finally stopping at a massive out-of-town shopping centre on the way to the coast. Stepping out of the lift, Brian noticed there weren't many children around. They would all be at school. Nervously, he took Ed's hand.

'You don't want to get lost here.'

'I won't get lost,' he answered with the cheerful optimism of childhood.

He was excited about their adventure, but Brian had grown fearful in case they were recognised. Having just gained Ed's trust, he wasn't prepared to give him up now.

'Come on, we can get everything we need in one department store.'

Ed agreed they didn't want to waste time shopping when they could be outside playing on a beach. They started off buying him some summer clothes and sandals for the beach. In the food hall, no one challenged them as Brian pushed a trolley round the aisles while Ed filled it with whatever he fancied: biscuits, chocolate bars, fizzy drinks, crisps and cakes. There was nothing healthy in his selection. Brian would have to educate him in how to eat properly. For now, all he wanted to do was finish the shopping and get out of there.

'Not at school today?' the cashier asked Ed as she rang up the items.

'He's got the day off,' Brian answered quickly. 'He's recovering from a virus.'

'He looks well enough to me,' the woman replied, smiling at him while speaking to Brian. 'You're obviously taking good care of him.'

'What's a virus?' Ed asked as they drove out of the car park. 'You said I had a virus. What's a virus?'

Brian smiled. 'It's nothing.'

'But you said I had a virus. I heard you. What's a virus?'

'It's a little illness, like a cold.'

'I'm not ill!'

'No, I know you're not.'

'Why did you say I was then? You lied.'

'Just a little.'

'Why did you lie?'

'You don't want to go back to school yet, do you?'

Ed shook his head vigorously.

'So when she asked why you weren't at school, I had to say something.'

'Why didn't you tell her the truth that we're going to the seaside?'

'Yes, I could have said that, but some people might not think that's a very good reason for staying away from school.'

'But you lied.'

Brian sighed. This was becoming irritating.

'You shouldn't ever lie,' Ed said solemnly.

'I won't lie again, all right?'

His companion shrugged and they drove in silence. After a while Ed began to grow impatient.

'When will we be there?'

'Soon.'

'How soon?'

'Not long now.'

'I need to pee.'

'Can't you wait a bit longer?'

'No. I need to go now.'

They pulled off the main road and drew up in a quiet country lane. No one would see him urinating there. Once out of the car, he changed his mind. The stop gave Brian an opportunity to fetch some snacks from the boot before they drove off. For the rest of the journey Ed crunched his way happily through two packets of crisps and a sticky bar of chocolate. Brian hoped he wouldn't be sick. Ed told him he had eaten far more than that before on car journeys.

'I once ate a whole bagful of sweets, I mean a really big bag, bigger than a carrier bag, full of sweets, all by myself, and I didn't feel the littlest bit sick,' he assured him earnestly.

At last they drove over the crest of a hill and saw the grey-blue vastness of the ocean stretched out beneath them. Ed cried out with excitement as they descended a long incline that led them straight down to the sea. Leaving the main road they followed a winding lane to a deserted stretch of coast. It wasn't exactly a beautiful smooth sandy beach, but Ed was happy clambering around rock pools, poking them with a stick. Every time he found a tiny creature in the water, or prised a crustacean from a rock, he shrieked with joy. He brandished his discoveries on the end of the stick while Brian made suitably admiring noises. After eating a whole tub of ice cream, he washed out the empty container with sea water so he could use it to store his treasures: a tiny crab, a spiral shell, together with an assortment of bits of stick and gritty pebbles.

Neither of them wanted to leave, but at last it grew dark. It was difficult to find their way among the rock pools without tripping over as they made their way back to the car.

'I don't want to go,' Ed whined.

Brian didn't want to leave either, but it could be dangerous to stay after dark. Someone might see them and call the police.

'Come on, you can sleep in the car.'

'I don't want to go to sleep.'

Like a cold shiver down his back, Brian heard him asking to go home.

'That's where we're going,' he replied softly.

'I want to see my mum.' He began to cry. 'I want to go home.'

'We're going home,' he whispered.

'I feel sick. I want to go back to mum.'

Wordlessly Brian led him back to the car. He put one arm round the boy's shoulders, glad that the darkness hid his expression.

'Come on, I'm taking you home,' he repeated softly as he opened the door.

Before long Ed was fast asleep on the passenger seat.

'I'm taking you home with me,' Brian whispered. 'You'll be safe there. I won't let anyone take you away from me, not ever. I'll take you to the seaside again whenever you want and we'll have fun, won't we? You and me. We don't need anyone else.'

At his side the sleeping boy didn't stir.

43

AFTER FORCING DOWN A miserable breakfast, Geraldine felt surprisingly clear headed as she drove along busy streets. She was almost cheerful at the prospect of getting stuck into work. Dave's case was as good as wrapped up. There was only the paperwork to go, and the legal checks. Reg was confident they had enough evidence to convince the Crime Prosecution Service to proceed. After her initial gut feeling to the contrary, Geraldine had to accept that Greg was guilty. There was no longer much room for doubt.

'It's all over bar the shouting,' Reg had assured the team.

Apart from Geraldine, the entire team had been convinced all along that Greg was guilty. She had already stuck her neck out over it and disagreed with everyone else on the team. Reg was difficult enough to get on with at the best of times, and he was an experienced investigating officer. If he was happy with the outcome of the investigation, she was in no position to challenge him. It was time to put that investigation behind them and focus on finding Nick's killer.

By the time she reached her office, the list of duties was already being discussed. Reg looked up as she entered the incident room and announced that he intended talking to Eve again himself. Geraldine took a deep breath and waited to hear if Nick's colleagues were to be questioned as a matter of routine. Lowering her eyes, she saw that her hands were trembling. She glanced around but no one else was paying her any attention. Not only were they all shocked at the loss of a colleague, Nick's murder raised the possibility of an aggrieved ex-con out to be avenged on the force that had put him away. They might all be at risk. Her hands probably weren't the only ones to be shaking that morning.

'We need to focus our resources on those outside the police force,'

Reg said. 'There's no point in wasting valuable time questioning each other. If anyone knows anything that might be relevant, you know we're all relying on you to come forward. You know how serious it is to withhold information, and we're all concerned to reach a speedy conclusion.'

He seemed to be staring directly at Geraldine as he spoke. Until that moment, she hadn't appreciated quite how stressed she was feeling. Deciding against coming forward to volunteer information was very different to telling an outright lie. She didn't think she could have avoided admitting the truth if she had been questioned. That would have provoked questions about why she hadn't spoken out two days earlier, when they had first heard the news of Nick's death. To be fair, she had tried to tell Reg about Nick's suspicion he was being stalked, but she hadn't tried very hard. She deeply regretted her reticence now. But there was no going back. In any event, Nick had admitted he had probably imagined he was being stalked. With a sigh, she tried to dismiss the uncomfortable memory and concentrate on her day's tasks.

Before she went home, she at first intended looking into Caroline's false claim that one of her sons had been kidnapped. Something about the episode made her uneasy. On reflection she realised that Caroline's false claim had been nothing more than a desperate cry for help. Caroline had virtually admitted as much when she talked about her struggle to cope without Dave. One of her sons coming home late had thrown her into a panic. She had been afraid that he had been taken from her as well. It was an irrational reaction, but understandable. In any case, Geraldine found it almost impossible to worry about Caroline now. She could hardly focus on anything, apart from getting through the day without breaking down in tears.

As she was about to find Max and set off to interview Nick's neighbours, Reg summoned her.

'Enter. Ah, Geraldine. Come in and close the door.'

This was it. He had discovered that Nick had spent the night with her. Soon everyone at the station would know. After years of slog and dedication, her reputation would be in shreds. If she could engage in a clandestine affair with a fellow officer, there would always be a question mark over whether she was trustworthy.

A promiscuous officer might allow herself to be influenced by a witness, or a suspect. She felt lightheaded. Reg's next words seemed to reach her through a haze.

'So on balance I think it's best you come with me.'

'Where?'

'To the interview.' He frowned. 'Are you listening? We're going to question Eve Williams properly. Find out what she can tell us, if anything. You're coming with me. A woman's touch and all that.'

For once, Geraldine wasn't bothered by his patronising tone.

'I thought about taking another female officer with me, but they all knew Nick for longer than you, and we need to keep a sense of detachment. You're not to go off at a tangent, pursuing your own line of questioning. We need to keep this strictly routine.'

Geraldine took a deep breath. 'I think Nick was worried about something.'

'We've talked about this before, Geraldine. I saw Nick the day he died. We went for a drink after work and then he went home and that's when it happened. I can assure you, he was in good spirits when he left the pub. Never better. He wasn't a worried man. I like to think I would have known, even if he hadn't said anything. Now, let's hear no more about it. Come on, his widow's waiting for us in an interview room. She might be more inclined to talk here.'

It was typical of Reg to try and intimidate a witness by questioning her at the police station, but Geraldine didn't say anything. Perhaps he was right. With luck Nick would have confided his fears to his wife. She followed Reg's large square figure along the corridor, trying not to think about Nick and his wife. They had lived in a three-bedroomed semi-detached house. It was possible they had been estranged, as he had claimed. But it was equally possible that Nick had lied about his relationship with Eve. It wasn't a subject she would be able to raise during the course of the questioning. Her whole working life was a striving to discover the truth. Not being able to pursue it was maddening.

Reg paused to have a word with a sergeant on the way to the interview room.

'Nothing,' he muttered as Geraldine joined him. 'They haven't found a murder weapon.' The way he spoke made it sound like an accusation.

Eve looked ghastly. Her skin seemed to be stretched tightly across her face, accentuating her high cheek bones. She stared vacantly at them across the table, as though she didn't recognise them. Reg greeted her gently and Geraldine followed him inside. Every so often Eve's eyes would flick to Geraldine as Reg questioned her.

'Did you notice anything unusual?' he asked.

She shook her head.

'Did anything happen the day before he died? Anything out of the ordinary?'

Geraldine held her breath. She was about to hear Eve tell Reg that Nick hadn't been home the night before he was killed. Reg would look surprised.

'Do you know where he went?' he would ask.

Eve would turn to Geraldine, her eyes burning with hatred.

'He went to her!' she would shriek, leaping to her feet and pointing to Geraldine. 'He was in her bed and then he was killed!'

Geraldine bit her lip. Eve couldn't possibly know that. Nick would never have told her. Eve saying she didn't know where Nick had been would only postpone the mortifying discovery. Reg would reassure Eve that they would find out where Nick had spent the night by tracking his car on CCTV through the streets of London. He might even put Geraldine in charge of the operation. Finally she would have to confess the truth. When Reg demanded to know why she hadn't come forward earlier, she could only mutter feebly that she had tried to tell him but he wouldn't listen. That would go down well.

'Nothing unusual happened,' Eve replied softly.

Geraldine choked back a gasp of relief. Oblivious to her reaction, Reg sat forward, his gaze fixed on Eve.

'Where were you on Monday evening?'

'Me?' she repeated.

'Yes, you.'

She smiled sadly. 'Nick used to say, "Never commit a crime unless you can prove you weren't there." You don't think I could have done it?'

'This is just routine, but we have to ask,' Reg said apologetically. 'Where were you on Monday evening, between eight and nine o'clock?'

She frowned. 'I was out visiting my aunt.'

'Would anyone be able to confirm that?'

'My aunt was with me all evening. I visited her at her home. It's about half an hour's drive away. I got there about seven, after they'd had their dinner, and stayed with her until she went to bed at nine. She's not all there, but she enjoys an occasional visit. I thought Nick would be out anyway...'

Her voice petered out and she dropped her head in her hands.

'That's all right,' Reg said gently. 'We'll leave you in peace now.'

He nodded at the female constable who had been keeping Eve company.

'I'll take you home,' she said.

44

ON THE WAY BACK to her office, Geraldine speculated about why Eve hadn't told them Nick had spent the night away from home the night before his murder. She might have been asleep and not realised he had been absent all night, especially if they slept in different rooms. It was also possible she might be aware that her husband hadn't come home that night, and be concealing his infidelity out of a sense of loyalty. There was certainly no reason for her to suspect that he had spent the night with a fellow officer, one who was involved in investigating his murder. It was only chance that Geraldine knew Eve was lying at all. But there could be another reason for her wanting to conceal the truth. Nick's adultery gave Eve a motive for hating him. His death could have been a crime of passion.

Geraldine hesitated to mention her suspicions to anyone for fear of revealing her own part in the drama. On impulse she stopped and turned to Reg who looked at her in surprise.

'Reg, there's something I've not told you. Nick came to my flat the night before he died.'

'What exactly are you telling me?'

'He came round for supper.'

'Did he? So did he say anything while he was there that might have a bearing on the investigation?'

'Yes.'

'Go on.'

Geraldine told him once again about Nick's concern that he was being followed. This time Reg listened without interrupting, a serious expression on his square face. She repeated Nick's account, word for word, as accurately as she could. When she had finished, Reg shook his head, his brows lowered in a frown.

'I can't believe he confided in you not me,' was his predictable response.

'I was just there,' she replied lamely. 'But it gives us a lead, if we can trace the van he saw.'

Reg nodded with renewed energy. 'Set a team to work checking CCTV following Nick when he left here the night before he spoke to you. You said it was the previous night he was followed, didn't you?'

'I'm not absolutely sure, but I think so. We can start there anyway, and then go back further if we don't find anything when he left work that evening.'

They walked on in silence for a few seconds.

'I still can't believe it,' Reg repeated at last. 'I had no idea you two were seeing one another out of work.'

'We were friends.'

'Just friends? Or is there more you haven't told me?'

'We were just friends. We went out a few times for a drink. He came round to my flat once for supper. We talked about work. That was all.'

Like Eve, she lied readily. There was no need for Reg to know more than that. No one need ever find out in detail what had happened between her and Nick. It had no bearing on the case. She should have thought of this before, but she had been too worried and upset to think clearly.

'After all, we did share an office.'

'Well, I know that, but for some reason I had the impression the two of you didn't get on that well.'

'I suppose we didn't to begin with.'

'It seems unbelievable that you became friends so quickly.'

'There's a lot about Nick that seems unbelievable.'

'And about you, Geraldine. It's important to be discreet, but being secretive is hardly helpful.'

She didn't remonstrate that she had tried to tell him about Nick's visit to her flat on several occasions, but he hadn't wanted to listen. As they arrived at his door, Reg detained her in the corridor.

'Hang on a minute. You told me you were friends with Nick. If you'd rather leave the investigation to colleagues who weren't so close to him, I'd understand.' He paused, uncertain of his ground. 'Like you said, you shared an office...'

'And that's all it was.' She didn't look at him, couldn't trust herself to stare levelly at the suspicion in his eyes. He must have known Nick's reputation with women. 'I'm fine, really I am. I want to work on this investigation. I owe it to Nick.'

'We all do,' he answered heavily.

'Don't take me off the case, please.'

'Very well. If you're sure. Let's not waste any more time.'

It sounded like a reprimand, which was hardly fair. Geraldine had attempted to tell Reg about Nick's visit to her flat before. On the point of making a stinging retort, she pulled herself up short. Reg was upset about Nick's death too. The two men had worked together for a long time, developing a close camaraderie. In his own way, Reg must be missing Nick as much as anyone. Now was not the time to lose her temper with him. Taking a deep breath, she nodded and agreed they must crack on.

They were able to establish an approximate time frame for Nick's last journey. He was killed outside his house between eight and nine on Monday evening. Before that, Reg had been with him in the pub until about six thirty. The detective chief inspector had only stayed for one pint. He had to get away to see his sister and brother-in-law, so he was able to be quite specific about the time he had left.

'There would have been hell to pay if I'd been home late,' he added ruefully.

Under any other circumstances, Geraldine would have smiled at the thought of the detective chief inspector as a henpecked husband. But today no one was smiling. Reg had left Nick still finishing a pint. No one else had noticed Nick leave the pub after Reg had gone. None of the bar staff could recall how long Nick had hung around after Reg left, or whether he had stayed for another drink or left straight away. It wasn't precise, but at least they could narrow down the time Nick had left to between six thirty and eight thirty, at the latest.

Geraldine sent Max to organise a team to watch CCTV of the roads leading away from the police station. She gave him specific instructions that they were to watch for the van Nick had mentioned. Then she set off to speak to Nick's neighbours. However long it took, she wouldn't stop searching until she found out who had killed Nick.

45

GERALDINE DROVE BACK TO West Hampstead slowly, struggling against her reluctance to revisit the scene of Nick's murder. It would be hard to look at the front yard where he had been battered to death, impossible not to be reminded of his warm body in her bed. Although she had resolved not to spend the night with him again, there was no way of knowing what might have developed between them if he hadn't been murdered. She was tormented by the memory of the touch of his lips on hers, his hands on her body. In a way it was almost worse than losing someone she had been seriously involved with. He would remain a fantasy partner who could never disappoint.

Reaching her destination, she parked and sat for a moment in the car, feeling thoroughly wretched. She wasn't sure she wanted to question his neighbours, but she could hardly have refused the task. At the same time, a masochistic urge to discover more about his relations with his wife drove her on. She told herself she would be pleased if she learned that they had been living together as a couple right to the end. Confirming he had lied to her might lessen the anguish she was feeling at his loss. But it wouldn't bring him back.

With a shiver, she clambered out of the car and set to work. Whatever her feelings, she had to remain alert and professional. She couldn't afford to miss any information, however insignificant it seemed. With a nod to a scene of crime officer who was still working outside Nick's house, she rang the bell of the house attached to Nick's. A grey-haired man came to the door. With an irritable scowl he asked her what she wanted. He was apologetic when he discovered who she was.

'It's a terrible business, a terrible business, struck down like that in broad daylight. But I've already spoken to a young woman in uniform. There's not really anything else I can tell you. I was here with the wife on Saturday evening.'

His wife came to the door and confirmed his account of their Saturday evening. Although they had been at home neither of them had heard anything unusual from the street. Geraldine took a deep breath and plunged in.

'We're trying to build up a picture of their life next door. It's routine, standard background information in a murder enquiry.'

It wasn't a complete lie. Any information could be helpful. But the neighbours were unable, or unwilling, to comment.

'We didn't know them that well,' the man said. 'I know we lived next door, but we didn't socialise with them. Not even drinks at Christmas. They weren't very friendly really, which suited us. We like to keep to ourselves.'

Geraldine spent several hours doing her best to build a picture of the lifestyle Nick and his wife had shared. It was heavy going. By the end of the afternoon she was convinced that they had been living as a couple. Seen returning from the supermarket together, and occasionally going out together in the evening, the neighbours who backed onto their property had even spotted them sunbathing hand in hand in the garden in the summer. Whatever else Nick might have been, he had been a liar. Sam had warned Geraldine that Nick had slept his way around half the female officers at the station, before Geraldine had invited him to spend the night with her. Feeling like a complete fool, she was determined that no one else would ever find out what had happened between them. It wasn't so very terrible, two adults choosing to spend a night together, but it would remain her secret. She told herself she was protecting his widow's feelings, although she knew it had more to do with her own reputation.

Back at her desk, Geraldine tried to write up her notes on her discussions with Nick's neighbours. Too distressed to concentrate, she struggled to summon up anger at Nick's deceit. He had lied, to her, to his wife, to everyone. But whenever she looked up and saw his vacant chair, the desk where he had done his work, the keyboard his fingers had touched, she felt only a deep sadness.

He had entered her life for such a brief time, and now she would never see him again, never hear his teasing voice or feel the lingering touch of his lips on hers. It was agony remembering how his eyes had met hers whenever she had looked up, as though he had been waiting constantly for her attention. To begin with she had resented having to share an office with him. Now she would give anything to have him back. His lies, his confused relationship with his wife, none of that mattered to her any more. She just wanted to feel his arms around her, and know that she mattered in his life.

Too restless to settle to anything, she went to see whether Max was making any progress searching for the vehicle that Nick had claimed followed him home from work the night before he was killed. The team watching the CCTV had spotted a small white van that drew away from the kerb shortly after Nick drove out of the police station car park. Geraldine started forward in excitement. She was disappointed when Max told her they hadn't been able to get a clear shot of the registration number.

'Look again,' she said. 'Surely you can do something to it?'

'We've been over and over it,' Max said wearily. 'There's nothing to see. There's too much traffic. We checked all along the route to Nick's house, but we didn't see it again until Nick reached home.'

'And then?'

The van had been visible briefly in Nick's street, but once again the team failed to establish the registration number.

'If it *is* the same van,' Max added. 'It could be, but we can't be sure, even with the image enhanced. There are no obvious distinguishing features.'

'Nick thought it was the same one.'

'He could've been mistaken.'

Geraldine swore. 'Look again,' she repeated and strode out of the room.

It was frustrating to learn that they had sighted the vehicle without being able to identify it. They had no way of following it up to establish whether it was connected to the murder. Nick had allegedly seen it, but that didn't help, because it could have been an innocent mistake on his part. What was worse, Geraldine was annoyed with herself for not having insisted Reg take her seriously when she had first mentioned Nick's concerns. He must think her incompetent, as though her judgement was questionable. It was his misjudgement, but she was left feeling responsible.

46

THEY FINISHED BREAKFAST and Brian cleared the table. He dumped
the plates and cutlery in the sink for later. If he messed around
stacking the dishwasher now, Ed might become restless. He was
already bored with cartoons on television. Since Ed had moved
in, mealtimes had taken on an unforeseen significance. However
much the youngster ate, he seemed to be permanently hungry.
They had stopped for him to throw up on the car journey home
from the seaside the previous day, but he had still insisted on
having crumpets and chocolate spread when they reached home.

They sat down at the table, and Brian set out draughts. The game
wasn't much fun for Brian, but he enjoyed watching Ed's face. He
was very competitive and grew sullen if beaten, exhilarated out of
all proportion whenever he took one of his opponent's pieces.

'It's only a game,' Brian reminded him.

'You said that because you're losing!' Ed crowed.

While he didn't appreciate the boy's gloating, Brian was pleased
he was enjoying himself.

'This is more fun than being at school, isn't it?' he asked and
immediately regretted his words as Ed's brow twitched with the
flicker of a frown. The less he thought about his past life, the more
quickly it would fade from his mind. Ed glanced up and stared past
Brian's shoulder.

'There's a man out there. He's looking at us!'

He stuck his tongue out and laughed, oblivious to the threat.
Brian spun round, fists clenched. Whatever happened he was ready
to protect his young charge. A draughts counter slipped from his
grasp to land on its rim and roll silently across the kitchen floor.

'You lost a go!' Ed shrieked gleefully. 'You dropped a piece so
that's two turns to me!'

Brian didn't care about the game. All he could think about was that their secret was no longer safe. He sprang to his feet and raced over to the window to see who was there. While there was no sign of an intruder, a ladder was propped up against the wall. Ed hadn't been making it up. He had said quite categorically that the man was looking at them. Ed had been sitting facing the window. A spy outside would have a clear view of him sitting at the table, and could easily have gathered evidence. It didn't need any special equipment. Anyone could take a photograph on a mobile phone. Brian turned to Ed.

'Did he take a picture?'

Ed shrugged, puzzled. The likelihood was that someone had spotted Ed out with Brian on their excursion the previous day and had sent a spy to investigate, under the guise of cleaning the windows. Brian had known he was sitting on a time bomb ever since Ed had come to his house. The clock had started ticking.

'We can't stop now,' Ed whined. 'I want to keep playing. It's fun.'

'It's time for a break.'

'Just because you're losing. That's not fair. I want to play now!'

'Be quiet.'

Ed was so surprised when Brian snapped at him that he stopped protesting at once. Brian had never spoken harshly to him before.

'I need to think,' Brian went on, more gently. 'Be good. Go in the living room and put the telly on. I've got to speak to the window cleaner. As soon as I'm done, we'll carry on. We'll leave the game here, just as it is, and you can have an extra go because I'm the one who's holding us up.'

'You're a cheat. I'll know if you've moved any of the pieces. I know where they all are.'

Grumbling under his breath, he trotted off. Brian waited until he heard the television was on before he opened a door that led to the side passage. He winced as it creaked on its hinges. Peering round the corner of the house into the back garden, he saw the long wooden ladder still in place. It trembled as someone moved on it. Brian squinted upwards. From that angle the man's feet looked impossibly large. If he had been sent round to the house to spy on them, he was doing a pretty good job of masquerading as a window cleaner. He might really be a window cleaner, paid to gather evidence that Ed was living there. Either way, he wasn't about to pass on that information. Climbing the ladder to fool them would prove to be his downfall. Literally.

With a burst of adrenaline, Brian dashed forward and seized the ladder. The wood felt rough and warm against his palms as he yanked it backwards. As the top of the ladder swung away from the wall, Brian flung himself sideways. There was a sharp thump as the ladder landed, straddling the patio. Regaining his balance, Brian staggered over to the house and leaned against the wall to recover his breath.

The man lay motionless on the patio. Brian tensed, half expecting him to spring to his feet and attack, after being momentarily stunned by the fall. He could be feigning, watching through half closed eyes until Brian came within reach of his long arms. He waited a moment, but the man still didn't stir. Trembling, he approached the prone figure and saw that he was thin with long limbs, and rough calloused hands. His head was turned to one side, his face a ghastly pale colour. Beside his cropped brown hair a trickle of blood had formed a small pool on the ground, staining it dark brown. If he had landed on grass, he might have survived the fall, but he had cracked his skull on a stone paving slab. Just to make sure, Brian pulled off his jumper, knelt down and held it firmly over the unresisting face.

The dead man couldn't stay there. The body was unlikely to be seen, with the garden screened on either side by tall trees. All the same, it was possible someone might look out of an upstairs window in another house and notice him. He had to be dragged out of sight as quickly as possible. Desperately, Brian grabbed the inert figure under his arms and pulled. The body barely budged. Brian tried again, straining with all his strength.

'What are you doing?'

Intent on his task, he hadn't heard Ed come out into the garden. Sitting up on his heels, he stared at the boy in a panic, wondering how much he had seen, and how much he had understood.

47

GERALDINE DID HER BEST to dismiss her suspicions about Nick's widow. Her own liaison with Nick would probably never have amounted to anything more than a brief fling. Yet without his wife standing in the way, their affair might have developed into a significant relationship. Her personal resentment towards the woman who had stood between them was bound to affect her judgement, however hard she tried to remain objective.

Reg leaned forward across his desk, staring mournfully back at her.

'I've met her before, several times,' he said. 'Only briefly, mind, and I never really spoke to her. She seemed a quiet sort, happy to sit back and let others do the talking. On reflection, I suppose she seemed a bit withdrawn, but I never really thought about it before.' He sighed. 'What did you make of her?'

Geraldine hesitated. Despite her decision to keep quiet, her resolve wavered when Reg asked her outright for her impression of Eve.

'Well, she does seem very quiet,' she agreed. 'It could just be that she's in shock, after what's happened. I mean I've only just met her. I don't know what she's usually like. What she was like before all this?'

It was hard to put into words what had happened to Nick.

Reg scowled. 'Don't beat about the bush, Geraldine. What do you think of her? Women's intuition and all that.' When Geraldine hesitated, he pressed her. 'Do you think she could know more than she's letting on?'

Neither of them mentioned Nick's reputation for womanising, but they both knew it could be a motive for hatred, and possibly even murder.

Geraldine admitted that she didn't know what to make of Eve. 'But she stands to gain a lot financially from his death. I'll check out her alibi.'

'Good. Hopefully we can eliminate her straight away. And if we can't... so, first the alibi.'

'Right away, sir.'

Eve had claimed she had gone to an old people's home to visit her aunt on the afternoon of Nick's murder. It should be relatively straightforward to discover whether she was telling the truth. Admittedly she had been in the company of an aunt who was in her nineties, but the old people's home would have a record of the time of her visit. This was an important point to establish, so Geraldine decided to drive out to the home herself. She went alone. The home was located in the leafy suburb of Pinner, about half an hour's drive from Nick and Eve's house.

The well turned-out manager looked up with a bright smile. She asked whether Geraldine had made an appointment to visit the home, or if she was there to visit one of the residents. She nodded, unworried, when Geraldine explained her enquiry. She didn't seem at all curious about why Geraldine wanted to see Eve's aunt.

'Jane Arkwright, yes she's here. Her niece did come to visit. Not often, but she came here sometimes. You can ask Jane about her niece. She knows who she is. She's physically very frail, but she's still got all her marbles. I'll take you along to see her. She's probably in her room. She hardly ever leaves it any more.'

Geraldine followed the manager along a quiet corridor. Nearby she could hear the muffled drone of a television. Apart from that, there was no sound in the building. The manager tapped on one of the doors and opened it without waiting for a response.

'Mrs Arkwright? I have a visitor for you.'

Geraldine followed the young woman into the room. Its occupant was sitting in an armchair beside the bed, her slippered feet resting on a footstool. She was gazing at the window, seemingly watching clouds scudding across the sky. The manager called her name without eliciting any response. She called out more loudly, whispering to Geraldine that Jane was a little hard of hearing. This time the old lady turned and looked at them with a vague smile.

'Hello,' she replied in a voice that quavered softly.

Geraldine introduced herself.

'Oh dear, the police, you've caught up with me at last have you?' Mrs Arkwright chuckled. 'How can I help you?' she added more seriously.

She confirmed that Eve Williams was her niece. 'Eve Browning she was, my sister's niece really, not mine, but she's the only family I have living in London now.' She sighed. 'My daughter's in Leicester. She comes to see me every month. She's a good girl.'

The manager returned to her office.

'You know where I am if you need me,' she said as she left.

The old lady was keen to talk, but she was too confused to be much help. She confirmed that her niece visited her from time to time.

'She's a good girl.'

'Did she come and see you on Monday evening?'

'Monday?'

'Yes. Today's Friday. We think Eve came to see you on Monday, four nights ago, earlier on this week. Is that right?'

Mrs Arkwright leaned forward. Reaching out, she placed one gnarled hand on Geraldine's arm.

'Has something happened to Evie?'

Geraldine hastened to reassure her that her niece was fine.

'Is she in trouble?' Mrs Arkwright smiled vaguely.

'No.' Geraldine refrained from explaining the reason for her visit, and repeated her question.

'Oh dear,' the old lady said, 'I'm not very good with days, dear. In this place, one day's much the same as another.' Still smiling, she gave a helpless shrug. 'My niece Evie visits me.'

Eve's aunt couldn't give her any more help so she went back to the entry hall and questioned the receptionist. She too confirmed that Mrs Arkwright's niece had been to visit her recently.

'Was she here on Monday?'

'Just a minute,' the girl said. 'I'll check the book. We ask visitors to sign in. Oh,' she broke off, flustered. 'I never asked you to sign in, did I? I thought, with you being a police officer, it would be OK

193

to let you in, and I didn't think.' She glanced around and lowered her voice. 'You won't tell anyone, will you?'

'Don't worry,' Geraldine reassured her. 'I won't tell. Now, about Monday evening. Can you confirm if Mrs Arkwright's niece was here?'

The girl nodded. Opening a large book that was lying on the desk, she checked it.

'Monday evening, yes. Here it is. Eve Williams, visiting Jane Arkwright.'

'Can you tell me the time of her visit?'

'Yes. She signed in at seven thirty, that's after the residents have their evening meal, and she left at nine when we lock up for the night.'

'Thank you.'

It seemed Eve was in the clear. They were no closer to discovering who had killed Nick.

48

Geraldine had thrown out the sheets that had been on her bed when Nick had stayed with her. She couldn't bear to use them again. Paranoid that samples of both their DNA might be discovered, she had been tempted to burn them, but wasn't sure where to do it without attracting attention. Instead she had to be satisfied with washing the sheets at a high temperature, stuffing them into a large black bag and disposing of them in an outside waste bin. She felt like a criminal. The following day she had watched the contents of the bin chewed up in a large waste disposal lorry. It was not so easy to get rid of her memories. The only way she could try to stop thinking about Nick was by filling her mind with work, but sitting at her desk she saw his empty chair every time she looked up.

To get out of her office, she went to see Max who was cross referencing villains recently released from prison against those whose cases Nick had investigated, searching for a known killer who might have hated Nick enough to kill him.

Max looked up and gave her a weary smile. 'Here's the list.'

He had a team of constables laboriously checking through every villain recently released from prison. Once they finished, they were going to look at those still behind bars who might have friends or family seeking revenge. It was a long shot, but someone had wanted him dead. So far they had drawn a blank. In all but one of Nick's cases, the killer was either still in prison, or dead. Geraldine herself went to interview the one possible suspect. He was an allegedly reformed murderer Nick had put behind bars.

Cameron Drew was in a hospice, suffering from terminal cancer. A softly spoken nurse took Geraldine to a conservatory which looked out on a well-tended garden at the back of the building. There were several patients sitting in cushioned wicker chairs, dozing, gazing out of the window, or reading. They all glanced up as she walked in with the nurse. Their eyes slid past her. She wasn't there for them. The nurse led her to a frail bald man seated in a corner near the French window. The nurse touched him gently on the shoulder and he looked up with a slight smile, removing his headphones. There was a wonderful air of serenity in the room. Geraldine wished she didn't have to break the silence, but she had a job to do.

The nurse hovered protectively as Geraldine sat down. Leaning forward and speaking in a low voice, she introduced herself. If he was disturbed by her intrusion, he didn't show it by so much as a flicker of an eye but continued smiling amiably.

'What do you want with me?' he asked evenly. 'I've served my time in the nick. And I won't be leaving here alive, if that's what you want to know.'

'I'm sorry.'

'Why? What's it to you?'

He was going through the motions of responding to her, but his dull eyes looked through her as though she didn't exist.

'Do you remember DI Nick Williams?'

The name brought a flush of pink to his pale cheeks. Behind her, Geraldine heard the nurse stir.

'Inspector...' she said, but her patient waved his skeletal hand feebly.

'It's OK,' he muttered. He turned to Geraldine. There was a flash of animation in his eyes. 'I should bloody well think I do remember him. He's the bastard had me put away for twelve years. And then I came out to this.' He raised his hand as though to wave it again, but let it drop back into his lap.

'DI Williams is dead.'

'Good riddance.'

'He was murdered.'

'Oh bloody hell. You're not saying you think I had anything to do with it, are you? For Christ's sake, woman, look at me.' He scowled. 'When did it happen?'

'On Monday night.'

'Monday just gone?'

'Yes.'

'What day is it today?'

'It's Saturday.'

He gave a hollow laugh. 'Do I look like I could overpower another man? I can't even hold myself upright.'

'Can you think of anyone who might have had a grudge against him?'

'Apart from me, you mean?' He shrugged. 'I'm sure there are enough of us, but I wouldn't give you any names, even if I could.' He turned away. 'Fuck off and leave me alone, will you? And next time you want to go pestering a dying man, do your homework first. You could've asked anyone here. Ask her, go on.' He looked up at the nurse. 'Ask her where I was on Monday. Where I've been since I left the hospital. She'll tell you. Anyone'll tell you.'

He leaned back in his chair, exhausted by his momentary anger.

'Inspector, I think you should leave,' the nurse said firmly. 'Come along, please.'

As soon as they left the conservatory, Geraldine put the question. 'I'm sorry, but this is a murder investigation. I have to ask. Was he definitely here on Monday evening? He couldn't have slipped out unnoticed?'

'Inspector, he can't get out of his chair unaided,' the nurse replied. 'He certainly couldn't walk out of the building on his own two feet. He's far too weak.'

'I hate to press you on this, but there's no possibility he could be stronger than he appears, is there?'

The nurse turned to her. 'Inspector, Cameron's dying. Can I make it any plainer? I told you, he can't stand up by himself.'

'Well, I hope you understand I had to be sure. I'm just doing my job, thinking about another man who's died. It's very peaceful here,' she added as she said goodbye to the nurse. 'No one would suspect they were all dying.'

'We're all waiting for death in our own way,' the nurse replied gently.

49

'WE'VE GOT AN INTERESTING development,' a constable called out to Geraldine when she returned to the police station, thoroughly dispirited.

Going over to see what he had found, she recognised the name straight away. Stacey Rawlings, Greg's girlfriend, had been accused by two boyfriends of causing them actual bodily harm.

'She's a nasty piece of work,' the constable said. 'You met her, didn't you? Vicious little cow according to this report. Look at that photo. Poor bastard. He should have restrained her.'

Geraldine nodded, remembering the girl's hostility. Although Stacey was a skinny little woman, Geraldine wasn't surprised to discover that she was inclined to be violent. It suggested an interpretation of Greg's injuries they had not previously considered.

'So it looks as though he's the victim of a violent partner,' she told Max, who raised his eyebrows.

'A man who lets himself get beaten up by a woman has to have a few screws loose,' he said. 'I mean, surely he could overpower her if he wanted to?'

'There's nothing to suggest he's a violent man. Quite the opposite, I'd say. And a man who puts up with being assaulted by his girlfriend is hardly likely to go and physically attack another man, is he?'

'Unless he takes his aggression out on other people because he can't, or won't, take it out on her.'

It was possible, but Geraldine was convinced her earlier suspicion had been justified. The man they had in custody for the murder of Dave Robinson was innocent.

Reg looked up and smiled grimly when he saw her at his door.

'Ah, Geraldine. About time. I was about to call on you and ask

you how you got on. You went to see the man Nick put away –
Cameron Drew, was it? I've checked with the prison governor and
he's been out for nearly a year. That's more than enough time to
track down the man who put him away and...'

'According to his medical records, Cameron Drew couldn't
possibly have done it.'

'What do you mean, his medical records?'

'He's terminally ill. He can barely walk. There's no way he could
have done it.'

'I see.'

Geraldine hesitated.

'Yes? What is it?'

'Well, there is something else, sir.'

Reg raised his eyebrows at her. She still sometimes fell into her
former habit of calling senior officers 'Sir', although it was all first
name terms on the Met.

'It's to do with the Robinson case.'

'Oh yes? I thought we had that one tied up.'

'Yes, we all thought that, but I'm not sure we've got the right
man.'

'Greg Hawkins?'

'Yes, sir – Reg. I don't think he did it.'

Reg gave one of his exaggerated sighs. 'Well, are you going
to find the man who did it then, Geraldine?' he added, his tone
unexpectedly gentle. 'If you'd rather not work on Nick's case, that's
perfectly all right. It can be difficult...'

'No, it's not that at all. I don't want to be taken off that case. I
want to work on it, really I do. I need to, for myself as much as for
Nick.'

'Good. I'd like to think I've still got my best officer on it.'

His compliment took her by surprise. She hoped her feelings
didn't show on her face. She found Reg patronising, and had always
believed he looked down on her both as a woman and as an officer
used to working in the Home Counties. Meanwhile Reg carried on,
apparently unaware of her reaction.

'OK then, so what's the problem with Greg Hawkins? He was in
an argument with the victim the day before his murder, wasn't he?

I know it doesn't place him at the scene, but we have a witness, and his injuries bear out the statement.'

'Well, we thought so, but there's a problem.'

'Go on.'

'First of all, the witness retracted. He said he did see them quarrelling, but the fight wasn't a physical one. He saw the victim throw a punch at the suspect who didn't respond but backed away. He issued verbal threats to the victim, but that's all we have. Greg didn't explicitly threaten violence. He just said, "This isn't over." That's all.'

'What about Greg's injuries? Even if the witness didn't see them fighting, we all saw his face. He'd been in a fight all right.'

'I think he might not have received those injuries in a fight. His girlfriend's been had up twice for ABH after she assaulted two previous boyfriends.'

'Oh shit.'

'Even if he did it, we'll never make it stick, not with what we've got.'

Reg shook his head. 'No, you're right. Let him go for now. But warn him not to go anywhere. And for Christ's sake, let's get some real evidence and put Dave Robinson's killer away for good next time.'

Reg had told her to find Dave Robinson's killer, and she was determined to do just that. It was a good way of distracting herself from thinking about Nick. There was nothing she could do to help the investigation into his death. Teams of uniformed officers were out questioning possible witnesses. An entire forensic laboratory had been assigned to the case. All Geraldine could do for now was wait. In the meantime, she was going to review all the statements connected to Dave Robinson's death.

It was too late to release Greg that night. First thing in the morning she would send him on his way. After that she would contact social services as a matter of urgency and alert them to the situation. Greg was at risk, and Stacey desperately needed help. The likelihood was that Greg would strenuously deny Stacey's violent abuse. The social worker sent to investigate would be too overworked to pursue the case. Making her report as forcefully as she could, Geraldine was aware that she would be powerless to influence what happened. There was a tragic inevitability about the course of events in Stacey's household. Yet with even a slim chance that her report might make a difference, she would persist. Without Geraldine's intervention, there was no chance for Greg and Stacey. With it, they might be offered the support they needed. Geraldine had to do whatever she could to trigger the process.

She worked late into the night, but made no headway with the investigation into Dave's murder. Every time she looked up from her files, she saw Nick's desk and his empty chair. Soon someone else would come and sit there. That would be hard enough. It would be unbearable if Nick was replaced before his killer was caught.

50

THE CELL STANK OF stale sweat and shit. There was one window that showed a tiny square of grey sky. She glanced up at the ceiling, whitewashed and bare apart from a small painted cross showing the signs of the compass so Muslims could face east when they prayed. Other than that one symbol, the cell was bare. Greg was so worked up he didn't pause to listen to what Geraldine was saying. Red-faced, hot and sweaty, he jumped up and began haranguing her as soon as the door to his cell swung open.

'I've been banged up here for a week, all for having a row with some poor sod who's gone and got himself killed, as though it's my fault someone clocked the bastard. Dave had it coming all right, but I never so much as touched the bloke, never laid a finger on him, and now I'm locked up. It's a bloody disgrace. Trying to make something out of this. So what? If every bloke with a black eye got banged up for murder, there'd be precious few people left out on the streets.'

Geraldine waited until he paused for breath before telling him quietly that he was free to go. Without giving him a chance to respond, she continued.

'If you're experiencing problems with physical abuse at home, we can arrange for social services to help you. Greg, listen to me, you don't need to live with abuse. Everyone has the right to feel safe. Please, for the children's sake as well as Stacey's, and yours, let us contact social services on your behalf.'

She had already begun her report, but it would be processed more effectively with his co-operation. Working without his consent, she could do less to help him. Geraldine entered the cell and invited him to be seated.

'What? On this thing?' He kicked the bed angrily.

'Sit down,' she repeated firmly.

He did as he was told.

'Greg, there are people who can help you.'

'Like you, you mean? Locking me up without any good reason.'

'I'm suggesting you go to the social services for help.'

'What the fuck are you on about?' he blustered. 'Like fuck I'd go to the social services. Bloody interfering load of bastards they are, interfering in things what don't concern them. Look,' he went on in a more reasonable tone, 'no one understands Stacey like I do. The poor cow doesn't need strangers breathing down her neck issuing bloody injunctions and fuck knows what else. It's all been tried before and none of it helps. Those social workers don't know fuck all. They come in, all blithering and blathering and it don't make a blind bit of difference. In the end they bugger off and good riddance, leaving me to pick up the pieces. They drive her over the edge. We're better off without their sort of help.'

Gazing at his eye, still swollen and bruised, she tried again.

'What about your eye?'

He raised a hand in an involuntary movement, wincing as he touched the reddened skin.

'Stacey hit you, didn't she? You told me that yourself.'

'I tripped,' he mumbled. 'It was an accident.'

If he insisted he had walked into a wall, there was nothing she or anyone else could do to help him.

'I fell over and banged my head on a wall, I tell you. Why the fuck won't anyone believe me? What do you think happened?'

'Greg, there are people who can help you.'

'All lying bastards, the lot of you. Being paid to lock up poor innocent blokes. You're all in it. Find some poor bloke, fit him up, and throw away the key. Another box ticked. Another crime solved. As long as you hit your bloody targets, you don't give a toss who's on the receiving end. You're only interested in making sure your trumped cases stick. I wish I *had* killed the poor bastard. At least I'd be behind bars for a reason. You're all lying bastards, the whole bloody lot of you.'

It was impossible trying to reason with him. Even the suggestion that Stacey's children might be in danger didn't persuade him to accept help. Geraldine accompanied him to the custody sergeant to collect his belongings before escorting him to the exit. All she could do was file a report and hope Greg thought better of his hostility when a social worker paid him a visit. Realistically, she wasn't optimistic, but there was nothing more she could do to help him.

'Why would anyone stay with a partner who abuses them?' she asked Max when she joined him later in the canteen.

He shrugged. 'Love?' he suggested. 'Masochism? Force of habit? People who grow up as victims of violent parents often choose violent partners.'

She was amused by his eagerness to answer her rhetorical question.

'Statistics in this area aren't very reliable,' he continued, 'because we only know about violence that goes on behind closed doors if it's reported. And even then it's usually one person's word against another's.'

'There would be physical evidence to back up an accusation.'

'What about mental and emotional abuse? There doesn't have to be physical violence. We studied this at uni,' Max said, with the assurance of a man who knew what he was talking about.

'The confidence of youth,' Geraldine thought. She wondered if her superior officers had found her equally presumptuous at his age. For all his brashness, she quite liked Max. He was certainly keen and bright. She was inclined to agree with Reg's opinion. With a few years' experience Max was going to shape up into a first-rate detective.

Geraldine thought it best to inform Caroline face to face that they had released the man arrested for her husband's murder.

'What do you mean, you let him go? What about Dave?' She sounded angry.

'New evidence came to light that confirmed the suspect was innocent.'

'Innocent? Who's innocent?'

She backtracked when Geraldine asked her what she meant by that.

'Oh, nothing. I didn't mean anything. I'm just disappointed, that's all. So the bastard who did for my Dave is still out there somewhere,' she added bitterly.

'We're doing everything we can to find him,' Geraldine assured her. 'We're following several leads and hope to resolve things soon. But these things take time,' she added illogically. 'We have to ask you to be patient.'

Without another word, Caroline slammed the door in Geraldine's face.

51

'WHAT ARE YOU DOING?' Ed repeated as he took a few steps forwards.

'Stay where you are. Don't come any closer.'

It was too late to hide the body.

'Why? What's wrong with that man? Did he fall off his ladder? Why did he fall off his ladder?'

'I think he was ill and it made him dizzy, so he fell off.'

'He was very silly to go up that ladder if he was feeling dizzy,' Ed said solemnly. 'It's a very long ladder. He's a very silly man.'

Brian shrugged. 'Silly' was a childish word to use in the circumstances.

'Yes, he is silly,' he agreed.

Brian turned back to the body, grabbed it beneath both shoulders, and pulled. The figure shifted slightly.

'Are you trying to make him get up?'

'No. I'm trying to move him.'

'Why doesn't he wake up? Is he dead?'

Brian sat back on his heels and squinted up at Ed, wondering what might be going through his ten-year-old mind at such a time.

'Yes,' he said simply. 'He's dead. He was a bad man.'

'Serves him right then.'

Silently Brian heaved a sigh of relief at his matter-of-fact tone. He had been afraid the boy would become hysterical, or insist on summoning the police.

'Anyway,' Ed went on, 'we had a dead man in our garden. He was in our shed. Only our dead man was my dad and...' His lips wobbled and tears welled up in his eyes, but he forced himself to carry on speaking. 'Our dead man was my dad, and he wasn't bad.'

Brian scrambled to his feet and ran over to him.

'Don't cry,' he muttered, putting his arms awkwardly round the boy and patting him on the back. 'It's all right. You're safe here with me. I'm going to look after you. Everything's going to be all right. You'll see.'

With a jerk Ed pulled away.

'What are we going to do with him?' he asked curiously, wiping his eyes on his sleeve.

'Who?'

'Him. The dead man. What are we going to do with him? Are we going to bury him here? I could dig a really really big hole to bury him in.' He paused uncertainly. 'If you want me to.'

Brian could have laughed out loud. The boy was priceless. Together they were going to bury the body, and no one else would ever find out what had happened in their garden that day. It would be their secret. All Brian had to do was think of a way of persuading Ed to keep silent about it, but that wouldn't be difficult. He'd think of something. On reflection, he wondered if it was such a good idea to bury the body in the garden. It would take some time, and they might be seen. They weren't overlooked at the back, but the houses on either side could see down right into their back garden. He glanced up at the windows of the house next door.

'I'll tell you what,' he said. 'Let's hide him in the bushes for now, and then we can think about what we're going to do with him.'

'OK.'

The body seemed impossibly heavy and cumbersome. Brian held him under his arms, and Ed clutched his ankles. It was a strenuous task, but between them they succeeded in dragging the dead man across the patio to the flower bed. It was even more difficult to manoeuvre him onto the earth. At the edge of the paved area, they knelt down side by side and rolled him over and over down onto the earth. He lay on the ground, tolerably well concealed beneath a bank of camellias.

'We could put leaves on his face,' Ed suggested. 'Then the foxes won't find him.'

Brian gave a taut smile. It wasn't foxes he was worried about. But he didn't want the boy to be traumatised by the sight of the man's face half chewed away by wild animals. It might give him nightmares.

'Covering him up with leaves is a very clever idea,' he agreed.

As soon as it was dark, they would drag him to the car and dispose of him, somewhere he would never be found. Meanwhile, he let Ed gather up a clump of leaves and drop them on the dead man's face. Brian crouched down and spread them out evenly. The leaves were cold and damp and mushy. Touching them with his bare hands made him shudder.

'That's very good,' he said as he stood up and straightened his aching legs.

'It's not very good for him,' Ed replied. He looked thoughtful. 'Was he very bad? Are you glad he's dead?'

Brian nodded. 'He was a very bad man. He came here to hurt you. Yes, I'm glad he's dead.'

'Why did he want to hurt me?'

'I don't know. No reason. Just because he was a bad man.'

'Did he hurt other children?'

'Yes. Lots of them.'

'Was he a paedophile?'

'I don't know. Probably. Yes, he was.'

'That's why you made him fall off the ladder, isn't it? To stop him getting in the house and hurting me.'

'I didn't make him fall. The ladder wasn't safe. It was wobbly. I tried to hold onto it and keep it steady, but I was too late to save him.'

'Why did you try to save him? He wanted to hurt me. He was a bad man, a very bad man.'

'Yes, he was very bad. He can't hurt you now. But it wasn't my fault. He did it to himself.'

'Serves him right. You shouldn't have tried to save him.' Ed's expression changed. 'My dad wasn't a bad man. He didn't hurt anyone.'

'Let's go inside,' Brian interrupted quickly. 'We'll wash our muddy hands, and then we can make some hot chocolate. Come on, we haven't finished the game. I'm going to win!'

'You're not. I am!'

Ed turned and raced back. After dragging the ladder into the garage, Brian hurried after him, calling out to him to leave his muddy shoes on the mat.

52

To begin with, Greg thought he must have misunderstood the detective. He stared into her large eyes, so dark the pupils were swallowed up by the irises. She was classy, way out of his league. A low voice was telling him he was free to walk out of his cramped cell, collect his possessions, and return to Stacey and the kids, or go to the pub and have a few pints. It was hard to take in. The inspector might have been talking about the weather, her voice was so quiet and steady as she mouthed the life changing words. After a moment she fell silent, waiting for his response.

'What?' he said stupidly. 'What's that you said?'

'I said you're free to go home. But don't think of doing a runner. Stay out of trouble, and let us know if you're thinking of changing your address.'

For a moment he couldn't move. He stood there, staring at her, thinking about what she had told him, imagining what his mates at work would be saying behind his back, and what the boss would be thinking of him. He spoke very slowly and clearly to impress on her the seriousness of the situation.

'You have to tell them.'

'Tell who?'

'Tell them at work. All of them. I been banged up here for days. Cost me a week's wages you have. I need you to tell them you screwed up royally. You got to tell them I done nothing wrong. Tell them I'm an innocent man, or they'll never take me back.'

'That's not a problem.' She spoke as if to a child, making him feel about two feet tall. 'Remember, you're not to go off anywhere or you'll be in trouble before you know what's hit you.'

Her expression altered. He bristled, understanding her pity, and muttered obscenities under his breath. What did a posh bitch like her know about trouble?

He had been lying in one position on a hard bench for far too long, and his neck was stiff. It felt unreal as he hobbled out of his cell to collect his possessions. Carefully he counted his cash, although he couldn't remember how much had been in his wallet.

'There's a tenner missing.'

'No, it's all there, mate, what you signed for.' Behind his desk the custody sergeant grinned with fake conviviality, as though he was standing behind the bar in a pub. 'No place like home, eh?'

Greg wondered why the guy bothered to try and sound friendly. He must know Greg hated his smug guts.

'Just give me the rest of my things.'

His shoes felt uncomfortably tight. Mustering as much dignity as he could, he straightened up and glowered at the sergeant.

'I'm a wronged man.'

'Best get off home, then, sir.'

Home. He half expected Stacey to have changed the lock, but his key turned easily. The three kids were creating havoc in the living room, chasing each other over the furniture. The television was blaring out a monotonous beat. Through a brief hiatus in the racket he heard a neighbour yelling at them to shut the fuck up. He strode across the room and switched the television off. The kids stopped careering round the room and turned to glare at him.

'What d'you do that for?'

'I was listening.'

'Mum said we could have it on.'

Greg turned to face them. 'Mum's not here now, I am.'

'Where you been then?' one of the little boys squinted curiously up at him. 'We thought you was dead.'

'We thought ninjas got you!'

One of the little boys launched himself at his brother and began pummelling him. 'You're stupid!'

'No, you're stupid!'

Greg ruffled the nearest child's tousled head.

'Oy, get off me! Pervert!'

Greg smiled. It was good to be home. That night he would sleep in a proper bed, with Stacey.

'Where's your mum?'

'Dunno.'

His mood altered. He went in the bedroom. One day he would find her there, stretched out on the bed, dead. But not this time. He could hear the rasping of her breath as she heaved herself up onto one elbow and stared at him with glazed eyes. Her bleached hair was tangled and straggly, in need of a wash.

He gave a tentative smile.

'Stace, it's me. I'm back.'

'What the fuck you playing at, buggering off...'

Her voice trailed away and she fell back on her pillows with a grunt.

'I been in the nick all this time. Don't you remember them bastards taking me away?'

'What did they get you for?'

'Well, it wasn't like I was nicked. I was, but they let me go. I done nothing.'

That made her laugh. 'You done nothing?' she spluttered, when she was able to speak. 'You done nothing all your life. You always was useless...'

She sat up properly and attempted to question him seriously, but her speech was slurred, and she struggled to find the right words. She scared him when she was like that. He ought never to have left her on her own.

'I said I want to know where you been all this time, leaving me on my own to deal with those damn kids, like you was free of us all... just do what the hell you want... you always do...'

Mumbling incoherently, she sank back on the bed again. Feeling wretched, he sat on the edge of the bed and pulled off his shoes. His feet hurt. In the next room the television began blaring again.

53

WINNING AT DRAUGHTS RESTORED Ed's good humour. He was soon laughing at a cartoon on the television while Brian sat quietly, working on a plan. The dead man couldn't stay in the garden for long. Insects must already have discovered the carcass. They would be busy burrowing into the flesh, depositing eggs. Soon larger urban scavengers would find him, rats and foxes, gnawing and biting him to the bone. Needing the boy's help meant moving the corpse before it became too unsightly to stomach. He had a vision of decomposing flesh falling apart in their hands as they tried to shift it. The body had to be moved as soon as it was dark. Apart from all the problems decomposition would bring, the longer it stayed where it was, the greater the risk of discovery.

Ed grumbled about going outside again. He wanted to stay and watch television, but Brian couldn't manage the task without his help.

'I'm tired,' Ed protested.

'You can go to bed as soon as we're done.'

'Not that sort of tired.'

He had to promise to buy ice cream on the way home before the boy would budge from his chair.

'Chocolate ice cream?'

'Any flavour you like, but we'll have to hurry or the shops will be shut.'

'Oh, all right.'

It was chilly outside. He was glad he had given Ed one of his jumpers to wear under his anorak, and a warm pair of gloves. Even so, Ed shivered when he saw the dead body.

'He looks yucky. Does my dad look like that?'

To Brian's relief, Ed seemed curious rather than upset.

'No, he's nothing like this. Your dad has been taken care of by an undertaker.'

'What's an undertaker?'

'He's a man who takes care of dead people, and sees them put to rest. Your father's at rest now. The undertaker made him comfortable so it's like he's sleeping peacefully now.'

'Is an undertaker going to make *him* comfortable?'

He pointed the toe of a dirty trainer at the body.

'No.'

'Why not?'

'Because he's a bad man.'

'Did an undertaker take my dad to heaven?'

'Sort of.'

'You're a liar. Heaven doesn't exist.'

A few flies were crawling across the dead man's face. Other than that the body looked untouched. There was a faint stench on the still night air as they drew close. It wouldn't be long before other scavengers arrived.

'Come on,' Brian said, stooping down and grabbing the dead man's arm. 'We've got to move him.'

The body was incredibly heavy. After strenuous tugging they managed to pull it back onto the patio. Under cover of darkness they dragged it across the paving stones. It seemed to take ages. Although it wasn't very far, Brian was terrified someone might be watching them. There were spies everywhere. The window cleaner was only the first. There would be more. Brian had to be on his guard all the time. They might be in the house next door, watching and waiting to trap him.

Once they had lugged the body into the garage, he breathed more easily. No one could see them now. Fishing in the dead man's pockets, he found a wallet and keys. After a moment's hesitation, he replaced the wallet.

Ed flatly refused to be left alone in the garage with the body.

'What if he wakes up?'

'He's dead. He can't wake up.'

'He can if he turns into a zombie.'

Brian was too wired to stop and argue about zombies. 'Come on then, come with me.'

Slamming the garage door behind them, Brian led the way to a dirty blue van that the window cleaner had parked outside the house. Ed jumped in and sat quietly in the front passenger seat as Brian backed the van right up to the garage. Without a word, they climbed out. Opening the back doors of the van, they returned to the body and began dragging it over to the van. Ed understood what was needed without a word being exchanged. Together they tried to lift the body into the back of the van. If anything it felt heavier than before. To make matters worse, the long limbs were beginning to stiffen, making it almost impossible to bend them.

Ed was convinced the dead man was turning into a zombie.

'He's not a zombie,' Brian insisted, trying to be patient.

'Why does he feel so hard then? My arms aren't hard. He's a zombie.'

Brian hesitated to explain that that was what happened to dead bodies. He was afraid Ed would ask him about his father's body.

'Let's try again.'

By dint of much heaving and shoving they managed to hoist it up and slide it along the floor of the van. Brian's back strained with the effort. Ed was trying, but he wasn't really much help. He kept losing his grip just when Brian needed him to give an extra push. He pressed his lips together, determined not to lose his temper. The boy was doing his best. In any case, he had no idea how important it was to dispose of the body without delay. His childish ignorance was becoming irritating. At last they had the body safely in the van. Brian slammed the doors.

'No one can see him in there,' Ed said.

'I know.'

'Is it a secret?'

'Yes.'

'He was bad, wasn't he?'

'Yes.'

'That's why he's turning into a zombie. I'm glad we didn't bury him in our garden. It wouldn't be safe.'

Ed objected loudly when Brian wanted him to stay behind.

Brian wasn't happy about it either. He was afraid they would come for the boy while he was away disposing of the body. One man had already turned up to spy on them. If someone else came for Ed while he was at home by himself, he might be snatched away, just as he was beginning to settle down. His father had been murdered. The poor boy couldn't cope with any more disruption in his life. Only by promising a daily supply of Jaffa Cakes and ice cream was he able to persuade Ed to go back inside.

'Don't turn the lights on, and don't open the door to anyone. Just watch telly and wait for me to come back. I won't be long.'

Using duct tape, he carefully changed the I on the van's number plates to T, and the F to E, checking to make sure the plates matched, front and back.

He drove slowly, without any lights, hoping no one would spot the dark vehicle. His thoughts whirled at the prospect of a police officer peering into the van.

'And what have you got in the back, sir?'

But there was no sign of the police as he drove down the road. He didn't go far. Apart from the risk of being seen, or stopped, he was going to have to walk back home again. At the end of Hervey Close he stole round the bend into Strathmore Gardens. From there he made a sharp right turn into a narrow lane that led down to an overgrown track separating a row of back gardens from a fenced off abandoned lake. The lane was well concealed between high wooden fences and a tall hedge that had spread across a wire fence that formed a barrier to the lake.

The night air was chilly and damp. As he strode quickly home along the deserted pavement, he thought about the hump lying motionless in the back of the van he had abandoned in the lane. It was insane to think he could get away with it. He should have called the police straight away, and told them the window cleaner had fallen from his ladder. It was true. There was no reason why anyone would suspect it had been anything but an accident. Only now he couldn't do that. He couldn't turn the clock back and make a different decision. From the moment he had concealed the body, the choice had been made.

As his legs carried him further away, he calmed down enough

to realise he had made the right choice. He couldn't have invited the police to come crawling all over his garden. They might have caught sight of Ed at a window. Far better to keep a low profile and not attract any attention from anyone. In any case, the police might recognise the window cleaner as a spy who had gone missing. Brian couldn't be associated with him, not if he wanted to keep the police away from Ed.

He was relieved to find his boy sitting quietly in the living room watching television. It was worth all the stress and effort to keep him safe. Hearing Brian come in, Ed looked up at him.

'When are we going to get the ice cream? And the Jaffa Cakes? You promised.'

Brian had been preoccupied with more important matters.

'The shop was shut.'

'But you promised,' Ed whined.

He didn't seem grateful for all that Brian had done for him, nor did he appreciate that Brian's patience might soon run out. For the first time it struck him that Ed might not be on his side after all. It would be a pity if he had to get rid of the boy.

54

It was a lovely sunny day. A hint of summer hovered in the warm breeze, a faint reminder of childhood holidays on the beach. There was barely space for two chairs on the balcony of Sam's flat. Smiling lazily, she popped a chocolate in her mouth.

'Mmm,' she grunted with satisfaction. 'These are gorgeous. Go on, have another one.'

Geraldine shook her head. 'I bought them for you.' She studied her colleague who had been off work for a month with a leg injury. 'When do you think you'll be coming back?'

Fluffing up her short spiky blonde hair with her fingers, Sam leaned back in her chair and closed her eyes against the glare of the sunlight. Geraldine waited. After a moment Sam raised her head, shielding her eyes with her flattened hand.

'My ankle's fine now,' she admitted, lifting her right leg and wriggling her foot in its bright green slipper.

'So?' Geraldine prompted her.

'Well, I'm not altogether sure I want to come back.'

'What?'

'You have to admit, this isn't a bad way to spend a Monday.'

Max was efficient, but Geraldine would be gutted to lose her regular sergeant for good. Sam was not only a reliable colleague, she was fun, and very kindhearted. When Geraldine had first transferred to London from the Kent Constabulary, she had found the capital a lonely place for someone on their own. Sam had become a friend, as well as a capable partner at work. But it wasn't Geraldine's place to put any pressure on Sam to return to work before she felt ready. Injuries sustained while on duty could cause psychological as well as physical damage.

'You mustn't come back before you're ready,' she announced,

doing her best to hide her disappointment.

Sam gave a mischievous grin. 'For God's sake, Geraldine, I'd have been back weeks ago if they'd let me. The bloody doctor kept saying it would risk permanently injuring my ankle if I came back before it was fully recovered. To be honest, I think I probably should have come back anyway. At least that way I wouldn't have risked losing my sanity. I've been going crazy stuck here at home for so long, with my mother coming round here all the time, fussing.'

Geraldine smiled with relief. 'So when are you coming back?'

As she spoke, she heard a faint bustle behind her. Turning, she saw Sam's mother in the room behind them.

'Oh God,' Sam muttered under her breath. 'What now?'

Mrs Haley smiled brightly. 'Hello, Geraldine. How are you?'

'I'm fine, thank you. I was just saying to Sam she mustn't come back to work before she's ready.'

'If she wants to come back at all,' Mrs Haley replied sharply.

'OK, mum, we've been through this. Geraldine doesn't want to hear it.'

Geraldine felt a flicker of doubt about her friend's intentions. Sam had been clear about wanting to return to work. Geraldine couldn't imagine she would allow her mother to bully her into leaving the force, but it was possible.

Geraldine pushed back her chair and stood up. 'Why don't you come out here and sit with Sam?' she suggested. 'I've got to get going...'

'You've only just arrived,' Sam protested.

'A detective's work is never done,' her mother said, with a hint of bitterness in her voice. 'You sit down, Geraldine. I'll go and put the kettle on. And then we'll squeeze in somehow.'

'Yes. I've had four people sitting out here before now. It's a bit of a squash, but it can be done.'

'You must have been sitting on top of each other,' Geraldine laughed.

'Anyway, the point is you must stay for a bit, at least for a cup of tea. You can't go yet. I've hardly seen you.'

When her mother had disappeared into the flat, Sam asked Geraldine how she was getting on with her investigation.

Geraldine sighed and shook her head. It was hard talking about Nick, especially as he and Sam had never seen eye to eye.

'Still no leads?'

She shook her head again.

'What about the wife?'

'Her alibi stacks up.'

'What was she doing?'

'Do you really want to know?'

'Of course I do.'

'She was visiting an old aunt in a nursing home for the evening.'

'So her aunt is giving her an alibi? Is she reliable?'

'Well, no, not exactly. She's a bit confused, you know how it can be with old people. She knew her niece had been to visit her but didn't know when. Still, the nursing home confirmed she was there all evening.'

'OK, that's her out of the frame. Although it's a bit convenient, isn't it? I mean, do we know how often she went to visit this aunt?'

It was a sharp question. Before Geraldine could answer, Sam's mother returned with a tray of tea. They shifted along the narrow balcony so she could join them. It was awkward, but they managed. With Sam's mother there, the conversation moved on to Sam and her injured ankle. As soon as she had finished her tea, Geraldine stood up to leave. She would have liked to talk about the investigation for longer with her colleague. It was so helpful to discuss the details with someone sympathetic who understood exactly what she was talking about.

'I can't wait for you to come back,' she told Sam.

'You and me both,' her friend replied.

Sam's mother gave Geraldine a cold smile.

'*If* she comes back,' she repeated plaintively.

This time, Geraldine didn't feel the slightest doubt about it. Sam's interest in the investigation was all the proof she needed about her colleague's intentions. Although she wasn't superstitious, Geraldine couldn't help hoping the good news about Sam's planned return would rub off on her investigation, and work like a lucky charm to bring in a result. They were certainly in desperate need of a lucky break.

'I'll show you out,' Sam's mother said, getting to her feet.

'I'll see her out. I'm not an invalid.'

'You're supposed to be resting.'

'Mum, my ankle's better. Stop fussing!'

Geraldine smiled to see her competent colleague revert to a sullen teenager, irked by her mother's attention. Despite the cross words, their mutual affection was evident.

'I'll show myself out,' she said. 'You two both stay here and enjoy the nice weather, while it lasts.'

55

A GREY-HAIRED MAN entered the police station and shuffled up to the desk, his face flushed and his eyes bright. The desk sergeant wondered if he was drunk. All the same, the sergeant put aside his paper and listened as the man launched into a breathless monologue. He spoke very fast, his gaunt face twisted with anxiety. He was worried about a boy who had disappeared. The sergeant sat forward when he understood that the man had come to report a missing child. It was the second such report in just over a week.

The sergeant interrupted urgently. 'Tell me about the missing boy. He's been gone since Saturday you say. How old is he?'

In the silence that followed, he was aware of tension growing in his neck and shoulders. He knew that every individual deserved equal consideration, but crimes against children worried him more than anything else. He had two kids himself. Observing the man's distress, he could barely control his impatience.

'He's...' The man screwed up his eyes as he worked it out. 'I was twenty-nine when he was born, so he's thirty-eight or thirty-nine. Does that make a difference?'

The desk sergeant put down his pen and sighed. This wasn't about a missing child at all. It was just some bloke who had gone on a bender. Nodding to show he was still listening, he allowed his attention to wander while the man continued his account of his missing son's movements. He was becoming increasingly agitated.

The sergeant waited for an opportunity to interrupt. 'I'm very sorry you've been upset like this, sir, but you wouldn't believe the number of reports like this we receive, and they all turn out fine in the end. I'm sure he'll be home soon. There's nothing to stop a grown man in his thirties from taking a break now and then, and no harm done.'

Words intended to reassure the man only seemed to provoke him.

'I don't think you understand. I haven't been able to get hold of him since Saturday, and it's Tuesday. That's four days.'

'Let's get down some details. What's your name, first of all?'

'Joe Henry Wright, Wright with a W.'

'And your son's name?'

'Robert Wright. Everyone calls him Rob.'

Carefully the sergeant went through his questions, writing down a detailed description of the missing man.

'If you can bring in a recent photograph of your son, that would be helpful. Have you tried contacting his friends?'

Joe nodded miserably. 'I've gone through everyone I can think of. I don't know what else to do.'

'We'll do what we can to find him, but you know it's not against the law for your son to go away for the weekend. We can't interfere in private matters...'

The man glared at him miserably. 'I told you, there's no way Rob would go off without telling me where he was.'

'Well, leave it with us, sir,' the sergeant replied patiently. 'We'll see what we can do.'

'You don't understand. I don't think you're listening.' Joe's narrow lips trembled and his voice rose in pitch. His face, already flushed, turned a darker shade of pink. 'The point is, his mother's not well. She's in hospital, really ill.' He leaned forward and lowered his voice. 'It's terminal. The end could come at any time. Rob knows that. He would never go away without making sure I could contact him, because what if something happens?' He sounded close to tears. 'I'm on my way to see her now. What if she asks for him and I still can't get hold of him? I know he would never do that to us, abandon her like that. Something must have happened to him. You've got to find him before it's too late.'

The desk sergeant picked up his pen again.

'I'm sorry about your wife, sir, and I do see that the situation must be very distressing for you. Now, let me check those details, and if you can give me a list of all his known contacts, then we'll see what we can do to help.'

Having noted down as much information as he could, he looked up and gave Joe a reassuring smile.

'I assure you we'll do our best to find your son, Mr Wright.'

'You'd better do more than just write down a few names, you'd better bloody well find him.' Joe stood there for a moment, staring at him. 'So, what are you going to do about it?'

'Leave it with us, sir. I suggest you go on home, and please do give us a call as soon as he turns up.'

'I'm telling you, there's no way he's going to return, just like that. Something must have happened to him. He wouldn't go off like that, not with his mother being so ill.' His voice quavered. 'He visits the hospital every day, and now – not a sign of him since Saturday. I just can't get hold of him.'

He turned abruptly and walked away, blowing his nose noisily as he crossed the foyer. The desk sergeant watched him until he disappeared. It sounded as though Rob had run away from the stress of dealing with his mother's illness. It was a rotten way to behave, but he didn't entirely blame the guy. In any event, no doubt he'd show up again before long, shamefaced and full of apologies. A bloke going off for a weekend wasn't exactly a cause for alarm. The fuss his father was making, he had thought at first that the bloke had lost a child. To be fair, he could understand the man being so emotional. His wife was dying. With a sigh, the sergeant filed his report. If the son had done a bunk, by the time they found him his mother might already be dead. He hoped the missing guy would return home in time to say goodbye.

56

GERALDINE WAS ANNOYED WITH herself for agreeing to drive all the way to the mortuary. Her irritation increased as she sat waiting in a queue of traffic. She didn't know why the young pathologist wanted to see her. All that he had told her on the phone was that another body had been found. She understood that it had turned up on her patch, but with two murder investigations on her hands, neither of which seemed to be going anywhere, she had more than enough to occupy her time. She had been tempted to refuse point blank to drive all the way to the mortuary unless the pathologist told her what this was about, but he had been so insistent, she hadn't liked to turn him down. It was important to stay on good terms with him. Not only was Miles Fellowes good at his job, he was willing to express opinions, unofficially. Geraldine recognised that his impressions might prove to be wrong. Certainly they couldn't be treated as any kind of proof. All the same, his instincts hadn't let her down yet. He had given her a few useful pointers when she had been in need of leads to follow up.

Miles' hazel eyes lit up when he saw her. He greeted her like an old friend.

'Geraldine, you're here at last. It's good to see you again. How are you?'

'I'm fine. A bit bogged down with work right now.'

'Sure.' He gave her a sympathetic smile.

She waited to hear his explanation of his summons, but he just turned and stared down at the body. The dead man was tall and lanky, with thinning light brown hair and cadaverous features. Lying flat out, naked, his legs and arms looked almost impossibly long. His belly was concave and his high cheek bones jutted out. Altogether he gave a bony impression that was singularly unattractive.

'He looks like a walking skeleton, doesn't he?' the pathologist commented, as though reading her thoughts. 'Although of course he's not walking any more.'

'Who is he?'

Despite her annoyance at being summoned to a post mortem when she was already overstretched, Geraldine was curious. Miles had been so insistent about seeing her.

'I thought you'd never ask,' he grinned. 'His name's Robert Wright, Wright with a W. Mid-thirties, unemployed – although he owned a van and from the state of his hands he did building work of some sort, odd jobs maybe. The body was discovered yesterday evening, dumped in a van at the back of some gardens in Finchley. The vehicle was reported as suspicious, and when the police arrived, they opened it up. It wasn't locked, and this is what they found.' He pointed at thc corpse. 'Must have been quite a shock for the poor constable who looked in the van.'

Geraldine was puzzled.

'If the Homicide Assessment Team called for a post mortem, they suspect there was something unlawful about this death. There must be a team investigating what happened to him.' She did her best to control her frustration at having her time wasted. 'To be honest, Miles, I don't know why you sent for me. I've got enough to be getting on with. This one here isn't my case. There must be a team working on it. I wouldn't want to interfere, even if I had the time.'

Unfazed by her outburst, Miles smiled.

'I called you straight away, because there's something here that's going to interest you. Trust me on this, Geraldine, you're not going to believe it.'

Miles' enthusiasm was infectious. In spite of herself, Geraldine was intrigued.

'Not going to believe what?'

'Well for a start, there's no doubt there was foul play of some sort here. The cause of death appears to be a fall from a considerable height resulting in several fractures. He fell backwards and the impact caused his skull to crack. He died from internal bleeding and head trauma.'

'So it's possible he sustained a fatal injury from an accidental fall and then crawled into the back of the van and died there?' Geraldine asked, interested in spite of herself.

'No, he was placed in the van – dragged in there rather clumsily – after he was already dead. And someone took the trouble to disguise the registration number of the vehicle with a neat job with duct tape.'

Miles paused, as though for effect. Geraldine waited. She knew he liked to rack up the dramatic impact whenever he disclosed particularly interesting or intriguing information.

'We found a trace of DNA on the body.' He lowered his voice. 'It wasn't his. I haven't talked to anyone else about this yet because the lab's only just confirmed it – at least they think they may have worked out what we're dealing with. I wanted you to be the first to hear about it.'

'Go on.'

'First of all, they matched the DNA to someone on the data base.'

'Yes? Go on!'

By now Geraldine had realised that this body must be somehow related to the investigation she was working on, but Miles' next words came as a shock.

'To begin with they matched it to David Robinson...'

Geraldine's jaw dropped, and he laughed.

'I thought that would surprise you.'

Carefully he explained how the DNA had, in part at least, been such a close match to Dave's that the lab had come up with his name straight away.

'It's only a partial match, but the body had been lying out overnight and they thought it could have been contaminated. So they were fairly certain – at least the probability was that they had identified the sample correctly.'

The blue van body had been discovered only about a couple of miles away from Dave Robinson's house, but the pathologist's claim made no sense.

'Dave Robinson's dead,' Geraldine said. 'He's been dead for two and a half weeks. Could his DNA be found on a dead man now? Could it have been a family member? He could have had a twin brother.'

It was common knowledge that twins tended to run in families.

Miles nodded. 'That's what I thought. So I queried it and asked them to look again. They said it was possible. Only Dave Robinson didn't have a brother, and this time they had a closer look and discovered long telomeres...' He broke off, seeing her expression. 'Put simply, DNA strands are copied each time a cell divides, and the telomeres protect the ends of the strands from damage when they divide. Each time a cell divides, the telomeres become a little shorter. The younger you are, the longer the telomeres are likely to be. It's not an exact science, and can only give an approximate indication of age, which isn't completely reliable, but the indications are that the DNA sample found on this body, the sample that is similar to Dave Robinson's DNA, comes from a boy who is young, maybe not yet into his teens.'

Geraldine stared at him in sudden understanding.

'Dave Robinson has ten-year-old sons,' she whispered, horrified.

Miles was sure the owner of the DNA had been in contact with the victim after his death.

'What about before he died?' Geraldine asked.

'It's impossible to say. But there was definitely contact after death.'

Geraldine struggled to accept what he was saying.

'So just to be clear, you're positive the young boy was there after the man died.'

'Yes.'

'How can you be sure?'

'There are flecks of the boy's dandruff on the dead man's face and a few landed in his eye. If he'd still been alive, he would have blinked and at least washed them down inside his eyelid, but they were right there, on his iris and one on his pupil. So the boy must have been standing above the body, perhaps leaning over it, after he died. But whether or not he was there when the murder took place, well that's for you to discover, isn't it?'

'Off the record, what do you think?'

'It's impossible to say.'

'Are you telling me a ten-year-old boy was involved in this man's death? A ten-year-old psychopath killed his father and then Robert

Wright, hitting them on the head?' Geraldine shook her head in disbelief. 'Could a ten-year-old be strong enough to overpower grown men like that?'

'Presumably he would have taken them completely by surprise.'

'Even so, would he have the physical strength?'

'That depends on the size and power of the boy.'

Geraldine thought about Caroline's twin boys. They had struck her as fairly slight. But there were two of them. The possibilities were growing more terrible by the minute.

'I thought you'd be interested.'

'Thank you,' she muttered.

Interested wasn't the word she would have chosen to describe her feelings.

57

RETURNING TO THE STATION, Geraldine decided to investigate Robert Wright's background. She was hoping to discover a connection between him and Dave Robinson's family. First she wanted to question Joe Wright who had reported his son missing the previous day. She went to find the sergeant who had taken the report. When he heard what she wanted to talk about, he became instantly defensive.

'How was I to know the bloke had been murdered? This man comes in to say his son's gone missing for the weekend, but a grown man going off for the weekend is hardly a reason to go raising the alarm, is it? I told him, there's plenty of blokes go off for a few days, especially at the weekend. There's nothing suspicious about it.'

'Why did he come in to report him missing? It seems a bit of an overreaction. Robert Wright was a grown man.'

'That's what I thought, but his father said he was upset about him disappearing like that, on account of his wife, Rob's mother.'

'What about his wife?'

He explained what the dead man's father had told him. 'OK, so his wife's sick, and his son shouldn't have gone off without telling them where he was, but there was nothing to suggest a crime had been committed. I wish I hadn't now, but I told his father to go home and not worry about it. I said I was sure he'd turn up. And now this. How was I to know the bloke had been murdered?'

Geraldine gave him a reassuring smile. 'You did nothing wrong. Like you said, you weren't to know something had happened to him. Now, where's the father's details? And has he been informed?'

Learning that the dead man's father had not yet been told about the murder, Geraldine decided to deliver the news herself. Before setting off, she conducted a brief investigation into the victim's background. Apart from a natural curiosity about a possible connection between Rob and Dave's sons, knowing a little about the dead man might help her to deal sensitively with his father. A bricklayer by trade, Rob was currently unemployed. The van in which his body had been discovered belonged to him. Besides the body, there were several cans of white paint, a bag of old sponges, and two large plastic buckets in the back of the van. She suspected the dead man had been moonlighting, doing odd jobs for cash. Whatever his activities while alive, he had never had any dealings with the police during his lifetime.

Before she had time to check his father's details, the desk sergeant called her. Rob's father had returned to the station demanding to know what the police were doing to find his son.

'He's not happy,' the sergeant warned her.

'I'll come over there straight away.'

She hurried down to the interview room where the sergeant had put Joe. He was sitting on a chair, gazing listlessly at the floor. He was thin, his bowed shoulders narrow inside a black jacket, his grey hair lank and greasy. Geraldine greeted him softly. When she introduced herself, Joe looked up at once. His eyes were bloodshot. Just in time, Geraldine remembered that Joe wasn't upset about his son's murder, but about his wife's illness. He hadn't yet heard that his son was dead.

'Joe,' she said gently, 'I'm afraid I have some bad news for you.'

'Is it my wife? I knew this would happen. She's dying, and he isn't even here. Where is he?' His face twitched in agitation. 'Is she dead yet? I need to get there.'

'This isn't about your wife.'

'Not about my wife? What then?'

'I'm afraid I have some bad news about your son.'

'Rob? Where is he? I'd rather he had the balls to come and tell me himself if he can't take it. It's not easy. It would be typical of him to bugger off...'

'Your son's not gone anywhere.'

'What do you mean? Where is he then?'

'Joe, I'm really sorry to tell you your son's dead.'

A shocked silence followed her announcement. Geraldine sighed, but there was nothing for it but to press on.

'I'm afraid your son's dead,' she repeated.

This time Joe shook his head. 'No,' he whispered. 'That's not right. It's not him. It's my wife. She's the one...' His voice tailed off and he stared at Geraldine with growing trepidation.

Viewing the dead didn't upset Geraldine unduly. They were past pain and misery. The people left behind were the ones who disturbed her, the ones whose torment would never end, as long as they lived. She spoke as gently as she could.

'I'm afraid it's true, Joe. Your son's dead. He didn't abandon you and his mother. He hasn't been to the hospital because he's dead.' She paused before adding helplessly, 'I'm sure he'd be here for you if he could.'

Joe seemed to gather himself together. His shoulders lowered slightly and he raised his head to look Geraldine in the eye. His voice remained steady as he asked what had happened. Geraldine hesitated to spell it out. Joe was already so vulnerable.

'We're investigating the circumstances of your son's death...'

'Investigating? What do you mean, investigating? Was he – is he – what happened? Tell me.'

Geraldine took a deep breath. 'Your son was discovered in the back of his van yesterday evening. He was dead.'

'Oh my God, this is so sudden. Was it his heart? I had no idea he was sick. He never said anything about it.'

This was the worst part of the job. Geraldine cleared her throat. There was no way to soften the words.

'We have reason to believe your son may have been murdered.'

The words were out. For a split second she was almost relieved that she had said it. Then Joe covered his face with his hands and let out a muffled howl. Geraldine waited. After a few seconds, he looked up at Geraldine with tormented eyes.

'What am I going to tell my wife?'

58

THERE WASN'T A GREAT deal of point in Geraldine going to inspect the van in which the body had been found, but she went along to the police vehicle pound all the same to look at a filthy blue van, scuffed and scratched in a few places. The interior was dirty. A dark stain indicated where the dead man's bloody head had been dragged across the floor. Apart from that, the van was empty. Two large plastic buckets and a grubby sponge had been taken away for examination. She studied photos of the number plates which had been altered with duct tape. Someone had been keen to disguise the identity of the van, which was registered to Robert Wright. The vehicle was taxed and insured. Everything about it was legal, apart from the murdered body of its owner in the back.

'It looks like he might have been a handyman,' a scene of crime officer commented. 'We found scratch marks and a few hard splinters that could have come from a ladder, but that's only speculation. It's the buckets and the cans of paint that gave us the idea, really. There's no evidence to substantiate it.'

Geraldine went to the local police station in Finchley Road to speak to the constable who had discovered the body in the back of the van. He was a young officer, barely out of training, who had been on patrol in the area. Bright-eyed, he was pumped about his recent discovery. 'Tell me exactly what you saw in the van.'

The constable looked surprised. 'There are lots of photos.'

'I know. I've seen them. But I want to hear from you, because you were there. You did see inside the van, didn't you?'

He grinned at that, glowing with self-importance. 'Oh yes, I was the first one there. I went right up and had a good look.'

Geraldine was slightly dismayed by his enthusiasm. A man had lost his life. It was not a subject for self-congratulation.

'Tell me what you saw,' she repeated.

She spent some time interrogating the young constable, but he could add nothing to what she already knew.

Her next visit was to Caroline. As she drove there, she tried to picture the two boys, one of whose DNA had been found on the dead man. It could have been DNA from both of them. Seeing them when she had met their mother for the first time, she had paid little attention to the two boys, and couldn't remember much about them. It had never even crossed her mind that one – or both – of them might be implicated in murder.

Caroline looked dazed, but her eyes flickered with recognition when she saw Geraldine. She made an involuntary movement to close the door.

'What is it?' she asked. Seeming to think better of her reaction, she added, 'have you found out who did it yet?'

Geraldine shook her head. 'May I come in?'

'Now's not convenient.'

Under the circumstances, it seemed a slightly strange response.

'Shall I come back later?'

'No. Say whatever it is you've come here to say, and then leave us alone.'

'Mrs Robinson, Caroline, we're doing our best to find out who's responsible for the death of your husband.'

Geraldine had the impression the widow's expression relaxed slightly. On a hunch, she asked if Caroline's two sons were home. Immediately the other woman's mouth tensed. The door she was holding onto inched towards closing. There was something Caroline wasn't telling the police about her sons. Geraldine took the plunge.

'I'd like to have a word with both your sons. It won't take a moment, but there's something they might be able to help us with. You can stay with them the whole time.'

'No, you can't see them. They're upstairs in bed.'

Geraldine was sure she was lying.

'Leave them alone,' Caroline went on with ferocious urgency. 'This has nothing to do with my boys. They've been through enough.'

Without any attempt to explain or excuse herself, she slammed the door shut. Geraldine couldn't be sure, but this struck her as more than a mother being protective towards her children. There was something wrong. She rang the bell again, but Caroline didn't come to the door.

'Of course there's something wrong,' Reg responded when she shared her concerns with him. 'The woman's husband's been murdered, and we don't know who did it.'

'I just think it was more than that. She was scared about my speaking to her kids.'

Instead of jumping down her throat for speculating without any evidence, Reg looked at her thoughtfully.

'Tell me what you're thinking,' he said.

With a rush of relief, Geraldine realised that she had passed some kind of unspoken test with her detective chief inspector. He was beginning to trust her judgement and listen to her impressions, ideas that he might quite reasonably have continued to dismiss as mere hunches. Gazing at a faint crack in the plaster on the ceiling, she considered how to word her concern.

'I'm thinking there's something going on that we don't know about.' She paused, aware that she sounded daft, but Reg didn't leap in to complain she was stating the obvious. 'Dave's widow didn't want me to speak to her sons, and we know their DNA was found on the body in the van. I just think we need to look into it. Is it possible...' She hesitated to say it.

'Is it possible a ten-year-old boy is implicated in two murders, including the death of his own father?' Reg finished her sentence. 'And the mother is covering up?'

Geraldine thought about her niece, not much younger than the twin boys who had lost their father, and frowned. She had believed nothing could possibly distract her from Nick's death, but this changed her mind. The evidence pointed to one or both of Dave's sons being involved in at least one murder.

'Where do we go from here?'

Reg sighed. 'I've been thinking about it and it seems to me it's time to bring Caroline Robinson in and see what she has to say.'

Geraldine nodded. This was going to be difficult.

59

MATTHEW WAS UPSTAIRS PLAYING on his old Xbox, when he thought he heard the doorbell. Dropping the game, he ran out of his room, eager to see if Ed had returned. It was boring at home without his brother. As he reached the stairs, he heard a stranger's voice. His mother had her back to the stairs and couldn't see him. The caller's head was hidden behind the door frame. He couldn't see her, so he guessed she couldn't see him, but he heard her say she was a police detective. Cautiously he lowered himself onto the top step, hoping to hear news of his brother. Neither of the women downstairs realised he was there, eavesdropping on their conversation. They were talking about Ed. He leaned forward, listening intently. His mother never told him anything. Anyway, he had a right to listen if they were discussing his twin.

The detective said she had come there to speak to him and his brother. His mother answered angrily. Saying nothing about Ed staying with a friend, she told the caller that both twins were at home in bed. Shocked, Matthew rose silently to his feet and stole back up the stairs to his room, wondering what was going on, and why his mother had lied about his brother. She would never have got away with it if his father had been there. Since his father's death, everything had become confusing. All he could be sure about was that his mother knew more than she was telling him. But what *did* she know? He stood at his bedroom door, straining to hear what the two women were saying, but all he could hear was a muffled murmur. Soon after, the front door slammed.

The next morning his mother barely spoke to him. That was fine with Matthew. She had been acting weirdly ever since Ed had disappeared. Ever since his dad had been killed, in fact. He made a half-hearted effort to complain again.

'How come I have to go to school and Ed doesn't?' he whined. 'It's not fair.'

'Nothing's fair,' she replied tersely.

'Where is he anyway?'

'Come on, it's time to go.'

'I haven't had breakfast.'

'It's too late.'

'But I'm hungry.'

'Get your shoes on now.'

He grabbed a couple of slices of bread and munched miserably as they walked.

His mother didn't remonstrate when he deliberately scuffed his heels on the pavement. Only when the school gate was in sight did she stop and look at him.

'Remember, you're not to tell anyone where Ed is.'

'How can I tell anyone where he is when I don't know? You won't tell me.'

'He's with a friend,' she replied vaguely, gazing around as though she was afraid someone might overhear their conversation.

'When's he coming home?'

'Soon.'

He remembered she had told a policewoman that he and Ed were both at home in bed.

'I don't believe you. You're a liar.'

She didn't answer, although he was standing right next to her.

'Go on, you'll be late,' was all she said.

'Who bloody cares?'

She didn't scold him for his bad language. She wasn't even listening. She didn't listen to anything he said. All she cared about was making sure Ed was off having a good time while he had to go to school by himself. He glared at her but she didn't react. He might just as well not exist for all the notice she took of him. Scowling, he spun round and raced towards school. At least he'd get lunch there.

His day didn't improve. Natty was being a dick, flicking bits of chewed paper at him. One of them hit Matthew in the eye and Natty sniggered. Matthew flipped. He leaped from his chair, which fell over with a clatter.

'Ow!' the girl sitting next to him shrieked. She pretended the chair had hit her leg, when it hadn't even touched her. Drama queen. Typical stupid girl. Matthew flung himself at Natty, pummelling him. Other kids started yelling out and laughing. Above the racket he dimly heard Miss shout that she was calling the headmistress. Meanwhile, Natty covered his face with his hands and backed off, crying. Satisfied, Matthew allowed a couple of the other boys to pull him away. They held on to his arms, while the rest of the class chanted, 'Fight! Fight! Fight!' They didn't shut up until the deputy head walked in.

Mr Dowling marched Matthew and Natty straight to his office. Natty was still crying. One of his eyes was half closed and puffy.

Aware that he was in trouble, Matthew went on the attack. 'He started it.'

'I didn't do nothing!'

'You were flicking bits of paper at me.' He turned to the deputy head. 'Ask anyone.'

Mr Dowling assured them that he would conduct a thorough investigation into their disgraceful conduct. Natty was sent to the school nurse to have his swollen eye seen to, leaving Matthew to face a boring lecture about appropriate behaviour in class, and proportionate response to provocation.

'What is your mother going to say about your disruptive and aggressive behaviour?'

There was a lot more along those lines. Matthew just shrugged. The days when he would have given a toss about upsetting his mother were over. She didn't care about him. It worked both ways.

Miss Threadgold asked to see Matthew at lunch break.

'What's your mother going to say?' she asked, gazing mournfully at him.

He didn't answer.

'Don't you think she's got enough to worry about right now?'

'It's all her fault.'

'No, Matthew. You have to take responsibility for your own actions,' she replied, and started on another lecture about treating other pupils with respect and all the rest of the stuff the teachers liked to rabbit on about. He just shrugged. Why should he care about other people? No one showed any respect for his feelings.

'She's a stupid bitch,' he said. 'She doesn't care about me.'

He was disappointed when the teacher didn't lose her rag with him. Instead she just looked sad and spoke very gently, as if he was some kind of retard.

'That's no way to talk about your mother. She must be finding it hard too, without your dad. I know it's difficult for you, and you've been very brave, but you can't go around fighting other boys. That'll only get you into trouble, and it's not going to make you feel any better, is it? If you want to talk to someone, I can arrange that.'

All at once he couldn't control himself any longer. It was such a long time since his mother had been kind to him. He wanted to shout that he never wanted to talk to anyone ever again, but instead he broke down in tears. Miss handed him a tissue, and he blew his nose loudly. He should have felt stupid, but he didn't care any more.

'It's only natural for you to miss your father. It would be strange if you didn't. It's painful, and it's hard, to lose someone you love. I really think it might help if you talked to someone about how you're feeling about what happened to your father.'

Talking wouldn't make things right. Of course he wished his life could go back to how it had been before his father died, but there was more to it than that.

He tried to explain. 'I'm not upset about my dad. I mean, I am, but it's not just that.'

He could tell she didn't believe him.

'What is it then?'

'It's not fair,' he snivelled.

'What's not fair?'

She was easy to talk to. It all came out in a rush, how his mother had let his brother go away, while he had to stay at home and go to school. It wasn't as though his mother was even being nice to him. His teacher was so sympathetic that he grew bold.

'I'm sure your mother cares about you both...'

'No she doesn't, and anyway she's a liar. She lies all the time. She lied about my brother. She told them we were both at home in bed yesterday, but Ed's not at home. He hasn't been there for ages.'

Miss looked puzzled. 'Who did she say that to?'

'A policewoman.'

He felt a flicker of triumph at having told the truth. His mother wanted him to keep his mouth shut, but why should he listen to her? She never listened to him.

60

THE FOLLOWING MORNING, AFTER the rush hour, Geraldine drove to Caroline's house. The twins were likely to be at school by the time she arrived, but that was fine. She wanted to talk to Caroline on her own first, to find out how much she knew. Any suspicion levelled at the children would have to be sensitively handled, and she needed to be sure of her ground before setting things in motion to question them. She was hoping there would be an innocent explanation for the child's DNA that had been discovered on the body in the van. But whatever the reason for the sample, there was no getting around the fact that one of the boys had been in close contact with the dead man after he was killed.

Caroline came to the door so promptly she could have been expecting a visitor. Dishevelled and bleary-eyed, she looked ill. Geraldine wanted to feel sorry for the recently bereaved widow, but it was worrying to think she was responsible for the welfare of children not much older than Geraldine's own niece. From her appearance, she looked as though she could barely take care of herself. This time she didn't try to shut Geraldine out. On the contrary, if anything she seemed to be in a hurry to invite Geraldine inside.

Once she had closed the front door, the difference in her demeanour was marked. She apologised at once for her hostility the previous day.

'I just don't want the boys to be involved in all this any more than they have to be. I mean, they've just lost their father. I don't want them to be upset with questions raking it all up again.'

It was reasonable enough for a mother to want to protect her children from further distress, after the violent loss of a parent. Recent events could hardly have been more traumatic for them.

If one of the children's DNA hadn't been found on another dead body, Geraldine would have been happy to leave them alone to cope with their loss as well as they could. As it was, she had to press on.

'I'm sorry, but we're going to need to speak to your sons. We'll do it very sensitively, and we'll be careful not to upset them. We have officers trained to speak to children.'

Caroline's smile vanished. Her eyes glittered warily and she took an involuntary step backwards, away from Geraldine.

'They're not here. They're at school. They didn't want to go back, but it seemed best for them to keep to their usual routine as far as possible.'

Geraldine inclined her head.

'That's why I don't want you talking to them. It'll only upset them all over again. Please, I'd like you to leave them alone. I don't want you – or anyone – talking to them about what happened. They need to be left alone to get over it. You're not helping!'

'I'm sorry, but something's come up that we think they can help us with. If you like you can bring them to the station after school. I can assure you they'll see an officer who's trained to speak to children, and you can be present the whole time. The last thing we want to do is upset them. Or we can come here, if you think they'll be more comfortable at home. We're just trying to establish what happened to your husband, and we think they may be able to help us. They won't be in any trouble, not at their age,' she added.

It wasn't an unreasonable request, given the circumstances, but the widow shook her head. With a scowl, she asked Geraldine to leave.

'Not until I have your assurance that we can speak to the boys.'

'They're at school,' she repeated, with a hint of desperation in her voice. 'Look, I want you to find my husband's killer, of course I do. But the boys were both with me all the time on Saturday. They were at football practice and then we came home and I made them supper and all the time he was…' She broke off in tears. 'I've told you all this. I gave a statement at the time. There's nothing more to say. Please, just leave us alone.' With a sudden burst of anger, she added, 'We're the victims here, me and my sons. You have no right to hound us like this. Now please, leave my house and don't come back until you've found out who killed Dave, and locked him up.'

Geraldine let herself out. It was true. Caroline was the victim. But the problem wasn't going to go away. There was no question about it. Her son's DNA had been found on another corpse. Until that point, Rob's death had appeared unrelated to Dave's. Now the whole murder investigation had taken a horrific turn. Geraldine drove away, resolving to return later, when the children would be home from school. There didn't seem to be much else she could do, short of going to the school and hauling the boys out of their lessons, which was unlikely to encourage them to talk.

Baffled and dejected, she returned to the station to resume going through documents but she couldn't settle to anything. She was troubled by an image of two young boys seated beside their mother, sobbing. She tried to picture the twins' expressions, wondering if there could be a clue there, but at the time she had focused on their mother and hadn't paid the children much attention. She hoped that hadn't been a mistake. In any case, the two boys were indistinguishable. Their DNA was identical. If one of them had been somehow implicated in murder, how would anyone be able to identify which twin was culpable? The whole situation was fraught with problems, and she couldn't see any way through it.

61

HE HADN'T SEEN HIS mother for ages. He missed her more every day, and he missed his brother so much it was a physical ache in his stomach, making him feel sick. They had never been separated before. At first it had been an adventure going off like that, all by himself. Brian had made him feel special because he had wanted only him, and not Matt. He had never gone away without his brother before. For the first time in his life he had felt independent, and free. Brian wanted to be called by his first name, not Mr Something, or Sir. It had seemed very grown up, addressing him by his name. The novelty soon palled.

It was over a week since he had gone home with Brian, and apart from the ice cream it was boring. Brian kept telling him his brother had gone away to another friend of their mother's, because she needed some time to grieve. Ed wasn't sure he believed him any more.

'How much longer do I have to stay here?' he asked.

Brian's face twisted so he looked ugly. Ed didn't like him any more.

'I'm disappointed in you,' Brian replied quietly.

Ed didn't care how Brian felt. He wanted to go home.

'Sit down. We need to talk.'

'I don't want to sit down. I don't want to talk. I want to go home.' He was close to tears.

'Sit down, I'll get you some ice cream, and then I'll explain why you can't go home.'

He spoke with an air of finality that scared Ed.

'I don't want any ice cream. I want to go home.'

Brian shook his head.

'You can't go home, not yet.'

'Why not? You can't stop me.'

'There's no point. The house is empty. Your mother's not there.'

'I don't believe you.'

'Why would I lie about it? Your mother's gone away to recover from the shock of losing your father. It's understandable, isn't it? She needs time to get over it. That's why you and your brother have come to stay with me and another friend of your mother's.'

'Why can't I see Matt? Where is he?'

Brian shook his head again, as though he was really sad about it. 'I'd like to take you there, and I would if I could, but it's too far away. And anyway, I'm not sure it would be a good idea to travel there right now.'

'What do you mean?'

Brian gazed at him earnestly. 'You know I care about you.'

Ed nodded his head, uncertainly.

'I promised your mother I'd look after you and keep you safe, and that's what I'm going to do, whatever it takes. There's something you need to know about. The people who killed your father, they want to kill you and your brother too. Matthew has been taken far away, somewhere they'll never find him, and the police have put your mother in a safe house. No one knows where you are. I managed to whisk you away in time, before the bad people caught wind of where you are. But it's not safe for you to go out of the house right now.'

Ed sat down. He thought about what Brian had said.

'What about the man who came looking for me here?'

'He was a scout. They must have sent spies out to all the people who knew your mother, all the friends she trusted. But he never went back to report he'd seen you.'

'Won't they wonder what happened to him?'

'They won't know for certain that he saw you. But they might find out what happened to him, and then they'll be back.'

Ed was really frightened now. He couldn't understand why Brian was talking so calmly. He jumped to his feet.

'We need to call the police.'

'No. We can't do that.'

'But the bad people might come back.'

'Yes. That's why we're going to hide you, somewhere safe, until this is all over. You have to keep very quiet if you hear anyone in the house, and not let anyone know where you are.'

'What if they see me?'

Brian smiled. 'Where you're going to be hiding, no one will see you. No one will know where you are but me. And I'm not going to give you away. You do trust me, don't you?'

Ed nodded although he wasn't sure if he trusted Brian or not. The first chance he had, he was going to run away. If he went straight to a police station, before the bad people saw him, he would be safe. He decided Brian was weird. He would never say as much to Brian, but he didn't trust him, not one little bit.

'Come on, then.'

'Where are we going?'

'Come with me.'

Pulling a torch out of his pocket, Brian led him to the hall where he opened a door to a narrow cupboard under the stairs. Ed had never looked in there before. Now he saw that it was packed with boxes and bottles of cleaning stuff. There was a broom, a dustpan and brush, a hoover and a bucket and mop. It smelled funny in there. With barely room for Ed to stand behind him, Brian opened a low door on the far wall. Crouching down, he clambered through the doorway and disappeared. His voice sounded echoey as he called out to Ed to follow him. Resisting an urge to turn and run, Ed manoeuvred his way past the broom and hoover, and squatted down on his heels to peer through the opening.

In the beam from Brian's torch, he made out a narrow wooden staircase that led down under the floor.

'Come on,' Brian called up to him. He couldn't see him in the darkness. 'It's a secret hiding place. No one but us knows it's here!'

Responding to the jubilation in Brian's voice, Ed felt a rush of excitement. This was a real adventure! Cautiously he made his way down the crude wooden staircase. The floor was dirty, covered in grey concrete. A few paces away, Brian face was lit from below. He looked ghastly, grinning in the white torch light.

'No one will be able to find you here, and you'll be safe as long as you stay quiet.'

Although it was an adventure, and Brian was with him, Ed was scared. Brian stepped back and was swallowed in darkness.

'I can't see,' Ed complained. 'I don't like it here.'

'I'll leave you the torch,' Brian said, suddenly brisk. 'There's a bucket when you need to go, and I've left you enough supplies to keep you going for a few days. No ice cream, because it would melt, but there's chocolate and sandwiches and fruit. It'll be fun, like camping. And you can sleep here.' He waved the torch around until it rested on a camp bed that was made up with blankets and a pillow.

'You'll be quite safe here,' he repeated. 'But you have to keep quiet. I'll leave you now but don't worry, I'll be back soon to see how you're settling in.'

He turned and walked towards the narrow staircase, the ground ahead of him illuminated in the beam of light.

'You said you'd leave me the torch!' Ed called out in a panic.

'Yes, I was just finding my way to the stairs. Here you are.'

He put the torch down on the bottom step, still switched on so its beam lit up the plaster wall. Hurriedly he climbed the stairs which were lit from above through the open door. Before Ed could remonstrate, Brian reached the top and scrambled through the opening.

'Wait,' Ed called out, 'wait! I don't like it here. I don't want to stay here by myself…'

The door closed with a sharp crack leaving him in darkness.

Cautiously he shuffled across to the torch. Seizing it, he tried to hold it steady, but the beam of light shook in his grasp making the shadows in the cellar move as though they were alive.

62

GERALDINE WAS ABOUT TO leave when she received a message that a woman was asking to speak to her.

'What's it about? Only I was just going to try and arrange to speak to Dave Robinson's sons – if we can get near them,' she added under her breath.

The sergeant who had brought her the summons grinned. 'That's what she said she wants to talk to you about.'

'I hope she's got them with her this time,' Geraldine said. 'I've heard enough excuses about why we can't speak to her sons.'

The sergeant shook his head. 'She's on her own.'

Geraldine set off for the interview room, prepared to be firm. Expecting Caroline, she was surprised to see a stranger waiting there. The woman didn't look much older than twenty. She had highlighted straight blonde hair that hung down to her shoulders, and a broad, pleasant face.

'Did Mrs Robinson send you?' Geraldine asked without any preamble.

'You mean Ed and Matthew Robinson's mother?'

'Yes. Did she send you to see me?'

'No. But I wanted to talk to someone about the twins.'

'What about them?'

'I'm their school teacher.'

Geraldine sat down. 'I'm listening.'

'I'm concerned about the twins, both of them. We all thought it was wrong to send one of them to school, and keep the other one off…'

'What do you mean? Weren't they both at school today?'

'No. Matthew came back to school almost straight away – possibly too soon – but we haven't seen Ed, not since their father's death.'

Geraldine hid her alarm.

'Where is Ed?'

'That's just it. We don't know. His mother told us he's staying with a friend of hers, which we all thought was a bit odd, keeping one son at home and sending the other one away, especially seeing as they're twins. But today Matthew said he heard his mother tell a police officer that Ed was at home. He might have got the wrong end of the stick, but if his mother *is* lying about it, I just thought maybe someone ought to look into it and find out exactly what *has* happened to Ed. Matthew genuinely doesn't seem to know where he is, and he's worried. He seems to think his brother just disappeared, so perhaps he has gone to stay with one of his mother's friends. I mean, it could be that Matthew misheard, or lied about what his mother said to your colleague. Kids do lie for all sorts of reasons, and it would be perfectly natural for Matthew to want some attention, given what's happened...'

Geraldine interrupted her. 'Matthew wasn't lying. I was the police officer their mother spoke to. I didn't realise Matthew was listening. His mother told me both boys were home and asleep in bed.'

The two women exchanged an apprehensive glance. There was no point in Geraldine trying to hide her anxiety any longer. She thanked the teacher for coming forward.

'Do you think something's happened to Ed?'

Deliberately Geraldine adopted a reassuring smile in an attempt to mask her true feelings. 'I'm sure there's a sensible explanation.'

It must have been obvious she was lying. She couldn't help wondering whether Ed was the twin who had been present when Robert's body had been moved. Perhaps he had seen too much. She thanked the young teacher for coming forward, assuring her they would keep her informed. As soon as she finished talking to her, Geraldine mustered a search team and returned to Caroline's house. She went to the door by herself. This time she didn't hold back.

'We'd like to come in,' she announced. 'I've got a team waiting outside. We can have a quick look around now, or we can come back later with a warrant and take the place apart.'

It wasn't much of a choice.

Caroline's face went white. 'The boys are asleep upstairs,' she blurted out.

As though to prove her wrong, one of the twins appeared in the hall behind her. He was fully dressed.

'Has Ed come home?' he asked.

There was no point in Caroline attempting to sustain her lie. Geraldine took a step forward and spoke softly so the boy couldn't eavesdrop again.

'Caroline, you need to tell me the truth. Something's happened to Ed, hasn't it?'

Caroline turned a stricken face to her, but said nothing.

'I can't help you if you keep lying.'

Tears welled up in Caroline's eyes, but her voice was curiously expressionless. 'No one can help me. Not now.'

'I will, if you tell me what's happened.'

Caroline turned and went inside, calling to her son to go upstairs. He just stood in the hall, watching. Geraldine followed her in and closed the front door. With a hurried glance at Matthew, Caroline ushered Geraldine into the front room and shut the door. She sat down facing Geraldine, and spoke quietly.

'Ed's been missing for eleven days.'

Geraldine was staggered. 'Eleven days? What do you mean?'

'He's been kidnapped.'

'You're telling me your ten-year-old son's been kidnapped and you didn't report him missing?'

Caroline glanced towards the door as though afraid Matthew might be listening. 'No, I did. I reported him missing.'

Struggling to control her sobbing, Caroline described how she had gone to the police station the day after her son's disappearance to tell them he had been kidnapped.

'It was the Monday. I went there as soon as Matthew was at school. I had to get him out of the way first because I'd told him Ed had gone to stay with a friend of mine.'

More lies. Geraldine wondered if Caroline could help it, and if it was reasonable to believe anything she said.

'I've been going out of my mind with worry,' Caroline burst out suddenly. 'Please, you have to help me.'

'Let's go through this step by step. When did this alleged kidnap take place?'

'Sunday night. And it's true. I know it is. He's called Brian.'

'Hang on, I want to go through this step by step,' Geraldine insisted. 'How did it happen?'

'I don't know. He went to the shop and he never came back.'

'How do you know he was kidnapped?'

'There was a note.'

'A note?'

'Yes. When he didn't come home, Matt and I went out looking for him and when we got home there was a note on the doormat. It was from Brian.'

'Have you still got it?'

Caroline pulled a scrap of flimsy paper out of her pocket. On it was written 'ED'. Nothing more.

'Is that it?'

'Yes. It was in an envelope but I don't know what happened to that.' She stared at Geraldine, appalled. 'I should have kept it, shouldn't I?'

Geraldine dismissed her regrets, assuring her the writer had probably been wearing gloves. The days of tracing criminals from their fingerprints were long gone. Geraldine picked up the slip of paper by one corner, and dropped it into her purse.

'So Ed disappeared on Sunday evening and you received this note through the door shortly after.'

'Yes.'

'And you said this note was from someone called Brian?'

Caroline explained how she had met someone from her junior school in the park, and he had kidnapped her son.

'What makes you think it was him?'

'I know it was.'

'And you said you went to the police ten days ago? What happened?'

'Nothing happened. They didn't believe me. I think it was because my headscarf looked weird.'

'Headscarf?'

Caroline described how she had worn a disguise when she had gone to the police station. The more the woman talked, the more far-fetched her story sounded, with a shadowy kidnapper threatening to kill Ed if she went to the police.

'I get it that the kidnapper doesn't want the police involved,' Geraldine said, as she struggled to make sense of the garbled account. 'But what *does* he want? Do you have any idea why anyone – why Brian might have wanted to kidnap your son?'

Caroline hesitated. 'No.'

Yet again Geraldine thought she was lying.

'Caroline, you have to tell me the truth.'

Caroline shook her head. Geraldine tried again.

'You're going to have to give me something more than that to go on.' Geraldine waited, but Caroline just began to sob. 'If you know anything, anything at all about the person who's taken your son, you must tell me.'

'His name's Brian and he went to Cartpool Junior School. We were there at the same time. And now he's taken Ed. That's all I know...'

Geraldine wondered if the woman was unhinged, whether by grief or guilt it was impossible to tell. If she hadn't already been mentally unstable before her husband's death, she might well be now.

'Did Ed have something to do with your husband's death?' she hazarded.

Caroline stopped crying abruptly. 'What do you mean?' She sounded genuinely shocked.

Geraldine pressed on. 'Did Ed know too much? Is your husband's killer the kidnapper? Caroline, help me out here. Why would anyone want to kidnap one of your sons? What's going on that you're not telling us?'

Caroline became agitated. She stood up in one swift movement and went to the door of the living room.

'I don't know what you mean. You have no right to come here making accusations. We're the victims here, me and my boys.'

'Caroline, you need to start telling me the truth. Is Ed here?'

'No. No. He's gone. He's gone. You have to find him. You have to find Brian.'

Bending double, she wrapped her arms around her waist and began to wail. That much at least was genuine.

63

MAX SAT, ONE LEG loosely crossed over the other, his head tilted on one side, listening attentively. Geraldine did her best to concentrate, but it was difficult to stay focused on the case with Nick's desk standing empty; the proverbial elephant in the room. For the time being at least the office was exclusively hers, but she didn't appreciate the solitude, not under these circumstances. No one was deliberately unkind, but her colleagues made it worse. Over and over again she had to listen to people telling her that she hadn't known Nick for as long as they had. Geraldine didn't disclose that it hadn't actually taken her and Nick very long to get to know one another.

Some officers were depressed about the loss of their colleague. 'I worked with him, on and off, for nearly twenty years,' a grey-haired detective constable said mournfully. 'You never had a chance to get to know him. He was a good officer. A great bloke.'

Others expressed anger about what had happened. Wherever she went in the police station she was met with the same refrain, 'You didn't really know him, not like we did.' She heard it so many times, she began to wonder if it was true.

'I shared an office with him,' she responded, but her colleagues just turned away, muttering that it wasn't the same.

'The same as what?' she wanted to shout. 'How about sharing my bed with him? Does that count as getting to know him?'

But she kept her feelings to herself.

It was true that she had only been in London for just over a year. Nick had been away when she had arrived. They had shared an office, on and off, for less than a year, and had barely exchanged civil greetings for much of that time. Their antagonism had begun with his flirting. Knowing he was married, she had resented his attentions. Her irritation had been fuelled by Sam's hostility towards Nick. Privately, Sam decried him as a womaniser who had slept his way around half the women at the station. Geraldine agreed with her. Conduct that would have been dubious in a single man was despicable in a married man.

Max nodded thoughtfully. 'Could she have killed her husband herself?' he wondered aloud. 'Perhaps the boy saw her, and she had to silence him?'

Geraldine was relieved that Caroline had an alibi for herself and her sons. The thought that a ten-year-old boy might be implicated in his own father's murder was hard to contemplate. Yet there was no getting away from the fact that a boy's DNA had been discovered on a second body.

'Perhaps it was him,' Max suggested.

'Yes, perhaps a missing ten-year-old boy has been battering grown men to death, felling tall men at a blow,' she replied gruffly. 'His mother discovered his secret, and is hiding him. But where is he?'

'Whichever way you look at it, it's all very odd.'

'Max, that's not helpful.'

'There couldn't be a mistake with the DNA, I suppose?'

She shook her head. 'We have to go with the evidence, however confusing or disturbing it is. But Caroline and the boys were at their football practice when Dave was killed.'

They gazed helplessly at one another. She wasn't sure whether to feel reassured to know that he was as worried as she was by the turn the case had taken.

A constable trained to question children had been interviewing Matthew. After listening to the recording, Geraldine went to speak to the constable.

'It was a bit awkward,' the constable admitted. 'Matthew's mother had told him Ed had gone to stay with a friend of hers. She's been doing her damnedest to cover up the fact that Ed's gone missing. Basically Matthew now knows she was concealing it from him, on top of everything else that's happened.'

'I suppose she didn't want to worry him.'

'He's hardly less worried now, knowing his brother's disappeared and his mother lied to him about it.'

'Do you think she knows where Ed is?'

The constable shrugged. 'It's difficult to be sure what she knows, because she's been lying all along, to everyone.'

It was time for Geraldine to interview Caroline formally. She had to find out the truth. A young boy's life might be at stake.

'No more lies, Caroline. We know you lied about Ed staying with a friend. That never happened, did it?'

Caroline sat motionless across the table from Geraldine in the interview room. Her face was dreadfully pale. She didn't answer.

'Caroline, it's imperative you tell me everything you know. We have to find Ed.'

An involuntary sob escaped Caroline's lips. At last she leaned forward and mumbled something. Geraldine asked her to repeat it.

'He never went to a friend. He was kidnapped.'

They were going round in circles. Geraldine spoke fiercely.

'Caroline, do you know where Ed is?'

The other woman shook her head. She looked too terrified to speak. Geraldine had a horrible feeling the woman was insane and had hidden him away herself – or worse. For the moment she decided to humour Caroline, and see where the line of questioning led.

'Can you tell me who kidnapped your son?'

'It sounds so final, hearing you say it like that.'

'Do you have any idea who's responsible?'

'Yes. I keep telling you. It was Brian.'

Caroline kept coming up with the same name. Geraldine suspected Brian's role in Ed's disappearance was a figment of Caroline's diseased imagination. Nevertheless she continued to act as though she believed what Caroline was saying.

'Where can we find him?'

'If I knew that, do you think I'd be sitting here, talking?'

'Tell me about Brian.'

Caroline launched into a convoluted account of a boy from her school she had met recently by chance on a park bench, where there were no security cameras. Caroline began to cry.

'He's not right in the head. He hasn't got any children of his own, so he's taken one of mine. You have to find him!'

Geraldine wondered whether this was another lie, to cover up for what she herself had done to her son. It was possible that she was a paranoid schizophrenic who had killed her own son and was blaming someone she had known years before. But there was also a chance she was telling the truth. The story she was telling was consistent with the earlier accounts she had given of someone called Brian kidnapping Ed.

'Does this have any connection to your husband's death?'

Caroline started, as though she had been slapped.

'No,' she whispered.

Once again, Geraldine was almost certain she was lying.

'Caroline, if we want to find Ed, you have to tell me the truth about everything.'

Caroline shook her head, weeping. 'I've told you what I know. Now you have to find Ed, please, before it's too late.'

64

THE ENTRANCE HALL TO the school looked pristine. It must have been recently redecorated. Glancing through the windows of several classrooms she passed, Geraldine saw that they were less well maintained. The signage led her to the headmistress' office. Seeing the door was open, she tapped on it and went in. The headmistress stood up to greet her visitor. She was a tall woman. With cropped grey hair and a square jaw, she could have been a man were it not for her calf-length plaid skirt and lipstick.

'Inspector Steel, is it?' she boomed, extending a large hand in greeting.

'Yes.'

'I'm Mrs Pennycook. I've been expecting you this morning. Now, what's this all about?'

Geraldine explained the purpose of her visit. When she finished, the other woman shook her head.

'I may look old enough to have been headmistress here twenty-eight years ago,' she said, smiling. 'I have been teaching for that long, but I'm afraid I've only been here for four years. Your enquiry goes back way before my time. You're looking for a boy called Brian? Do you have a surname?'

It was Geraldine's turn to shake her head. 'I'm afraid the only information we have is that he was called Brian, and he attended school here. That, and the fact that he has fair hair.'

'You're talking about a long time ago, and names can be unreliable.'

Geraldine understood Brian could have been a nickname. People sometimes changed their names. Nearly thirty years had passed since Caroline had known a child called Brian at school. But Brian was all they had to go on. She enquired whether the school kept records going back nearly thirty years.

'We should have complete records going back that far, yes.'

'Then we can look it up and see if there was a child called Brian in that year group.'

It took about twenty minutes to establish that the relevant list was no longer accessible.

'It must have been missed out when we moved everything onto computerised records,' the headmistress apologised. 'The only other thing I can suggest is that you talk to Betty Collins. She worked here for over twenty years, and she still lives just up the road. She retired when her husband died. He was school caretaker when I arrived. She might remember something, although I'm not sure how reliable her memory is these days. She still visits. She keeps a kind of archive of the school, school photos going back for years. She might be able to help you.'

Betty lived in a slightly rundown block of flats two streets away from the school. When Geraldine explained the reason for her enquiry, the old woman invited her in at once. Bright-eyed, sprightly in her movements, her face was wrinkled, her fingers twisted with arthritis.

'Ah, the children,' she said, with a sigh, as they sat down in her cluttered front room. 'We loved those children, Bert and me.' She leaned forward confidentially. 'Who did you say you were, dear?'

Her memory seemed more reliable when they moved to the subject of her time at the school.

'Brian? I'm not sure.' Her beady eyes grew distant. 'Oh yes, there was a Brian once, funny little thing he was.'

'Can you remember his full name? Please think. It's very important.'

The old woman shook her head.

'Now let me put my thinking cap on. His real name. Let me see. It's all a long time ago... the other children were very unkind to him, although he brought it on himself really. Nasty little lad he was. They used to tease him about his ginger hair. He used to cry a lot. The teacher – what was her name? – anyway, she called him a crybaby. Mrs Whittaker, I think it was at that time. Was it Mrs Whittaker?'

Geraldine asked to see the school photo from the year Caroline left the school and the old lady bustled off, returning with a box file labelled 1990s.

'I keep them all in the right boxes,' she explained with a touch of pride. 'Bert and me, we used to do it together. He was a stickler for keeping things in order.'

Alert now, she rummaged through the box and brought out a photograph of a class of children.

'Here you are, dear, this is the date, isn't it? Is this what you wanted?'

Geraldine stared at the faded photograph.

'And here's my list,' Betty went on. 'You'll see we kept them all in order, me and Bert.'

Geraldine studied it. Caroline's name was there, listed under her maiden name. There was one boy called Brian, who must have been the former classmate Caroline had spoken about. Assuming she hadn't been lying, they had met up again recently, just before Caroline's husband was murdered. It was hard not to jump to conclusions. Looking at the faded image, Geraldine was reminded of the old photograph she kept hidden in the top drawer of her bedside cabinet. It was a tenuous link to the mother who had given her up for adoption at birth. At the time, her decision to give her baby away had been made with her daughter's interests at heart. As long as the search continued, Geraldine could cling to the hope that her mother only continued refusing to have any contact with her out of a sense of shame. But she knew that might not be true.

Returning to Caroline's classmates, she studied the faded image closely.

'Can you tell me which one's Brian?' she asked, curious to see what he had looked like.

The old lady frowned. 'Let me see,' she said.

Propping her glasses on her nose, she peered at the picture, consulting the list clutched in her other gnarled hand.

'I remember Pamela,' she said at last, pointing out a mischievous-looking girl with short dark hair. 'She was a real tomboy. And that's Tommy.' She broke off with a cackle of amusement.

Geraldine tried to control her impatience. 'And Brian?'

Betty pointed to a boy with a pale pinched face and light hair.

'There he is, that's him.' Betty pointed to the boy then consulted her list. 'Brian Stanbury.'

'Brian Stanbury,' Geraldine repeated softly. 'I wonder what happened to him.'

The old woman shook her head and bent to retrieve her glasses.

'I don't know what happened to him. None of the children ever came back to visit, not once they left us.'

Geraldine thanked the old lady before she too left her. She had a name. Before long she was staring at an address too.

65

SITTING ON THE BOTTOM step, he cried until he felt as though someone had stamped on his head. His eyes throbbed when he closed them. When he opened them, the darkness scared him. He was frightened to move in case he knocked into something and hurt himself. He could bleed to death on the dirty floor, and no one would know. Brian had promised to come back soon, but he had been gone for ages. Ed didn't trust him. He said he had locked Ed up in the cellar to keep him safe, but he didn't feel very safe, alone in the dark. All he wanted to do was to go home to his mother and father and brother. Only that could never happen, because his father was dead. Nothing made sense any more. He didn't know why the people who had killed his father wanted to kill him too. Brian said it was because they were wicked, but that didn't explain anything.

Brian had assured him his mother and brother were safe. Ed hoped that was true, but he wasn't sure whether to believe it. Brian had promised he would be back soon, but Ed had no idea where he was, or how long he had been gone. If Brian had lied about returning, he might have lied about Ed's mother and brother too. In the beam of the torch, he made his way across the cellar to the bed Brian had shown him. It was just a hard wooden trestle bench pushed up against the wall, covered with a sleeping bag. He turned off the torch to conserve the battery and placed it under the bench where it would be easy to find. Then he lay down on the hard bunk, on top of the sleeping bag. He had to keep very still. The bench was so narrow he was afraid he might fall off if he moved. Lying perfectly rigid, he began to cry again.

He wept silently, in case the bad people returned. If he sobbed out loud they might hear him. After a while his nose felt bunged up and his head began to ache from crying, but he couldn't stop. He must have dozed off in the end because a noise woke him. He sat up, vaguely aware that he had heard a loud bang. It might have been in his dream. All at once he froze. There was no doubt this time. He could hear noises, the clumping of footsteps above his head and then a woman's voice, talking. He almost cried out, thinking it might be his mother. Just in time he remembered Brian's warning. The bad people might have returned. If they found him, they would kill him. Hearing more footsteps, he felt on the floor for the torch. Stealthily he crept across the floor, careful not to make a sound. Reaching the narrow staircase, he made his way up very slowly, holding the torch in one hand to light his way. If he fell he would make a din, and everyone would know he was there.

All was silent when at last he reached the top of the steps. Putting his head against the rough wooden door, he listened. There were muffled voices, but he couldn't distinguish any words. Gradually he was able to recognise Brian's low tones. The woman didn't sound like his mother, but it was difficult to hear her clearly. She must have been standing further away from the door under the stairs than Brian.

'I don't know why she would mention my name,' he heard Brian say. There was a muffled response and then Brian said, 'Yes, that's true. We did. Anyhow, it's all very sad.'

The woman moved within earshot. 'If you hear anything, let us know,' she said. 'We need to find this boy.'

There was another muffled exchange. He couldn't catch what the woman was saying but he distinctly heard Brian say, 'I would if I could, but he's not here. And I'm sorry to hear about Caroline.'

That clinched it. The woman wasn't Ed's mother. She must be another spy, out looking for him. He stood very still, remembering what Brian had told him about not being heard. There were more footsteps. The front door creaked open. Before it closed, he heard the woman's voice again. She was facing the hall now, so he could hear her quite clearly.

'Here's my card. Call the police station straight away if she contacts you again.'

The front door slammed shut. Too late Ed realised the woman was a police officer. She must have come to the house looking for him. If he had shouted, she would have rescued him. As disappointment seized him, he heard someone moving just the other side of the door. Before he could clamber back down the stairs, the door slid open and a bright light shone in.

'There you are,' Brian said softly. 'What are you doing on the stairs?'

'I heard voices,' Ed replied truthfully.

'I told you to stay still and quiet.'

'I never made a sound. Can I come out now?'

'No. That was another spy. They'll be back.'

Ed didn't want to play any more. 'I want to go home,' he said.

For answer, Brian closed the door. Ed was in darkness again. He pushed against the door but it stayed firmly shut. Miserably he switched on his torch. The narrow beam of light waved around the stairs and down into the cellar. It was like a dungeon. He was trapped. The police had come looking for him and Brian had sent them away. They wouldn't return. He began to cry again. But even as he shuffled wretchedly back to his bunk, snivelling, a plan was forming in his mind. He wasn't going to sit there and rot. Brian would have to return at some point with more food and water. When he did, Ed would be ready. Slowly he shone the torch all around the cellar, searching. After a while he shuffled over to the bunk bed where he sat down, weighing the torch in his hand.

66

AFTER TELLING MATTHEW TO stay put and not answer the door to anyone, Caroline ran down the drive and fumbled to unlock the car. Flinging herself behind the wheel, she turned the key in the ignition with a shaking hand. The engine purred into action straight away. She eased her foot off the brake and hurriedly manoeuvred the car away from the kerb. The other car was nearly out of sight by the time she set off in pursuit. There were no other cars driving along the side street where she lived. Having almost caught up with the inspector, she eased her foot off the accelerator to keep a discreet distance behind the other vehicle. She couldn't afford to be spotted. Several times Caroline had driven to the police station complex in Hendon and waited outside the car park, hoping to see the other woman emerge. Sooner or later, she hoped the inspector would drive to Brian's house. When that happened, Caroline wanted to be right on her tail, but so far she hadn't seen her leaving the police station. This time the inspector had come to her. It was too good a chance to miss.

At the end of the road, the inspector turned left onto Ballards Lane. Caroline hesitated to follow her too closely, and missed a gap in the traffic. Fretting about losing her target, she waited impatiently for another chance to turn onto the main road. The inspector wasn't driving especially fast. Even so, it was difficult to stay on her tail. Caroline couldn't stay directly behind her without risking discovery. What with anxiety about losing sight of the inspector, and fear of being seen, she was so stressed she had to make a conscious effort to drive sensibly. The knuckles on her hands looked almost white, she was clutching the steering wheel so tightly. She was feeling sick, but she had no choice other than to continue the terrifying journey. Convinced Brian had kidnapped Ed, she was desperate. Her only chance of discovering where he lived was to follow the inspector. Waiting at home doing nothing was driving her insane. Her plan to follow the inspector around might fail, but she couldn't think what else she could do.

It was quite likely the inspector was headed to another destination entirely, but if she wasn't going to Brian's house now, then she might do so later. Caroline determined to stay on her tail until the inspector led her to the house where she was convinced Ed was being held captive. The police didn't believe her when she told them Ed had been kidnapped. She had no alternative but to take matters into her own hands. She would never normally have had the guts to chase a police car through the streets of London. At every second she was afraid the inspector would slam on her brakes and demand to know why she was being followed. But more terrifying than the prospect of being challenged was her fear of losing sight of the inspector.

The car she was following drew to a halt outside a house just a few streets away from where Caroline lived. Edging into a parking bay a few spaces away, Caroline sat hunched over her steering wheel, shaking. Her relief at having reached the end of the journey was so strong she wanted to cry. The inspector climbed out of her car and crossed the road. Tense with hope and fear, Caroline watched her walk up to a front door. She paused on the doorstep, apparently talking on her phone. While the inspector was hanging back, Ed might be locked up, hungry or in pain. He was bound to be frightened. Under her breath, Caroline cursed the inspector for being so slow. At last she reached out and rang the bell. Caroline held her breath.

For a long moment, no one came to the door. Tormented by anxiety, Caroline sat, waiting helplessly. The chances were that she had followed the inspector to a house that had nothing to do with Brian. She could be visiting a friend, or a family member, or following up a lead in another case entirely. Caroline's hands dropped from the steering wheel. She crossed her fingers. It was equally possible that Ed was in there, out of sight, concealed inside that house, behind those brick walls. She stared keenly at each of the windows in turn, willing Ed's face to appear. Darkness gaped back at her, giving nothing away.

She seemed to have been waiting for hours when the front door finally opened. Whoever was in the house remained obscure, shielded by the caller. Caroline shifted in her seat, trying to see past the inspector. As though to accommodate her, the detective moved to one side to reveal a man with a head of straggly ginger hair. From that distance Caroline couldn't make out the man's face, but she could see enough to know that the inspector was talking to Brian. They stood on the doorstep for a few minutes. Finally the police inspector followed Brian inside the house and the door closed behind them.

'Find my son,' Caroline whispered. 'Come back out with my son. Don't you dare come out without him.'

At last the inspector emerged, tall, dark and elegant. She was alone. Numb with disappointment, Caroline watched her stride across the road to her car, and drive off down the road. Ed wasn't with her, but Caroline had discovered where Brian lived. No longer worried about being spotted, she sat up and watched the other car vanish into the night. The inspector had brought her to Brian's house. All at once, she felt a wild excitement.

67

BRIAN STANBURY LIVED SIX blocks away from Caroline's road. The fact that he lived so close to Caroline meant it was quite likely they had bumped into one another recently. That might have given her the idea to use his name to throw the police off the scent if she herself was guilty of some wrongdoing. Geraldine was convinced she was hiding something, she just couldn't tell what it was. And at the centre of Caroline's secrecy, a small boy had disappeared.

After Nick's death, they had all been warned to be especially careful. There was a possibility that someone was targeting police officers. Under normal circumstances, such a warning would have been unnecessary because Geraldine was usually deliberately conscious of her surroundings. Distracted by the investigation, she hadn't been as alert as usual. Walking down the path, she noticed a car parked opposite. Someone was seated at the wheel, and was watching her. With a shiver, she hurried to her car. Nick had believed someone was following him shortly before he died. Now it seemed to be happening to her. When she looked up again, the figure had vanished.

She drove away fast. There was only one other car travelling along the side road where Caroline lived. For a few moments it appeared to be following her, but when she turned onto the main road she lost the other car in traffic before she could see its registration number. She wasn't sure whether she ought to report the incident, but decided to wait and see if she noticed anything else suspicious. So far she had no grounds for her paranoia, apart from a general awareness of the need for increased vigilance.

The man in the doorway raised his eyebrows inquisitively

without speaking. His face relaxed into a tentative smile when she identified herself.

'How can I help you?' he asked in soft, cultured tones.

He was skinny, and his fair complexion was pock-marked from past acne. With pale watery eyes, and light ginger hair, he wasn't good-looking, but his gentle voice inspired confidence. At least he hadn't reacted aggressively to her presence on his doorstep. Increasingly, members of the public were hostile when the police came calling. Older officers grumbled about the lack of respect they were shown. In some areas the situation had become so volatile members of the force were reluctant to make house calls on their own. The change in the public perception of the police was an issue that exercised the higher powers within the force but, as in all the services, it was the officers on the ground who bore the brunt of the dwindling deference they were accorded on the streets.

Brian appeared to entertain a healthy old-fashioned respect for her position.

'I'd like to ask you a few questions. May I come in?'

He hesitated for only a second before nodding his head. Walking quickly, he led her to a small kitchen at the back of the house. When they were both seated, Geraldine brought up Caroline's name. Initially he looked puzzled, then he nodded in recognition.

'Oh yes, Caroline,' he said. 'We were at school together, but it was all a long time ago. I haven't seen her in years – that is, I hadn't – and then we bumped into each other in the park the other day. I recognised her straight away!' He smiled fleetingly. 'But what's this about? I really hardly knew her. We just happened to be in the same class at school. Longer ago than I care to remember – it must be more than twenty years ago. It was only chance that we happened to meet again, after so long. Why? Has something happened to her? I'm sorry, I'd like to help, of course, but I can't see how I can. We were only children. I don't know anything about what she's up to these days, or what happened to her after we left junior school.' He paused, thinking. 'She had some children with her the other day, so she might have changed her name since I knew her, got married I mean. She was Caroline... no, I'm sorry, I can't remember her surname at school. It was a long time ago.'

'Caroline gave me your name.'

'Did she?' He looked perplexed, but not at all worried. 'Why?'

He smiled and put his head slightly on one side, waiting for her to respond. He was intrigued. Geraldine hesitated. Apart from a pipe creaking and gurgling somewhere above their heads, the house was silent. It was hard to believe a healthy ten-year-old boy was being held prisoner there against his will. She pressed on, unsure of her ground.

'Caroline has lost one of her sons.'

'Oh dear. How did he die?'

Geraldine explained that Ed had disappeared.

'You mean he's gone missing? That's awful,' he stammered, visibly shocked. 'Poor Caroline. What a terrible thing to happen. I thought her children were quite young – too young to run away from home. But it seems kids grow up so fast these days. The influence of television, perhaps? But how can I help?'

'We have reason to believe the boy's been kidnapped.'

'Kidnapped? Are you sure? He couldn't have fallen and hurt himself, or lost his memory? Because who would do such a thing? I mean to say, I didn't get the impression she had much money, but then you can't always tell, can you? I suppose you've contacted all the hospitals, and searched everywhere? If she lives round here, well, there's a park just a few streets away…'

Geraldine nodded. A search party had been deployed and another team was busy going door to door, asking if anyone had seen the missing boy.

'We're doing what we can.'

'Yes, I'm sure you are. I'm sorry. I shouldn't be telling you how to do your job. It's just so shocking when anything like this happens to a child. I mean, it's terrible when something bad happens to adults too, but somehow it seems worse to hear about crimes against children. But are you sure he hasn't had an accident? What makes you suspect he was kidnapped? That's not common around here, is it? I've lived here for over ten years and I've not heard of any children being kidnapped before.'

Geraldine shrugged. The only evidence that Ed had been kidnapped had come from Caroline, and she was hardly a reliable witness. Leaving aside the fact that she appeared to be distraught at her son's disappearance, there was a chance she had levelled the accusation against Brian to divert police attention away from herself. If her son had discovered she had arranged her husband's murder, bumping into a loner like Brian might have seemed like a godsend. Living alone, gentle, and amenable, he could be an ideal scapegoat. Having met Brian, Geraldine couldn't help thinking it even more likely that Caroline was responsible for Ed's disappearance. In seeking to silence her son, Caroline was hiding something. And it was pretty clear what that was.

'I'm sorry to have troubled you,' she said, getting to her feet.

She wondered whether she should ask for permission to search the house.

'If there's anything I can do...'

'I'd like to have a quick look around, while I'm here.'

For the first time, he looked worried. 'It's all a bit of a mess,' he said.

He led her from the kitchen through the hall to a small living room and dining room. Both were empty.

'I've seen places that are far untidier than this,' she assured him, and he smiled, relieved.

Upstairs was similarly empty. He pulled down a ladder so she could stick her head into the loft and shine her torch around. There was nothing up there except a few cardboard boxes.

'Is there a shed in the garden?'

'No. You can see the garden from in here.'

As he led her back into the main bedroom, his phone beeped.

'Oh no,' he burst out, sounding exasperated. 'Look, I'm really sorry, but I need to go out. I'm supposed to be meeting someone. You're welcome to come back and look around some more another time, although I don't know what you're hoping to find here.' He shrugged, almost dismayed that he had nothing to show her.

'That won't be necessary.'

They went back to the hall. Glancing around, she noticed a small door under the stairs. Visions of Harry Potter's bedroom flashed into her mind.

'What's in there?'

He grew jittery, and glanced at his watch.

'That? Oh, that's just the broom cupboard. You can look inside if you want to. It won't take a second. But then I really do have to go.'

He gave a shamefaced shrug and muttered something incoherent about going on a blind date. Quickly she stepped across to the door and pulled it open. With a glance she took in a hoover, broom, dustpan and brush, ironing board and iron. She closed the door.

'I told you it wasn't very interesting,' he said, almost apologetically.

He was sweating slightly, anxious not to be late for his date.

'Thank you, Mr Stanbury. I won't keep you any longer.'

She considered wishing him good luck on his date, but decided to maintain a professional detachment. He had been embarrassed enough by her intrusion.

68

THE CRASH OF THE slamming front door reverberated in his ears. Brian stood in the hall, staring at the discoloured wallpaper, shaking with fury. After all he had done for Caroline, it was hard to believe she had let him down so badly. Disregarding his warnings, she had gone blabbing to the police. He had been a fool to trust the bitch. Not after this. He glared around wildly. He would have to leave the house before the police came back. He didn't trust that detective. Whatever she had said, he knew he hadn't seen the last of her.

Still trembling, he raced upstairs into the spare room and found his suitcase, dusty and brown, at the back of the cupboard. He had been afraid his wife might have thrown it away. As he yanked it out, a faint mist of dust rose from it, making him sneeze. In the doorway he turned his head to look back over his shoulder. The spare room looked empty without the boy there. He felt a pang of loneliness, but this was not the time to hang around feeling sorry for himself. He had to get out of there quickly, before the police returned. Fighting to control his panic he ran into his own bedroom, flung the case on the bed and opened the wardrobe. Hurriedly selecting clothes, he folded them quickly and stuffed them in. The case had wheels which meant he would be able to cram it full and still be able to drag it around with him. Ignoring anything formal, he packed jeans, shirts and jumpers. With no idea where he was going, he had to be prepared for all climates. He wouldn't be able to take much with him apart from clothes but that didn't matter. Most of the stuff in the house had belonged to his wife. He had no need of her clutter.

A thought struck him and he hurried downstairs to fetch his spare trainers. Shirts and trousers would be easy to replace, but he had no idea if he'd be able to buy comfortable shoes where he was going. If he could get to America, all well and good. He would be able to speak the language and buy whatever he needed. That said, he had to be prepared to end up anywhere. The more remote his destination, the less likely he was to be traced. Off the beaten track, decent shoes might be difficult to come by, even if he could explain his requirements. He pounded back upstairs and shoved his trainers in the bottom of the case, underneath his clothes. He pulled open the second drawer of his bedside cupboard. Passport, driving licence, even his birth certificate was there. He thrust them all into the black leather bag and put it down on the bed. It had a long strap that enabled him to wear it slung over one shoulder. That way he could keep his hand over it. He had bought it for travelling, back in the days when he was still married. His wife had laughed at him, calling it his 'man bag'. He had never used it, but he was glad now that he hadn't chucked it away. At last he closed his case and lugged it downstairs. It was time to go.

Now that he was ready to leave, he hesitated over whether to take the boy with him. He would miss his company if he left him behind, but he couldn't ignore the fact that the boy had been difficult all along. He had never really settled, constantly whining and nagging to go back to his mother. The reality of their friendship had never lived up to Brian's wishes. In common with everyone else Brian had ever met, the boy had disappointed him. Given time, things could have turned out very differently. Seduced by the idea that he and Ed might go travelling around the world together, Brian had done his best to establish good relations with the boy. But time had run out. Caroline had put paid to that. He had to abandon the idea, as he had done with so many other dreams.

He would have liked to deliberate for longer, but he had to make up his mind quickly. The only sensible option was for him to leave by himself. Apart from any other considerations, it was hard to imagine he could succeed in taking the boy out of the country without attracting attention. The police were bound to be looking for a man travelling with a ten-year-old boy. Going alone would enable Brian to get out of the country safely. Even if Ed agreed to accompany him quietly, it would be too risky. He paused in the hall and looked around for a moment. This house had been the scene of his only real happiness in life, and his most desperate grief. The walls resonated with the extremity of the emotions he had suffered while his wife was alive. It would be a relief to get out of there and start a new life somewhere else. He should have done so years ago. He took a deep, juddering breath and opened the front door. He had no idea where he was going. He only knew that he had to get as far away from the house as possible, before the police came back. He would leave, abandoning the property to the many species that lived there unseen, rats and mice under the floorboards, ants and woodlice that would crawl out of the skirting boards, spiders and beetles and other kinds of insects.

And the boy in the cellar.

69

GERALDINE WAS GOING THROUGH everything, step by step, checking and cross checking. So far she had failed to put the fragments of information they had gathered together in the right order, missing a vital lead. She wasn't optimistic as she drove back to the old people's home where Eve's aunt lived, to double check Eve's alibi. All the same, someone had lied to them. She couldn't take anyone's word at face value. The London roads seemed to be more congested every day, but at last she reached her destination. The exterior of the brick nursing home was unprepossessing, but well-maintained. Inside there was a pleasant atmosphere. The manager saw Geraldine through the window and recognised her straight away.

'You're here to see Jane Arkwright, aren't you?' she asked with a bright smile as she came out of her office into the foyer. 'You won't go upsetting her, will you? She's very frail.'

Geraldine reassured her without giving away the reason for her visit.

'She's not been getting into mischief, has she?'

The manager laughed, but there was a slight edge to her voice.

Lowering her voice confidentially, Geraldine explained that she was interested in tracing the movements of Jane's niece on the evening of her visit to the home.

'May I ask what this is about? This isn't the first time you've been here asking questions, and we don't want to go upsetting our residents. Is Jane's niece suspected of being involved in some trouble? Nothing illegal, I hope. Only we have a duty of care...'

'I'm afraid the reason for the investigation is confidential. All I can tell you is that we're looking into the movements of a number of people, and at this stage we're simply eliminating possible suspects. In fact,' she added firmly, 'Jane's niece is voluntarily helping us with our enquiries. I'm afraid I really can't tell you any more than that.'

After remonstrating half-heartedly about being busy, the manager took Geraldine into a small office. The visitors' records confirmed that Eve had visited her aunt on the evening of Nick's murder. She had arrived at seven and left just before ten.

'We don't usually have visitors staying so late. The residents get tired,' the manager said.

The timing of Eve's visit was certainly convenient, given that Nick had been killed between eight and nine that evening.

'Did she usually stay so late when she visited?'

The manager frowned. 'Her visits have tended to be on and off, in the long term. She'll visit fairly regularly for about six months, then we won't see her for a while, and then she starts coming again. She made some excuse about not being able to drive for a while but, to be honest, it's not unusual for visitors to be unreliable.' She sighed. 'It would help the residents so much if visitors would be more consistent, but you can't make people turn up regularly. Everyone leads such busy lives these days.'

Geraldine gave a sympathetic nod, thinking guiltily how rarely she made time to visit her sister.

Once she had agreed to co-operate, the manager became quite chatty.

'We see a lot like that. Family members who rarely visit frequently suffer a sudden attack of guilt – often brought on by the prospect of an imminent inheritance,' she added in an undertone.

Geraldine enquired about Eve's other recent visits. Although she had been hoping to hear the date of Dave Robinson's murder, she was nevertheless shocked when she heard it in the list the manager read out. After arranging for scans of the entries in the visitors' book to be emailed to her, Geraldine went to speak to Jane Arkwright. A question was beginning to form in Geraldine's mind about Eve, but she had to be sure her theory stacked up before taking it to Reg. He might be reluctant to accept that the killer they were hunting for was his dead colleague's widow.

This time the manager didn't escort her to Jane's room.

'You know the way. It's along the corridor to your left, four doors along. You'll see her name.'

'Thank you.'

The old woman was seated in exactly the same position as she had occupied on Geraldine's previous visit. Ensconced in an upholstered armchair, with her feet resting on a foot stool, she barely stirred when Geraldine entered. Gazing around the impersonal decor and furnishings, Geraldine could understand why someone might prefer to sit gazing out of the window all day, even though the view wasn't spectacular. Through the window, a narrow path was visible. It ran between a tall hedgerow and a small patch of mown grass. A reasonably fit adult could sprint along the path in a few minutes. By skirting the hedge, they might reach the street without being seen from Jane's room.

Seeming to notice Geraldine for the first time, Jane looked up and smiled vaguely at her.

'Do I know you?'

Eve's aunt was unlikely to be much help as a witness. Mumbling reassuring platitudes without really knowing what she was looking for, Geraldine went over to the window. The sill was low, the single pane of glass quite large. With a quick jerk of the handle, she pulled the window wide open. It would be easy enough to climb out of it. For a moment she was lost in a mental image of Eve straddling the window sill before vanishing into the darkness outside.

Jane's querulous voice recalled Geraldine to the present.

'There's a bit of a draught. I don't like to have the window open. It's not safe to leave it open. What if someone gets in?'

The old lady sat watching with a worried expression as Geraldine closed the window.

Back in the office, Geraldine thanked the manager and said she was leaving.

'Well, if there's anything else we can help you with, just give me a call.'

Geraldine spoke in as casual a tone as she could manage. 'There is one more thing. What kind of security do you have in the ground floor rooms?'

'I'm not sure what kind of security you mean,' the manager

replied, at once on her guard. 'We have a burglar alarm, as well as smoke alarms, and alarm cords in every room. Our residents are perfectly safe here. We had an outstanding inspection report...'

'The burglar alarm is on at night, presumably?'

'Every night.'

'But what about during the day? What's to stop residents walking out?'

'There's always someone on duty here, keeping an eye on the exit. I'm really not sure...'

'Someone could leave through a window?'

The manager laughed. 'Most of our residents can barely walk through the door. I can't see any of them climbing out of a window!' She laughed again, genuinely amused.

Geraldine didn't stop to explain that she hadn't been thinking about a resident leaving the building unseen.

70

As she drove to Nick's house, Geraldine tried to make sense of the recent events. Uppermost in her mind was the missing boy. Brian appeared to be on the level, and Caroline's accusation sounded implausible. There seemed to be no reason why Brian should have randomly kidnapped Ed. Yet there was evidently something connecting the two former classmates. They both admitted to having met by chance, just before Dave's death. Still puzzling over it, she drew up outside Eve's house. Only a couple of weeks ago it had been Nick's house. Every day, Geraldine's grief grew sharper. Usually she coped with any personal problems by immersing herself in work. Now, whenever she sat in her office, his empty desk beside her was a constant reminder of his absence. Even without that she would have found it impossible to stop thinking about him, since she was involved in the investigation into his murder.

Several times she had considered telling the detective chief inspector that she wanted to step down. Before taking the case on, she had been confident she could cope. She had been desperate to hunt for Nick's killer. By the time she had realised that the case was too personal for her to manage in a detached manner, it was too late to withdraw. She would have had to admit the truth about her relationship with Nick, exposing herself as a liar as well as promiscuous. Her reputation would never recover. She had to leave Reg ignorant about her emotional involvement with Nick. As far as he was concerned, they had been no more to each other than colleagues who had established friendly relations after a difficult start. They hadn't known one another for long. She had no choice but to tough it out and see the case through to its conclusion, however difficult it was for her.

Identifying a killer who had claimed more than one victim was always urgent. This time it was even worse than usual. Until the case was over, it was impossible to drive out the memory of her night with Nick. It haunted her waking thoughts and plagued her dreams. Once she woke in the morning expecting to see him lying in bed beside her. Returning to reality was painful. Her colleagues were all in various states of shock over what had happened to Nick. No one paid any attention to the signs of exhaustion Geraldine saw when she glanced in the mirror.

Geraldine had never seen Nick's house while he had lived there. Now her curiosity was like an uncomfortable itch. She wanted to see where he had worked at home, where he had relaxed in the evenings, and where he had eaten. She was desperate to know whether he had lied about no longer sharing a bedroom with his wife. She tried to concentrate on Eve, who reiterated her account of where she had been on the evening of Nick's murder.

'How often did you visit your aunt?'

Eve looked slightly uncomfortable. 'Not as often as I should,' she admitted.

'And how long did you usually stay?'

'I don't know. I didn't time my visits.' She paused. 'It just depended on how she was feeling.'

'And how was she feeling on that evening in particular?'

'Fine. Now if that's all, there's really nothing more I can tell you. I'd like to help you, but I can't.'

Remembering the window in Jane Arkwright's room, Geraldine considered the possibility that Eve was guilty. She looked fairly fit. She could easily have climbed out through the window without anyone knowing, run to her car, driven home to kill Nick, and returned to the old people's home without being seen. Her aunt was too confused to notice what had happened. It would have been risky, but it was possible.

'Did you kill your husband?'

Eve's cheeks flushed dark red. Her eyes brightened with suppressed outrage.

'I can't believe you're asking me that. You do know who my husband was?' She stood up, her voice quivering with indignation. 'How dare you speak to me like that? My husband was an inspector.

I don't think Reg is going to be very impressed when he hears what you've been here accusing me of.'

'I'm just doing my job, Mrs Williams. We need to eliminate you from the enquiry. The quicker we can get through this, the sooner I'll be off.'

'Eliminate me by accusing me of murdering my own husband,' Eve muttered, but she sat down again. 'I've told you where I was. You can go there and check.'

Geraldine didn't say that she had done just that, and her visit hadn't helped Eve's case. She leaned forward in her chair. 'Help me out here, Mrs Williams – Eve. I'll be frank with you, we're all at sea. Why would anyone have wanted to kill Nick?'

Eve shrugged. 'I don't know. Haven't got the faintest idea. That's your job, isn't it, to find his killer? One of the criminals he arrested, I suppose.'

'Have you ever met a man called Dave Robinson? Or his wife, Caroline?'

'That's the victim of another attack, isn't it? Do you think the murders are linked?'

'Have you ever met him or his wife?'

'No. I'd never heard the name until Reg mentioned it, and of course it's been all over the news. The papers are saying there's a serial killer, but why target a police officer and then some plumber or electrician?'

She sounded genuinely baffled. Geraldine tried one more time.

'You must have known your husband was unfaithful.'

Eve stared straight at her, unblinking. 'Was he? That's an extremely nasty rumour to go spreading around about a man who can't answer for himself.'

'It's more than a rumour. How did it make you feel?'

'Your opinion of my husband is of no interest to me. It's not your place to spread gossip and lies. I don't want to hear it. For the purposes of your elimination process, I didn't kill my husband in a jealous rage. Why would I have done? He wasn't unfaithful. We were happily married. I didn't kill him, I didn't kill that other man; in fact, I'm sorry to disappoint you if you've got it into your head that I'm a serial killer, but I haven't killed anyone. Now, get out of my house.'

Geraldine wanted to ask her why she had lied about Nick staying out the night before he was killed, but there was no point. She could only challenge Eve by admitting how she herself knew Nick hadn't been home that night. Even if she established Nick's whereabouts, Eve would claim ignorance. She could easily say she had fallen asleep and not realised he hadn't been home that night. Or she might accuse Geraldine of lying, and complain about her. Geraldine turned to a different line of enquiry.

'A ten-year-old boy has disappeared.'

'Well, I'm sorry to hear that, but it has nothing to do with me. I'd like you to leave.'

There was no reason for Geraldine to stay. If Eve was innocent as she claimed, then she would be quite within her rights to report Geraldine for inappropriate conduct, knowing that Reg would listen sympathetically to her. She could dress it up as harassment or something. But Geraldine couldn't shake off the suspicion that Eve was guilty of killing Nick. Her alibi gave it away. That, and the fact that she lied about Nick's infidelity. She had to have known about it. But Geraldine couldn't accuse Eve of lying without admitting her own relations with Nick. She wasn't sure if it was worth the risk. Not for the first time, she bitterly regretted the night she had spent with Nick.

71

GERALDINE WASN'T ON duty on Sunday but she drove to the office to discuss her theory with Reg, judging it better to approach him face to face. He wasn't in a good mood. Nevertheless, she broached the subject of her suspicions concerning Eve Williams. Reg listened without interrupting, a strained expression on his face.

'You think she's guilty because she has an alibi?' he repeated, a quizzical frown on his face.

'I checked her alibi. It doesn't stack up.'

'Well, alibis aren't always watertight. Plenty of innocent people don't have alibis at all. A dodgy alibi means nothing. It's certainly not evidence of guilt.'

'Eve's visits to her aunt were often infrequent, but she went there five times in three weeks, and two of her visits were at the times Dave and Nick were murdered. It can't be coincidence...'

'Well, it can be, and it clearly is. Coincidences are not as rare as you might think.'

'Plus we know she lies.'

'Indeed?' He raised his eyebrows.

Ignoring the menace in his tone, Geraldine ploughed on. 'Eve insists Nick was faithful to her.'

'And for all we know he was.'

'He wasn't.'

'You mustn't believe all the tittle tattle you hear around the station.'

Geraldine bit her lip.

'You do realise what you're accusing her of?' he asked.

'I realise I'm suggesting that Nick's wife may have killed two men, including Nick.'

Her voice wobbled at the end of the statement. Reg looked at her thoughtfully. She thought he was about to say something, but he appeared to think better of it.

'You really think she climbed out of the window of the home where her aunt is living, drove all the way to Finchley, and West Hampstead, on two separate occasions, killed two men, on two occasions, and drove back to her aunt's home, all without anyone seeing her?'

'I don't know,' she admitted. When stated so baldly, the idea sounded unlikely. 'All I'm saying is that it's feasible. Not only would it have been physically possible, but she went to the home on both evenings, providing herself with an alibi for the times of both murders, although she hadn't previously visited her aunt that often.'

Reg frowned. 'Well, I can see why you might find that suggestive,' he conceded.

Expecting strident opposition to her suggestion, Geraldine was relieved.

'We need to proceed carefully,' he warned her. 'Officers higher up the chain than me knew Nick, and would have known his wife too. Have you mentioned this to anyone else?'

'No.'

'Good.'

Geraldine suppressed a flicker of unease, wondering whether Reg was actually giving any credence to her theory. He might be putting on a show of taking her seriously when he was really only concerned to keep her quiet. She waited for him to tell her to leave it to him, but he didn't.

'Look into it if you must, Geraldine, but be discreet. And don't mention it to anyone else, least of all to Eve herself.'

Geraldine nodded. Her head was spinning. She decided it might be best not to admit that she had already as good as accused Eve to her face of murdering Nick. What she really needed was a break from the investigation. It was so hard to tell whether her suspicion of Eve was based on professional instinct, or personal resentment.

Leaving the police station, she set off on the drive to Kent, to visit her sister. Every few weeks, Celia liked to make a Sunday roast with all the trimmings. It made for a pleasant family get together. Geraldine couldn't always make it, but she tried to go there once in a while.

'I know you're busy,' Celia complained, prompting Geraldine to promise to take her niece out for the day as soon as she could.

Geraldine responded with her own stock response to Celia's habitual grouse. 'I promise I'll take her out for the day as soon as this investigation's finished. No, let's make it a weekend. I'll take her to the coast. She'd like that. Somewhere nice. Bournemouth or Brighton or somewhere.'

Celia grinned, caught up in Geraldine's transient excitement. A weekend at the seaside with her niece would be fun, and Chloe would certainly remember it.

'You promise?' Celia repeated.

'I promise. Cross my heart and hope to die.'

'Don't say that, please,' Celia pleaded, with a mock shudder.

Geraldine laughed. She was forever reassuring her sister that being a detective inspector was nowhere near as dangerous as it appeared on detective series on the television.

'Are you going to stay a detective all your life? Can't you at least tell them you need more time off?'

Geraldine squirmed. 'It doesn't work like that. If I'm on a case, I have to be there. I have no choice.'

She didn't add that more often than not it was her own decision to work overtime. When someone had been murdered, investigating their unlawful death took priority for Geraldine over every other possible consideration.

'If there's someone walking around who's committed a murder, they have to be arrested and locked up. It's not just a question of justice, retribution and all that, but we have to protect everyone else. Otherwise the streets wouldn't be safe for anyone. Killers would rule society.'

'As opposed to politicians? How can you tell the difference?'

They both laughed.

'It's my job to catch killers, not politicians,' Geraldine insisted firmly, but she was smiling.

Celia took her for a stroll around the garden while Chloe was on the phone to a friend.

'All we've done is talk about me,' Geraldine said. 'What about you? How are you feeling?'

'Excited, scared, and sick!'

'But everything's all right?'

'Everything's fine. We want to call the baby after mum, if it's a girl.'

Geraldine smiled. Celia was so predictable. 'I think that's a lovely idea.'

'Oh good. Only I didn't want to use mum's name without checking you were OK with it.'

'Of course I am. It was nice of you to ask, but this is your child we're talking about. Anyway, I'm fine with whatever you want to do.'

'Thank you.'

Geraldine smiled. 'Don't start going all weepy on me just because you're pregnant.'

Celia laughed, her eyes shimmering with tears.

'I said don't,' Geraldine repeated with mock severity.

Admiring Celia's swelling belly, she wondered what she would have done if she had fallen pregnant after her one night with Nick. She shook her head as though to bat the thought away.

'What about you?' Celia asked. 'How are you, I mean really?'

'Oh, I'm fine.' Another lie.

Before Celia could respond, Chloe came running out of the house. 'Mum! Mum! Stephanie says I can go to her house after school tomorrow.' She ran up and flung her arms around her mother. 'Please let me go.'

Without warning, Geraldine thought of Ed. She felt as though she had been hit in the guts.

72

BRIAN HAD BEEN GONE for ages and ages. Ed didn't understand why he had stayed away for so long. He guessed Brian was punishing him for wanting to go home. It reminded him of how his father used to send him to his room when he misbehaved, except that there had been a light in his room, and he could play on his Xbox to pass the time. Not only that, he could have opened the door and gone out onto the landing at any time, if he had dared. He might have ended up in even worse trouble with his father, but at least his father had never locked him in his room. Thinking about his father made him want to cry. It was even worse when he thought about his brother. He missed Matt more than anything. They had never been separated before. He felt as though he had lost a part of himself. He couldn't help missing his mother as well. The thought of her made him want to cry all over again, but he managed to restrain himself.

He had cried so much lately, his head hurt and his eyes were sore. If he cried any more he was afraid he would damage his eyes. He might already have gone blind. He switched the torch on and turned it off again almost straight away. If the battery failed, he would be completely helpless. There was nothing to see down there anyway, just the bed and the stairs, and the foul bucket that made the place stink worse than the toilets at school. The smell made him feel sick. His mother always nagged him and Matt to wash their hands after going to the toilet. For once, he wished he could.

He lay perfectly still on his bunk, thinking. His supply of food was nearly all gone, so Brian would have to come back soon. Brian might be mean, but he wouldn't leave him there to starve. He had taken him to the seaside, and was protecting him from bad people who had killed his father. Brian was his friend. Yet he had locked him in the cellar. That was a very mean thing to do. It was very confusing. One thing was certain, it was horrible being shut up in the dark. He couldn't stay there much longer. It would drive him nuts. Rather than stay locked up in the dark he was prepared to take his chances out on the street. He would just have to hope his enemies didn't find him before he found his way home to his mother. Meanwhile, he had to think of an escape plan.

Switching on the torch he climbed cautiously up the stairs and examined the door. It had no handle, and no keyhole. Gripping the torch in his left hand, he placed his right hand flat against the smooth surface of the door. He pushed gently at first, then with sudden force. The door didn't budge. He put the torch down very carefully at his feet and gave the door a shove with the heels of both hands. Still it didn't move. He tried again and again. He was crying now. With sudden rage he kicked the door with one foot and only managed to jar his ankle painfully. Next he tried putting his shoulder against the door and pushing. Although he knew it was futile, he had to try everything. The door didn't even quiver.

Even though he hadn't expected the door to open, he was bitterly disappointed. He was no more trapped than he had been a moment before, but he had been clinging to a desperate optimism. Now even that glimmer of hope had gone. The cellar was like a cupboard. Once the door was shut, it couldn't be opened from the inside. He might as well be locked in a prison cell. But two could play at that game. Slowly a plan began to take shape in his mind. The next time Brian opened the door, Ed would be waiting for him at the top of the stairs. He would trip Brian and send him hurtling down the steps. As he fell, Ed would dash out and slam the door behind him, leaving Brian in the cellar. See how *he* liked being locked up in the dark. It would serve him right. After that all Ed had to do was find a phone and call 999. It was so simple. He couldn't believe he hadn't thought of it before.

By the light of the torch he studied the narrow area in which he was confined. There were some empty wooden crates stacked in one corner. Next to them was the stinking bucket, and beside that some boxes of cereal Brian had left for him. To begin with Ed had enjoyed scoffing handfuls of dry coco pops and sugar puffs, but after a while their sweetness made him feel sick. The rolls Brian had left him were too stale to bite into, and he had finished the store of cheese and apples. There were several large bottles of lemonade left, but he was sick of drinking it. He had to force himself to swallow the sugary liquid.

His watch said ten o'clock, but he didn't know if it was ten in the morning or ten in the evening. He felt as though he had been there all his life. All he could do was cling to his plan. There was nothing else he could do. Reluctantly he switched off the torch and settled down to wait.

73

AT FIRST CAROLINE HAD resisted the suggestion that they film a reconstruction of Ed's last known movements. No one in Morrisons could recall whether Ed had arrived at the shop on the day he disappeared, and one of the CCTV cameras in the shop wasn't working, so that was inconclusive. Reg was keen to broadcast an image of him walking along The Ridgeway, crossing at the lights, going into the local Morrisons, and returning home again. With an identical twin, it would be easy to recreate the scene. Reg did his best to convince Caroline this was the best way of seeking to establish Ed's whereabouts. She was reluctant to go along with the suggestion, which would see Matthew retracing his brother's last known footsteps. At last she caved in. If filming Matthew might help rescue Ed, they had to go ahead.

'You don't have to do this,' Geraldine told Matthew. He stared at her, white-faced. 'We can find another boy who looks like Ed.'

'I'm the only one who looks like him.'

'Of course you are, but we can find another boy who looks similar, if you don't want to do this.'

'If it helps get Ed back, then I want to do it,' he insisted, his face rigid with determination.

During the filming Geraldine watched Caroline tremble as her son appeared around the corner. Matthew's face was unnaturally pale in the bright lights. He looked very small and very frightened. Holding himself upright, he marched like an automaton, his arms swinging stiffly. His eyes swept across the spectators, pausing only when he saw his mother, who let out a low moan. As he marched past, one of her hands jerked forward in an involuntary movement. It wasn't clear which of her sons she was reaching out for. As soon as the filming finished, she bent over, as though doubled up in physical pain. Matthew went and stood beside her, scuffing the ground with the toe of one shoe. After a moment, he reached out and patted her awkwardly on the arm.

'You can stop crying now, mum,' he said. 'We've done it, so they'll bring Ed home soon.'

The broadcast provoked a flurry of phone calls. More people claimed to remember seeing Ed on the day he disappeared than could possibly have been on that street that day. Several callers claimed to have seen the boy being bundled into cars of different makes and colours, but no one had thought to record the registration number. There were conflicting descriptions of men and women allegedly dragging the boy off the street. After a few hours the calls tailed off. They had resulted in no useful leads.

Geraldine wasn't sure what to do next. The investigation seemed to have reached an impasse. They were sitting around waiting for further results from forensic tests of fibres and fabrics, analysis of scenes of crimes and reports on CCTV. Hours and hours of film had been closely scrutinised. Rob's blue van had been sighted driving along Ballards Lane, close to where Caroline and Brian lived, but not all the traffic cameras were working, so they could only establish its presence in the area. It couldn't be placed at any specific address at the time Rob was killed.

'What's the use of all these fucking cameras when they don't bloody work,' Reg fumed.

Halfway through the morning Reg summoned Geraldine to his office where he warned her off questioning Eve again.

'You upset her,' he said heavily, gesturing to Geraldine to take a seat. 'Keep away from her from now on. Unless you come up with some real evidence, you have to drop this. She's threatening to make a formal complaint against you for harassment. She doesn't need this right now, Geraldine, and nor do you, and frankly, nor do I.'

Geraldine couldn't argue with him. He was right. She didn't have any evidence to substantiate her suspicions of Eve. With no other leads, Geraldine took Max with her to speak to Caroline. After that they were going to question Rob's father again to see if he could shed any light on the connection between his son and the twins. The missing boy was the priority right now.

Caroline didn't look surprised to see Geraldine and her sergeant again so soon. She didn't recognise Robert Wright's name.

'He's been murdered, and we think he may have known one or both of your sons.'

Caroline shook her head, her expression blank.

'We discovered a few flecks of your son's dandruff on Robert Wright's body suggesting they were in the same room at some point. That doesn't mean your son was in contact with the dead man *after* his death, of course,' she added untruthfully. 'Are you sure you don't know Robert Wright? That's Wright with a W.'

Staring at the photograph Geraldine had shown her, Caroline shook her head. 'It doesn't ring a bell. I told you Brian's taken Ed. Please, you have to find him. I went round there,' she went on, suddenly animated. 'He wouldn't let me in, but you could get in. You can go anywhere, can't you?'

'You told me you didn't know where he lives.'

Fighting back tears, Caroline described how she had followed Geraldine to Brian's house.

'Ed's there. I know he is! He has to be!'

Leaving Caroline, they went to question Rob's father. He said he had never heard of Caroline or her sons.

'Rob knew all sorts of people,' he added unhelpfully.

Having investigated Eve as far as she was able, Geraldine turned her attention to Brian. Looking further into his background, she discovered that his dead wife had a sister living in Milton Keynes, a woman called Mary Drysdale. Family members could prove a useful source of information, so she decided to talk to the woman face to face. It was an excuse to get out of the office, and away from Nick's empty desk. Sometimes a change of scene helped her to think.

Mary Drysdale was a thin woman with greying blonde hair and a sharp-featured face. At first she seemed reluctant to speak to Geraldine.

'I know I agreed to meet you, but there's really nothing I can tell you about my brother-in-law. I haven't seen him for years.'

'What did you think of him? Anything you can tell me about him might be helpful.'

'But you can't tell me why you want to know?'

'I'm sorry. But please...'

'Well,' Mary said, appearing to relent, 'to be honest I hardly ever met him, but I never liked him. And if you're asking about him because you're reopening the investigation into Susan's death, I still don't believe it was suicide, whatever they said at the time. It wasn't like her at all. I knew my sister, Inspector. She loved life. What she ever saw in that Brian...' She pulled a face. 'It was bad timing. She was on the rebound when she met him. She'd been seeing a married man, poor cow. When that all went wrong, she settled for Brian, far too quickly. I knew it was a mistake. I think she did too, deep down. Anyway, she took up with Nick again, and then suddenly she was dead. It didn't make sense. Why would she have gone and killed herself?'

Mary was clearly still distressed by the loss of her sister, but Geraldine's attention had been caught by something else.

'Nick?'

'Yes. That's the man she was seeing, before she met Brian. He was messing her around, telling her he'd leave his wife, and then letting her down. More fool her for letting him. You know the story, it's hardly original, but he was breaking her heart. That's the only reason she married Brian, she said she wanted someone safe, someone who would always put her first. Only then it all started up again with Nick...'

'What was his other name?'

'Who?'

'Nick. The man she was seeing. The married man. What was his surname?'

Mary shrugged. 'I don't know.'

'Think, please. This could be very important.'

But Geraldine already knew the identity of the married man who had been in a relationship with Brian's dead wife. He was the missing link that connected the murder of her colleague to the murder of Caroline's husband, and to Rob the odd-job man who had somehow become caught up in the spiral of killings.

'Was it Williams?'

Recognition registered in Mary's face. 'Nick Williams, that was it. Susan told me he worked for the Metropolitan Police.'

By the time Geraldine reached London, her reservations about Brian had grown into a firm conviction that he was involved. She would have waited until the morning to follow it up, but concern for the missing boy lent urgency to her actions. If Caroline was right, Brian was keeping Ed captive. Although hard to believe, it was possible. And if Geraldine's hunch was correct, Brian was capable of murder as well as kidnap. Meeting Brian's former sister-in-law had crystallised her thoughts. There was no time to lose. Ed's life might be in danger.

74

PEOPLE WERE MILLING AROUND, watching the departures board, or striding purposefully towards the platforms, dragging cases behind them. Brian's train wasn't due for another twenty minutes. He perched on the end of a bench, head lowered, one hand resting on his suitcase, waiting. Gazing around through dark lenses, he couldn't spot any security cameras in that corner of the station. He had selected Scotland as his destination, having once seen a film of *The Thirty Nine Steps* in which the hero had evaded capture by moving around remote places in the Highlands. He fancied he could do the same. He wasn't travelling straight there. Instead he would start his journey by going west. At the counter he used his credit card to buy a ticket to Oxford. By the time the police were on his trail he would have arrived in Oxford and bought an overnight ticket to Inverness, making a cash purchase that would be difficult to trace.

There was an airport at Inverness. From there it must be possible to leave the country. It would involve taking a bus to the airport, or another train, or maybe both. He might hire a car if he could do so without disclosing his identity. Perhaps it would be best to 'borrow' a car, without the owner's permission, of course. That way he would be able to travel without leaving any tracks, at least until the owner of the vehicle reported it missing. He could fly straight to Europe from Inverness, and stay overseas until he was no longer in the news and the police lost interest in him. He could quite happily spend years renting a room on the coast somewhere sunny, biding his time. He would be in no hurry to return to England. He might never come back. When his money ran out he could get a job, working in a bar, or teaching English.

He was going to leave the UK before the police came back and searched his house. It was a pity that by the time they discovered the boy it would probably be too late to save his life, but there was nothing Brian could do about it now. It was all for the best really, because if he *had* been found alive, the boy would have been able to tell the police how a man had fallen to his death in Brian's back garden. They couldn't prove Brian had deliberately caused the man's death, but the boy could describe how they had heaved the body into the van, and how Brian had driven it away. It was a pretty damning account.

His platform came up, and he walked quickly to the turnstile, taking care not to jostle anyone, or do anything that might draw attention to himself. He was an unremarkable man embarking on an unremarkable journey. When two British Transport Police passed him, he didn't flinch. One of them glanced at him as he walked by, trailing his case behind him. He lowered his eyes and hurried on, like any other traveller. The train was busy. He found a seat near a luggage rack, sat down and buried his face in a free newspaper he had picked up on the underground. There wasn't much room, but he extended his legs as far as he could, arching his back and rotating his head gently. For the first time he wondered how the boy was feeling, cooped up in his cellar. Dismissing the thought, he turned to look out of the window at the countryside flashing past.

Thinking about leaving the country, and wondering where to go, he reached for his leather bag. The strap on his shoulder wasn't there. With a sick feeling he realised what he had done. In his rush to get away, he had left the bag on his bed at home. He could picture it lying there, the black strap snaking across his pillow. There was nothing else for it. He had to go back and get it. He would slip round the back of the house under cover of darkness. Leaving his suitcase concealed behind the low wall of his narrow front garden, he would race upstairs to the bedroom, and be out of there again before anyone saw him. It was going be dangerous, because the police were bound to be watching the house, but he would manage it. He had no choice. Without his passport he was stuffed.

Heaving his suitcase off the train at the next stop, he made his way across to the opposite platform where he waited for a train to take him back to London and the quiet house where his documents lay, all ready, packed into a leather bag. He had been an idiot to leave them behind, but there was no point in getting worked up about it. Now more than ever he needed to keep a clear head. The worst was happening, and he had done it to himself, but there was still time to retrieve the situation.

'Failure is not an option,' he muttered furiously to himself. He kept his head down, afraid that an inquisitive official might notice he had arrived at the station only to turn round immediately and return to London. He wished he had gone to sit in the waiting room, out of sight, although there were probably cameras in there. CCTV cameras were everywhere on the train lines. It had probably been a blunder, travelling by train, but it hadn't occurred to him that he would have to go back to London. He should have been in Oxford by now, buying his ticket to Inverness.

At last his train was announced and he clambered aboard, lugging his suitcase which seemed to be much heavier than it had been when he left home. He was tired, and his arms were aching. He was tempted to unpack some of his clothes and leave them behind on the train. He didn't need them. But there were other people in the carriage and he was wary of attracting attention. So far no one seemed to have noticed him, sitting quietly behind a newspaper. With a twinge of fear, he saw a train guard coming down the aisle towards him. He didn't have a ticket for the return journey back to London. His carefully planned day was fast degenerating into a nightmare. With one swift movement he was on his feet, walking away from the guard. He kept going until he reached a toilet. It stank in there, but he stayed crouching on the seat with the lid down, until he heard an announcement over the tannoy. They were approaching the London terminal.

No one even glanced at him lugging his case off the train.

'I seem to have lost my ticket,' he muttered to the station official at the barrier. 'Can you let me through please?'

He didn't suppose any of the station staff would remember him, and the police would hardly be expecting him to be returning to London from Oxford.

The barrier guard didn't even look at him. 'Go to the excess fares counter over there. You'll have to pay the maximum fare.'

The ticket was a rip off but he didn't protest, and was soon hurrying down to the underground. The nearer to home he was, the more anxious he became. He could feel his shirt clammy with sweat beneath his overcoat, and his head began to hurt. He was probably dehydrated, but he didn't stop to buy a bottle of water. Shops all had CCTV, and the police were bound to be looking out for him this close to home. Carefully he turned his head away from the cameras in the station, pulling his coat collar up to his chin.

It was the obvious place to wait, in the park across the road. At last the sun set and darkness swallowed the empty expanse of grass. It was just past nine o'clock when he rose to his feet and stole silently along the pavement towards his house. The street was deserted. No one knew he was there. This might be easier than he had expected. All he had to do was run upstairs, grab his bag, and leave. He wouldn't so much as look at the door under the stairs. He just wanted to slip away quietly. He hoped the boy would do the same.

75

MATTHEW HAD KNOWN ALL along that something awful had happened to Ed. He was deeply upset that his mother had lied to him about it. When he demanded to know the reason, all she could say was that she had wanted to protect him.

'Protect me from what? I can look after myself.'

'I wanted to protect you from being upset.'

Now he was even more upset, because she had kept the truth from him about Ed being kidnapped.

'Why did you lie to me? Why?' he repeated.

'I thought you'd be upset.'

At last he calmed down enough to listen to her.

'What are we going to do?' he asked.

'What do you mean?'

'We can't just sit around doing nothing. He's been gone for ever! We have to save him!'

Caroline was infected by his enthusiasm. She knew it was a mistake as she blurted out that she knew where he was being kept. Matthew jumped up.

'Come on then!' he shouted.

Caroline shook her head. This could all go terribly wrong. She hadn't told Matt that Brian wasn't just a kidnapper. He was a killer as well. Matt began pestering her to tell him where his brother was being held captive. To her relief he yelled at her that they had to go and tell the police. She had been afraid he wanted to rush round there and confront Brian himself.

'How come you haven't told them yet? Don't you want Ed to come home?'

'Of course I want him home. I went to the police days ago, but they didn't believe me.'

Another mistake.

'Well, I believe you. Come on, if the police won't help us, we'll go and rescue him ourselves!'

'At least let's wait until it's dark,' she said, playing for time.

Somehow she had to persuade her son it was too dangerous even to try. If the police couldn't save Ed, there was nothing a woman and a ten-year-old boy could do. The last thing she wanted to do was put Matt in danger as well. Yet despite her trepidation, she couldn't help feeling excited. With Matt's help, there was a possibility they might succeed. Together they began to plan Ed's rescue. Matt was adamant that he would accompany her.

'That way one of us can distract him while the other one rescues Ed.' It sounded like a sensible plan. 'Then we can kill him and chop him up in little pieces and feed him to the rats, and dissolve his bones in a vat of acid,' he concluded, in a sobering reminder that he was just a child. 'Or we can feed him to pigs. They eat everything, bones and all. They crunch the bones up with their teeth!'

She couldn't help smiling at his childish enthusiasm. 'Where are you going to find pigs?'

He stopped capering round the room. 'You can find them. That's your job. I'm the ideas man.'

'And you have some very good ideas, but I think we should concentrate on finding Ed, and leave his kidnapper for the police to deal with.'

'You said the police didn't believe you.'

'But if we rescue Ed...' She paused, struck dumb by the enormity of what they were discussing.

They might already be too late. The idea of Matt stumbling on his twin brother's corpse was too horrific to contemplate. On the pretext of making some tea, she went into the kitchen and poured herself a generous slug of whisky. Her husband had been the drinker, not her. But since his death it had been the only way to deaden her anguish. Feeling slightly tipsy and very brave, she returned to the living room to confront her son.

'You can't come with me,' she announced firmly.

'What?'

'I can sort this out on my own.'

'But it has to be two of us so one of us can distract him while the other one rescues Ed. That's our strategy. It's what we agreed. You said. There has to be two of us.'

'No. It's too dangerous.'

'You're going.'

'He's my son.'

'He's my twin.'

There was no arguing him out of it.

They waited until it was dark before driving to Brian's house. Leaving the car parked a few doors away, they hurried across his front garden. It was only nine o'clock but there were no lights on in the house. Caroline hesitated. She hadn't thought about whether they should try and break in, or march up to the front door and ring the bell. Now they were there, she was terrified Brian would see them. He had already taken one of her sons. She wasn't prepared to risk Matt's safety as well.

'Round the back,' she whispered.

Matt nodded to show he understood. Cautiously she led the way to the side gate. It wasn't locked. She activated the torch on her phone. By its narrow beam of light they shuffled along the passageway that led down the side of the property. There were glass patio doors at the back of the house, flanked by two windows, all divided into small square panes. She tried each one in turn. They were all securely fastened. The only way they could get in was by breaking a window. She would have to do it without making any noise. She swung the torch around, looking for something to use. She wished she had come better prepared. Most of their planning had revolved around ways to dispose of Brian's dead body in the absence of any acid, or pigs, or convenient quicksand.

There was a low dry stone wall surrounding a small rockery at the side of the garden. Crouching down, she selected a sharp stone. As she raised it, Matt put his hand on her arm to stop her. Without speaking, he pointed to a different area of the window. In the darkness his face looked ghastly, wide-eyed and pale. She looked to where he was pointing, and nodded. She had been about to smash the large central pane of the window. He had guided her to the pane beside the window catch. If she broke the glass there, it should be easy to reach inside and open the window.

Matthew was only ten, but he was more clear thinking than her. She blinked, feeling muzzy-headed, regretting having downed so much whisky before coming out. She hoped she would be able to drive home without crashing the car. That would be just perfect.

The sound of breaking glass seemed to echo across the still night air. She winced. Without a word, they both stood with their backs pressed against the back wall of the house. There was a chance they might escape notice if anyone looked out. Nothing happened. In the moonlight, high tree branches stirred silently in the breeze. No lights came on, no voices yelled out from neighbouring houses demanding to know what was going on. They waited. At last, Caroline turned her attention to the window. Concentrating on keeping her arm steady, she reached in through a jagged hole in the glass and carefully pulled the window latch. For a terrible second she was afraid it was locked in place. Then, with a jolt, the catch lifted.

The delicate skin on the underside of her forearm brushed a jagged sliver of glass. For an instant she felt nothing, then a fierce pain stabbed her. Too late, she lifted her arm. Infuriated, she wiped the blood on her T-shirt. It was only a scratch but it stung dreadfully. Worse, she had left a smear of blood on the broken glass. Shining her torch on the teeth of glass that bordered the hole, she spotted the one she had caught her arm on. Carefully she knocked it out of the window with her stone, and caught it in her outstretched T-shirt. Carrying it to the rockery, she scrabbled at the dry earth with her fingers, and buried the pointed sliver of glass. The police might still be able to prove she had been there, but she was damned if she was going to make it easy for them.

'Come on,' she whispered as she reached in and opened the window. 'Be careful. There's broken glass on the floor under the window. Don't cut yourself.'

Gingerly they clambered into the silent house.

76

THIS TIME GERALDINE WAS careful to register her destination with Computer Aided Despatch herself, so the nearest patrol car would reach her quickly if she summoned backup. On the way to Brian's house she called the station. As she had expected, Reg wasn't at his desk. Even though it was after nine, she called him at home. To her relief he answered the phone almost straight away. Quickly she told him what she had learned from Brian's former sister-in-law, and why she felt unable to wait until the morning to investigate further.

Reg expressed surprise at hearing that Nick had been sleeping with Brian's wife. It was easier to speak to him about it when she couldn't see him glaring at her. Even so, she held back from telling him about her own affair with their dead colleague.

'He was a good officer, Reg, but he was a serial adulterer.'

'You know that, do you? It's not just rumours and…'

'It's true. There's no doubt. Ask anyone.'

Reg grunted. She didn't mind that he sounded put out. After all, she had disturbed him at home, in the evening. At least he was listening to her. Once she accepted what she was saying, he couldn't ignore the significance of the connection.

'So you think Brian killed Nick because his wife had an affair with him?'

'I think it's possible.'

'But Brian's wife died years ago.'

'It was over three years ago. Alleged suicide…'

'Alleged?'

'That was the coroner's conclusion, but the deceased's sister didn't believe it was suicide.'

'She wouldn't, would she?'

'No. Of course it's perfectly reasonable to suppose it was suicide, and I suppose we'll never know...'

'Unless he confesses...'

Geraldine smiled. Reg was taking her accusations seriously.

'Brian may not be our killer, but he has to be a suspect now.'

'So how does the missing boy fit in with all this?'

'I don't know how he fits in,' she admitted, 'it's just that Caroline accused Brian of kidnapping him. She must have had a reason for suspecting him. Perhaps the boy saw something and Brian needed to make sure he couldn't talk. Unless she's lying to cover up for herself.'

'Like you say, we can't be sure of anything yet. But too many fingers seem to be pointing at Brian. We need to look into him. And given Caroline's accusation, we need to move fast. Send a message to all traffic police, train stations, bus depots and airports, nationwide, to be on the lookout for a man and a boy travelling together, with descriptions of the missing boy and Brian Stanbury, just in case he tries to take off with the boy.'

'I'll get onto Max right away.'

'Circulate his description, and say he might be accompanied by the boy.'

Neither of them suggested that Ed might already be dead.

'As soon as I've spoken to Max I'll take a look around,' Geraldine said. 'I'm outside the house now.'

Reg warned her to wait for backup, and she promised to be careful.

'You know where I am.'

'Yes, but you're on your own there, Geraldine. Wait for backup. That's an order. I can't afford to lose another inspector. They'd string me up for being careless!'

Behind his joking tone, she could hear fear in his voice. Whether it was on her account or his own no longer mattered. They were on the same team.

'I won't go in unless I have to, but if I think the child is in immediate danger...'

'Call for backup now!'

The house was in darkness. Geraldine stood outside the front gate, waiting for the backup team. Brian could be in bed, but there was a chance he had become alarmed and fled. She hoped she hadn't arrived too late. He might have gone away, taking the boy with him. As she waited, she heard the sound of glass breaking at the back of the house. It seemed she wasn't the only visitor to Brian's house that evening. She ran to the front door and rang the bell to warn Brian about the break in, but there was no answer. She tried the lock. After a few seconds of fiddling, one of her keys turned with a loud click and the door swung open. She pressed herself against the wall beside the door and waited, listening. There was no sound. Cautiously she stepped forward and peered inside. Nothing was moving. The backup team would be there at any minute. Leaving the door ajar for them, she went inside.

There was a street lamp right outside the house. Light shone through the fanlight above the front door, illuminating the hall with a dim orange glow. Geraldine gazed around. She had been there before, but everything looked different at night. From outside, the faint drone of a passing car reached her. She stood perfectly still, listening. The car didn't stop. Her colleagues hadn't arrived yet. She hesitated. The obvious course was to stay in the hall and prevent anyone escaping that way onto the street. No one was covering the back, but her presence at the front door was better than nothing.

As she waited she heard voices. They were speaking so quietly it was hard to make out the words. She inched forward until she reached the door to the kitchen where the sound was coming from.

'I told you to wait there,' a woman's voice muttered angrily.

'I want to come with you. He's here, I know he is.'

The door was open. All Geraldine's instincts prompted her to rush forward. It was an effort to remain perfectly still, watching and listening.

More alert than Matthew, Caroline was first to notice Geraldine standing in the doorway. Her eyes widened.

Matthew broke the silence. 'What's she doing here?'

'Same as us, I expect,' Caroline answered. A faint smile curled her lips for an instant.

'But...' Matthew began then fell silent, evidently recalling where he had seen her before.

'More to the point, what are *you* doing here?' Geraldine asked, although the answer was obvious.

Caroline stepped forward, but before she could speak the boy replied.

'We've come to get Ed.'

Quickly Geraldine explained that backup was on its way. There was nothing for Caroline and Matthew to do but leave matters to the police. They would search the house, taking it apart brick by brick if necessary. She didn't add that this was no place for Matthew. As she was insisting Caroline took Matthew away, they heard footsteps pounding up the stairs. Someone else was in the house, and it didn't sound like a team of police officers.

77

THE FIRST THING THAT RAN through Geraldine's mind was that Brian had come home. With a sickening lurch in her guts, she remembered that she had left the front door ajar. If Ed was concealed somewhere in the house, dead or alive, Brian would hardly have forgotten to shut the front door when he went out. On his return, he would have noticed the door was open. She guessed he had run upstairs to check whether Ed had escaped while he was out. But she had looked in every room. There was no one upstairs. If Ed was being kept in the house, there was only one possible explanation for his silence. She couldn't work out why Brian would have gone upstairs instead of legging it as soon as he realised someone else had been in the house, and might still be there.

'He's here, I know he is. Let me look for him,' Matthew said.

The thought of Matthew discovering his dead brother was too terrible to contemplate. Before anything else, she had to protect the living. She turned to Caroline and gestured to her to leave.

'Take Matthew and get out of here now,' she hissed. 'My colleagues will be here soon. We can deal with this. You'll only get in the way. Go!'

Before either of them could stop him, Matthew darted from the room. Caroline grabbed for him, but she was too slow. Geraldine charged after him. At her heels, she heard Caroline panting. Matthew ran straight for the stairs. He bounded up them two at a time, with Geraldine racing after him. Reaching the landing, she stopped. There was no sign of Brian or Matthew. Caroline started forward but Geraldine put her hand on the other woman's arm to stop her.

'Come with me.'

To her relief, Caroline obeyed without question. She looked

terrified. Geraldine couldn't afford to lose sight of her as well. They looked in the nearest bedroom. It was empty. As they turned, a figure darted out of the bathroom and went haring down the stairs. It was the boy. Brian was still upstairs. Geraldine ran into the bathroom expecting to see him in there. Caroline followed her. The bathroom was empty. Geraldine's best option was to run back downstairs and wait there. Wherever Brian was, she had to make sure he didn't leave the house. If she didn't succeed in finding him by the time backup arrived, he would stand no chance once the search team were in place. They would arrive at any moment. She turned and whispered to Caroline.

'I'll make sure he doesn't get away. You go and find Matthew and keep him away from the hall. It could be dangerous.'

Caroline was sobbing uncontrollably. As Geraldine urged her to hurry, Brian bounded past them. Geraldine swore. She dashed forward but the momentum of his leap had already taken him out of reach. By the time she started down the stairs he was at the open front door. There was no one outside. All her muscles tensed, poised to leap. If she mistimed her landing, he might yet escape her.

A thin voice rang out. 'Wait!'

To Geraldine's surprise, Brian stopped in the doorway and turned round. Below her, she could see the top of Matthew's head and Brian, staring at the boy as though transfixed.

'Ed,' he called out, stepping back into the hall. 'Come with me.' He gave a tentative smile and reached out his hand in a gesture of entreaty.

Caroline started forward. Geraldine seized her by the arm to stop her. Motioning to Caroline to stay where she was, Geraldine edged silently down the stairs, one step at a time. Brian's gaze was fixed on Matthew who stood scowling at him across the hall.

'Come with me,' Brian repeated. He sounded desperate.

He edged towards Matthew. One more step and Geraldine would be able to reach out, grab his arm and twist it up behind his back to incapacitate him. She stood, poised to lunge.

'We can go to the seaside again,' he urged. 'You liked that, didn't you? And I'll buy you ice cream, as much as you want.'

Caroline swore. At the sound of her voice, Brian seemed to come to his senses. He blinked in surprise. As Geraldine sprang forward there was a commotion below her. A burly uniformed constable charged in through the front door, yelling, followed by more officers. The backup team had arrived.

Brian's gaze never left Matthew, not even when the constable seized his wrists. Caroline darted forward and slapped Brian's face so hard he almost lost his balance. At the same instant, Matthew ran forward, screaming, 'Where is he? Where is he?'

The constable lifted Matthew easily off his feet, and put him down out of Brian's reach.

'Now,' Geraldine said firmly. 'You need to tell us where Ed is.'

Standing right in front of Brian, she heard him expel all the air from his lungs. His shoulders drooped and he hung his head. But he didn't answer.

'Make him tell, make him tell!' Matthew cried out. 'Torture him until he tells!'

Fleetingly, Geraldine wished she could. Instead, she issued instructions for the search team to set to work. Immediately the hall was full of uniformed men and women. Half the team raced upstairs, the others began spreading out downstairs.

'We need to get Matthew out of here,' Geraldine told his mother urgently.

'It's OK, mum,' Matthew said. He was crying. 'Ed's OK. I know he is. I'd know if he was hurting.'

Geraldine and Caroline exchanged a worried glance.

'Come on, son, we'll wait for him at home.'

78

'IN HERE, MA'AM!' A woman's voice rang out above the background noises of footsteps and muttered exchanges.

Geraldine ran over to the cupboard under the stairs.

'There's a door at the back there,' the constable said. 'It's locked, but it looks as though it's recently been opened.'

The constable shone her torch onto the back wall of the under stairs cupboard. Standing side by side, they stared at a small door almost hidden behind a hoover and an ironing board resting up against it. The floor to either side of the door was dusty, but a central pathway leading to it was relatively clean, as though someone had recently made their way over to the door a few times.

'He could have just been using the ironing board,' the constable said.

'Open it! No, wait, stand back. I'll do it. We don't want to frighten him.'

The constable moved out of her way, and Geraldine approached the door at the back of the cupboard. It was illuminated by the powerful beam of her colleague's torch. Quickly she shifted the hoover and the ironing board, wondering if this was exactly what the killer had done. She shivered, seeming to sense his presence in the cramped space. It didn't take her long to force the lock. Cautiously she pulled the door. It opened slowly. A musty odour of damp and faeces assailed her. As she was raising her hand to cover her nose and mouth, the door flew back on its hinges so suddenly it nearly bowled her over.

Before she could regain her balance, a small figure leapt out of the darkness. He was brandishing what looked like a club in his right hand. Reacting swiftly, Geraldine reached out and grabbed his skinny forearm. She shook it until, with a squeal of rage, he dropped his weapon and began pummelling her in the chest with his other fist. Looking down, she saw the weapon he had dropped: a metal torch. If he hadn't been dazzled by the constable's light, he might have caused her a serious injury.

Gradually Geraldine relaxed her hold on his arm. He was trembling so much he could barely stay on his feet. Nevertheless he continued to punch her.

'It's all right, Ed,' she said softly. 'I'm a police officer. We've arrested Brian. He'll never be able to hurt you again.'

He didn't look like his identical twin right now. Blue eyes stared balefully at her from a face dark with dirt. His blond hair was grey with grime. He squirmed and grunted in her grasp like a feral child.

'Come on,' she said, 'we're going to take you to hospital to make sure you haven't been hurt.' At least they could check him for physical injuries. The mental trauma would take longer to heal. 'They'll give you lots of nice things to eat. Whatever you want. Your mother will be waiting for you there.' She nodded at the constable who pulled out her phone to call Caroline. 'And after that your mother's going to take you and your brother home.'

At the mention of his mother, Ed finally stopped wriggling and hitting. He collapsed against her chest and began sobbing noisily. Tears left pale runnels in his dark face.

'All he left me was Coco Pops,' he mumbled, bending double and clutching his stomach. 'It hurts.'

Relieved at finding Ed alive, Geraldine cursed her own poor judgement in having trusted Brian. Ed had been in the house all along and she had walked away, leaving the poor child imprisoned there. She was even more relieved when the doctor who examined Ed found no evidence of sexual abuse. Ed insisted that Brian had never touched him. It seemed Brian's worst crime was multiple murders. That was bad enough. If there was any justice in the world, he wouldn't leave his cell until he was carried out in a box. Prison was too good for him. Geraldine hoped he would be branded a paedophile as well as a murderer. It would make his stay in prison less comfortable.

She spoke to his mother while Ed was asleep. Caroline was

anxious to get back to his bedside. She kept glancing at the door, to see if a nurse had come to fetch her.

'They said I can be there when he wakes up.'

'I just want to ask you a few questions. It won't take long,' Geraldine reassured her.

That wasn't strictly true. She had a lot of questions for Caroline. She did her best to control her curiosity and focus on the priority.

'Tell me everything you know about Brian Stanbury.'

Caroline shook her head. 'I don't know anything about him, except that he's an evil bastard. Really, I've only seen him a few times in the last few weeks. And before that we hadn't seen each other since junior school.'

'Tell me about your recent meetings.'

Distracted, Caroline gave a garbled account of her meetings with Brian in the park.

'It was all my fault. I was an idiot. If I hadn't let him take that bloody photo of the two of us together – he said he was going to show it to Dave to make him sit up and take more notice of me. He had his arm round me!' Her eyes widened and her nostrils flared in outrage. 'How was I to know what he was going to do? There was no reason to suppose he was going to do that, was there? I mean who would do that? Kill a complete stranger, and lock up a child...' She paused. 'And he wanted me to do it too. Kill someone, I mean. He said that was our deal, but I never said I'd kill someone. Why would I? Why would anyone?'

When a nurse came and told Caroline she could see Ed, she jumped up and ran out without a backward glance. Only then did Geraldine realise how tired she was. She wished she could just go home and sleep, but first she had to write her report. She would have to word it carefully.

79

AS SOON AS CAROLINE revealed that her proposed victim had been a police officer, Brian's motive became clear. The whole tragic episode had been driven by his jealousy of the man his wife had loved. He had killed Dave with the sole intention of persuading Caroline to kill Nick in exchange. As long as they were both careful to leave no clues at the scene, there would be nothing to connect them to their victims. The plan was ingenious but evil. When Caroline had refused to carry out his demands, Brian had kidnapped Ed in an attempt to persuade her to kill Nick, and ensure her silence. For a time it had worked, but he had run out of patience and carried out the second murder himself. With Nick dead, there was no reason for Brian to keep Ed locked up. He refused to be drawn on what had happened between him and the boy. All Ed would say was that Brian was horrible, and had shut him up in the dark. Brian's reaction on seeing Matthew in his hall was the only clue they had about the feelings he had developed for Ed. Suffering from paranoia, at some point he had turned against the boy and locked him in the cellar.

His reasons for killing Rob remained unclear. Ed had given a convoluted account of how they had disposed of the dead body of an enemy agent who had been spying on them. Neighbours on one side of Brian's house confirmed that Rob had cleaned their windows on the day he had disappeared. He had never reached the property on the other side of the house. It seemed that, unlike the other two, Rob's murder had not been planned. If Ed's account was accurate, Brian had killed Rob in the paranoid belief that he was a spy. Brian himself refused to discuss what had happened.

'Ed told us you dragged the body into the back of his van and drove away with it.'

'Ed's lying. Who's Ed? I don't know anyone called Ed.'

'Ed's the boy you locked in your cellar.'

'There's no one in my cellar.'

When Geraldine assured him she was telling the truth, he sat back in his chair and crossed his arms. 'You would say that, wouldn't you? You're in on it with them. You're all in on it. You think I can't see that? Do I look like a mug?'

'From where I'm sitting I'd say you look like a calculating killer who planned two murders, and then carried out a third when you thought an innocent man had seen the kidnapped boy in your house...'

'I don't know what you're talking about. You can't prove any of this.'

'Do you deny you kidnapped Ed Robinson?'

'I don't know anyone called Ed.'

'I was there when you saw Matthew and mistook him for his identical twin,' Geraldine reminded him softly. 'I was there when you recognised him. You said you'd taken him to the seaside. We checked with him and he's corroborated your story. You did take him to the seaside. Just to be sure, we're checking CCTV. Once we find your car, and see where you were headed, we'll do extensive door-to-door questioning and find out where you went. It won't be difficult, and we'll find out what we need to know, however long it takes. You must have stopped for food or petrol at some point. Maybe both,' she added, catching sight of Brian's expression. 'There's no point in lying any longer. You'll only make the case against you worse. If you tell us the truth now, the court may treat you more leniently.'

Brian gave a derisive snort. Geraldine pressed on.

'What about Nick Williams?'

She hoped her voice didn't betray her anguish at naming her dead lover. Brian's eyelids flickered. At her side, she heard Max stir.

'Did you kill him too?' she asked gruffly.

'Someone had to do it. He deserved it. I should have done it years ago.'

'You mean you killed DI Nick Williams?'

'That's what I just said. He had it coming. It was only fair.'

The rest of the interview passed in a blur. It didn't matter. Brian had confessed to knowingly murdering a police officer. It was over.

Geraldine was sitting in her office, tidying up her documents, when Reg knocked and entered. He looked grim.

'Eve wants to see him,' he said.

'What?'

'Eve's asking to see Brian.'

'Is that a good idea?'

'She says she has a right to speak to the man who murdered her husband. She wants to look him in the eye and ask him how he could do it.' He heaved a sigh. 'Nick was a good man.'

'I know, but surely she can't see him. In the interests of everyone involved we have to protect...'

'I think we can make an exception in this case,' Reg interrupted heavily, 'under the circumstances. Nick meant a lot to all of us here.'

Her discomfort must have shown on her face.

'She's Nick's widow, for Christ's sake,' Reg burst out. 'How can I refuse her anything? Take her in there, Geraldine. That's an order.'

Geraldine was uneasy about Reg's decision, but he was her superior officer. Besides, guilt at her earlier suspicions of Eve made her reluctant to argue against granting her request. Ignoring her qualms, she nodded at the custody sergeant to open the door and allow Eve into the cell.

'Just for a minute,' Geraldine said. 'We'll go in with you.'

Eve insisted on going in alone.

'I'm afraid that's out of the question.'

'Reg said I could have a moment alone with him.'

Geraldine wasn't sure whether to believe that or not. As she hesitated, Eve ran in, slamming the door behind her. Geraldine wrenched it open just in time to hear a shot. Brian lay slumped on the floor, clutching his shoulder and screaming. He wasn't dead. Eve turned, still aiming the gun at Brian. Beads of sweat dotted her forehead, but her voice was steady. 'Nobody move!'

Geraldine was only vaguely aware of alarm bells ringing as Eve raised her hand so the gun was pointing at Geraldine. The custody sergeant swore under his breath. Geraldine's mouth felt dry. She blinked and passed her tongue over her lips. It was an effort to speak. She had no idea what she was going to say, but she had to say something. There was no way she was going to die without remonstrating.

'Eve, what are doing? It's not worth it. Nick's dead. It's over.'

'He wasn't worth your devotion,' Brian gasped, his eyes sharp with pain. 'He was at it with my wife!'

'Eve, he was never faithful to you,' Geraldine echoed.

'I knew about his affairs. How could I not know what he was up to? He was my husband. But that doesn't mean I stopped loving him. And he never stopped loving me. Never! He would never have left me. He looked after me.' Her voice trembled. 'How can I live without him?' She turned back to Brian, still pointing the gun at him. 'I was just waiting for them to find out who killed him, so I could make you suffer. Killing's too good for you.'

She whipped the gun up to the side of her own head and a second shot rang out. Brian yelled in alarm as Eve fell, blood splashing the wall and floor.

The gun dropped from her grasp with a faint clang.

80

GERALDINE FELT GUILTY FOR having suspected Eve of murder. It was
a terrible conclusion to have reached without any real evidence. All
she had been able to say was that it would have been possible; the
same could be said of any husband or wife. It was too late to make
amends now. She couldn't help feeling she had let Eve down. Nick
had let his wife down too. The whole case seemed to have lurched
from one betrayal to another. She was glad it was over. Although
Ed had been returned safely to his mother, there were likely to be
long-term consequences to his experience. He was young. With
family counselling, he might come through relatively unscathed in
the long term, but the brutal murder of his father made that unlikely.
One way and another, it had been a depressing investigation.

She wasn't in the mood for going to the pub with the rest of the
team, but it would be churlish to refuse. Reg came over to join her
as soon as she entered the bar.

'I told you Nick wasn't like that,' he said quietly.

'Like what?'

'Oh come on, Geraldine, don't play dumb. I said all along he
wasn't cheating on his wife.'

'But...'

'You can't deny they were loyal to each other right up to the
end. Why else would she have shot Brian and killed herself?' He
looked thoughtful. 'I don't suppose my wife would do that for me.
Anyhow, it just goes to show they were faithful to each other to
the end.'

Unsure whether Reg really believed what he was telling her or
not, she nodded.

'Let's have a last drink together,' he went on, more cheerfully.

'What do you mean, a last one?'

'Allowing Eve in to Brian's cell didn't go down too well.' He glanced around before leaning down towards her, lowering his voice. 'Keep this between us for this evening – I've been suspended pending an investigation. We didn't even search her. Who would have thought she'd be carrying a weapon? A woman like that, married to a DI. But that's no excuse. I should never have allowed my emotional state over losing Nick to have affected my judgement like that. Don't worry,' he added, seeing Geraldine's consternation, 'I'm taking full responsibility. I'll tell them you challenged me and I overruled your reservations. My career's over anyway. I don't want to drag anyone else down with me. If I agree to go quietly, I might get to keep my pension. No one wants any adverse publicity, least of all the chief. To be honest, I'm relieved to be getting out, and it looks like I'll be getting off quite lightly, given the circumstances. Now,' he went on in a louder voice, 'let's get you that drink, Geraldine. You deserve it.'

Watching his broad shoulders as he made his way to the bar, pausing to congratulate other members of the team on his way, she thought how badly she had misjudged the detective chief inspector. It was true she had been acting on his instructions, but he hadn't been present when Eve had entered Brian's cell. A less scrupulous man might have tried to salvage his own career at the expense of hers. With friends higher up, he might have succeeded in using her as a scapegoat. She had a lot to be thankful for, but all she could feel was sadness at the fragility of human happiness. Caroline's encounter with a former school friend had destroyed so many people's lives, the dead and the living. Reg was just one more victim of Brian's quest for vengeance.

'Cheer up,' Max broke her reverie. 'You aren't drinking. What can I get you?'

Geraldine smiled sadly. 'Reg is looking after me.'

In reality, no one was looking after her. Nick had offered her a fleeting glimpse of happiness. No sooner had she opened herself up to him than he had been snatched away from her. Every night she went home to an empty bed.

'What about Geraldine?' she heard Reg ask.

'That's a good point,' Max replied. 'Geraldine, what's the policy on pets in your place?'

'What?'

'Nick and Eve had a cat,' he explained. 'We're trying to find a home for it or it'll have to be put down.'

Emotion took Geraldine by surprise. Turning, she dashed out of the bar and only just managed to reach her car before she broke down in tears. Soon she would pull herself together, dry her eyes, fix her make-up, and return to her normal routine. But she wasn't ready to face the world yet. First she had to deal with a grief she could never share. The thought made her feel more alone than ever. As she was pulling herself together enough to drive home, her phone rang. It was a familiar number.

'Guess what?' Sam sounded excited.

Stifling her regret at having answered the call, Geraldine switched the engine off.

'What is it?'

'The doctor's said I'm fit for work.' Sam paused, clearly waiting for Geraldine to crack a joke. 'Are you all right?'

'Yes, I'm fine. That's great news.'

'What's wrong? You sound terrible. It's because of Nick, isn't it? Where are you?' Sam didn't even pause for breath. 'I'm coming round. And don't even try to stop me. I'm setting off right now.'

'There's no point. I'm not at home.'

'Well, where are you then? We can meet anywhere you like. Let's go out and get pissed and celebrate my return to the land of the living – oh shit, sorry – my return to the world of work, I mean.'

Geraldine had missed Sam. There was an infectious excitement in her young colleague's joy at the prospect of returning to work. Despite all the human tragedy of her recent case, Geraldine felt her mood lighten. Brian's tormented vengeance, Caroline's grief for her unfaithful husband, even the pain of her own loss began to fade, almost imperceptibly. Tomorrow it would feel ever so slightly less raw than today.

'I'm not up for it tonight, Sam, but we'll go out soon,' she promised.

As she hung up, she realised she was smiling.

A LETTER FROM LEIGH

Dear Reader,

I hope you enjoyed reading this book in my Geraldine Steel series. Readers are the key to the writing process, so I'm thrilled that you've joined me on my writing journey.

You might not want to meet some of my characters on a dark night – I know I wouldn't! – but hopefully you want to read about Geraldine's other investigations. Her work is always her priority because she cares deeply about justice, but she also has her own life. Many readers care about what happens to her. I hope you join them, and become a fan of Geraldine Steel, and her colleague Ian Peterson.

If you follow me on Facebook or Twitter, you'll know that I love to hear from readers. I always respond to comments from fans, and hope you will follow me on **@LeighRussell** and **fb.me/leigh.russell.50** or drop me an email via my website **leighrussell.co.uk**.

That way you can be sure to get news of the latest offers on my books. You might also like to sign up for my newsletter on **leighrussell.co.uk/news** to make sure you're one of the first to know when a new book is coming out. We'll be running competitions, and I'll also notify you of any events where I'll be appearing.

Finally, if you enjoyed this story, I'd be really grateful if you would post a brief review on Amazon or Goodreads. A few sentences to say you enjoyed the book would be wonderful. And of course it would be brilliant if you would consider recommending my books to anyone who is a fan of crime fiction.

I hope to meet you at a literary festival or a book signing soon!

Thank you again for choosing to read my book.

With very best wishes,

Leigh Russell

noexit.co.uk/leighrussell